THE LOST CHILD

PATRICIA GIBNEY

sphere

SPHERE

First published in 2017 by Bookouture, an imprint of StoryFire Ltd.
This paperback edition published in 2019 by Sphere

1 3 5 7 9 10 8 6 4 2

A CIP catalogue record for this book
is available from the British Library.

ISBN 978-0-7515-7248-3

Printed and bound in Great Britain by
Clays Ltd, Elcograf S.p.A.

Papers used by Sphere are from well-managed forests
and other responsible sources.

MIX
Paper from
responsible sources
FSC® C104740

Sphere
An imprint of
Little, Brown Book Group
Carmelite House
50 Victoria Embankment
London EC4Y 0DZ

An Hachette UK Company

www.hachette.co.uk
www.littlebrown.co.uk

Kathleen and William Ward, my parents,
for your love, support and encouragement.

The seventies: The Child

'You have to be quiet. Please. Don't cry again.'

'But… but she hurt me. I want to go back to our other mummy.'

'Shh. Shh. I do too. But if we're good, this mummy won't hurt us. You have to be really, really good.'

More crying. 'Too hard to be good. I'm so hungry. Hic… hic.'

'Don't get hiccups. Don't. You make her so mad.'

I wrap my arms around my twin's small, thin body and stare into the blackness. It is too dark in here. When the mummy woman turned off the hall light, even the little crack at the lock was filled with blackness. I lean into the folds of the vacuum cleaner bag, try to make a pillow for my head, but it is too lumpy, my body too bony. Pins and needles prickle my arm where my twin's head rests.

I am too cramped to move. The weight of my twin lying on me would be very light for the big people, I think, but it feels like a monster to me.

A spider lowers itself from a web, down on to my nose, and I scream. My twin slips from my grasp. A head cracks loudly against the wall. We are both screaming now.

In the confined space of the hall cupboard, our screams are loud and shrill. Neither of us knows why the other is howling. Neither of us can stop the other crying. Neither of us knows when the horror will end.

And then… the sound of the lock opening.

*

Carrie King puts her hands over her ears. Will they ever shut up? Sobbing, crying, screaming. Little brats. After all she has done for them. Given up her drugs. Stopped drinking. Become someone she isn't. For them. To get them back. She had to do it, especially after the others were taken from her. Fought so hard for them.

'Shut up!'

She uncorks the whiskey bottle and fills a glass. Two gulps later, she feels the warmth seep into her veins. That's better. But she still hears them. Another gulp.

'Enough!' She runs from the kitchen. Bangs on the door of the cupboard in the hallway.

'I said, shut up! If I hear one more word, I'll kill the two of you,' she screams.

Leaning against the white chipboard, her chest rising and heaving from the effort, she listens above the thumping of her heart. Still crying, but softer now. Whimpers.

'Thank God,' she sighs. 'Peace at last.'

She drags herself back to the kitchen, dirt and crumbs sticking to her bare feet. Standing at the clogged sink, peering out through the smeared window, she pops an acid pill, but she really needs a smoke. Pulling the small bag of weed from her skirt pocket, she rolls a joint and takes two hits from the spliff in quick succession.

Her legs weaken at her knees. She can see two windows, or is that three? The bread bin hops along the bench and the sweeping brush is begging for a dance partner.

She laughs, and lights a candle. This is seriously good shit, or is it the acid? Turning, she grabs the whiskey bottle and drinks from its neck. It doesn't taste so sharp now. She opens the book lying by her hand, before closing it again. She can't remember when she last read, but this looked good. She liked the little pictures. Now, though, it is mocking her.

The racket from the hallway has ceased and she hears the angels singing. Up there, lying in white fluffy clouds on her ceiling. They look kind of cute. Not like the twin bastards that have cost her so much of her life. At least she got them back. Away from their foster mother. That was a laugh. That woman had no idea how to raise children.

'Hello, little angel friends,' she chirps at the ceiling, her voice an octave higher than normal. 'Have you come to shut the brats up?'

That's when she hears screams. Scrunching her face in confusion, she stares blindly around the kitchen. The angels have fled.

Carrie King takes another slug of whiskey, following it with a drag on her joint, and grabs hold of the wooden spoon. As she flees the kitchen, she doesn't notice she has knocked over the candle and the bottle.

'I'll give you two something to cry about. So help me God, I will.'

DAY ONE

Early October 2015

CHAPTER 1

The evening was the best time to study. A glass of wine by her hand, phone in the dock spewing soft music, blinds pulled down halfway, the fields beyond the house in darkness. Light reflected off the glass and she could see all around her. Alone with her books. In her own home. Safe.

Marian Russell had to admit that social studies wasn't her course of choice, but she loved the genealogy module. Everything else was too highbrow for her stupid brain. She *was* stupid. Arthur had kept telling her that, so now she almost believed it. But she knew it wasn't really true.

Smiling to herself, she popped two pills into her mouth, swallowed them with her wine and lit a cigarette. Since she'd secured the barring order against her husband, she was beginning to take hold of her life again. A twenty-five-hour-a-week contract in the supermarket helped, and she had the family car. The bastard had lost his licence, so he hadn't put up much of a fight over it. She'd succeeded in getting her mother to sign the house over to her before ensconcing her in a flat. Out from under her feet. And she had her studies. And her wine. And her pills.

The front door opened and slammed shut.

'Emma, is that you?' Marian shouted over her shoulder. She needed to have a sit-down with her daughter. At seventeen, Emma was beginning to take liberties with her curfew. She checked the time. Not yet nine o'clock.

Marian sipped her wine. 'Where did you go?'

Silence. No matter how much trouble she got into, Emma always stood her ground. A trait inherited from her father? No, Marian knew where she got it from.

Standing up, she turned to the door. The glass fell from her hand. 'You!'

CHAPTER 2

Carnmore was a quiet area, situated on the outskirts of Ragmullin. The main road had once run through it, but after the ring road had been constructed, it was cut off and mainly accessed by residents, or used as a rat run by those aware of its existence. Almost five hundred metres separated the two houses built there and only every third street lamp remained lit. On a night like this, with rain thundering down to earth, it was a bleak and desolate place. Trees shook their wet branches free of their remaining leaves and the ground was sludgy and black.

The crime-scene tape was already in place when Detective Inspector Lottie Parker and Detective Sergeant Mark Boyd arrived. Two squad cars blocked the house from the view of any curious onlookers. But the area was quiet, except for garda activity.

Lottie looked over at Boyd. He shook his head. At over six feet tall, he was lean and well toned. His hair, once black, now shaded with grey, was cut close around his ears, which stuck out slightly.

'Come on,' she said, 'let's get out of this rain. I hate calls late at night.'

'And I hate domestics,' Boyd said, turning up the collar of his coat.

'Could be a home invasion. A burglary gone wrong.'

'Could be anything at this stage, but Marian Russell's had a barring order against her husband, Arthur, for the last twelve months,' Boyd said, reading from a page dripping with rainwater. 'An order he has flouted on two occasions.'

'Still doesn't mean it was him. We have to assess the scene first.'

She pulled her black puffa jacket tight to her throat. She hoped this winter wasn't going to be as bad as the last one. October could be a lovely time, but currently there was a storm warning, status orange, and forecasters intimated it could change to red at a moment's notice. Being surrounded by lakes, Ragmullin was susceptible to flooding, and Lottie had had enough of the rain over the last two weeks.

After a cursory look at a car in the drive, she approached the house. The door was open. A uniformed garda barred the entrance. When he recognised her, he nodded.

'Good evening, Inspector. It's not a pretty sight.'

'I've seen so much carnage in the last year, I doubt anything will shock me.' Lottie pulled a pair of protective gloves from her pocket, blew into them and tried to ease them over her damp hands. From her bag she removed disposable overshoes.

'How did he get in?' Boyd said.

'Door isn't forced, so he might have had a key,' Lottie said. 'And we don't know it's a "he" yet.'

'Arthur Russell was on a barring order; he shouldn't have had a key.'

'Boyd… will you give me a chance?'

Bending down, Lottie inspected a trail of bloody footprints leading along the hallway to where she was standing. 'Blood tramped the whole way out.'

'Both ways.' Boyd pointed to the imprints.

'Did the assailant come back to the door to check something, or to let someone else in?'

'SOCOs can take impressions. Mind where you walk.'

Lottie glared at Boyd as she stepped carefully along the narrow hall. It led to a compact old-style kitchen, though it appeared to be a relatively new extension. Without entering further, she shivered at the sight in front of her. She welcomed the sense of Boyd standing close behind her. It made her feel human in the face of such inhumanity.

'It was some fight,' he said.

A wooden table was turned upside down. Two chairs had been flung against it, and one had three legs broken off. Books and papers were scattered across the floor, along with a phone and a laptop, screens broken, smashed as if someone had stomped on them. Every movable object appeared to have been swept from the counter tops. A combination of sauces and soups dripped down the cupboard doors, and a tap was running water freely into the sink.

Drawing her eyes from the chaos, which evidenced a violent struggle, Lottie studied the corpse. The body lay face down in a small pool of blood. Short brown hair was matted to the head where a gaping wound of blood, bone and brain was clearly visible. The right leg stuck out to one side at an impossible angle, as did the left arm. The skirt was torn and a red blouse was ripped up the back.

'Bruises visible on her spine,' Boyd said.

'Badly beaten,' Lottie whispered. 'Is that vomit?' She looked down at a splurge of liquid two inches from her feet.

'Marian Russell's daughter was—' Boyd began.

'No. She couldn't get in. She'd forgotten her front door key and didn't have the one to the back door. She yelled for her mother through the letter box. Ran round the back. After heading back up the road to her friend's house, she called the emergency services. So the report says.'

'If she didn't go inside, then one of ours spilled his guts,' Boyd said.

'No need to be so explicit. I *can* see it.' Lottie went to run her fingers through her hair but the gloves snagged. 'Where's the daughter now?'

'Emma? With a neighbour.'

'Poor girl. Having to see this.'

'But she didn't see—'

'The report says she looked through the back door window, Boyd. Saw enough to never have a decent night's sleep for the rest of her life.'

'How do *you* sleep? I mean, with all you witness in the job. I know I pound it out on my bike, but how do you cope?'

'Now's not the time for this conversation.' Lottie didn't like Boyd's probing questions. He knew enough about her already.

Stepping into the kitchen, she realised they were compromising a scene already contaminated by the first responders. 'Are the scene-of-crime officers on the way?'

'Five minutes or so,' Boyd said.

'While we're waiting, let's try and figure out what happened here.'

'The husband broke in—'

'Jesus, Boyd! Will you stop? We don't know it was the husband.'

'Of course it's him.'

'Okay, for a second, say I agree. The big question is why. What drove him to it? He's been barred from the family home for twelve months and now he goes mad. Why tonight?' Lottie sucked on her lip, thinking. Something wasn't right with the scene before her. But she couldn't put her finger on it. Not yet, anyway. 'Has Arthur Russell been located?'

'No sign of him. Checkpoints are in place. Traffic units have the car registration. Our records show he's banned from driving, but the car isn't here so we can assume he took it. We'll find him,' Boyd said.

'If your hypothesis is correct, then who owns the car in the drive?'

'Registration is being checked as we speak.'

Hearing a commotion behind her, Lottie turned. Jim McGlynn, SOCO team leader, was beside her in two strides, his large forensic case weighing him down on one side.

'Are you two retiring any time soon?' he asked.

Lottie squeezed against the wall, allowing him to pass. 'No, why?'

'Death seems to follow you around. Stay outside until I say you can come in.'

Gritting her teeth, Lottie forced the words she wanted to say to stay in her mouth, and waited as McGlynn's team laid down foot-sized steel pallets so they wouldn't add anything else to the crime scene. She eyed Boyd rubbing his hand down his mouth and along his jaw. Burning to say something. Putting her finger to her lips, she shushed him.

'Who does he think he is?' Boyd whispered in her ear.

'Our best friend at the moment,' Lottie said.

They stood in silence and watched the forensic team work the scene for evidence. After twenty-five minutes, Jane Dore, the state pathologist, arrived, and McGlynn eventually turned the body over.

It was then that Lottie realised what was wrong. The body could not be that of Marian Russell. It was a much older woman.

'Who the hell is that?' Boyd asked.

CHAPTER 3

'Blunt-force trauma to the back of the skull.' Jane Dore tore off her forensic suit and stuffed it into the paper bag held out for her by her assistant. At five foot nothing, the state pathologist made up in expertise what she lacked in height. 'Find the weapon and I can match it to the wound.'

'Any idea what the weapon might be?' Lottie asked.

'Something hard and rounded.'

'Anything else you can tell us?' Lottie tried not to plead. 'We still have to identify her.'

'Well, *I've* no idea who the victim is. I'll schedule the post-mortem for eight in the morning. Maybe the body can tell us something. Come along and see for yourself.'

'I will. Thanks.' Lottie watched the pathologist walk out into the rain, her driver holding a wide umbrella over her head.

'There's a ladies' raincoat hanging on the stair post. It's damp,' she said to Boyd as he stood outside the front door. He lit two cigarettes and handed her one.

'So?' he said.

She took a drag. She didn't smoke. Not really. Only when Boyd gave her one. A double vodka would go down nicely, she thought. She had tried to give up alcohol, numerous times, but in the last few months she'd found herself slipping back into old habits. She took a double pull on the cigarette and coughed out the smoke.

'Whoever she is, she called to visit and maybe disturbed a burglar. That must be her coat in there,' Lottie said.

'Brute of a night for social calls,' Boyd said.

'There's no handbag. Nothing to tell us who she is.'

'Someone will know her.'

'Where's Marian Russell? According to her daughter's report, she was here when Emma left to go to her friend's house.'

'Where does the friend live?'

'Next house down.'

'That's about a mile away,' Boyd said.

'More like five hundred metres,' Lottie corrected him.

'It's dark and wet. Why would she let her child walk home?'

'Emma Russell is seventeen years old.' Lottie quenched the butt between her fingertips and handed it to Boyd. He placed both butts into the cigarette packet. She added, 'We need to find Marian Russell.'

'Kirby's working on it.'

'Let's have a look around the back yard.'

'I'll get McGlynn to switch on the outside light.' He headed inside.

The rain eased slightly but still Lottie found herself sloshing in and out of puddles as she made her way around the gable of the house. The building seemed to be a converted farmhouse, but the farm was long gone. A wide hedgerow provided the boundary as far as she could see, which in the dark wasn't far.

As she stepped into the yard, the external wall light blinked on, filling the space with an amber hue.

'Oh my God,' she said.

Boyd came out of the back door. 'What did you find?'

On the ground just outside the door lay a baseball bat, blood draining from it in the rain. Beside it was an old-fashioned black leather handbag, with an open brass clasp on top, its contents spilled out onto the paving stones.

'The weapon,' Boyd said. 'Someone was in a hurry.'

'And if this isn't Marian's handbag, it must belong to the victim inside.'

Lottie crouched down and with gloved fingers carefully turned over a plastic card lying on the saturated ground.

'Blood donor card. Tessa Ball,' she said. The name sparked a recognition nerve somewhere in her brain. But at the same time, she was convinced she had never met Tessa Ball.

'What are you doing to my crime scene?' McGlynn stood in the open doorway, towering over her. 'Don't touch a thing. I need everything photographed first.' He shouted for a tent to be erected.

'Okay, okay.' Lottie stood up. 'Keep your knickers on,' she added in a whisper.

As McGlynn approached, she sidestepped him and followed Boyd back to the front of the house.

'We need to speak to Emma,' she said.

'You need to slow down,' Boyd replied.

'I will, when I find whoever killed that old woman.'

CHAPTER 4

Emma Russell's hair hung long and limp over her shoulders. Lottie watched Emma's eyes following her through plain-framed spectacles. A woman stood behind the girl's chair.

'Bernie Kelly,' the woman said. 'Please sit down.'

'Thanks for taking care of Emma,' Lottie said, sitting on the couch. She introduced herself and Boyd and said, 'As soon as I can organise it, I'll assign a family liaison officer. Are you okay to have a chat with us, Emma?'

Emma sat forward on the armchair, her arms hanging between her denim-clad legs, twisting a tissue round and round her fingers. She nodded.

The sitting room was small and sad, stuffed with furniture and ornaments. A coal fire blazed in the open hearth, and it seemed to Lottie as if its heat was pulling the walls in on top of them. An oil diffuser did little to lighten the smell of smoke.

'I know you've had an awful shock,' she said, 'but it's important for us to talk to you as soon as we can.'

'Okay,' Emma whispered.

'First off, do you know a woman called Tessa Ball?' Lottie asked. Within the last fifteen minutes they had positively identified the victim from the driver's licence found in the handbag. And the registration plates proved the car in the drive belonged to her too.

'She's my granny,' Emma said, raising her head.

'Your granny?' Lottie turned to Boyd. He sat forward.

'Oh my God!' Emma gasped. 'That was her, wasn't it? Lying like that… on the kitchen floor. Who would do such a thing?'

'I'm so sorry. I didn't know,' Lottie said, mentally kicking herself. 'Can you tell me what you saw?'

'I… I don't really know.' Tears slipped down Emma's cheeks. She removed her spectacles and wiped the glass with a piece of the torn tissue, then shrugged Bernie's hand from her shoulder.

'Are you sure you're okay to discuss this? I'm sorry if it seems harsh, but we need to act immediately.' Lottie felt Boyd nudge her in the ribs. She inched away from him, but there was nowhere to go.

'You need to find my mum.'

'We have people out looking for her. Do you have any idea where she might be?'

'I don't know.'

'Okay. Emma, I need your help to establish what happened.'

Emma looked up, eyes wide. 'I don't know anything.'

'Tell me about your evening. Start at the beginning.'

'Do we have to do this now?' Bernie asked, her hand landing lightly on Emma's shoulder once again.

'I'm doing everything possible to find out what happened to your grandmother and to find your mother.' Lottie directed her answer to Emma. 'You might remember something you think is inconsequential, but it may in fact help us. You okay with that?' She lowered her head, trying to see the girl's eyes.

Emma spoke haltingly. 'I came straight home after school and went to my room. Did my homework. I heard Mum come in from work around five. She called me for dinner at six. We had lasagne. The ready-made kind. Horrible crap, but I ate it, to keep her happy. She said she needed to work on her stupid course. I took the hint, made a cup of coffee and sat in the sitting room for a few minutes before Natasha rang me and I came over here. Watched the telly. That's all I did.'

'What time did you go home?' Lottie asked, glancing at Boyd to make sure he was taking notes.

'Mum told me to be home by nine, but I think it was maybe after ten thirty by the time I got back. She's usually okay if I'm late as long as she knows where I am. I couldn't find my key. It's never a problem, because Mum is always at home at night…' Emma's voice trailed off and she looked up at Lottie. 'Where is she?'

'That's what we're trying to determine,' Boyd said.

'Why aren't you out looking for her, instead of sitting here asking me stupid questions?' Emma hung her head. 'Sorry.'

'I know you're upset, Emma.' Lottie reached out to touch the girl's hand.

Emma grasped it. 'Please find my mum.'

Squeezing her hand, Lottie said, 'It's upsetting, I know, but can you tell me what you did when you reached your house?'

Emma pulled her hand away, sniffed and rubbed her nose. 'I rang the doorbell. No one answered. I went round the back. Looked through the glass in the top half of the door. I saw… I saw…'

'You're doing fine,' Boyd said.

'No, I'm not! What would you know about it? It was horrible. Seeing a woman like that – on the kitchen floor. And now you tell me it was my granny. Who did that to her? Who killed her? And where is my mum?'

Where indeed? Lottie thought.

'So you didn't go inside at all?' Boyd said.

'Are you deaf or something? I had no key. I couldn't get in.' Emma glared, eyes flashing. 'I saw the… body on the floor. I didn't see anyone else around. It was raining and dark. I ran back to Natasha's. Then I rang 999.'

'Why didn't you phone from outside your own house?' Boyd asked.

'Didn't stop to think. I was scared. I just ran.' The tissue disintegrated into confetti and fluttered to the flowery carpet.

'When you were at the back of your house, are you sure you didn't see anything? Nothing on the ground?' Lottie asked.

'It was dark. I didn't see anything.'

'I know you had no key, but did you try the back door? Check if it was locked?'

'N… no. I didn't stop to think. I assumed it was locked but I didn't try it. Oh God, maybe Granny was alive and I could've saved her.' Emma curled up, arms around her chest, heaving back sobs.

'There was nothing you could have done, Emma,' Lottie said, reaching out to the girl. 'You did exactly the right thing, leaving the premises.' Now I've frightened her even more, she thought. Wild eyes stared back at her. If the fragility of the girl's mind mirrored her body, she was ready to collapse.

'Could he have been waiting for me?'

'No, pet. He was gone. But we need to take your fingerprints and DNA. Just to rule you out of the investigation.'

Emma's eyes widened to balls of fear. 'Why would you need my DNA? I didn't do anything.'

'It's procedure,' Lottie said, then relented. 'For now, though, I think you need to rest.'

'How can I rest when all I see is… is…'

Leaning over, Bernie Kelly squeezed the girl's elbow. 'Try not to fret too much.'

'I know this isn't easy, Emma,' Lottie said, 'so thank you for speaking to us. You've been a great help. This is my card with my number. Call me if you remember anything else.'

'Just find my mum.' The teenager convulsed into sobs.

At the door, Lottie turned. 'Your dad, when did you last see him?'

Emma looked up, confusion skittering across her face. 'My dad? Surely you don't think he did this?'

'Not at all. We have to follow up with everyone. Where might we find him?'

Shaking her head, Emma shrugged. 'I've no idea where he is.'

Lottie exchanged a look with Boyd. She dearly wanted to interrogate Emma further, but another girl had appeared in the doorway. Lottie assumed the tall, gangly teenager with red hair tied up in a ponytail was Natasha.

Bernie Kelly ushered the two detectives to the front door. 'I think Emma needs some rest, don't you, Inspector?'

'Yes, of course. But if she remembers anything at all, contact me straight away.' Lottie handed over another card. 'Like I said, there'll be a family liaison officer allocated to stay with her,' she added.

'No need for that. I'll look after her. I do most of the time anyway.'

'What do you mean?' Lottie pulled up her hood against the rain hammering down.

'Poor Emma. When she's not at school or working part-time in the hotel, she's here with Natasha. I don't think Marian has been well since… you know…'

'I don't know.'

'Since that business with Arthur.'

'You mean the barring order?' Lottie wondered where this conversation was going.

'Yes, and the other stuff.'

'Mrs Kelly, can we go back in to talk?'

'I really ought to watch the girls. I've said too much already.' Bernie Kelly turned to go back inside.

Lottie put a hand on the woman's arm, stalling her.

'You haven't said near enough. Emma's grandmother has been murdered, her mother has disappeared and we have no idea where Arthur Russell is. Do you know where Marian might be?'

'No. Sorry.'

'I can do with all the help you can give.'

'I don't know anything.' She made to close the door. Lottie thought of blocking it with her foot, but decided she would speak to her tomorrow.

'You know an awful lot more than you might think. Call in to the station in the morning. I can take a full statement then. Ten suit you?'

'I'll have to stay with the girls.'

'The family liaison officer will be here. Ten a.m. See you then.'

CHAPTER 5

Lottie crept up the stairs and listened. Not a sound. Thank God. She slipped into her room and eased the door shut. Without removing her jacket, she slumped down on the bed and breathed a sigh of exhaustion. After a hurried meeting at the station to set up an incident team, she'd called it a night and Boyd had dropped her home. Everything was in place to resume investigations in the morning, while searches were ongoing through the night to find Marian Russell.

She jerked her eyes open. Her brain wouldn't ease down. Hopefully the SOCOs would find something for them to go on, but her first priority was locating Marian Russell and her husband. Then she might have a better idea of just what had gone on in that house.

'Shit,' she said, jumping up. Her jacket was wringing wet. She tore it off and saw the damp patch on her duvet. 'This is all I need.'

Scooping up the Argos catalogue from Adam's side of the bed, Lottie dumped it on the locker. The heavy book gave her the sense of someone in the bed beside her. A feeling that she wasn't alone. Sometimes it was the little things that helped. She fluffed up the duvet, flipping it over so the wet patch was now at the bottom, on Adam's side. He wouldn't mind. He was dead. As she went to replace the catalogue, she paused. Four years was long enough to mourn an empty space. Her breath caught in her throat as she nudged the book under the bed. Four years *was* a long time in some respects, but the life she'd lived with Adam was still as fresh in her mind as if it were yesterday. A shroud of loneliness settled on her shoulders as she pulled off her damp clothes, dragged an old T-shirt over her head and got into bed.

A cry from the room beside hers told her Katie's baby was awake.

'Ah, God, not again,' Lottie whispered at the ceiling.

Katie's footsteps reverberated as she walked around her room soothing little Louis. Should she get up to help? No. Katie was adamant she wanted to care for her own baby.

The clock showed 3.45 a.m. Tapping her fingertips against her forehead, Lottie willed sleep into her brain. No use.

She sat up.

Opening the bedside locker, and without turning on the light, she felt for the bottle. A few sips wouldn't do any harm. Help her sleep, that was all. Medicinal. Yeah.

Two paracetamol for good measure, and a few more slugs, and she was soon fast asleep.

*

He watched the tall detective get out of the car and enter her house without switching on any lights. The other detective drove away.

He waited five minutes.

Saw a light go on in an upstairs bedroom and a shadow move around behind the blinds.

He waited a further five minutes, then made a phone call.

Like he had done every night for the last ten months.

When he was satisfied, he switched on the engine and drove away.

The mid seventies: The Child

They placed me in here and threw away the key.
The walls speak to me and I have no voice to join in their conversation.
I don't know how long I've been here. Do you?
The voice in the wall is silent now.
Do you know how long I've been here?
Silence.
My little fingers are sore.
I look down at the gown they've put on me.
I want my twin.
I want my own clothes.
They were all burned in the fire.
What fire?
The one your mother started, or maybe you did it?
I didn't do anything.
No one answers me.
Are the voices I hear only in my head?
I begin to cry. Big kids don't cry.
But I'm just a little kid.
Little kids should be seen and not heard.
I want my mummy…
Or do I?

DAY TWO

CHAPTER 6

A new day. Same old shit. Lottie's head ached and her mouth felt like something had slept in it overnight. She spied the empty vodka bottle lying like a discarded doll on the bed beside her.

Dragging her weary limbs into the shower, she avoided looking at her face in the mirror. Confusing the direction of the dial, she felt her body being blasted with freezing water.

'For feck's sake!'

She twisted the switch the correct way and stood to one side in the small glass cubicle until she felt warmth come from the stream of water. Stepping under the flow, she closed her eyes and breathed out, blowing a soft spray of water up to her nose. Feeling slightly dizzy, she leaned with the palms of her hands against the slippery tiled wall and allowed the water to hammer her spine.

I so deserve this, she thought. Stupid. Stupid. Stupid.

When she had enough energy, she lathered shampoo and conditioner into her hair, rinsed off and stepped from the heated cube to the cold bathroom.

No towel.

Rushing to get one from her room, she banged her toe against the door jamb.

And so her day began.

*

Pulling down her hood at the door to the mortuary, which everyone called the Dead House, Lottie ran her fingers through her hair. Her head thumped like mad. Seriously, though, she had to get her act together. She knew how an isolated slip-up turned into a downward spiral. Did she really want to go down that rabbit hole again? No. But one swig could ease the pain. Or a pill, if she had one.

The rain had continued unabated during the night, and it had crashed against the windscreen as she'd driven the forty kilometres to Tullamore, where the state pathologist was located. Buzzed in, she hurried down the icy corridor with its antiseptic smell masking the underlying pungent scent of death.

Jane Dore had already started the post-mortem and was walking around the steel table that held the seventy-plus-year-old body of Tessa Ball.

'Good morning, Detective Inspector.' The pathologist's voice was sharp and professional. 'I'll continue, if you don't mind.'

'Fire ahead,' Lottie said, suiting up and perching herself on a high stool beside a stainless-steel counter. Jane Dore and her team worked to a set routine. Viewing, touching, poking, sampling, recording.

The room seemed to be tipping on its axis as Lottie said impatiently, 'Any definitive cause of death? I'm assuming it is murder.'

Jane Dore turned and stared. 'You and I know that in my business I don't assume anything. I let the body tell me its story. And that is all I can work with.'

'I know, but I'm kind of busy and I've a team meeting to get to, so it would help if you…' Lottie's voice trailed off; she was aware she was slurring her words. Jane Dore's glare bored through her.

'Go, if you wish. I'll email my findings.' She turned back and continued her examination.

'Blunt-force trauma?' Lottie offered. 'That's what you said last night.'

With a sigh, Jane walked over. 'Okay. I can see your mind is elsewhere. I understand how busy you are, but I can't be rushed. As it stands, I've prioritised Mrs Ball's PM so that you'll have something to work with.'

'Thanks, Jane. Honestly, I appreciate it, but I don't feel the best and—'

'Cause of death will most likely be blunt-force trauma to the head. Satisfied?'

'Thank you. Any indication of the type of weapon used?'

'As I surmised last night, something hard and rounded, applied with great force. One strike. It either killed her or caused a massive stroke. I'll know more later.'

'Could it be the baseball bat we found at the scene?'

Jane stared. Lottie knew she couldn't alienate the state pathologist. She needed Jane to do something for her. Off the books, so to speak. And if she stayed here while Jane was cutting up the body, she would contaminate more than their friendship. Her stomach contents were already settling into her throat.

'Thank you,' she said and made for the door. 'One more thing. Sexual assault?'

'I'll take swabs, but I don't think it likely. You'll have my preliminary report this afternoon.'

With a final glance at the jaundiced-looking corpse, Lottie rushed from the autopsy room. The only consolation, as the rain drummed down, was that she hadn't vomited all over the shiny stainless-steel counter or the white-tiled floor. No, she'd waited until she reached the car park to spew up between two parked vehicles.

No more drink.

CHAPTER 7

The rain cleared a little and Ragmullin emerged from the mist, a smoky grey silhouette. The cathedral's twin spires spiked the clouds to the right and the landscape deformity of Hill Point protruded to the left. Lottie's one-time friend Doctor Annabelle O'Shea worked there. Pills. She needed a few Xanax to get her through the day – every day. Shaking herself to dislodge her cravings, she floored the accelerator and sped into town.

In her office, she tore off her jacket, hung it on the overflowing coat rack and headed to her desk.

'Anything from Mrs Ball's post-mortem?' Detective Larry Kirby asked.

Lottie stopped mid-step, noticing the big, burly detective, his wiry hair standing on end, chewing on an electronic cigarette.

'What're you doing with that?' she said.

'Trying to give up the cigars.' His fingers swallowed up the device and he pushed it into his shirt pocket.

'I've nothing from the PM yet,' Lottie said, pulling out her chair. 'I thought you were on door-to-door enquiries?'

'I was, but you called a team meeting for ten. I'm here. Is it still going ahead?'

Shite. In the space of the half-hour drive from Tullamore, she'd forgotten what she'd been rushing back for.

'Of course it is. Incident room. All of you.' She looked around. Her detectives were staring back at her. 'What?'

Boyd leaned over her. 'Are you okay?'

'Of course I am. Why?'

'You seem a bit… rattled.'

'I'll show you what rattled is.'

Detectives Boyd, Kirby and Lynch shuffled out of the office. Lottie waited until they had disappeared before sitting down and pulling out her desk drawer. She rifled through the mess. One, she thought. Even half of one. Dragging out files and pens, she ran her hand over the bottom of the drawer. Nothing. Yanked it out and turned it over. Yes! Sellotaped to the underside she found half a Xanax. Her safety net. As she tore it from the sticky tape, it began to crumble. No, she thought, I need you. Glancing around to ensure she was alone, she shoved the pill, still stuck to the tape, into her mouth. She let her tongue suck the residue and then spat out the tape. Catching sight of her reflection in her computer screen, she wondered who the wild woman might be. She looked a sight.

Standing up, she grabbed a bottle of water from Boyd's desk, gulped it down and headed for the incident room.

*

The notice boards were back in place, lining the end wall of the incident room. Hanging side by side, the death-mask photograph of Tessa Ball and an image from Emma's phone of her mother, the missing Marian Russell.

'Do we know if any of the blood at the scene is Marian Russell's?' Kirby asked.

'This is real life, not *CSI*,' Lottie said. 'It'll be days before we have the analysis. SOCOs are still on site this morning.' She pinned up photos of Russell's kitchen.

'Looks like a riot occurred,' Kirby said.

Lottie turned to rebuke him, but instead she said, 'Tessa Ball. Blunt-force trauma to the back of the head. Marian Russell. Last seen by her daughter Emma around six thirty p.m.' She tapped Marian's photo. 'We'll try to get a better photograph later today.'

'Did Marian kill her mother and skip town? Or was Tessa Ball in the wrong place at the wrong time?' Boyd asked.

'We can only work with the facts we have. Tessa Ball lived alone, across town, in St Declan's Apartments. No mobile phone in her handbag. A wallet with fifty-five euros and loose change. Keys, and reading spectacles in their case. A prayer book with a multitude of memoriam cards, and rosary beads.'

'A bible thumper,' Kirby said.

Lottie closed her eyes, counted to three and continued. 'One of the keys opens the car parked outside the house, and we can assume the other is the key to her apartment. We'll carry out a search there. We also need to trace her last known movements.'

Boyd piped up. 'Report just in from McGlynn. SOCOs have recovered a phone from the car.'

'Good. Get the data analysed.'

'Will do.'

'What does Emma have to say?' Detective Maria Lynch asked.

'She was very distraught last night. You'll have a transcript later of my interview with her.' Lottie eyed Boyd and smiled. A reminder for him to type it up. He nodded.

'Is the family liaison officer with her?' Lynch said.

'I'm glad you asked. The regular FLO is on sick leave. I was going to suggest maybe you could stand in for her, Detective Lynch.'

'Oh, no. I know I have the training, but I've so much work to be doing.' Lynch flicked through the files on her knee.

'Will you do it for today, please? Emma is at the Kellys' house. You can head over after we finish and see what you can get out of her.'

Lynch tugged at her ponytail, not a bit happy. Tough shit, Lottie thought. She didn't trust Lynch. The reason stemmed from a long time ago and she didn't want to think about it. Not now, anyway.

'So that's agreed,' Lottie said. 'Have we an address for Arthur Russell?'

Boyd said, 'He's been staying at a Bed and Breakfast. I spoke with the landlady. He's there at the moment.'

'We'll go and have a word with him.'

'It's not likely he had anything to do with the attack.' Boyd again.

'Why not?' Could he not shut up and let her get on with it?

'Doesn't make sense. If he did it, he'd be long gone by now.'

Lottie thought for a moment. 'We need to check where he was last night, and then we can look at means, opportunity and motive.'

Superintendent Corrigan appeared at the back of the room.

'Go ahead, Detective Inspector Parker. Don't let me interrupt you.' He leaned against the wall and folded his arms over his large stomach.

'Thank you, sir,' Lottie said, dropping the sheets of paper she'd been holding. She didn't trust herself to bend down to retrieve them. Her head was swimming enough already.

Boyd moved to pick them up. She cut him with a look. He sat back down.

'Looks like a domestic to me,' Corrigan said.

'Looks can be deceiving.' Did she really just say that to her superintendent?

'I feckin' know that,' Corrigan said, staring straight at her, rubbing a hand over his bald head.

Maybe she should have stayed in bed.

'Until forensics are complete, we're not in a position to speculate,' she said. 'Post-mortem is occurring as we speak, but the state pathologist confirmed that blunt-force trauma to the head is the most likely contributor to Mrs Ball's death.'

'Blunt-force trauma? With what?' Corrigan asked, unfolding his arms and striding through the room towards Lottie. He jabbed a thick finger at the crime-scene photo. 'Show me.'

'We found a potential weapon outside the back door, sir.' Lottie pointed to a grainy night-time photograph. 'It's being forensically examined.'

'A baseball bat. This is Ragmullin, not feckin' Chicago. Who owns the bat?'

'We haven't determined ownership. Yet. Sir.' Digging her nails into her palms, she repeated a silent mantra. *Keep the fuck calm.*

'You seem to have determined feck all.'

'We're working flat out, sir.'

'Not flat out enough. I want Russell in a cell before the day is out. And I want his wife found. Can you determine *that*, Detective Inspector Parker?'

'Yes, sir.'

'Then get to it, the feckin' lot of you.' With a smug sniff, he straightened his shoulders and marched out of the door.

'What was all that about?' Boyd asked.

'A load of bollocks,' Kirby said.

'He's the boss,' Lynch said.

'I'm the boss of this investigation,' Lottie said, throwing her arms upwards in despair. 'Will someone track down Mrs Ball's friends and interview them? Kirby? And find out who owns that baseball bat.'

He nodded.

Her phone rang. Desk sergeant.

'What's up, Don?' Lottie asked.

'There's a Bernie Kelly in interview room one. She's been there this half-hour. Did you forget about her?'

'Shit!' Lottie gathered up her papers, phone between ear and shoulder. 'I'll be down in one minute.'

As she left the incident room, she said, 'Lynch, head over to the Kellys'. I don't want Emma Russell left alone. Boyd, come with me.'

Kirby said, 'What will I do?'

'Find Tessa's friends and the owner of that baseball bat.'

'Can I fly to Chicago?'

CHAPTER 8

'I'm so sorry for keeping you, Mrs Kelly.' Lottie pulled out a chair and sat facing Bernie Kelly, who was sitting with her arms folded. She looked to be mid-forties, a thick layer of foundation obscuring her natural colour and eyebrows pencilled in. Her lips were pale. Lipstick forgotten or by design? Lottie didn't know, but she knew an attack was imminent.

'Do you think I've nothing to do and nowhere to be? Thirty-five minutes I've been sat here.'

Received, over and out. Her strawberry-blonde hair was matted to her scalp and her mac-type jacket was still dark from the rain.

'Please accept my apologies, but we're at the beginning of a murder investigation. It's a bit chaotic. I'm sure you can understand.' Smile in place, Lottie switched on the recording equipment.

'What's with all that stuff?' Bernie nodded toward the machine. 'I'm not a suspect, am I? Do I need a solicitor? I only came in because you asked.'

'And I appreciate you taking time out of your busy schedule.' See how that sits, Lottie thought. 'Now, what can you tell me about Marian Russell?'

'There's not much to tell.' Bernie shrugged her shoulders, a shadow of indifference falling over her green eyes.

Lottie eyed Boyd from the corner of her eye. Not one of those interviews, she hoped, where she had to extract a statement word by word.

'What *can* you tell me?'

'Like I said last night, I don't think Marian has been too well.'

'In what way?'

'You know.' Bernie pointed to her temple. 'Up here.'

'What makes you say that?'

Bernie sighed and lowered her eyes. 'She became reclusive. Wouldn't go out any more. At one time we used go to the pub for a drink on Friday and Saturday nights. The only place she goes now is work. When she's not there, she stays at home. Won't even answer the phone to me any more.'

'What does Emma have to say about her mother?'

'Emma is a bit harsh at times. I don't think she gets that Marian could be depressed. She's always been a daddy's girl. She blames her mother for the trouble at home, not her father.'

'What kind of trouble?'

'I'm sure you can access the court files. Marian took Arthur to court and got him barred from the house.'

'We will get the files, but it would help if you could tell me what you know.'

Bernie leaned over the desk conspiratorially. 'Beat her black and blue. Saw the bruises with my own eyes.'

'How did you see them?'

'Emma came crying into my house one evening, saying her mammy had made her daddy mad and she thought he was going to kill her. That's the only time I've heard her speak ill of her father.'

'What did you do?'

'Got my phone and ran to their house. The door was wide open. Marian was curled up in a ball beside the cooker and Arthur was marching around the kitchen with a poker in his hand.'

'Had he hit her with the poker?'

'I don't know what he hit her with, but she was fierce frightened. I said to him, "Arthur Russell, you get out of this house. I've called the guards." I hadn't, but maybe I should have.'

'What happened then?'

'He turned round and glared at me like a wild bear – not that I've ever seen a wild bear – then dropped the poker and ran out the back door. I got Marian to a chair. She wasn't bleeding, just badly bruised. Said she didn't want a doctor or the guards. Asked me to keep Emma at mine for the night and to call her mother.'

'And what did you do?'

'I did as she asked.'

'And you didn't report the incident?'

'Marian told me not to.'

'You said you thought Marian was depressed. What way did you notice that, besides her not going out for a drink with you?' If Marian was in fear of an abusive husband, it was understandable that she might retreat into herself, but it didn't mean she had to be depressed.

'I'm not sure I should speak ill of the dead…'

'We have no evidence to suggest Marian is dead.'

'I mean her mother. Tessa Ball.'

'What about her?'

'She was a right nag when she wanted to be. Didn't agree with the barring order. One of those old-fashioned biddies who believed in "for better, for worse" even when the worse was so bad you had to lock your husband out.'

'So she was nagging Marian over Arthur?'

Bernie nodded.

'But she was the person Marian wanted the night she was assaulted?' Boyd said.

'I wondered about that. I think Marian had to show her mother just how brutal Arthur could be.'

'Makes a kind of sense,' Boyd said, scrunching his eyebrows together.

'Any other instances of domestic violence in the Russell home that you can recall?' Lottie asked.

Bernie sighed and looked down at her clasped hands.

'Is there something you have to share with us?' Boyd urged. 'Rest assured everything is confidential.'

'Yeah, right. Until I read it in the newspaper or online.'

'You're here to help us. We need to find Marian,' he said. 'To make sure she is safe. Something you say may help us locate her.'

With another sigh, Bernie said, 'I think Tessa Ball beat Marian too.'

Lottie exchanged a glance with Boyd. 'Why do you say that?' she asked.

'It's just something Emma told Natasha once. About how it was such an injustice the way the courts treated her dad, when he was like a puppy compared to her granny.'

'But you have no eyewitness account of Mrs Ball beating Marian?'

'No. But after what happened last night, I think I can believe it.'

'You think Marian attacked her mother and left her dead on the kitchen floor?' Lottie asked.

'It seems like it from where I'm sitting.'

'Is there anything else you'd like to add?' Boyd asked.

'No. I want to go home now.' Bernie Kelly picked up an umbrella from the floor and shook it.

'Of course,' Lottie said. 'I'm sending a family liaison officer to stay with you until we find somewhere for Emma.'

Bernie's cheeks flared red. 'I've told you we don't need a babysitter.'

'Emma needs protection until we find her mother.'

'She says she wants to go home.'

'That's not possible. Not at the moment.'

'She can stay with me as long as she wants. And I don't want any guards in my house.'

'And I've to do my job. Thanks for coming in.' Lottie stood up to complete the interview protocol. 'I'm sorry for leaving you waiting earlier.'

Bernie Kelly stood too. 'I'd nowhere else to be anyway. Except being at home watching the girls.'

CHAPTER 9

The garda technical van was still parked on the road outside the Russell house, and spotlights were casting tunnels of yellow light up at the grey-black sky. Jim McGlynn was standing outside the door, instructing his assistant to head upstairs.

'Hi, Jim. Did you see a teenager hanging round here this morning?' Detective Maria Lynch asked, holding the umbrella over both of them. 'I've been up at the Kellys' but there seems to be no one there.'

He ducked away. 'That thing is dripping all over me. Who is it you're looking for?'

'Emma Russell. Granddaughter of the victim. She might have been with a friend.'

'Ah, yes, saw someone. Around ten o'clock. Wanting to get in. The cheek, like.'

'Do you know where they went?'

McGlynn said, 'I was busy trying to finish up here so I didn't pass any remarks. Is it your job to be minding the young one?'

'Yes, it is. And I can't find her,' Lynch said. A gust of wind took hold of her umbrella, blowing it inside out.

'Rather you than me, then, having to tell DI Parker you lost her.' McGlynn chuckled to himself as he hurried inside the house.

'For fucks sake,' Lynch said. She was already in Lottie Parker's bad books – God only knew what for – and now this. She'd wring Emma Russell's neck when she found her.

And then a terrible thought struck her.

She dropped the inside-out umbrella into the ditch and started to run back up the road.

CHAPTER 10

Arthur Russell strummed his guitar and listened through the headphones. It was beginning to sound good. Beginning to sound like something worth recording. He still had dreams. Forty-nine and acting like a wannabe world-famous guitarist. That's me, he thought. Too late to change now.

Flicking a couple of the red switches and sliding a lever on the sound desk, he began again. Crooning to the soft music straining through his headphones.

Still not quite right. Sighing loudly, he tugged at his wiry grey-flecked beard and closed his eyes. When he opened them again, two people were standing before him. He pulled off the headphones, scraping the skin on his shaved head.

'What do you want? How'd you get in here?'

'Mr Russell? Arthur Russell?' said the woman with rain-soaked hair.

'Who's asking?' He placed his guitar on its stand, folded his arms and gently swivelled on his stool.

'Detective Inspector Lottie Parker,' the woman said.

He liked the sound of her voice. Deep and melodic. He wondered if she could sing.

'Detective Sergeant Boyd,' said the tall wiry man.

He looked more groomed than the woman. Odd pair, Russell thought.

'You're trespassing on my property. How did you get in?'

'Your landlady. Nice set-up you have here,' the detective inspector said.

'Mrs Crumb is a loony old bat. What do you want? I haven't done anything.'

'Breach of a barring order strike any bells?' The woman's voice was higher now. Sneering at him.

He said, 'I haven't been next, nigh nor near that house. Ask the wife. Oh, maybe she sent you to shake me up for a few more euros, is that it? Hard luck. I'm broke.'

'When did you last see your wife?' the male detective asked.

He wasn't a singer anyway, Russell mused. And what had this to do with Marian?

'My wife?'

'Yes, Mr Russell. Your wife.'

'Saw her in court about four months ago. Why don't you ask her?'

'We would if we could find her.' The inspector again.

'Try Tesco or up at the house. Only two places Marian goes.'

'She's not at either. When did you last see your mother-in-law?'

'Hold on a minute… What's this about?'

'Answer the question.'

'No, I won't answer the question. You've no right being here, asking stupid shite. Now get out before I call a solicitor.'

The inspector stepped towards him. Arthur stood his ground.

She said, 'It's in your own interests to answer our questions.'

'Why? Any time I've had anything to do with your lot, it's ended up damn expensive. You and your like cost me my family. I can't even see my daughter without giving a month's notice.' He rolled his fists into tight balls. Chewed hard on the Nicorette gum in his mouth. Blood pumping up through his chest and arms, boiling around in his head. The muscles in his legs making his knee twitch.

'Why are you so angry?' The inspector – what was her name? Parker. Yeah. Bitch –took another step into his space. One more and I'll flatten you, he thought. He shrugged his shoulders instead.

'I want no trouble.'

'Where were you last night between six thirty and, say, eleven?'

'Do I need a solicitor?'

'Up to you. Have you something to hide?'

Arthur banged his fists against his thighs. 'You come in here and ask me all these questions. Makes me nervous, that's all. What would you feel like if someone came into your music shed and did that to you?'

'I don't have a music shed,' she said.

'Figures.'

'What do you mean?'

Arthur stood up, his patience finally snapping. 'You look like you're too far up your own hole to chill with music. Am I right or am I right? Ha.'

Gone too far, he thought, as she grabbed his shirt and pulled him close to her. He smelled the mint she'd been sucking, masking the staleness of alcohol. A drinker. All the guards were the same. Alcoholic bastards.

'Take your hands off me this second,' he said.

She released her grip, dropping her hand without moving away. 'I'm taking you to the station to make a statement.'

'What am I supposed to have done, because I sure don't know?'

'You refused to answer our questions,' said the lanky male detective. 'Last night, where were you?'

Russell picked up his guitar and sat down. 'I was at work yesterday in Danny's Bar and I had my dinner with Mrs Crumb around seven thirty. After that, I worked on my music in here. Now get the hell out of my privacy.'

The two detectives looked at each other. Deciding what to do? Pricks, Arthur thought, and put his headphones on. He wheeled the stool away from them, faced his desk and began to sing.

When he turned around again, they'd gone. But he knew, as sure as day follows night or whatever the saying was, they'd be back.

He spat out the gum. Rooted around in his guitar case, found a pack of cigarettes and lit one. His head began to swim and he knew he needed something stronger than nicotine.

'Fuck you, Marian,' he said, tugging off the earphones again. 'You scheming bitch.'

*

'He's a piece of work,' Boyd said, struggling to light a cigarette in the rain.

'With his hillbilly tartan shirt and his scraggy beard… Who does he think he is?' Lottie said, pulling up her hood against the downpour.

'He could do with a wash,' Boyd said.

'I couldn't smell him.'

'I'm not surprised.'

'What do you mean by that?'

'Lottie, you're drinking again. I'm not blind or stupid. What's going on?'

The concern etched on his face disturbed her. But she didn't need him to feel sorry for her. She'd fight this her own way. Like she always did.

'Mind your own business.' She ran to the car. Got in and slammed the door.

Boyd joined her. 'I'll only say this once,' he began. 'I'm here if you need me.'

'Start the car. We need to do the paperwork on Arthur Russell and check out his so-called alibi.'

'Your wish is—'

'Start the car, Boyd.'

'Maybe we should've told him about his dead mother-in-law and his missing wife.'

'Maybe we were right not to. Let's see what he does next.'

'Do you think Marian killed her own mother?'

'When we find her, why don't we ask her?' Lottie stamped her feet up on the dashboard and wondered where she could get more pills.

'Where to?' Boyd said.

'Tessa Ball's flat.'

'What about Danny's Bar? To check Arthur's alibi.'

'It can wait. We'll have lunch there.'

'Might get it on the house.' Boyd put the car in gear.

'You're a mean shite.' But she had been thinking the same thing.

'Bet you were thinking the same,' Boyd said.

Lottie attempted to hide her smile, but failed. She had to listen to him laughing all the way to St Declan's Apartments.

*

Lynch ceased her banging on the door and turned round, coming face to face with a woman, key in hand.

'Can I help you at all?'

'I'm the temporary family liaison officer assigned to Emma Russell. Do you know where she might be?'

'I told the other one that we don't need… Oh, come on in.' The woman opened the door and ushered her inside. 'I'm Bernie Kelly.'

Taking off her coat, Lynch hung it over a heap of others on the stair post. 'I was ringing and knocking but no one answered. I even went down to check at the Russells'. Where is Emma?'

'In bed, I should think. I don't know how she's going to cope with it all.'

'Can I check?' Lynch grabbed the other woman's arm and steered her towards the stairs. 'I want to be sure she's safe.'

'Of course she's safe in my house. Why wouldn't she be?'

'Please have a look.'

'Emma? Natasha? Are ye awake yet?' Bernie sauntered up the stairs. Lynch wanted to push past her and run into every room.

'What's up, Mum?'

Lynch assumed this was Natasha. The girl appeared on the landing, a black T-shirt for a nightie and her hair a tangled mess around her shoulders. Both thighs were tattooed with a dark red heart dripping blood from the dagger piercing it.

'Where's Emma?' Lynch almost sent Bernie tumbling back down the stairs as she barged past her.

Natasha squinted through one eye, the other seemingly stuck closed with sleep. 'Who are you?'

'Detective Maria Lynch, family liaison officer. I need to see Emma. Where is she?' She couldn't stop the panic sharpening her voice.

Emma's bedroom was empty.

'Is she in another room?' Without waiting for an answer, she checked the other rooms. All empty. She whipped out her phone and bounded down the stairs past an open-mouthed Bernie Kelly, tapping her phone for Lottie's number.

'Hey, just a minute, you, this is my house.'

Lynch felt her ponytail being tugged, and whirled round to launch an attack just as the back door opened and in walked a teenager, holding a plastic supermarket bag in her hand. The smell of fresh bread preceded her entrance.

'Are you Emma?'

The girl nodded.

'Where the hell have you been?' Lynch shouted, disconnecting the call before Lottie could answer.

Emma shrank back against the door. Tears suffused the whites of her eyes. 'Shopping.'

'And *you've* just assaulted a member of the gardaí,' Lynch snapped at Bernie Kelly.

'This is my house! You can't go barging around like you own the place.' Bernie marched past Lynch into the kitchen. 'Come on, let's have a cup of tea and we can all calm down.'

And that made Lynch even madder.

CHAPTER 11

Tessa Ball had lived in a modern two-bedroomed apartment complex next door to the disused St Declan's Hospital. Lottie squirmed as a shiver wormed its way between her shoulder blades. She didn't like to dwell on her most recent case which had culminated inside the closed-down hospital.

'What's the matter with you?' Boyd asked. 'You look like a rat crawled over your face.'

'Very funny, Boyd.' She unbuckled her seat belt. 'Second floor. Apartment 6B.'

She tried to avoid splashing in puddles. Her boots would never dry out at this rate. In the clean, square foyer, smelling strongly of disinfectant, they were met with the steel door of an elevator. She pressed a button, stepped inside and waited for Boyd to join her.

The elevator trundled slowly up to the second floor. They exited into a corridor lined with doors.

Stepping into the apartment, Lottie felt around the wall for a light switch and flicked it on. They were standing in a living area. Curtains drawn across the window. The room was split in half by a breakfast bar, behind which lay a galley-type kitchen. A couch piled with cushions in knitted covers was pushed up against the bar. There was a single armchair too, and the floor was covered with flowery deep-pile carpet.

'Like a return to the seventies,' Lottie said. 'I thought these were relatively new apartments?'

'Built about ten years ago, maybe less. She must have decorated it herself.'

'I wouldn't call it decorating; not in the modern sense.' She appraised the acrylic paintings on the wall and sniffed the air. 'Wintergreen.'

'To mask the fusty smell, or maybe she had muscle problems?' Boyd shrugged and lifted up a newspaper from the coffee table. 'Yesterday's *Irish Times*. No *Sun* for this lady.' A basket with wool and knitting needles sat beside the newspaper.

Lottie moved to the window and drew back the brocade curtain. It didn't add much light to the room. One of those days that refused to brighten up. A moth escaped the darkness and fluttered up to the glass chandelier.

The kitchen counter top was clean and the sink empty. One by one she opened the mahogany doors of the cupboards. Pulling out a few pots, she checked there was nothing hidden.

'What are we looking for?' Boyd asked, opening the refrigerator.

'Make sure you check the freezer box,' Lottie said, recalling how they'd overlooked evidence in an earlier case.

'Not even an ice cream.'

She walked down the narrow corridor and opened the first of three doors. Bathroom. She searched the cabinet. No prescription medicines. A packet of paracetamol, a brown bottle containing iron tonic, and a tube of wintergreen. Shampoo bottle on the floor of the green-mosaic-tiled shower. The chrome handrail made her think perhaps Tessa was feeling her age.

The next door appeared to be a spare room. Single bed, neatly made up with a white candlewick bedspread. One locker, empty. Free-standing wardrobe, empty. No boxes on top and nothing under the bed.

'This one must belong to the lady of the house,' Boyd said, opening the door.

Lottie bit down a sarcastic retort. Her head was pounding and she needed to get out of the suffocating air as quickly as possible.

Mrs Ball's bedroom was what she had half expected. An old brass bed, made up with a spread similar to the spare room. A picture of the Sacred Heart hung above it, with the requisite red lamp lit beneath. Lottie got down on her knees, scrabbling beneath the double bed. She sneezed. Mrs Ball's tidiness hadn't extended to hoovering under here. Her fingers touched a cardboard box – a shoebox. As she dragged it out, another cloud of dust rose up.

Boyd ran his hand underneath the mattress. 'Nothing.'

'I thought all little old ladies stored their life savings under the mattress.'

'What's in the box?' Boyd knelt beside her.

Lottie shook it. 'It's light.'

'Are you going to open it or bag it?'

Lifting the lid, she peered into the rectangular space that had once held size seven black court shoes, according to the label. A bundle of letters held together with a rubber band, sticky with age.

'She hadn't touched these in years,' she said.

'Old memories?'

'Bad memories?' She got a plastic evidence bag from her handbag and placed the bundle inside.

'Not going to have a sneaky look?'

'No time now.' Claustrophobia tightened her airways. 'I'll check the cabinet and wardrobe. You search the living room.' She stood up to let Boyd edge out and noticed he was careful not to let their bodies touch. Her imagination?

She opened the door of the wardrobe. Ran her fingers through the hangers. Polyester and wool dresses, blouses and coats. Marks & Spencer Classic range trousers and sweaters folded on a shelf. On the floor, three pairs of well-worn black shoes. She closed the door and turned her attention to the three-drawer bedside table.

On top of it sat a ticking alarm clock, set for seven a.m. A lamp. A small leather purse with gold lettering proclaiming that it came from Lourdes. Inside was a string of rosary beads. How many did she need? A laminated prayer to St Anthony was taped to the side of the locker. Lottie supposed Mrs Ball had recited it when she'd been in bed at night. Could this religious old woman really have beaten her adult daughter? Nothing would surprise her any more.

She opened the top drawer. It was kept tidy, with plastic separators for loose change, and an assortment of pill bottles. Aspirin, blood pressure and sleeping pills. She shut the drawer. The next one held underwear and tights. The bottom drawer was lined with a selection of paperback novels.

'Mrs Ball was an avid crime reader,' she called out to Boyd.

'Really? I thought she'd be the type to read the Bible. I don't see one here.'

'Don't worry – I've found one.' She flicked through the pages of all the books. Nothing fell out.

She joined Boyd in the living room. 'Find anything?'

'Nope.'

'We'll examine what we've got back at the station. Switch off the light on the way out.'

'Hey, Lottie?'

'Yes?'

'Look at this.'

She joined him hunched down at a dark cabinet squeezed between the armchair and the breakfast bar.

'I thought it might be one of those cupboards that you hide a television in,' he said, slowly opening the door.

'Christ!' Lottie said. 'That most definitely is *not* a television.'

CHAPTER 12

The bread was brown, soft and fresh, but the tea was weak. Lynch made no comment on either. Across the table, Emma gulped Red Bull from a can, her eyes wide with apprehension. Or was it fear? Lynch wondered.

'So who was with you down at your house earlier?' Lynch asked.

'What? I was only at the shop.'

Lynch couldn't help rolling her eyes. 'Well, it wasn't Natasha, because she was in bed. Tell the truth. Who was with you?' She tried to remember if McGlynn had in fact confirmed that someone had been with Emma. But then she recalled that he didn't even know Emma.

'I don't have to tell you anything.'

'Might help us find your mother.'

'Do I need a solicitor?'

'A solicitor?' Lynch spluttered into her mug. 'Why on earth would you need a solicitor?'

Emma shrugged her shoulders. 'Dunno. They always say that on the telly.'

Sitting forward, hands clasped to keep her impatience locked in, Lynch said, 'Emma, this is very serious. Your gran is dead. Your mum is missing. You can't just go waltzing round the shops. You could be in danger.'

The girl's eyes seemed to pop behind her spectacles. 'I want my dad.'

Bernie Kelly said, 'I don't think you should be frightening the life out of the poor girl. Isn't it your job to keep her calm?'

'I just want to know where you went this morning, Emma.'

'Buying bread.'

'There's plenty of bread here,' Bernie said. 'No wonder you're half drowned. You need to get out of those wet clothes.'

'It's a long walk to the shops. Why did you go out for bread if there was some here?' Lynch persisted.

'I like it fresh.' Emma dropped her eyes.

'Who was with you?'

'No one.'

'Listen, Emma, I know when a teenager is telling me lies.' Lynch was kicking herself for not getting more details from Jim McGlynn. 'I need the truth from you. Now.' Then she'd have to ring Lottie and tell her the girl had been out, alone or with someone.

'Bernie, could you make us two very strong cups of tea? This might take a while.'

*

Boyd stopped outside the station to let Lottie out of the car. She picked up her bag from the footwell. 'Register everything. We'll go through the letters later on.'

'Will I get forensics to check the apartment?' Boyd idled the engine.

'No harm giving it the once-over. But I don't think they'll find anything. It looked untouched since the last time Tessa was there.'

'What was a little old lady doing with a handgun?'

'Breaking the law. And don't forget she had boxes of bullets. Protection? Fear? I don't know why she had it or where she got it from. But get everything printed and organise a ballistics test. See if it was fired recently.'

'No one's been shot around here. Recently,' Boyd said pointedly.

'Check if it's *ever* been fired.'

'Sure. Where are you going?'

Lottie got out of the car and pulled up her hood. 'I need a coffee. A proper one. None of that office shite. Won't be long.'

'You sure it's just a coffee you're after?'

She slammed the door without reply.

*

The water on the footpath lapped up over her boots, saturating them. Rain dripped from the hood of her jacket down on to her nose. It was gone midday, but it was persistently dark and wet. Light from shop windows cast amber shadows on the flood streaming down the road into drains clogged with fallen autumn leaves. An umbrella-wielding passer-by prodded Lottie in the back of the head and she quickly entered the coffee shop.

She ordered and sat at a table by the window to mull everything over. She could do with Boyd to bounce stuff off, but he was being a pain in the arse. When her coffee arrived she stirred in three sugars and on impulse asked for a cream bun. Two garda sergeants came in, nodded acknowledgement and settled into a corner booth by the far wall. They reminded her of her dad. Though she'd only been four when he died – when he killed himself – she remembered him in uniform. Or was that a trick of the mind? Did she only remember him from photographs? She couldn't be sure.

The coffee was too strong but she forced it down. Her thoughts were focused on her father. What would he look like today if he was still alive? Would he have made detective? She liked to think so. But he'd be well retired by now. Would he be proud of her? Rubbing her forehead, as though it could eradicate the pain thumping inside, she wondered how different her life might have been if he hadn't killed himself. She had to find out what had made him do it. The box was still in her bedroom. His papers. Stuff from his desk. She'd gone through it many times since her mother had given it to her almost five months ago. Conducted her unofficial investigation, but no one she'd spoken to remembered anything. Selective amnesia? She didn't know. It was maddening

She put down the cup with a clatter, pushed away the uneaten bun. Her stomach could just about cope with liquid.

Her phone rang. Lynch.

CHAPTER 13

Standing outside the coffee shop, Lottie slipped her phone back into her bag.

Lynch had had one job – one goddam job – and she seemed to have messed it up. Emma had left the house and Lynch had no idea where the girl might have been. Pulling up her hood, Lottie turned towards the station. It was dark enough for the street lights to be on, but they weren't. She glanced up at the cathedral spires, which appeared to look down on her – two eyes warning of impending doom.

She heard a siren screeching down the road towards her. Boyd. He drew the car alongside, and she leapt back against the wall to avoid being drowned in the splash of water from the road.

'Get in,' he shouted, pushing open the passenger door.

Lottie jumped in. 'What's the rush?'

'Marian Russell's been found.'

'What? Where? Is she okay?'

'Too many questions.'

'Okay, one at a time.' Lottie held up one finger. 'Is she alive?'

'I don't know.'

Two fingers. 'Where's she been?'

'I don't know.'

She abandoned her fingers. 'Where the hell are we going?'

'The hospital.'

'Explain.'

'She was found outside the front door of the hospital. She was wearing a bracelet ID because she's diabetic. Her name was on it. Security guard had the sense to call us.'

'She's alive so.'

'She was when we got the call. I'm not so sure now.'

'Boyd, stop it.'

'I don't know what's going on,' he said. 'We were told she's been taken through to the emergency department and they're working on her. Sounds serious.'

He parked the car in the ambulance bay and Lottie was first to jump out and run to the revolving hospital door.

'Come on,' she shouted at the inanimate glass as Boyd squeezed in behind her.

'Which way?' he asked.

'Follow me,' she said.

'Detective Inspector Lottie Parker,' she shouted into the intercom speaker at A&E. 'Open up.' The door swished inwards.

Trolleys with patients lined the walls of the corridor. Lottie crashed along. She grabbed a passing nurse.

'Where can I find Marian Russell?'

'I'll have to check. Take a seat,' the nurse said.

'I have to find her. Now.'

'As I said, I'll check. And you need to calm down.'

Lottie took a deep breath. 'Please,' she said, trying to conjure a smile.

'We'd better wait.' Boyd guided her to a reception area.

The nurse looked at a computer screen, tapped the keyboard and said, 'She was triaged and taken upstairs for surgery.'

'She's alive then.' Lottie exhaled.

'She was when she left here,' the nurse said. 'Now if you'll excuse me, we're busy today.'

Lottie barely heard the words. She turned, ran out of the A&E department and scanned the notice board on the wall.

'Third floor,' she said, heading for the stairs.

By the time they reached the third floor, Lottie thought the elevator would have been a better option. Too late now. She leaned her bottom against the wall, bent over in two, struggling to catch her breath. Boyd was walking in circles, not a hair out of place, breathing normally.

'Press the buzzer.' Lottie wiped drool from her chin.

'You need to give up those cigarettes,' he said.

'I don't smoke.'

Boyd made a display of taking out his pack of cigarettes and counting them. She snatched it from him and shoved it in her bag as the ward door opened.

'We're here about Marian Russell,' Lottie said.

'Are you family?' The nurse checked down a list on a clipboard in her hand.

'We're detectives.' They showed their ID.

'She's in surgery. Leave your details and I'll give you a call as soon as she—'

'Look,' Lottie interrupted, 'this is a murder investigation.'

'She's not dead,' the nurse said.

'I know, but her mother is and we need to speak with Mrs Russell as a matter of urgency.'

'I don't think she'll be in any state to speak to anyone for a long time.'

'Can you tell us what injuries she presented with?' Boyd asked.

The nurse began to close the door. 'I've told you, Mrs Russell is in surgery. That's all I can say for now.'

Lottie stuck her foot in the door. 'What are her injuries?'

'Detective…?'

'Detective Inspector Parker,' Lottie said, showing her ID again.

The nurse conceded. 'She has severe head injuries. And her tongue was cut out. Sorry, but I must get back.'

Lottie removed her foot and allowed the door to swing closed. She looked up at Boyd. He was standing against the wall, mouth open, running his hand up and down his chin.

Neither of them could speak.

And if Marian Russell couldn't speak either, where did that leave their investigation?

CHAPTER 14

'I need a cigarette, now.' Lottie hopped from foot to foot at the front door of the hospital.

'It's a non-smoking campus.'

'And you're parked in an ambulance bay. Give me a cigarette before I scream.'

Boyd searched his pockets. 'You took them.'

She rooted around in her bag, found the pack and handed it to him. He lit two and gave her one. She inhaled too quickly and curled up in a fit of coughing.

'For someone who doesn't smoke, you have a hell of a smoker's cough.'

'I feel sick. Her tongue was cut out, her tongue! First her mother is murdered. Then Marian disappears and turns up at the hospital with horrific injuries.'

'And where was she? Who was holding her? Why?'

'First things first.' Lottie blew out a ring of blue smoke. 'Get Arthur Russell into the station. We need to have another chat with him.'

'Okay.'

'And interview whoever found Marian. Check the CCTV to see if she was dropped off or staggered in.'

'I'll call Kirby.' He pulled out his phone.

'I want an armed detective guarding her room. If she survives surgery, that is.'

'I'll draw up a roster when I get back to the station.'

'Get someone to come now.' Lottie paused for breath. 'And contact Lynch. Emma Russell has to be watched twenty-four seven.'

'Righto.'

'No one goes in or out of the ward.'

Boyd nodded agreement.

'We need to go back and search the Russell house,' Lottie added.

'SOCOs were there all morning.'

'They're looking for evidence of a domestic dispute gone tits-up. This is something much bigger than that.' She turned to head for the car. 'Ah no. This is all I need.'

Cathal Moroney, crime correspondent for the national television station, was running towards her.

'Detective Inspector Parker, I'm glad I caught you,' he panted, coming to a stop beside her.

'Well, I'm not, and it's no comment, no matter what the question is.'

'Just a quickie.' He struggled with a super-sized umbrella as he beckoned for his cameraman to get out of the van with the satellite dish on top.

Lottie glared at him. 'Out of my way, Moroney.' She attempted to get around him. Blocked by the cameraman.

'One minute, that's all,' the reporter insisted. He flashed his sparkling white teeth. Were they false? Lottie wondered.

'I've nothing to say to you. You'll get a press release like everyone else. Now move.'

'I've been doing a little investigative work. You might be interested in it.'

Lottie felt her phone vibrate in her bag.

'Sorry, I have to get this.' She took out the phone, waved it in his face, then glanced at the screen. Her daughter, Katie. She moved out of earshot of the reporter.

'What's wrong?' she hissed. 'I'm very busy.'

'Where's the Infacol, Mam? Louis won't stop crying. Granny said he has wind.'

'Jesus, Katie. I'm up to my neck with a murder and you're looking for Infacol?'

'You gave it to him yesterday. Where did you put it?'

Pausing, Lottie leaned against the parking ticket machine. Rain poured down her sleeve onto the phone. Infacol. Where had she put it?

'The cupboard over the fridge, I think.'

'I looked there.'

Lottie glanced at the hospital entrance gate. A large unmarked garda car was speeding into the set-down area. Superintendent Corrigan.

Straightening her back automatically, she said, 'Katie, I have to go. Sorry.'

'Mam, he needs it!'

'Go to the pharmacy and buy some, okay? I really have to go now.'

Feeling guilty, she hung up and raced to the front door, where Boyd was attempting to keep Moroney at bay. Shaking her head frantically, she tried to draw his attention to the superintendent's car. Boyd returned a blank stare.

Moroney jumped in with his microphone. 'Detective Inspector Parker, can you inform the public if you have anyone in custody regarding the murder of Tessa Ball?'

'No comment,' Lottie said. 'Superintendent Corrigan has just arrived. I'm sure he'll speak to you.'

'Where is he? Oh, I see him. Great. Thanks.' Moroney took off at a gallop, splashing through puddles.

Lottie moved just as quickly in the opposite direction. Grabbing Boyd by the elbow, she dragged him into the hospital foyer and up the stairs.

'Did you get it all sorted?' She tried to catch her breath as she took two steps at a time. Not a bad place to be if she suffered a heart attack.

'I'm still trying to reach Lynch. Two uniforms are on the way.'

'OK. We need to stay here until they arrive. We can't leave Marian Russell alone.'

'She's in surgery,' Boyd pointed out. 'She's not going anywhere.'

'Right, but I don't want to risk anything else happening to her.'

'I get that, but can't you take it easy? Slow down.'

She stopped on the top step, panting to catch her breath, hand on her heart. A young man pushed through the swing doors.

'Are you all right, missus?' he asked.

'I'm fine,' Lottie snapped.

*

A uniformed garda and a detective arrived. Lottie posted them outside the ICU with clear instructions.

'No one enters without clearance from me.'

'What about the doctors and nurses?' Boyd said.

'Get a list, with ID photographs, of everyone working the ICU shifts. Only those can go in. Got it?'

The two men nodded and took up their positions.

Before leaving, Lottie got an update on Marian Russell's condition. Not good.

'Boyd?' she said.

'Yeah?'

'I need a drink.'

CHAPTER 15

The lights were on at Danny's. Silver hues glinted off the bottles behind the bar.

Lottie slid onto a high stool and Boyd sat beside her. She dropped her bag on the floor hoping, too late, that it was shut. Shrugged out of her wet jacket and zipped down her black hoodie. Felt like pulling the hood up over her head, but thought she might be barred if she did.

'Your stuff is all over the floor.' Boyd leaned down to scoop up her belongings.

'Double vodka,' she said, through gritted teeth. The bored barman stared back at her, twisting his wrist as he dried a glass.

'She doesn't want vodka,' Boyd said, banging his head on the underside of the counter as he got up. 'Soda water.'

'It's a bar, Boyd. Where people drink alcohol.'

The barman took a step back, put down the glass. 'So what's it to be?' he said, hands on hips.

'Two vodkas,' Lottie said.

With an audible sigh, Boyd agreed, nodding his head. 'What about a sandwich? I'm starving.'

'I feel ill,' Lottie said.

'Don't puke on me,' Boyd said.

'Her tongue, Boyd. Her tongue.'

'Keep your voice down.'

'*She's* got no voice to keep down.'

'She might be able to write out what happened to her.'

'The doctor said it could be a week before they'll be able to take her out of the induced coma.'

The door opened and a blast of wind brought rain in through the door. The barman put the drinks on the counter. Lottie stared at the clear liquid slipping over the ice. She let her fingers glide up and down the glass.

'Is that all?' the barman asked.

'Do you know Arthur Russell?' she said.

'He works here. Why are you asking?'

'Just something I'm following up. Was he working yesterday?'

'He was. But he's off today. You might catch him later on. He plays music here some nights.'

'What time did his shift end?'

'Yesterday? Let me think. My shift started at six thirty, so he would've finished up around then.'

'Did he leave straight away?'

'Sometimes he has a drink before he goes. Why?'

Jesus, Lottie thought, why do barmen always have to be asking questions? 'Can you find out for me?'

'Can't you ask him yourself?'

'Right. Thanks.' She raised her glass and the barman walked off. 'Does vodka smell?'

'You should know. You drink enough of it,' Boyd said.

Twisting round on the stool, Lottie glared at him. 'Take that back.'

'Sorry.'

'Screw you, Boyd.' She stood. Downed her drink, picked up her bag and coat and stomped out into the rain.

*

The office was suffering from everyone's bad mood. The deteriorating weather wasn't helping. Her hair was stuck to her scalp and Lottie hadn't the will to go to the locker room to find a dryer. Dampness lined the neck of her shirt and her jeans were glued to her legs.

'Probably catch a cold now,' she muttered.

'Did you say something?' Boyd asked, coming in and hanging up his coat.

'Did you find out anything on the gun from Tessa Ball's house?' she asked before he could return to the argument they'd had in the pub.

He checked his computer. 'It's still with ballistics for testing.'

'The letters I found under the bed. Do you have copies of them?'

'In the incident room. Be back in a minute.' Boyd rushed out of the office and Lottie took a deep breath.

She didn't like arguing with him, but did he not realise how hurtful he'd been? Glancing at the time, she realised that home and bed were a distant prospect. She needed a pill. Something to calm her brain; stop her hands from shaking. She thought of her friend, Dr Annabelle O'Shea, whom she had fallen out with ten months ago. They'd met a couple of times since, in the street. Passed themselves, as her mother was apt to say. Maybe now was the time to rekindle the bond.

'Here they are,' Boyd said, jolting her out of her daydream.

Picking up the photocopies, Lottie flicked through them. She noticed they were not dated. And there were no envelopes.

'They're all unsigned.'

'I spotted that.'

'Who'd send a letter without signing it?'

'Anonymous letters can be a warning or a complaint. Why don't you read them and see what they're about?'

'That's what I'm trying to do.'

'I give up.' Boyd turned and marched out of the office.

The pages in her hands were crushed. Lottie flattened them out and realised she'd crumpled them herself. She started to read the first one. It appeared to be a love letter. Short and sweet.

Boyd appeared back at the door. 'Arthur Russell has arrived. Prepared to give a voluntary statement. You want to interview him?'

She put the letters into a folder and slipped it into her drawer.

'Has he a solicitor with him?'

'Yes.'

'Shit.'

*

As usual, the air in the interview room was stifling. Arthur Russell had showered and dressed in clean clothes. Lottie could smell fabric softener and wondered if his landlady did his laundry for him as well as cooking.

'Your mother-in-law, Tessa Ball, is dead,' she said, after conducting the formalities.

He nodded, unsurprised. 'So I've heard. Good riddance is all I can say. She was bad news from the first day I met Marian.'

Russell seemed comfortable in the intimidating room. Must be his solicitor's presence, Lottie thought.

'You didn't much care for your mother-in-law?'

'Hated her. Doesn't mean I killed her.'

She glanced over at Boyd. He shrugged. She focused her attention back on Russell.

'Can you account for your whereabouts last night? Six thirty p.m. until eleven.'

'Told you this morning, when you interrupted my music.'

'For the tape, please tell us again.'

'I didn't kill the old biddy.'

'No one said you did. We're just gathering evidence.'

'What evidence? I told you, I did nothing.'

Russell rubbed his head with one hand and tugged his beard with the other. Worry lines deepened around his eyes. The reality of his situation was sinking in, Lottie thought. Good.

'Your wife—' she began.

'Back up there a minute,' Russell said, raising a hand. 'What evidence?'

He thumped the table and jumped up, crashing his chair back against the wall. His solicitor put a hand on his arm. Russell shrugged it off. Lottie tapped her index finger on the table until he sighed and sat back down, glaring like a cornered bull.

She said, 'Your wife is in hospital. Know anything about that?'

Russell slammed his fist on the table again. 'No, I don't. What's wrong with her? Grief?'

'Mr Russell, please.'

'Maybe *she* killed the old woman.' He leaned back and folded his arms over his chest, a smug smile spreading across his face.

'Do you own a baseball bat, Mr Russell?' Lottie asked quickly. She was truly fed up with his antics.

His eyes darted around the room. The solicitor nodded his white head for him to answer.

'Yeah. I do.' Uncertainty flickered in his eyes. 'Not a crime, is it?'

'Not when it's used for a sport, no. Though there's not much scope for playing baseball in Ragmullin, is there?'

'I bought it for Emma. About five years ago, when I was on a trip to the States. It's been in the shed at home… her home, ever since. I haven't touched it in years. Doubt she has either.'

'Interesting.' Lottie wondered if Emma could have wielded the bat at her grandmother's head. She doubted the slight girl had the strength needed to cause such a serious injury, but she'd check with Jane.

Russell's eyes were full of suspicion. 'Why am I here? I never laid a finger on Tessa.'

'What about your wife? You ever lay a finger on her?'

Sucking on his bottom lip, bristles catching between his teeth, Russell was silent.

'Mr Russell? Are you refusing to answer?'

'She barred me from the house. Got a restraining order. Is that why you're asking me if I hit her?'

'Did you appeal it?'

'I sure did. That woman's mental. Doing drugs and stuff. If you want to know the truth, it was her started out beating me. But no one believed me.'

Boyd grunted.

Lottie said, 'Last night, I believe you went to Marian's house, murdered your mother-in-law, then abducted and violently assaulted your wife.'

Russell jumped up for the second time. 'What the hell?'

'Sit down. Now,' Lottie said, lacing her voice with grit.

The solicitor grabbed Russell by his shirtsleeve and eased him back into the chair.

Shaking his head vigorously, Russell said, 'Where's Emma?'

'You haven't asked what happened to Marian. Is that because you already know?'

'I don't like your tone,' Russell said. 'And I told you, I haven't been near that house in months. I did nothing.'

The oppressive atmosphere in the small room was grating on Lottie's nerves. She wanted to reach across the table and beat a confession out of Russell. That clearly couldn't happen; his solicitor was present. She tried to quench the frustration wrenching her chest into a knot by taking a few deep breaths.

'Mr Russell, tell me about you and your wife. The type of relationship you shared. How the separation has affected you.'

Leaning forward, hands clutching each other, Arthur Russell lowered his head as if in surrender and spoke into his chest.

'Volatile, that's how I'd describe it. We married young. But when we had Emma, even the rows were worth it. That girl is the light of my life. Whenever I can get access, that is. Marian is a bitch. I mean that, Inspector. An out-and-out bitch. Like mother, like daughter, eh?'

Lottie thought of her own mother, and hoped that sentiment wasn't true.

'Back to last night. Outline your activities.'

'One, I was nowhere near that house. Two, I don't know what happened to Tessa, and three, I've no idea what you're talking about, saying Marian was abducted and assaulted.'

'We want to know what you did yesterday,' Boyd said, and shifted in his chair, clearly fed up with the suspect.

'You're persistent, I'll give you that,' Russell said.

'Mr Russell—' Boyd began.

'Okay, okay.' He held up his hands. 'I got up. Had breakfast. Went to work for ten o'clock and was there until seven.'

'You work in Danny's Bar, that right?' Lottie said.

'Yes. I do the stock in the mornings and then my shift behind the bar. Some nights I play music there as well. Mainly weekends.'

'I assume you weren't playing last night?' Lottie said, knowing that if he had been, he'd have already offered an alibi and the dopey barman would have mentioned it.

'No, unfortunately. I went back to my digs. Landlady can confirm I ate my dinner there around seven thirty.'

'And?'

'Went to my shed and played music until I hit the hay. I'm repeating myself here, you know.'

'It's for the tape. What time did you go to bed?'

'Not sure. Probably around one.'

'So no one can corroborate your whereabouts from seven thirty onwards?'

'Landlady?'

'When my detectives interviewed Mrs Crumb she said she last saw you at seven forty-five, when you finished your dinner. Nothing after that.'

Russell raised his head. 'I'm fucked so.' His eyes were watery, and for the first time since she'd entered the interview room, Lottie felt something other than anger emanating from him. Despair?

'We need to take a sample of your DNA. That okay with you?'

Russell glanced at his solicitor, who nodded.

'Okay, I suppose.' He gave a wry laugh. 'It'd make me look guilty if I didn't.'

'Very good,' Lottie said, tidying up her notebook. 'We'll take a buccal swab. What did you do after we left you this morning?'

'Stayed inside, making music. All day. Then some of your lot arrived again and I agreed to come here.'

'Fair enough, for now. You can go for now but don't leave town. We'll have more questions later.' Lottie knew they hadn't enough evidence to hold him.

She stood up and gave Boyd a knowing look. If Russell was prepared to give a DNA sample without a fight, did that mean he was innocent?

Russell said, 'Where's Emma?'

'She's staying with a neighbour.'

'Who?'

'I'm sorry, I can't give you that information.'

'Only one neighbour on our road. That Kelly one is as daft as a brush.'

'You seem to think everyone has a mental problem, Mr Russell. I'm beginning to think you're the one with the problem.' Lottie opened the door.

'Can I see my daughter?'

'I'm sorry, Mr Russell, the answer for now is no.'

CHAPTER 16

'Kirby?' Lottie shouted as she rushed back into the office. 'Where's Kirby when I need him?'

He stuck his head around the door. 'You looking for me?'

'Yes, I am. Can you do an extra shift tonight?'

'I can, but if you're thinking of asking me to babysit a teenager, I'm not doing that.' He sat down, shoving his e-cig into the top pocket of his shirt.

'I've had a bitch of a day and I need you to do this one thing for me. Jesus!'

'Hey, boss. Calm down.'

She slammed the desk. 'Don't tell me to calm down.'

'I'll ask Gilly. She has the training; she might do it.'

'You're *friends* with Garda O'Donoghue now, are you?' She stared at Kirby, who blushed. 'Okay. Ask her.'

'Sure.' Kirby looked like he was glad to escape.

Lottie sat down. Breathe. Her phone rang. Lynch. 'I've got cover for you,' she said, pre-empting Lynch's question.

'Thanks.'

'Did you get anything from Emma?'

'She and Natasha are sticking to their story. In all evening, watching Netflix. This morning, Emma left the house. Said she went to get fresh bread in the shop, but Jim McGlynn thought she was trying to get access to her home.'

'Did he know for sure?'

'No. I tried ringing him to check, but he's not picking up.'

'I'll try him later on. Emma is not to be left alone until we figure out what is going on.'

'I'll make sure of it. Who's replacing me?'

'Garda O'Donoghue,' Lottie said, crossing her fingers and hoping Kirby could work his magic. Doing double shifts wasn't to be recommended, but until the appointed FLO returned from sick leave, she had to work with whoever was available.

'I'll stay until she arrives. But Inspector, I'm not doing this tomorrow.'

'Just do what I ask.' Lottie disconnected the call.

She thought about Arthur Russell's interview and couldn't decide if he was telling lies to cover his arse, or if he was innocent and painting Marian as the wicked witch in order to get access to his daughter. With her nerves frayed and no ideas popping magically into her brain, she made a phone call.

Then she grabbed her jacket and raced for the door.

*

The rain had eased to a soft veil, falling in inverted V's beneath the street lamps.

She started to walk, unable in that moment to recall where she'd left her car. She bit her lip, trying to conjure up strength. To face whatever foe was out there in the miserable night. Someone had murdered Tessa Ball. Someone had cut out a woman's tongue and left her to die on the front porch of a hospital. Someone was sending a message, loud and clear. Only problem was, she had no idea who that someone was or who the message was for.

A car drew up alongside her, drowning her with water.

'You eejit!' she screamed.

Boyd rolled down the window. 'Get in, you madwoman.'

'I need air.' She kept on walking.

'Get in, Lottie.' He kept pace with her.

She stopped and breathed in, then looked skywards and breathed out.

'Right. You can give me a lift,' she said and opened the door.

CHAPTER 17

'Well look what the cat dragged in.' Annabelle O'Shea grabbed Lottie in a hug. 'Missed you.'

'Hi, Annabelle.'

'Give me that wet thing. You'll get your death.' She took Lottie's jacket. 'Leave your… em… boots by the door.'

Glancing down at her soggy Uggs, Lottie wondered if her socks were presentable enough to walk on Annabelle's pristine tiles. She pulled off the boots and noticed that water had seeped into her odd socks. What the hell, she thought, and moved down the hall after her friend, leaving damp footprints in her wake.

Annabelle said, 'Would you like a drink? Oh, sorry, I forgot, you don't drink. Cup of tea?' She picked up a kettle and busied herself pouring in water.

'That'd be grand,' Lottie said, without correcting her friend. She'd seen little of Annabelle since they fell out in January, and since then she'd led an investigation into a horrific series of murders. On the night of the memorial service for the victims, she'd downed a bottle of wine. That was the start of it. Now she tried to control it; keep it secret. Not easy living in a house with three teenagers and a baby.

Sitting at the black-granite-topped breakfast bar, Lottie admired how it blended in with the decor. Everything matched. Figured. Dr Annabelle O'Shea was the epitome of designer chic.

The stainless-steel kettle began to hiss on the stove. Annabelle moved in her ridiculously high-heeled boots across the black-and-white-tiled floor and placed black mugs on the table.

'Where is everyone?' Lottie asked.

'The twins have after-school study groups. Cian is upstairs working. Developing some new game or… I don't know what he does up there.'

Cian was Annabelle's husband, and Lottie didn't really care much for him. She wasn't sure if that was because of the picture Annabelle painted of him or because she just didn't like him. She sensed Cian O'Shea was too good to be true. A man whose smile never succeeded in reaching his eyes.

'How did the twins get on with their exams?' she asked, immediately regretting it. Now she'd have to tell Annabelle about Chloe's.

'All A's, the both of them. Isn't that amazing?'

'Yes,' Lottie said. 'They're very bright.'

'How did Chloe do?'

'Not too bad. Considering all that happened.'

'What did happen?'

Did Annabelle live under a stone? Lottie thought everyone knew what had gone on last May in Ragmullin. Maybe she was being diplomatic.

'It doesn't matter. It's all over now.' Lottie rolled up the sleeves of her long-sleeved navy T-shirt. The kitchen was stifling.

Annabelle poured the tea and sat, expectantly.

It was a long time since they'd last spoken properly. But Lottie had lifted the phone earlier and called Annabelle. Swallowed her pride and everything else. She needed something more important than her damn pride.

'Oh, how stupid of me,' Annabelle gushed. 'You're a granny! Congratulations. Boy or girl?'

You know right well, Lottie thought. 'A boy. Louis. He's three weeks old. I worry about Katie, though. She's not coping very well but she won't let me help her.'

'If she has post-natal depression, she needs to see her doctor. Or tell her to call in to me.'

'I'm not sure she will, but I'll try talking to her about it.'

Lottie knew Katie imagined that because she had turned twenty in August and was no longer a teenager, she now possessed special powers. But she didn't want to get sidetracked about this with Annabelle. She would talk to Katie tonight.

'You're very quiet,' Annabelle said. 'What can I help you with?'

'I'm not sure,' Lottie began. 'It's so hot in here.'

'Is it? I didn't notice.' Annabelle, her blonde hair hanging loose over her shoulders, wore a black polo-neck jumper and skin-tight blue jeans. Her knee-high leather boots finished the look. Lottie didn't know whether to be jealous or suitably happy in her trusted old clothes.

'How's work?' she asked.

'Not as busy as it used to be. Not since the media publicised the fact that a brothel was being run from the building beside the surgery. Doesn't matter that it disappeared in a flash.'

Lottie caught the knowing look from her friend. But she wasn't about to admit anything. 'Do you have milk?' she asked.

Annabelle jumped up, fetched a jug from the refrigerator and sat down again. 'How's your mother?' she asked.

Lottie paused, jug in hand, and stared at Annabelle. After a moment she said, 'She's fine. Why? Do you know something?'

'I may be her doctor, but I'm just being polite.'

'She's fine.' Lottie sipped her tea. Silence wrapped around them, broken only by the soft hum of music emanating from somewhere in the depths of the house. 'Do you ever see Tom Rickard?' she said, her voice a whisper.

'No… Why would you ask that?' Annabelle had also dropped her voice and looked around furtively before getting up to close the door leading to the hallway. 'Jesus, what's got into you, Lottie? I haven't seen you for months, and then you come into my home asking about my former lover. Things are bad enough. Give me a break.' Her words swished through clenched teeth.

'Ease up. I was only wondering. You know his son was Katie's boyfriend, and therefore Tom is the baby's grandad.'

'I may be blonde, but I'm not stupid.'

'I think he needs to know about Louis,' Lottie said.

'Last I heard, Tom had moved abroad, and I've no idea where Melanie is.'

'That figures. I drove by their house once or twice and saw the For Sale sign. But I didn't think they'd left the country.'

'Surely you could have snooped around a few databases and found out where they'd gone?'

'Thought I'd ask you first.'

Annabelle threw back her head and laughed. 'You're so weird, Lottie. God, I've missed you. More tea?'

'No thanks.' Lottie clutched the mug with both hands. 'There was something else I wanted to ask.'

'Fire ahead.'

Before she could say another word, the door burst open.

'Somebody's left footprints on the hall floor, and I thought I told you not to close… Oh, I didn't know you had a visitor.'

'Sorry,' Annabelle said, picking up a tea towel. 'Lottie must have closed it when she came in.' She wiped the perfectly clean counter.

Lottie stood up. 'Hi, Cian. I'm just leaving.'

Cian O'Shea, at six foot three, had to duck his head under the ornate lighting arrangement hanging from the ceiling. He held out

his hand and shook Lottie's in a crisp, hard shake, then brushed her
cheek with his lips.

'Long time no see,' he said. 'What brings you here?'

'Just popped in for a chat.' She thought his eyes looked a lot
darker than she remembered, with circles of blue-grey around
them.

'Well, it's nice to see you,' he said.

Lottie doubted the sincerity of his words. It was the way he looked
at her when he said them. She glanced at Annabelle, frozen, cloth
in hand, watching Cian watching her. Bizarre.

'Don't let me disturb your chinwag.' He turned on his brown
leather loafers and took himself out of the kitchen and back up the
stairs, leaving the door wide open.

'Don't mind him.' Annabelle rushed into motion, sweeping her
hair on top of her head and wrapping it up tightly with a bobbin.
'Work pressure.'

As her friend cleared away the mugs, Lottie said, 'Is everything
okay?'

'Why wouldn't it be?' Annabelle dried her hands, checked a pot
boiling on the stove then shepherded Lottie back to her boots at
the front door.

'Does Cian know about Tom?'

'Shh!' Annabelle put a finger to her lips, opened the door and
shoved Lottie out on to the step. 'Yes, he knows, but there's no need
to remind him. I'll see you in town. Soon. For a coffee?'

'Yeah, sure,' Lottie said, standing in her saturated socks, boots
in hand.

The door closed before she could ask the question she had come
to ask.

*

'What did *she* want?'

'Cian, you know right well her name is Lottie.'

'Always sounded like a dog's name to me. Where's dinner?'

'Ready in ten.'

Annabelle backed up to the counter. She hated it when Cian was in this kind of humour, and it seemed to be happening more often. Since he'd discovered about her affair with the property developer Tom Rickard, he had made her life a living hell. It hadn't even been her first affair – just the first he'd found out about. If it wasn't for the twins, she'd have left long ago.

She turned her back to him and checked the saucepan, stirring the vegetables around and around and gazing vacantly at the swirling water. She knew that her indiscretion with Rickard had elevated Cian's wrath to a new level, and for the sake of her sanity she had made a conscious decision to make her marriage work. But all her efforts seemed to be failing. Badly.

She put the lid back on the saucepan, turned down the heat. Behind her she could hear Cian clattering the sweeping brush around the kitchen floor. Before she knew what was happening, her legs were whacked from under her, and she was sprawled on the black and white tiles, her husband standing over her. She shielded her face as he rained blows down on her legs with the handle of the brush.

'Stop, please stop!' she pleaded.

'You're a slut,' he snarled. 'Spreading your legs for scum, and then you try to deny me in bed.' He reached down and pulled her hair free of the topknot. Wrapping the long blonde strands around his fingers, he pulled her up to her feet. 'And then you bring your detective friend around here, snooping. For what?'

'You're insane,' she spat.

'I'm perfectly sane. I just want what is mine. Mine!'

When he let go of her hair, she slumped against the cupboard, her legs like jelly. There was only so much a person could take. She would have to leave him.

'Where's your Lottie friend now? Woof, woof.'

'Cian, we need to talk.' She held up her hands, appealing to him. Annabelle had never begged for anything in her life. But maybe now she was begging for her life. She shrugged off the tremor scuttling up her spine. Ignored the pain in her legs. Her husband might be all macho with the handle of a sweeping brush in his hand, but when she slammed the divorce papers in front of him, then she'd see what he was really made of.

'Talk? Now you want to talk?' His laugh was stoked with derision. He grabbed her chin and held her throat. She felt his other hand pulling at the zipper on her jeans.

'What the fuck? Get off me, Cian!'

'Shut your mouth.' With a kick, he spread her legs and thrust his body up against hers.

'I hate you,' she hissed. She struggled against him, but she was no match for him. Crushing her body against the granite, he pulled at her jeans. When he couldn't get them down, he stood back and hit her in the stomach with the brush handle. Doubling over in pain, she felt the wood smash into her back. She bit her tongue, and blood seeped out of the side of her mouth. She wouldn't cry. He could beat her and mock her, but by God, she wouldn't give him the satisfaction of seeing her cry.

The pot on the stove whistled. She twisted round on the floor to see Cian standing over her, the pot in his hand, steam rising in a cloud from the boiling water. Rolling her body into a ball, she held out her hands, pleading.

'No! Cian… no!'

CHAPTER 18

'Something's not right with the O'Sheas,' Lottie said.

'What makes you say that?' Boyd drummed his fingers on the steering wheel.

'Cian was acting a bit… off. He was always funny, but this was different.'

'Funny ha ha?'

'More like creepy. Are you going to start the car or start up a band?'

'I'm thinking about it,' Boyd said.

'Why would he want the door left open?'

'Who?'

'Annabelle's husband.'

'What door?'

'We were talking in the kitchen,' Lottie explained. 'Annabelle closed the door when I asked her about Tom Rickard. Then Cian comes charging down the stairs giving out about the door being shut.'

'Maybe he likes listening to his wife chattering nonsense with her friends?'

'Whatever it is, I think something isn't right in that house.'

'You've enough to be concerned about without getting involved in other people's business.'

'That's not what I meant. Oh, you're not even listening to me.'

'Come on, Lottie. You and I both know Annabelle O'Shea. No one tells her what to do. Not even her husband. Drop it.'

But Lottie couldn't get the look on Annabelle's face out of her mind. 'She was scared. Why did she blame me for closing the door? Outright lie. Why do that?'

'Why didn't you ask her?'

'I didn't get a chance. She rushed me out of that house like it was on fire.'

'If it's bothering you that much, ring her or call into her surgery.'

'I think I will.'

She caught Boyd's look – his eyes wide with warning.

'On second thoughts,' he said, 'don't get involved.'

'I said I'll think about it. Let's go.'

'Can we go get—'

'Food? No. I have to get home.'

Before she could even put her seat belt on, he was out on the main road, whizzing back towards town.

*

The smell of burning toast hit her as she walked through her front door. At least the smoke alarm wasn't blaring.

'What's going on in here?' she asked, dropping her bag and unplugging the toaster. She flapped a tea towel around to clear the air. Maybe the alarm needed a new battery. She'd have to check that later.

The kitchen was full of bodies. Chloe was sitting at the table on her phone. Katie was rocking baby Louis in his Moses basket. He wasn't crying, for a change. Lottie gave him a kiss and began clearing the mess of bread, knives, butter and bottles from the counter.

'Katie, you have to clean up after you make the bottles. And who was this for?' She held up the blackened piece of bread. No answer. The stench of dirty nappies rose from the bin. 'I told you to use the bin outside for nappies.' Still no answer.

The steriliser needed to be cleaned. The carton of baby formula was almost empty. 'Did you go shopping?'

'Mam! How could I? I've been busy with Louis all day. Please keep your voice down. I've only just got him to sleep.'

'You could've put him in his buggy and walked to the shops.'

'Did you see the rain?'

Stepping on a pile of swept-up dirt by the door to the utility room, Lottie went to get the brush and dustpan. The washing basket was overflowing with baby clothes and towels. She loaded the machine and switched it on.

'Where's Sean?'

'Over at Niall's,' Katie said.

Lottie was pleased that her fourteen-year-old son was once again out mixing with friends. He'd been through so much, but the counselling sessions seemed to be helping. She glanced over at Chloe. She still wasn't sure if her daughter was on the road to recovery. Her self-harming had reached a critical point in May, before Lottie had realised what was going on. Chloe had assured her she was better, but even so, every now and then Lottie tried to catch a glimpse of the girl's arms. There didn't appear to be any new cuts, but there were plenty of places she couldn't see. She just had to take Chloe's word for it while being vigilant for the signs.

She sighed, knowing she needed to give a lecture. They would have to assume roles in the household; she couldn't be expected to do everything while working long shifts. Just as she was about to open her mouth to begin her speech, the baby screamed.

'Now look what you've done.' Katie jumped up and grabbed a bottle.

'What?' Lottie stood in the middle of the floor, hands raised to the ceiling.

*

Baby Louis spewed milk on his clothes, his blanket, on Katie and the floor.

'Here, give him to me.' Lottie took the crying child. She undressed him, changed his nappy and dressed him in clean clothes. She cuddled and soothed him, and when he was calm, Katie took him back.

'It's quiet in the sitting room, feed him in there,' Lottie suggested. It felt like ten people had left the room when Katie took Louis out.

As she swept the floor, Lottie turned her attention to Chloe smiling at her phone, and it struck her how long it had been since she'd seen Annabelle's twins. One time, maybe not so long ago, now that she thought about it, the two families had been close, brought together by the kids' activities – hurling, drama, ballet and art. Memories of Adam surfaced. The pride he had taken in their children's achievements.

'What's so interesting on your phone?' she asked.

'Just checking stuff for my history project,' Chloe said.

Lottie couldn't see any sign of school books.

'What's the project about?'

'History.'

'Get much done?'

'Loads,' Chloe said, pocketing her phone.

'What am I going to cook for dinner?' Lottie asked.

'Something quick,' Chloe suggested. 'I'm starving.'

*

The stir-fry concoction Lottie threw together was barely edible. Sean arrived home with his friend Niall and they disappeared into his bedroom. Katie took Louis to hers and Chloe claimed homework as an excuse to escape up the stairs. It was 8.30 by the time Lottie had the kitchen half tidy and to herself. She sat in the kitchen armchair and listened to the silence.

The doorbell rang, a key turned and the door opened.

Her mother. Rose Fitzpatrick. At seventy-five, she was usually sprightly and energetic. Tonight she just looked drowned.

'Hello, Mother,' Lottie said. 'How are things?'

'Things are fine.' Rose placed her umbrella in the sink and took off her dripping mac. 'I didn't get to stay long today. I had my knitting class.'

'That's good.' Lottie didn't want to talk. She needed five minutes to herself. Five minutes' peace.

'One of the women in the group said Tessa Ball was murdered last night.'

'That's right.'

'In her own home?'

'No, in her daughter's house. Marian Russell.'

'That's a relief.'

'Why do you say that?' Please don't let her want tea, Lottie thought.

'I'll make tea.' Rose filled the kettle and switched it on. 'I thought she was killed at home. She lived alone. I was worried it might be someone targeting older people.'

'Did you know her well?'

'The state of this kitchen.' Rose started rinsing mugs under the running tap. 'Do those girls do nothing at all? I'll come over in the morning for a couple of hours. And I noticed the washing machine is off, but it looks full.'

Lottie jumped up. 'I forgot. I put Louis' clothes in.'

In the utility room, she heaved a deep sigh. Why did her mother make her feel so inadequate? Barely two minutes into a conversation and she'd already started. She emptied the clothes into a basket and slowly hung them on the airing rack.

Back in the kitchen, Rose was sitting down, two mugs of tea and a milk carton on the table.

'So did you know Tessa well?' Lottie asked again.

Rose sipped her tea. Eventually she said, 'No. Not at all. Just through the knitting club. She was involved in a lot of religious societies. Eucharistic minister, she was. Bit two-faced, if you ask me.'

'Why?'

'I shouldn't have said that.' Rose fidgeted with the handle of the mug.

'Mother?'

'Well, she was contrary.'

Lottie kept her mouth firmly shut. She could use that same word to describe her mother.

'Was she violent?'

'Violent? No,' Rose said. 'I mean, I don't know much about her…'

'Any idea if she had a job at any time?'

Rose looked around the kitchen before letting her eyes drop back to her mug of tea. 'I think she might have been a solicitor, back in the day.'

Lottie raised a quizzical eyebrow. 'I didn't know that.'

'Problem with you, Lottie, is you think us older folk were always old and never had jobs.'

'I don't think that. You were an excellent midwife,' Lottie said, 'back in the day.'

'How's the investigation going?'

'It might be a domestic. Her daughter, Marian Russell, was missing.'

'Was? Did she turn up?'

Lottie wondered how much she could say, and decided the less her mother knew, the better.

'Eventually.'

Rose stared vacantly at her tea. 'Maybe something from Tessa's past returned to haunt her.'

'What…' Lottie stopped and thought for a moment about what her mother had just said. Could it be that? No. Arthur Russell was her number one suspect, with his wife barely alive in hospital. This was a domestic situation that had spiralled out of control. 'I hadn't thought of that.'

'No? You don't think, do you? You need to slow down and look after those children of yours and your little grandson. You have responsibilities.'

Lottie cringed. She wasn't letting Rose get away with that.

'I have a job to do. I'm the only breadwinner in this family. You should understand that. After all, you had to work after Dad died to put food on the table for me and Eddie.'

Rose got up, washed her mug and dried it. She put it in the cupboard and without turning round said, 'I know how things can end up, Lottie. That's all I'm saying.'

'End up? What do you mean? That one of my kids will go off the rails like Eddie did? I don't think so.'

'I see the signs. Look what happened to Katie. Look what happened to Chloe. To Sean. Need I say more? Think about your family and start putting them first.' Rose folded the tea towel over and over until she had one neat square. She placed it on the counter.

Gazing up at her strong, rigid mother, for a second Lottie could see an image of herself standing there in thirty years' time. She looked away, staring down at her hands, noticing she had been digging her nails so hard into her palms they had left indented crescents. She wouldn't let her mother bully her. No. She was tougher than that.

'Mother,' she began, but when she looked up, Rose had gone.

Lottie went to the counter, picked up the tea towel and unfolded it. Scrunching it into a ball, she flung it across the kitchen, then sank to her knees. Deep breaths. One, two, three. She needed to regain control. She needed space and time. She needed a drink.

'What are you doing, Mum? Praying?' Chloe said as she came into the kitchen. 'I'm hungry. Is there anything else to eat?'

*

He walked to his car at the end of Windmill Road, phone to his ear.

'She's at home. The mother just left.'

He listened, taking further instructions.

'Right so. I'll follow the old woman to make sure she goes to her own house. And will I continue surveillance back here then?'

He waited for the reply, then said, 'Sure, that's no problem.'

Snapping shut the cover on his pre-paid phone, he slipped it into his pocket and took out his car keys. Climbing behind the wheel, he folded up the fast-food wrappers, then shifted the car into gear and headed after Rose Fitzpatrick.

CHAPTER 19

Alexis put her phone down on the desk. With a freshly manicured nail, she tapped her computer awake, then clicked on the screen so she could see the images in four different squares. One remained black, her own reflection glaring back at her. She turned up her Meryl Streep nose in annoyance and patted her lightly curled grey hair, cut tight at the back with a neat quiff at her brow.

Why wasn't that camera working? She pressed a button on her desk phone and asked the question. After a few seconds the square brightened and what she had initially expected to see appeared. All was well in her world, or it would be if people stopped interfering with the past.

Satisfied with what she'd seen, she powered down the computer, picked up her phone and walked over to the window. It was an expensive office, commanding views of Lower Manhattan. Image was everything for someone in her position. She could afford it. Beyond her reflection in the plate glass, she watched the late-afternoon lights come on and workers head home.

She turned away and picked up her full-length black coat. Pulling it on over her designer black jersey dress, she buckled it tightly. She liked black. It highlighted her best features – her inky blue eyes. Smiling to herself, she picked up her bag. She knew that some called her the black widow. Didn't matter that she'd never been married, let alone widowed, but she supposed she was a little like the spider. Dark and dangerous.

She left the light on. Her secretary could switch it off. Alexis knew the young woman was in awe of her; quite possibly she thought that someone of sixty-six should be retired and joining others of her age in a book club, or even a knitting club.

She grinned. She knew of one such woman who wouldn't be going to a knitting club ever again.

CHAPTER 20

As Rose Fitzpatrick entered her house, she noticed it was pitch dark. She flicked the light switch. Nothing. She opened the drawer in the hall table. Her fingers touched the small torch and she clicked it on.

The fuse box was above her head. She dragged a chair from the kitchen and climbed up to inspect the trip switches. The one for the lights was down. She flicked it up and the hall light flashed on immediately.

Throwing the torch back into the drawer, she closed the front door behind her and brought the chair back to the kitchen. Turning on the stove, she idly stirred the large pot of soup, waiting for it to boil. She was getting weary of the nightly soup runs for the homeless. I'm too old for this lark, she thought. But then Mrs Murtagh, who had started the venture, was over eighty and addled with Alzheimer's.

When she was happy with the soup, she switched the stove down to simmer and took two chicken breasts from the refrigerator. She placed them on a baking tray and put it in the oven. One would do nicely for a sandwich when she got back. The other for tomorrow's dinner.

It was only then that she realised she had forgotten to take off her coat. She shuffled out of it, and as she hung it up on a hook in the hall, she thought she saw car headlights outside, flashing in through the small V of glass on the front door. She glanced up at the fuse box. Had someone been in her house?

The lights outside disappeared and she went back to the kitchen, thinking about Tessa Ball. She'd known Tessa years ago, when her husband, Peter Fitzpatrick, was still alive. But that was so long ago it couldn't have anything to do with Tessa's death. No, poor Tessa must have been the victim of a burglary at her daughter's house. That was it.

She filled the flasks with soup. When she had them all ready, she buttered a couple of slices of bread to make her chicken sandwich.

Opening the oven door, she stared at the raw meat. She'd forgotten to turn on the oven.

Not for the first time, Rose Fitzpatrick wondered whether she was losing her mind.

CHAPTER 21

Emma curled up against the wall and stuffed her fist into her mouth to stem her sobs. What was this nightmare all about? Who could have done that to her granny? And now they said her mum was in hospital. Why couldn't she visit her? Her stomach hurt and her eyes felt like someone had thrown sand in them. She wanted her dad. And she wanted to go home. But that wasn't possible, so the detective said. Her stupid mother had destroyed her life. Again.

She heard the front door open. Chatter in the hallway. Then the door closed. Maybe the detective had left. She rolled off the bed and crept to the top of the stairs. Coming towards her was a young woman in a garda uniform.

'Who are you?' Emma asked.

'Hi, Emma. I'm here for your protection.'

'You can go away. I can mind myself.' Emma turned back into the room.

'Sorry, but I'm afraid you're stuck with me for the night.' The guard hovered in the doorway. 'I'll be downstairs if you need anything, or if you'd like to talk.'

'I don't want to talk to you. Leave me alone.'

Lying on the bed, Emma pulled the pillow over her face and listened to the muffled footsteps making their way back down the stairs.

Her granny was dead, her mother was probably dying and her dad was going to be a convicted murderer. Her life was gushing down the drain. Fast. Too fast.

She really had to speak to her dad.

There was something he had to know.

CHAPTER 22

When everyone else was settled down for the night, Lottie was still pacing her bedroom. Three steps one way, three steps the other. She could do with somewhere other than her room. If she lived in a house like Annabelle's, she would have plenty of space to think.

At her window, she looked down on the road below. Rain fell in sheets of grey to the ground. Maybe she could go for a run. Wash the cobwebs out of her brain. Don't be stupid, she admonished herself. She thought about Tessa Ball. Why had she recognised the name? And her mother had known her. Well, that was nothing new. Rose Fitzpatrick knew everyone over the age of sixty in Ragmullin.

Leaning against the wall, holding the curtain, she nursed the glass of vodka. Secret drinking. She was back there again and she didn't like it. But she couldn't help it. Spying the box sticking out at an angle from beneath her bed, she placed the glass on the window ledge and knelt down. Dragging out the box, she lifted the lid. Files, photographs, notebooks. Her father's pipe. She lifted it to her nose. It was stale and fusty; it didn't resurrect memories of the smell of his tobacco. It could have belonged to anyone.

Her fingertips feathered over a small, square, hand-made wooden box with rusted hinges. She knew what was inside but opened it anyway. Two trays of fly-fish hooks. All created by her father's hands. He would have got on well with Adam. They had both loved fishing. She closed the box and took up an old notebook. Sitting back against the wardrobe door, she reached up to the window ledge for her glass and started at page one.

She'd been through it so many times recently, she almost knew the words off by heart. Her father's notes on cases. All solved, as far as she'd discovered from her covert investigations. Had she seen Tessa Ball's name in this notebook? It had to be somewhere and it must have been something inconsequential, because she hadn't followed it up.

And then, more than halfway through, she found it. Belfield and Ball, Solicitors. Main Street. Ragmullin. Neatly inscribed in her father's schooled handwriting. In the centre of a page, written over a sentence, between two blue lines. She read back over the script. The name of the solicitor bore no relation to the text. Why had her father written it here? Had he been at his desk, taking a phone call perhaps; opened the first thing to hand, scribbled it down to remember for later? She had no idea.

Taking another sip, she closed her eyes. For the last few months she'd been asking questions. Interviewing old people in nursing homes. People who had once worked with her dad. Now Tessa Ball had died violently and her daughter, Marian Russell, had had her tongue cut out. It might not be related to her dad, but Lottie couldn't help wondering if she had opened up a can of worms with her private investigation into her father's death.

*

Taking the bobbin from her ponytail, Detective Maria Lynch let her hair hang loose about her shoulders. She was sitting in her car outside her home. It was in darkness except for the hall light. Ben usually got the children to bed early, and when she wasn't home, he'd retire to bed with either work or a book.

Gathering her phone into her bag, she took the keys from the ignition and wondered about Lottie Parker. During the last two big murder cases they'd investigated, Lottie had made a lot of errors of judgement. Lynch didn't like being on a team that made mistakes.

Okay, everything had worked out in the end and they'd caught the killers, but did that make how they'd reached those positive conclusions correct?

This case was probably a domestic dispute that had gone south, but Lottie Parker was on edge. And Lynch knew that that was when mistakes were sure to be made. Perhaps it was time to have a word with Superintendent Corrigan. One thing was certain: she was not going to sink on Lottie Parker's ship.

*

Boyd had a quick shower after his nightly workout on his turbo bike. Once the rain cleared, whenever that might be, he'd be back on the road with his racer. Pounding tarmac to exorcise the torment of his work.

Lottie Parker was at it again. He feared for her when she was in this state. She never knew when to stop. He half expected to find her curled up on his doorstep, or for his phone to ring with her babbling incoherently.

Dressed in a white T-shirt and baggy jogging pants, he sat on his couch and took out his phone, scrolling to Lottie's name. He wanted to talk to her. To make sure she was sober. But maybe she'd be asleep. He glanced at the time on the phone. 10.22 p.m. No way Lottie Parker was asleep.

The apartment walls were swallowing him up. He pulled on a pair of trainers and plucked a jacket from the hall stand.

There was only one place Boyd could go dressed like this, at this hour of the night.

CHAPTER 23

Lottie opened the door and stood back to let Boyd in.

'The state of you. What do you look like?' she laughed, then, seeing the serious lines etched on his face, she added, 'Something wrong?'

'I need a drink,' he said.

'You're driving.'

'One won't kill me.' He hung his jacket on top of a multitude of coats on the stair post.

She ushered him into the kitchen, filled the kettle and switched it on.

'Wait here,' she said.

'Where are you going?' He leaned against the refrigerator, and she noticed his eyes travelling the substantial length of her legs.

'To put on some clothes.'

'You don't have to do that. The view is quite good as it is.'

She thumped his shoulder and made for the door, glad she'd only had the one drink. 'I'll be back in a moment.'

She returned after a few minutes wearing a hoodie and pyjama bottoms, and carrying a sheaf of papers.

'What's all this?' Boyd asked, handing her a mug of tea.

'My father's stuff. I want to show you something.'

They sat at the table and she passed over the notebook. 'See that line there?' She pointed.

'Belfield and Ball, Solicitors. Right. Are you going to make a will?'

'Belfield and Ball.' Lottie emphasised each word. 'You don't get it, do you?'

'Ball,' he said. 'Any relation to our Tessa?'

'Well, my mother told me she used to be a solicitor.' She put down her mug. 'Why are you here anyway?'

Boyd sipped his tea. 'Missed you.'

'Don't be an ass.'

'If this Ball solicitor was Tessa, or someone related to her, has it any bearing on what happened to her, or to your father, seeing as the name is in his notebook?'

'I don't know, and answer the damn question. Why are you here?' Seeing the look that crossed his face, Lottie wished she could take back her words.

'I just wanted to have a chat with you, that's all.'

Lottie bit the inside of her cheek. 'What you mean is you wanted to check if I was drinking. Boyd, I don't need a minder.' She glanced up at her wedding photograph hanging on the wall. If Adam was still around, she wouldn't be in this situation. She missed him, but she had to let him go. She could live with the memories but not with the ghost.

'Sorry,' Boyd said.

'And while you're being personal, you need to sort out your situation with Jackie.'

'I don't want to talk about my ex-wife.'

'You have to proceed with the divorce.'

'Enough. Back to these.' Boyd looked at the post-mortem photographs Lottie had handed him. 'He was definitely shot. How can you bear to look at these?'

'Alcohol helps,' she quipped.

'Was there residue on his hands?'

She passed him another page.

'Not very conclusive,' he said, scanning the report.

'I'd love to get my hands on the full PM file,' she said.

'Ask Jane Dore. I know it's a long time ago, but there may be records somewhere in that Dead House of hers.'

'Yeah, I thought of that.' She scooped up the pages and stuffed them into a folder.

He took it from her and lined up the pages neatly before handing it back.

'I always knew you were good for something,' she said. 'Do you want another cup of tea?'

'I have to get home.'

'You're lonely.'

'And you're not?'

'We both are.'

She wanted to reach across the table and hold him. He looked so lost. She caught a glimpse of the photograph hanging on the wall, and fought an urge to turn it round or take it down.

'What are all these?' Boyd held up a bundle of newspaper cuttings held together with a bulldog clip.

'Court reports, sports reviews, usual stuff,' she said. 'All dated around a year before my dad died. I've gone through them like a hundred times.'

'The *Irish Press*,' Boyd said. 'That's a blast from the past. And the *Midland Tribune*. Bring them in tomorrow and we'll photocopy them. Then we can go through them without damaging the originals.'

'I can't see what use they'll be.'

'You never know until you look. It might be an idea to check the archives of the local paper too,' Boyd said. 'See what, if anything, they reported about your father's death.'

'That's an idea.'

'Or talk to old Willie "The Buzz" Flynn. He used to work at the paper. Kirby knows him. He might have known your father.'

Lottie closed her eyes, trying to conjure up her father. But all she could see was the pathologist's photographs. She heard Boyd moving. When she turned round, he was standing beside her chair. She scrutinised his face, searching for a sign. But he just looked serious.

'Thanks for the tea. Thanks for the company.' His hand slid around her shoulder. 'You're a good friend. And I appreciate it.'

A friend? Shite. She was the one who'd been keeping him at a distance, and now here she was acting like a needy teenager. Time to get a grip, Parker.

'I have to go.' He kissed her forehead chastely.

In that moment, she could have reached out and held him until morning. But she just sat there unmoving. Not even an eyelid fluttered until he walked away.

She heard him shuffling into his jacket and the door closing behind him with a soft thud.

Sitting in the kitchen, listening to the rain, the light reflecting off the dark windows, she sipped her cold tea, wishing it was alcohol, and sifted through the file on the table. When all the pages were messed up again, she felt a little more comfortable. Just a little bit.

And she knew she needed help.

The mid seventies: The Child

With a shove to the small of my back, I am propelled into the small square room. The sound of the door being locked behind me causes my heart to leap in my quivering chest. A woman lies on the bed, bound in an off-white thing that looks like a sweater with the sleeves crossed over the chest and tied behind her back. Only it's not a sweater.

With small steps, I shuffle forward, one foot at a time. Slowly. The shoulders of the woman on the bed twitch. When I am close enough to reach out and touch her, she screams and leaps up like a cat. I whimper and retreat.

'So she didn't take you! Ha! Figures. Who'd want a creature like you? No one. That's who.' She doubles over with laughter and falls from the bed to the ice-cold concrete floor.

I rear up against the door and cry out.

'Let me out! Please!'

My tiny fists pound the door, but my voice reverberates off the stone walls and hangs in the air as if suspended by spider's webs.

No one comes.

'It was an accident,' the woman says. 'Oh, I know they're saying I purposely set the house on fire. But why would I do that? I had the two of you. Tried to love you, I did, you ungrateful brat.'

She shuffles closer to me on her buttocks and snarls like a rabid dog. Like a desperate chained-up dog trying to escape. She is not like my mother at all. Though I know that is who she is.

I cry out once more. Turn my face towards the door to blot out the sight of the foam oozing from the side of her mouth.

'I want to go back to my own bed. Please…'

'I want to go back to my own bed,' the woman mimics, before her voice convulses in a long cough. 'Come here and help me, sweetie pie. Open the buckles. You know how to do that, don't you? I showed you once, didn't I? With the buckles on your shoes.'

My whimpers dissolve into choking sobs.

'Please… I want to go home.'

'This room is soundproofed. No one can hear you, my little baby. Only me.'

'I w-want to g-go home.'

'This is your home now. Maybe I will finish what I started, and this time I just might kill you.'

Another strangled laugh. More foam. A gurgle. Broken breaths.

I stare at the steel door without turning around.

I remain standing facing the door until someone comes and opens it.

Twenty-four hours later.

DAY THREE

CHAPTER 24

The clock on the old whitewashed wall showed the men it was 5 a.m.

'They'll be here soon,' the older man said.

'I'm a bit nervous,' replied the younger one. 'Such an awkward time to have a meeting.'

'Have a pull on this. I made it extra strong.'

'I will. What's the point if we can't test the product?'

'Now you're sucking diesel.'

'I hope no one found out.' The young man took a long drag and let the familiar feeling float through his veins. He took two more drags, the taper desiccating between his bloodstained fingers. 'We've done what we were asked. I don't see the point of this meeting.'

'Will you shut your gob?'

'But the old woman. That wasn't supposed to happen, was it?'

'I think it might've been part of the plan all along. Can't bring her back to life, can we? She was old enough to kick the bucket so stop going on about it.'

The young man laughed nervously. Had he really signed up for all of this? Once you're in, there's no backing out; that was what his friend had told him. All the same, he had never been that violent before. It must be the drugs. Not him. Someone else had inhabited his body. An alien. Yeah, that was what it was. A big green alien.

'What're you laughing at, you eejit?' the older man said.

The young man kept laughing. After a while, his companion joined in.

They were laughing so loudly they didn't hear the door open, or see the figure in black clothing enter, a knife clutched tightly in one hand and a jerrycan of petrol in the other.

CHAPTER 25

Emma couldn't hear any rain. The house seemed to be resting in silence. She struggled to her knees and peered out through the slit in the curtains. A pall of smoke was rising far in the distance, a grey mist rooting it close to the earth.

She wished she could go out and walk, allow the softness of the morning to fog up her spectacles and her feet to splash in puddles. But she wasn't five any more and she was stuck in Natasha's house. Sitting back down on the bed, she dragged the duvet to her chin and remembered the rows she'd had with her mother. About her dad, and her granny. That woman could shout when she wanted. And the rows she'd overheard. The words that had been flung to the four walls. Words that had seeped through bricks and mortar and settled in her brain.

Her home had been much quieter since Tessa had moved to her own apartment and Daddy had left. But a strong ache stabbed at Emma's heart as she thought of what was facing her.

Another day with Natasha and her mum, and of course her guard. Why did she have to be here? She felt perfectly safe.

The tears threatened again. She pulled the duvet over her head and let them flow.

CHAPTER 26

The morning broke without rain. The first time in over a week. But the sky bulged with heavy grey clouds and Lottie could see a mist hanging around the cathedral spires.

'Annabelle, I hate to be annoying you, but can you fit me in today?'

'I'm free before surgery starts. Now. Can you get here in the next five minutes?'

'Sure. I'm outside.'

She put away her phone, opened the door and entered the building. The receptionist nodded and Lottie made her way into Annabelle's surgery.

'What happened to you?' she asked.

'Oh, this?' Annabelle put her bandaged hand down on her lap, under the desk. 'Knocked over a kettle of boiling water.'

'Are you okay?'

'Yes. Enough about me. Sit down and tell me what's up.'

Lottie shook off her jacket and hung it on the back of the chair. 'I hate asking, because I know you don't want to do it, but…'

'But what? I've a full roster for the rest of the day, so you'd better be quick.'

Taking a deep breath, Lottie said, 'It's like this. I'm… I'm drinking again. Just the last few months. I'm trying to quit. It's hard, Annabelle. Very hard.'

'You've quit before.'

'I know, but it's worse this time. I need something to shave off the bristling edge.'

'And you want me to give you that something?'

'Just for a week or two. Until I get the alcohol out of my system.'

'You know as well as I do that substituting alcohol with a narcotic isn't going to help.'

'I'm not a druggie. I just need a few Xanax. To get me through the bad patches.'

'You need rehab.'

'I'm not an alcoholic!' Lottie folded her arms and turned down her mouth in disgust. No, she wasn't an alcoholic. She just couldn't do without it. Big difference.

The desk phone buzzed.

'I've a patient to see.' Annabelle took up a pen. 'Against my better judgement here is a script for one week. One a day. Twenty-five milligrams. Okay?'

'Can't you make it fifty?'

'No.'

'For two weeks?'

'Lottie, you need help. Professional help.'

'You're a professional. That's why I'm here.'

'You don't give up.'

'Never.'

Lottie watched as Annabelle tried to write out the prescription with her bandaged hand, her other hand shaking as she held down the page.

'What's wrong, Annabelle?'

The doctor raised her head. Blackness circled her eyes through a sheen of foundation.

'Wrong? Nothing is wrong with me.'

'Keep telling yourself that and you'll believe it. I'm the expert on that hypothesis.'

'Honestly, everything is fine.'

Lottie took the script, folded it up and shoved it into her bag before Annabelle could change her mind. 'You have my number. If you ever need to talk. About anything. Understand?'

'Up until a few days ago, you were hardly speaking to me.'

'I'm always your friend, even when we argue. So ring me if you need me.'

Annabelle nodded. If Lottie didn't know better, she could have sworn her friend was about to cry.

'Are you sure everything's all right? With you and Cian?'

'Why wouldn't it be?'

Lottie laughed. The sound seemed to take away the tension. Annabelle laughed too. They both knew things hadn't been right with Cian for a long time. Hence Annabelle's numerous affairs. 'Maybe we can go for dinner sometime.'

'You get off the drink and get yourself sorted out first.'

Lottie pulled on her jacket. At the door, she turned.

'You get yourself sorted too.'

Outside, the clouds burst and rain crashed down from the heavens.

CHAPTER 27

The cottage, situated in Dolanstown, a couple of kilometres from Ragmullin, was a smouldering wreck. Water from fire hoses flowed down the potholed road and settled in puddles on the leaf-clogged drain.

'How long do you reckon it's been raining for?' Kirby said, getting out of the car. He yanked up his trousers to keep the ends from getting wet and buttoned his coat.

'A week,' Lynch replied.

He zapped the car locked. Patted his pockets; found his e-cig. Twisted it, trying to get it to work. 'Feckin' bollocky yoke.'

'Try a mint, or gum,' Lynch offered.

Getting it ignited at last, he inhaled and blew out white smoke before dropping the metal tube back into his pocket.

'Meant to ask, why didn't you relieve Gilly from her duty at the Kelly house this morning?'

'Come on, Kirby. It's a bum job. And she's young enough to cope with doodling on her phone all day.' Lynch looked over at him. 'Did you have to cancel a date with her last night, or what?

'Or what.'

She laughed. 'You never learn.'

Kirby tried to keep up with Lynch's short, quick steps. They stopped beside a fire truck and surveyed the scene.

'You smell that?' he asked, sniffing the air.

'I smell burning. Wood, smoke, plastic and…'

They looked at each other.

'Cannabis,' they said together.

Kirby scratched his bushy damp hair. 'A grow house?'

Lynch agreed. 'Could be.'

They approached a small, thin man with a peaked cap. Kirby eyed the brass name badge and introduced himself.

'So, Chief Cox, what do we have?'

'Single-storey nineteen fifties cottage. Roof's about to cave in.'

'Any casualties?'

'One deceased and another who should be dead but is somehow still alive.'

'Male or female?'

'Both male. The dead man is just inside the back door of the house. Charred bone, that's all that's left of him.'

'Where's the man who survived?' Kirby asked.

Chief Cox pointed to the ambulance firing up its engine with a *whoop-whoop* of its siren. Lights flashing, it began to move.

Kirby ran. 'Hey, you… wait.'

The ambulance halted. Kirby leaned against the door, breathing in bursts. 'I need to speak to the patient.'

The paramedic lowered the window and leaned out.

'Who are you?'

'Detective Larry Kirby.'

'Look, I'm sorry, but if I don't go now, you'll be speaking to a corpse.'

Kirby debated his options and nodded. 'Which hospital are you headed for?'

'Ragmullin is the nearest, though he might have to be airlifted to Dublin. Bad burns and no fingers.' He shifted the ambulance into gear.

'No fingers? Burned off?'

'More like hacked off with a saw.'

As the ambulance drove away in a blaze of lights and wailing sirens, Kirby turned to Lynch. She shrugged her shoulders. Chief Cox joined them.

'When can we look around?' Lynch asked.

'It'll be a few hours before we deem it safe. As I said, the roof is about to collapse. Structure is unsound. But the fire's out.'

'Any idea how it started?' Kirby was pulling on his e-cigarette again as he eyed the tendrils of smoke creeping up from the house.

'Damage is substantial. Either they had an unprotected gas heater jammed up against the door, or someone poured petrol through the letter box. That's a guess at this stage.'

'Like a petrol bomb? Jaysus. Who lived here, do you know?'

'No idea.'

'Who called it in?'

'Neighbour. Lives a mile or so up the lane. Saw the flames blasting into the sky early this morning. You'd best have a word with him. As I said, it'll be hours yet before anyone can go on site.'

'Thanks, Chief,' Kirby said. 'I'll get my people to stand guard.'

'That's him, over there.'

A man wearing a green waxed jacket, and jeans tucked into mud-covered wellington boots stood leaning against an old Land Rover. He was chewing on the end of a fat cigar.

'A fellow after my own heart,' Kirby said. 'Lynch, contact the SOCOs to tell them we'll need them out here.' He pointed to the car parked haphazardly in the drive. 'And see if we can find out who that car belongs to.'

He marched over to the man and whipped out his ID.

'Detective Kirby,' he said.

'Mick O'Dowd.' The man tipped his flat cap with one work-roughened hand, offering the other in a shake.

Kirby looked into a face twisted in a knot of anger and guessed that the man was around the seventy mark. Bushy eyebrows with grey strands poking out and a nose that told the tale of a whiskey drinker. His cheeks were mottled with blood spots.

'You noticed the fire early this morning, then?'

'I did. On my way out to my cows sometime around five fifteen. It was like a firework display. Put my whole morning's work back hours. Cows still haven't been milked.'

Was this the reason for his anger?

Kirby said, 'Did you hear anything before that?'

'Like an explosion?'

'Exactly.' Kirby found his e-cigarette and began pulling hard.

'No. Never heard a thing.'

Kirby sighed, a cloud of smoke exhaling with his breath.

'You know who lived there?' he asked, nodding towards the smouldering building.

'Always been rented out. The original owner moved to the States, must be forty years ago now.'

'That's a long time to be renting out a property.'

'It's not my business. I've enough of my own troubles without concerning myself with others'.'

'Don't suppose you know who the estate agent is?'

O'Dowd pulled at his chin, thinking. 'No. Don't know.'

Kirby sighed again, deflated. 'Here's my card. We'll need to take a formal statement. And if you remember anything else, please contact me.'

'Told you all I know. I've work to be doing now.' O'Dowd turned to his Land Rover.

'You sure you've no idea who those men were?' Kirby persisted.

'Wouldn't I tell you if I did?' O'Dowd delved into the pocket of his jacket. 'I think you might like this.'

Kirby smiled, nodding his head. He rolled the cigar around in his hand before slamming it into his mouth. O'Dowd handed him a plastic lighter, then climbed into the Land Rover and set off down the lane.

Kirby walked back to Lynch, cigar between his teeth, smoke rippling from the side of his mouth.

'Grand man, but he's like someone with anger management issues.'

'What makes you think that?' asked Lynch.

'It was like he was itching to box the face off the first one who crossed him.'

'He's probably a very busy farmer who doesn't like having his morning's work interrupted.'

'Know a lot about farming, do you?' Kirby pinched out the cigar between two thick fingers and carefully placed it in his inside coat pocket.

'I thought you'd given them up?' Lynch eyed him suspiciously.

'I did. A few puffs do no harm.' Kirby marched back to the car. 'We'd better get to the hospital before that fella dies on us.'

'I had a look at the body,' Lynch said.

'Dead, was he?'

'Jesus, Kirby.' She stomped around to the other side of the car. 'The man was burned to death. Have you no compassion?'

'Oh, I've plenty of that. Did you find any sign of the cannabis we smelled?'

'There's a concrete shed down the garden. But the whole place is a swamp after the rain and the fire crew. Uniforms will have to remain here, and then we've to wait for the SOCOs to get clearance before they can work the site.'

'We? Ha, you'll be acting FLO for the rest of the day.'

'Not if I can help it.' Lynch shut the door with a smug bang.

CHAPTER 28

Glancing into her old office, which one day would be her new abode, Lottie noted that it had been painted. At last. A ladder stood against the wall with a decorator's paint-splattered table in the middle of the floor beside her old desk. All it needed now was new furniture and plenty of storage cabinets. She was sick of falling over box files. All on order, so she'd been told. Then she would have her own space back. Somewhere to think without an audience. Still no door, though. The plans dictated it would be full-length glass. Too late to order a solid one? For now she was stuck with her three stooges, as Katie had once called her colleagues.

Hanging up her jacket, she noticed that hers was the only one on the rack. Odd, she thought, that no one else was here yet. She carefully picked her way around the files stacked on the floor. Switched on the photocopier and copied the fragile newspaper cuttings from her father's box. Two copies of each, so she could give one lot to Boyd. Well, he'd offered, hadn't he? When she'd finished, she put a set on his desk and the other into her deep, cluttered handbag. She'd look at them when she got time. If she ever got time. She put the originals into her desk drawer. Opening the pharmacy bag she'd picked up on the way back from Annabelle's, she sighed with relief at the sight of the blister packs of pills.

Boyd arrived, hung up his jacket and sat down at his desk without a word. No chance of taking her pill, then. Maybe later.

Writing her report on yesterday's activities, Lottie couldn't concentrate. Peering over the top of her computer screen, she saw Boyd lining up pages neatly into a folder on his desk. When he seemed content that they were straight, he took a packet of disinfectant wipes from his drawer and began wiping his keyboard.

'What the hell, Boyd? What's up with you?'

He glanced up, a look of surprise creasing his eyes, as if he had only just become aware of her.

'Up? Nothing. Why?'

'You're in your OCD mode. Something is up.'

'Where are Lynch and Kirby?'

He was diverting her, but she let it go. 'I'd love to know.'

She rang Lynch and listened to the call go to voicemail. Maybe she'd already left to relieve Garda O'Donoghue. She tried Kirby. No answer.

Out of the office and into the incident room. Quiet as a churchyard at midnight. She stuck her head into a few of the other offices. 'Any of you seen Lynch or Kirby this morning?'

'They might be at that house fire,' one garda offered.

'House fire? I heard nothing about a house fire. What are they doing there? For feck's sake! I'm trying to run a murder investigation.' Lottie made her way back to her office.

Boyd called up the incident report log on his computer.

'House fire. Dolanstown. They're there. First responders called for detectives to attend. One male deceased at the house, another badly injured. Suspicion of arson.'

'This is all we need.' Lottie slammed a bundle of reports she hadn't had time to read onto the already crowded floor and planted her foot on top of them. She didn't have the resources to lend to an arson attack, body or no body. And she needed the hospital CCTV checked. Someone had to have dropped Marian Russell off there.

'There's another incident report here.' Boyd read from the screen. 'A car found burned out early this morning, at Lough Cullion car park.'

'Could it be Marian Russell's car?'

'Don't know.'

'Find out. Then get everyone in for a team meeting.'

*

The incident room was packed within half an hour. No sign of Superintendent Corrigan. Good.

'Let's get this house fire out of the way,' Lottie said. 'Kirby, enlighten us.'

'Cottage fire. Chief fire officer thinks it's malicious. One dead male. Dental records will be needed to identify him. The second male is in hospital. Badly burned and minus a few fingers.'

'Minus a few fingers? Explain?'

'That's all we were told.'

'Do you think someone tried to burn the men out of the house?' Lottie asked.

'Hard to know until SOCOs have a look.'

Lynch said, 'We suspect it might have been a grow house. Strong smell of cannabis above the stench of burning.'

'Interesting. Maybe they owed money, or were skimming. Hope we haven't got a drug feud about to explode in Ragmullin. Put someone on the injured man's ward. Just in case.'

'At this rate, we should all relocate to the hospital,' Kirby said.

Lottie thought for a moment. 'We have reports of a car burned out in the car park at Lough Cullion. It could be Marian's. We'll know later on.'

'Or it could've been used by the scum who burned down the cottage,' Lynch offered.

'Why aren't you at Kelly's?' Lottie said. 'You need to relieve Garda O'Donoghue.'

'Can't someone else do it?' Lynch folded her arms defiantly.

'The FLO is still off sick,' Lottie reminded her. She flinched as Lynch swiped her bag from the floor, cracking the strap against the desk. 'Wait until we're finished here, but then you'll have to go. And remember, you're still part of this team.'

'Right so,' Lynch said.

'I need Emma watched for her own protection. Until we find out what actually happened to her mother. I'm going to have another look around the Russell house. Boyd, come with me. Kirby, find out what you can about that house fire and the occupants and investigate the car. Then we can hand it over to another team.'

'Okay,' Kirby said.

'And draw up a list of Tessa Ball's friends and interview them. Did you trace her last movements?'

'Working on it.'

'Do it. Also, find out if Tessa had anything to do with Belfield and Ball, Solicitors. And follow up on the gun we found at her apartment yesterday. Am I talking to myself?'

Boyd stood up. 'Report is in on Tessa Ball's phone. The final activity was a call she received at 21.07 on the night she was murdered.'

'And?' Lottie asked.

'It was from Marian Russell.'

CHAPTER 29

SOCOs had already been all over the Russell house, and Lottie had checked around the night of the murder, but now she wanted to have another look, in daylight. It was a converted two-storey farmhouse. A narrow hallway led to the extension, which housed the kitchen. Before the kitchen, a door opened into an anonymous-looking rectangular sitting room. Brown leather three-piece suite and a long coffee table.

'Minimalistic, isn't it?' Lottie said.

'Bit bare, all right,' Boyd said, stepping onto the teak timber floor.

Lottie moved towards the iron-framed mirror hanging over the fireplace. She looked at her reflection before quickly turning to lift a couple of paperbacks from the coffee table. John Connolly novels. Beside the books, a mug containing an inch of cold coffee displayed evidence of the SOCOs' handiwork. A half-eaten biscuit lay beside an open packet of cookies. Traces of life, halted mid-cycle.

'Emma said she came in here because her mother was working in the kitchen. And then Natasha called and asked her over to her house.' Lottie opened the door of the stove insert. 'It's very clean, isn't it?'

'Compared to the carnage in the kitchen, yeah.'

Leaving the lounge, they headed up the stairs. Four rooms. One obviously belonged to Emma.

'Typical teenager,' Lottie said, and closed the door on the mess. It didn't seem right to search the girl's things. She'd been through enough already, with more heartache to come.

The next room seemed to be a guest bedroom, followed by a bathroom. In the master bedroom, Lottie inspected the contents of the wardrobe, checking the pockets of the jackets. Nothing.

The bottom two drawers of the dressing table held T-shirts and underwear. Opening the top drawer, Lottie observed sterling silver and costume necklaces with matching earrings.

'I don't think this was a burglary,' she said.

Boyd was standing at the window, looking out. 'Nice piece of land.'

Lottie closed the drawers. She joined him at the window and pointed down into the yard. 'What's that behind the shed?'

'Looks like an oil tank.'

'Don't think so. They use solid fuel,' she said, recalling the fire in the sitting room.

Boyd said, 'It's one of those containers for storing coal.'

'We'll have a look inside it.' She glanced around the room again before dropping to her knees to look under the bed.

'Anything?' he asked.

'Dust,' she said, getting up and wiping her knees. 'Did you search the bedside cabinets?'

Boyd lifted a book, glanced at it and opened one of the doors. 'A few pill bottles.'

'Here, let me see those.'

'Paracetamol,' he said.

'Oh.' Lottie looked into the second cabinet. 'This one is empty. Must've belonged to Arthur.' She ran her fingers under the pillow and between the mattress and the base of the bed. Nothing.

Boyd opened a door beside the wardrobe. 'En suite.' Stuck his head inside. 'Clean.'

'Jesus, I hope I'm never murdered,' Lottie said. 'You'd have to fumigate the place before you could go looking anywhere.'

'Nothing of note here,' Boyd said, closing the en suite door.

'What was that book?' Lottie went back to pick up the hardback Boyd had moved a moment ago. '*Culpeper's Complete Herbal*. Interesting. Quite an old book, too.'

She flicked through the pages. 'Such small font. Beautiful plant illustrations. Wonder why she had it?'

Boyd looked over her shoulder. 'Healing remedies?'

'I'll bag it. Might be something, might be nothing,' Lottie said. 'Let's check out the yard.'

*

The rain had begun to spit again. Lottie bent down and opened the flap in the bunker. A couple of nuggets of coal rolled out at her feet.

'Told you,' Boyd said, leaning against the shed.

'Make yourself useful and hand me that log.'

Boyd rolled it over to her.

'Hold on to it. I don't want to fall.'

Stepping up onto the log, Lottie lifted the top of the bunker.

'Flashlight?'

Boyd switched on the one on his phone and handed it over. 'Don't let it fall in.'

She swept the light down and around the cavern. 'Jesus.'

'What's in there?' Boyd tried to peer over the edge.

'Plants of some sort. We need to get the SOCOs back out here.'

'As soon as you hand me back my phone.'

'We'd better have a look inside the shed, too.'

While Boyd made the call, Lottie jumped off the log, headed into the wooden shed and snapped on the light switch. A myriad of paint cans and tools lined the steel shelves on one wall. Logs were stacked against the back wall.

Standing in the clutter, she wondered about the plants and the Culpeper book. Had Marian Russell got a little sideline going here?

If so, it might make sense of someone trying to stop her, but it wasn't a reason to murder Tessa Ball. And Kirby had thought the cottage set alight earlier might have been a grow house. Interesting.

'I want those logs moved,' she told Boyd. 'There might be something beneath them. How soon before SOCOs arrive?'

'Not long.'

'Good. We might be getting somewhere at last.'

'You might be, but I'm not.'

'You wait for the SOCOs,' Lottie said. 'I want to speak to Emma.'

*

At Bernie Kelly's house, she was greeted at the door by Garda O'Donoghue.

'Gilly,' Lottie said. 'Where's Detective Lynch?'

'I haven't seen her since yesterday, and I really need to get home to shower and change.'

'Go ahead. I'll stay until you get back, or until Lynch gets here.'

Gilly grabbed her belongings and escaped.

'Tea, Inspector?' Bernie Kelly asked.

'No thanks. Just a word with Emma.' Lottie stepped into the claustrophobic sitting room.

'Make yourself at home, why don't you?' Bernie said with down-turned pale lips. 'I'll tell her to come down.'

'Still in bed?'

'Teenagers.' She attempted an eye roll; Lottie thought Bernie's plucked eyebrows made her look like a strained prune.

Emma sauntered into the room and flopped onto an armchair. Her hair was a mess and the clothes she was wearing looked too small for her. Poor girl. She needed some of her own stuff soon, Lottie thought.

'How's Mum?' Emma asked.

'Still in an induced coma.'

'I want to see her.'

'I can take you,' Lottie said.

'And my dad? Where's he?'

'He's helping us with our enquiries.'

The girl shot out of the chair. 'Why? He didn't do anything.'

'Please sit down, Emma.' Lottie placed a hand on her arm. Emma shook her off.

'Have you arrested him?'

'No, but we're exploring all possibilities. Your grandmother has been murdered. I need to find out what you know.'

Emma's eyes widened. 'I don't know anything. I want to see Mum and Dad. You've no right to keep me cooped up here. I'm a free citizen, last time I checked.'

'It's for your own safety.'

'Yeah, I've heard that before.'

Lottie wondered how she'd missed the memo where it said teenagers no longer had to respect their elders.

'Did Garda O'Donoghue or Detective Lynch tell you about your mother's injuries?'

Emma bit her bottom lip. Tears loomed in her eyes. She nodded.

'And you've no idea who would do something like that to her?'

A shake of her head, with a sob. 'It's all my fault. I just want to see Mum.'

'How could it be your fault, Emma?'

'I wasn't nice to her,' the girl cried. 'I sided with Dad all the time. I know she's not the best mother in the world, but she's my mum and I made her life a misery.'

Lottie wanted to put an arm around her, to comfort her, but after the previous rebuff, she kept her hands firmly in her pockets.

'The night of your granny's… death, are you sure you saw nothing unusual around the house?'

'No, nothing.'

'Why were you so late going home? Was it usual for you to be late?'

Emma shrugged. 'Depends on what me and Natasha are watching on the telly.'

'So you were watching Netflix, is that correct?'

Emma hesitated, eyes searching out the corners of the room. 'Yup… I think so.'

Lottie watched her closely. '*Orange is the New Black*?'

'What?'

'The programme you were watching?'

'Oh, yeah. That's what we watched.'

'You're sure of that?'

'Yup.'

'So you were here with Natasha and Bernie from six thirty p.m. until you went home around half past ten?'

'Yes. Well, no…'

'That's what you told us originally. Is there anything you want to change or add?' Lottie studied the girl carefully; she was sure there was a lie in there somewhere.

'I was here and we watched the telly. Can I get some clean clothes? Natasha's are a bit small.'

Lottie wanted to press on, but her motherly instinct warned her to relent. That way Emma might trust her more. Later she could grill her about the strange plants growing in the coal bunker.

'I'll go to your house and get some clothes for you. Then we'll drive to the hospital and see if they'll let you see your mum.'

Emma nodded.

'I'll be back in a few minutes.'

Lottie was glad to escape from the suffocating house.

CHAPTER 30

She was winded by the time she arrived back at the Russells'.

'Only five hundred metres and I'm fecked,' she said.

'Thought you were babysitting,' Boyd said.

'Just picking up some clothes for Emma.' Lottie scanned the yard, now busy with life. 'Find anything?'

'They're going to start looking soon.'

'What if the attack here is linked to the cottage fire?'

'Maybe when we get to see what's in there,' he pointed to the shed, 'and what's at the cottage, we'll have a better idea.'

'Maybe,' Lottie said doubtfully.

'I'll get back to work,' Boyd said.

She watched his retreating back before heading inside.

Upstairs in Emma's room, she pulled on her protective gloves as a precaution and rooted around for suitable clothing. She decided on a pair of jeans, a T-shirt and a hoodie, then searched through the shoes. Nothing really appropriate for bad weather. A pair of blue Nike trainers would serve better than white Converses. As she was putting them in a gym bag she'd found at the bottom of the wardrobe, her fingers rubbed against something inside one of the trainers. Letting them drop, she jumped back, falling onto her bottom, sure that it was a mouse.

It wasn't a mouse. A roll of cash lay on the floor beside the trainer, held together by a hair bobbin. She picked it up and put it into a plastic evidence bag she had plucked from her pocket. The outside note was a fifty. A lot of money for a teenager, she thought. Had robbery been the motive after all? And why did Emma have it secreted away in the bottom of her wardrobe?

Putting the plastic bag with the money into her handbag, Lottie scanned the room for a jacket. Not seeing one, she went downstairs and rummaged through the rack of coats in the hall. She noticed a man's black North Face jacket among the feminine attire, and wondered if it belonged to Arthur Russell.

Inspecting it, she found the outside pockets empty, but in the inside breast pocket her fingers touched a piece of paper, neatly folded, nestling at the seam. It looked like a receipt. Opening it up, she found that it was a receipt, dated the day of the murder. From Danny's Bar. Arthur worked there. The time on the receipt was 19.04. She put it into another small plastic evidence bag.

Unhooking a jacket for Emma, she stuffed it in the gym bag and rushed outside.

'Boyd?'

He stuck his head out from behind the shed door. 'What?'

'There's a black North Face jacket hanging in the hall. Get it bagged, tagged and brought in for forensic examination.'

'Sure,' he said.

Lottie set off up the road to prepare Emma for the visit to her mother. First, though, the girl had a few questions to answer.

*

At Bernie Kelly's gate, she met Detective Maria Lynch.

'You took your time,' Lottie said.

'I'd things to sort out regarding the cottage fire. I'm sure Garda O'Donoghue won't mind. I'll take over now.'

'I relieved her.' Lottie held up the gym bag. 'I just ran down to get fresh clothes for Emma. I'm bringing her to visit her mother.'

'Are you sure that's wise?'

'Why not? She wants to see her. I can't deny her that. But now that you're here, you can take her.'

Bernie Kelly opened the door.

'Takes two of you now, does it?' she said, folding her arms.

Lottie walked past her into the house.

'I'll give this to Emma.' The sitting room was empty. 'Upstairs, is she?'

Bernie looked from Lottie to Lynch. 'I thought you took her home to fetch clean clothes. Didn't you?'

'No.' Lottie glanced into the kitchen. Natasha was sitting at the table, munching on burnt toast. 'Lynch, check upstairs.'

Lynch ran up the stairs. She shouted back down, 'No one here.'

'Where is she?' Lottie asked frantically.

Bernie shrugged her shoulders. 'When I came in here, both of you were gone. I assumed she went with you.'

'Where would she go?' Lottie tried to stem the panic gathering in the pit of her stomach.

'Maybe she went on ahead to the hospital,' Bernie said.

'Has she got her phone?' Lottie tapped in Emma's number. 'Nothing. It must be switched off.' She swung round to Lynch. 'Did she pass you on the road?'

'Not that I noticed.'

Rushing back into the kitchen, Lottie towered over Natasha. 'Where is Emma?'

'Hey, wait a minute, Inspector.' Bernie Kelly grabbed Lottie by the arm. 'No need to go accusing my daughter of anything.'

'Natasha.' Lottie ignored Bernie and leaned down to the wild-haired teenager. Looked her in the eye. 'Where would she go? Has she other friends she hangs out with?'

Natasha shook her head. 'Don't know,' she mumbled.

Lottie looked up at the ceiling and closed her eyes. Think.

'Lynch, go to the hospital. See if she's there.'

As Lynch left, Lottie rang Boyd. Emma hadn't appeared there either.

She turned back to Natasha. 'I know you know where she is, so you'd better tell me, young lady.'

Natasha glanced at her mother. 'She took my bike,' she said.

Bernie's face was red. 'Natasha, I told you to—'

'Tell me!' Lottie shouted.

The teenager melted into her chair. With toast crumbs stuck to her lipgloss she said, 'She might be with her boyfriend.'

CHAPTER 31

Lottie collected Boyd from Marian Russell's house. So far nothing had been found buried beneath the timber in the shed. But the plants in the fuel tank had been taken away for testing.

'She has a boyfriend?' Boyd clipped in his seat belt as Lottie took off down the road, wipers swishing trying to keep up with the rain.

'Natasha admitted it. Lorcan Brady. We need to check him out.'

'We should have found out about this boyfriend earlier.'

'Boyd. Don't.'

'Shouldn't he be at school at this hour of the day?'

'He's twenty-one. Unemployed, according to Natasha. We'll run his name through PULSE database later.'

'Did you get his phone number?'

'Said she didn't have it.'

'Isn't this a bit far for Emma to walk?' Boyd said, following the road with his eyes.

Taking a turn at the hospital, Lottie headed along the cemetery road. 'She took Natasha's bike.'

'All the same…'

'She might have arranged to meet him somewhere and he picked her up,' she said. 'Wonder if he has a car?'

Three minutes later, Lottie pulled into the drive of a two-storey house. It looked uncared for, she thought, if not abandoned.

She stepped out on mud flowing towards the road. A lazy-looking collie dog lay on the front doorstep. It didn't move. A red 2010 Honda Civic was parked at the side of the house.

'If that car was any lower to the ground, you'd have to tow it.' She noted the registration number to check later. 'Souped-up exhaust pipe too.'

'You'd hear it before you see it,' Boyd said.

Lottie knocked on the door. No bell. No answer, either. They walked to the rear of the house. The dog followed silently.

The yard was piled high with black rubbish bags. Some bitten through by the dog or maybe vermin; tea bags and bits of vegetable peelings were scattered around. Picking her steps carefully, Lottie peered through the window.

'No one home?' Boyd said.

'Curtains are drawn. It looks deserted.' She hammered on the door. Waited. No one appeared.

'Emma's not here. Hospital next?'

'Yes. Lynch should be there now.'

When she got back into the car, her phone rang. Lynch. 'Emma's not here at the hospital, but you…'

'What?' Boyd asked.

'Shush,' Lottie said.

Lynch was still talking. Lottie said, 'We'll be there in a few minutes.'

She looked at Boyd as she hung up. 'I think we just found Lorcan Brady.'

'Where?'

'He's one of the fire victims.'

*

Huddling in the hospital corridor, Lynch updated Lottie. Boyd lounged against the wall.

'So one of the guys is Lorcan Brady,' Lottie clarified. 'But you don't know which one yet?'

Lynch nodded.

'How were you able to get the name?'

'I ran the registration of the car found at the cottage.'

'But we've just come from Brady's place. There's a red Honda Civic there.'

'Maybe it belongs to the other fellow. We still have no positive ID on either man.'

'We'd better run the Honda plates.' Lottie walked around in a circle, tapping her phone against her leg. 'Is the victim still unconscious?'

'Yes. Severe burns and fingers hacked off.'

'So it might be Lorcan Brady and it might not.'

'Affirmative.'

'Brady is in the system. See if anything else matches to this guy. Is his room still guarded?'

'Yes, and Marian's.'

'This is getting complicated,' Lottie said. 'Brady was Emma's boyfriend and he's possibly either a burned man or a dead man.'

'You only have Natasha's word, though,' Boyd said.

'But if it's true, it could link Tessa's murder to the fire. I'm going to have a look at the cottage now.'

'What will I do?' Lynch asked.

'Find out who owns that Honda and get the burned victim identified. Put out an alert for Emma Russell.'

Boyd said, 'Do you want me to go back to Marian Russell's house? See if SOCOs have unearthed anything?'

'Follow it up. Main priority is to find Emma. That little madam has been economical with the truth from day one. God knows what she's into or who she's into it with, but I want her found.'

Without waiting for a reply, Lottie pulled her bag around her chest and ran down the stairs.

CHAPTER 32

It was nearing four in the afternoon and the sky was bulging with black clouds when Lottie arrived at the burned-out cottage.

Looking over at the wet embers, now cordoned with crime-scene tapes, she zipped her jacket to her neck and tucked her hair into the hood. The temperature had dropped significantly and an east wind was gathering pace across the miserable fields.

Listening to the roaring wind and the rainwater drip-dripping from the bare branches above her head, she stretched her arms and legs. She felt like she'd been cooped up in the office all day, when in fact she had been out for most of it. Once her name was ticked off by the garda standing at the small iron gate, she walked towards the cottage.

The roof had caved in, which didn't make much difference as the internal structure and personal effects had been either burned or saturated by fire hoses and the elements. But once it was deemed safe to do so, it'd be searched. SOCOs would have a hard job going through it, she thought.

A glare of lamps was lighting up the rear. She headed there. Gardaí and SOCOs were busy bagging and tagging the plants found in the insulated outhouse. Just as well the fire hadn't reached that far.

To the left of the outhouse she noted a galvanised shed. Three walls stood haphazardly and its front lay open with a sagging line of washing hanging beneath the roof. Denim jeans, jogging pants and T-shirts. All blackened with smoke. They might be dry by Christmas, she thought.

She walked up to the SOCO standing with a clipboard in his hand.

'I'm assuming you wouldn't get those in a garden centre,' she said.

'Definitely not,' he replied. 'Cannabis plants might be a tad expensive for the likes of those places.'

'Not very discreet about it, were they?'

'Out here in the countryside you can grow just about anything without anyone passing the slightest remark. They're just plants, if you don't know any different.'

'Was it locked?'

'Chains and combination lock, nothing a good pair of shears wouldn't cut through.'

He turned to check off another bag of plants being dragged by one of his colleagues to the waiting technical bureau van.

Lottie walked around the yard. From the hedge she could see smoke rising from the chimney of a house in the distance. There wasn't anything to done here, and as she returned to her car, she wondered if Mick O'Dowd knew what was growing close to where his cows grazed.

*

The Land Rover was parked haphazardly at the side of the farmhouse. Net curtains were draped across sash windows, and the front door had been painted green a long time ago, going by the weather-beaten look of it. The satellite dish on the chimney creaked eerily in the growing gale.

A dog, big and black, raced out and circled the wheels of her car. Lottie switched off the engine and got out, praying it would back off. It didn't.

'Go away. Shoo. Scram. Good doggie.' She twisted in circles, trying to keep the animal from jumping up on her. A Rottweiler with yellow teeth, dripping drool. 'Get off, dog!'

'What's all the commotion?' A man turned the corner of the house. 'Down, boy. Mason, lie down.'

The dog snarled and threw Lottie a lingering look before turning and strolling to its master.

'Who are you?' he said, chaining the animal to a hook on the barn wall. Wisps of long grey hair poked out from beneath his peaked tweed cap. Lottie surmised he must be at least seventy.

'Detective Inspector Lottie Parker.' She flashed her ID. 'And you are…'

'I think you already know who I am.'

'Your dog doesn't seem to like me, Mr O'Dowd. But I'm not too bad once you get to know me.' She smiled at the attempted joke.

O'Dowd's grimace curled his face into an unreadable expression. 'I hope you won't be here long enough to get to know.' He glanced at the ID and his hand swallowed hers in a firm shake. 'What can I help you with?'

She tried not to visibly recoil as the wind carried his body odour towards her. He smelled like someone who hadn't washed after sex. Lottie shuddered, thinking it was probably a long time since O'Dowd had engaged in such an activity.

Planting her feet firmly and facing the rising wind, she said, 'I was in the area. Wondered if you knew anything about the cottage up the road, the one that burned down?'

'Spoke to a detective this morning.' He sniffed, shaking his head. 'Do you not talk to each other?'

He turned and walked towards one of the large sheds.

Lottie followed. 'We do, but I'm the curious sort. Like to hear things first hand. If you don't mind.'

'I do mind, and I'm very busy. My day's been upset enough already. I've cows in the milking shed waiting for me.'

'Don't let me delay you. Go ahead. I'll watch, you talk.'

He kept walking, hand raised, directing her. 'You need wellington boots around here.'

'So this is a milking shed, is it?' Lottie scanned the large barn. Two rows of cows, heads through wrought-iron bars, chewing hay, their teats connected to milking machines behind them.

'I'm sure you don't want an agricultural lesson.' He took off his waxed jacket and hung it on a post, then began checking the machines, tightening and loosening as he went.

She loitered at the door. 'How many cows do you have?'

'Thirty. Used to have up on two hundred. Not much business in dairy any more, but it keeps me busy. I do a bit of beef farming as well. Heifers and bulls.' He pointed to a row of animals away on the far side of the shed.

'Jesus, they're huge,' Lottie said, sizing up the animals standing on a slatted floor. They seemed to be as wide as they were tall. She turned back to the cows being milked. 'Do those things... hurt the cows?'

He laughed sardonically. 'Why don't you ask them?'

Folding her arms, she leaned against the wall. 'Maybe another time,' she said. 'Tell me about the cottage. Who lived there?'

'Never saw anyone. Heard a car with a heavy exhaust, couple of times a week. Carving doughnuts on the road, no doubt. But they didn't bother me. So I never had reason to call anyone about it.'

'Until this morning.' She unfolded her arms and stepped further into the enclosure, holding on to one of the bars. The cow beside her lifted its tail.

'Righto. Until this morning.' O'Dowd looked over. 'Wouldn't stand too close if I was you.'

'Why not?' Lottie jumped out of the way as shit flowed from the cow's arse down to the straw-covered floor. 'Okay, I get it.'

He laughed. She thought it sounded more in derision than amusement. Resuming her vigil by the door, she had to shout above the noise of the machinery.

'You were at home when you saw the flames, that right?'

'I was in my house, getting ready to start the day. Looked out the window. Like Bonfire Night up there, it was.' He nodded his head in the direction of the cottage. 'Got into my Land Rover, so I did. Rushed up the road. Once I saw how bad it was, I rang the fire service.'

'Did you notice anyone in or around the cottage?'

'There was a car out the front, but I wasn't sure if there was anyone inside the cottage or not. And the flames were raging. I'm not young, nor a daredevil, so I didn't venture past the gate.'

Lottie watched O'Dowd working his way down the line of cattle, kicking up straw as he went.

'So you didn't go closer to see if anyone needed help?' she asked.

The muscles of O'Dowd's broad shoulders seemed to constrict under his tartan shirt before he trekked back to her. He wiped his hands on a clump of hay and pulled on his jacket.

'I'm no hero, Inspector.'

'Do you know who owned or rented out the cottage?'

'Haven't a clue. Maybe through an estate agent?'

Outside the barn door, the beast of a dog eyed Lottie suspiciously and growled.

'Why do you need such a dangerous animal?'

'I live alone. It's isolated out here. Mason is partly for company, mainly for protection. He's a good guard dog.'

Lottie was going to ask if he had a dog licence, but decided not to push her luck.

'He doesn't chase your livestock?'

'I have him well trained.' He untied the chain and held it in his hand, the dog straining on the end of it. 'Was there anything else?'

'You live alone. Married?'

'No.'

'Kids?'

'Why all these questions?'

'Like I said, I'm just curious.'

He looked up at the clouds rolling across the sky. 'There's a storm coming. You should head back to town.'

'What are those?' Lottie pointed to three large blue plastic barrels standing near the second barn.

'Propcorn.'

'Popcorn? You're having me on?'

'Not popcorn. Propcorn. It's an acid. To mix in with the oats and barley for the cattle feed. I use the barrels to collect rainwater once they're empty of the acid and washed out.'

'What's that machine over there?' She pointed to a large piece of equipment with massive steel rotors.

'A free course in agriculture you want, is it?'

'Just—'

'Curious. It's a slurry agitator. Are you finished now? I'm very busy.' He loosened his hold on the chain and the dog snarled.

Her brain was squeezing with an uneasy sensation. Was O'Dowd hiding something? Or was he just a citizen who had reported a fire?

'Can I use the bathroom?' she ventured, a ruse to get inside the house for a snoop.

He took a step towards her, the dog circling his legs. 'Doing a bit of decorating inside. You can use the outside one, though I wouldn't recommend it.'

He pointed to an open door on the side of the shed. Lottie could see the ground running green.

'Ah, it's okay. I'll manage until I get back. You'll have to give a formal statement about the fire. You could do it now if you like.'

'No, I don't like. Told all to your detective.'

'That was informal. Call into the station, or I can send someone out to you tomorrow.' By now, Lottie was fed up with him.

'I'll go in when I get time. Satisfied?'

'I suppose you heard about the murder and abduction over in Carnmore?'

'Aye, I did.'

Was that a flicker of a shadow rolling across his face? Or was it just the wind churning light through the trees?

'Did you know Tessa Ball?'

He lowered his head and was silent so long she thought he had slipped into a trance. At last he looked up from beneath wrinkled eyelids, crow's feet imprinting deeper lines. 'Everyone of an age knew Tessa.'

'Care to tell me about her?'

'Nothing to tell. She's gone now, that's all.'

'Oh, come on. I can't find out much about her.'

'You're better off. Now let me get back to work.'

'Farming here long?' Something was keeping her from leaving. A gust flung a steel bucket across the yard and the dog barked.

O'Dowd paid no heed. 'All my life. Worked with my father until he died way too young. I kept the farm going.'

'And your mother?'

'You do ask a lot of questions, don't you?'

'Part of my job.'

'My pedigree has nothing to do with you. And you'd do well to mind your own family history, Inspector Parker. Not all coated in the white paint of glory, is it now?'

Lottie had been about to head to her car. Now she stopped and half turned to O'Dowd, feeling the blood drain from her face. He knew he'd struck a chord, because she saw him raise a hand. In apology?

'What do you mean?' She scrambled the words through her lips.

'Nothing. Just shooting my mouth off.' He laughed. A feline tinkle, like breaking glass.

She stepped towards him. The dog strained on the leash. She didn't care. Walking into O'Dowd's space, her voice a whisper in the gale, she said, 'What do you know about my family?'

'Look, drop it.' He tightened his grip on the chain, rolling it up a notch, dragging the dog closer to his leg. 'I just meant we all have skeletons in cupboards we want to keep locked away from prying eyes. Yourself included.'

Lottie's jacket buffeted open and the wind cut through her like a sharp blade.

'I'd really like to know what you mean.'

'I think you already do. Now if you don't mind, I've a busy evening ahead. I'll call into the station tomorrow when I'm in town.' He tipped the peak of his cap and motioned with his free hand to her car. 'You'd best be getting off with yourself before the storm grabs a hold of you.'

Still feeling as if a claw had snatched at her heart, Lottie got into her car and reversed out of the gate. As she drove away, she could see in her rear-view mirror O'Dowd standing watching. A curtain twitched at an upstairs window. The wind? Or someone there?

She shook off the shiver. Had he threatened her? Did he know something about her father? Or was it about Eddie, her dead brother? Whatever it was, he had spiked her interest in him when she felt he was in fact trying to divert her.

And the fire. Wouldn't any normal human being ensure there was no one inside the burning cottage? Do all in their power to rescue them? But O'Dowd had apparently watched the place go up in flames while one man was burned to death and another was left hanging on to life by his fingertips. Another shudder up her spine. He had no fingertips.

*

O'Dowd watched the inspector's car crest the hill, heading into town. He sighed with relief. She hadn't noticed the bicycle at the side of the house. He wheeled it into the second shed, beside the milking parlour. Closed the door. Tied up the dog.

He pulled off his boots, banged them against the step, scraping away most of the cow dung and muck, and left them to dry out. The kitchen was clean but empty. Moving into the hall, he shouted up the stairs.

'You can come down now, girleen. The guard is gone.'

He waited a moment before seeing her pop her head over the banister.

'No need to be afraid.'

She pushed her spectacles back up her nose, and with wariness in her steps as well as her eyes came down the stairs.

'Sit yourself down and I'll make you that cup of tea now,' he said, and went to boil the kettle.

CHAPTER 33

Lottie had swung a U-turn when she'd reached the main road, and headed to the Dead House in Tullamore. O'Dowd, whether intentionally or otherwise, had got her thinking about her father.

Jane Dore poured boiling water over a camomile tea bag.

'So, what is it you want help with, Lottie?'

Lottie held the cup in her hand, letting the warmth thaw out her fingers.

'The body that came in this morning. Have you carried out his PM yet?'

'He's on the table. Badly burned. But he didn't die in the fire.'

'What?'

'I found a few nicks on his ribs. I've more tests to run, but in my opinion he was stabbed. No smoke in what's left of the lungs, and that suggests he was dead before the fire.'

Lottie digested this information. Murdered. She had already suspected as much, seeing as the other victim had had his fingers hacked off.

'Drug gangs,' she said, half to herself. This would bring the GNDU – the Garda National Drugs Unit – to her district. 'But it seems a bit extreme for a shedload of cannabis.'

'I'll email the preliminary results in the morning.'

'How can we identify him?'

'I've captured his dental impressions. Should have something for you later today or tomorrow morning.'

'Thanks, Jane.' Lottie sipped her tea, allowing it to relax her slightly. Only slightly.

'Is there something else you want to discuss?'

'It's about my dad. You see, in 1975, he supposedly killed himself.'

'I'm sorry.' Jane eyed her quizzically. 'You said supposedly.'

'Over the last few months, I've been privately investigating the circumstances of his death. Following up with his former colleagues. Asking questions. Poking my nose into old people's lives. Getting nowhere.'

'Why are you doing that?'

'I'm trying to figure out why Dad shot himself. I was only four, and my brother was ten.'

'Was he suffering from depression? Stress at work?'

'His colleagues, those still alive, say they can't remember. It's like they don't want to talk about him. And my mother won't tell my anything.'

'Have you tried talking to her? Nicely?'

Lottie smiled. 'Yes. I'd been trying to find out for years what happened, and a few months ago she handed over a box containing my father's things.'

'Did that give you any clues?'

'I can't pinpoint anything. A few newspaper cuttings. Notebooks. No suicide note. Mother says there wasn't one.'

'Was there an investigation at the time?'

'An inquest. I suppose, because he was a serving garda sergeant, there doesn't seem to have been too much of a fuss. Top brass probably wanted it all hushed up at the time.'

'What was the verdict?' Jane asked.

'Suicide by lethal weapon. I'm surprised he even got a Catholic burial.'

'Where did he get the gun?'

'Took it from the weapons cabinet at the station. Stole the key and stole the gun.'

'I'm assuming there was a post-mortem. Do you want me to check it out?'

'Please. I have some photos and a death certificate. It'd be great if you could see what's archived.'

Jane glanced at the certificate. 'I'll have a look.'

'Thanks, Jane.'

'I can't promise anything.'

'I know, but I thought that if you could examine the file, you might be able to tell me, one way or the other.'

'Where did he do it?' Cool and professional. Lottie winced at Jane's aloofness.

'In the tool shed at the bottom of the garden.'

'In my experience, a police officer who commits suicide most often carries out the act at their place of work. Unusual that he would bring it on the family like that.'

'That's what I thought.'

'I'm only speculating here, Lottie.'

'I know, but anything you can give me is appreciated.'

'You really want to know why he did it?'

'If he did it,' Lottie said.

'I deal with facts and evidence. I'll check our archives.' Jane sipped her tea. 'Who found his body?'

Lottie was silent for a moment. An image flitted across her eyes. A memory? No, she'd been too young then.

'My brother Eddie. According to Mother, it changed his personality. He ended up in St Angela's Institution, where he was murdered.'

'Sad family history you have, Lottie.'

'I know. Too sad that my mother won't help me.'

'I'm sure if you sit her down and tell her how it has affected you, she'll talk to you.'

'You don't know my mother,' Lottie said with a grim smile.

'She gave you the box of memorabilia, didn't she?'

'After years of begging for answers, that's all she offered. I still don't know what prompted her to hand it over.'

'Probably you discovering your brother's bones.' Jane picked up the two mugs. 'Speak to her about the days and weeks leading up to your father's death. If anyone can get her to talk, Lottie Parker, you can.' She slipped down off the stool and put the mugs into a sink.

'Thanks, Jane.' Lottie clutched her bag.

'I can't promise anything on your father's suicide, but I'll have the prelims over to you in the morning.'

'Prelims?' Lottie turned around, brows knitted together.

'On the burned body.'

'Oh, yes.'

Leaving Jane and the Dead House, Lottie headed out to the car park and was almost blown off her feet by the wind. The storm had arrived.

CHAPTER 34

The office was quiet when Lottie returned from Tullamore, her car having been bustled and buffeted along the motorway. It felt like a hurricane was blowing through her brain. She needed to ask Kirby about his impressions of Mick O'Dowd.

At her desk, she quickly typed up a statement of her conversation with the farmer, leaving out his veiled insinuations about her family. The photocopier was silent, the phones unusually quiet and none of her detectives were around. Out searching for Emma Russell, she hoped. If Emma wasn't at Lorcan Brady's house, and Brady was the man in the hospital or on Jane Dore's stainless-steel table, then where was she?

Opening her drawer and spotting her father's newspaper cuttings, Lottie remembered that she needed to go through Tessa Ball's letters. After shifting some of the clutter from her desk, she found the copies. Would they give her a clue as to why the old lady was murdered?

'I've looked through those,' Boyd said, coming in and sitting sideways at his desk. He shoved his long legs out in front of him and leaned back, yawning.

'Of course you have.' Lottie swore silently. He was always one step ahead of her. 'And?'

'And nothing.' He rolled up his shirtsleeves. 'Love letters by the look of it. When did her husband die?'

'How would I know that?'

'I do.' Boyd smirked. 'Timothy Ball died four years after they were married. 1970. Heart attack.'

'Long time to be a widow.' Lottie thought of her own mother, who had been a widow almost the same length of time as Tessa. Neither had remarried. Would she?

'But all the letters are undated and unsigned,' Boyd said.

'Anonymous? Why would she keep them?'

'We can't ask her, can we?'

'Very funny,' Lottie said, but neither of them was laughing. She scanned over the copies. 'They do read like love letters. Why not sign them?'

'In case her husband found them?'

'But they might've been written after he died. So that doesn't make sense. When we find Emma, we can ask her about her grandmother. Any word on Marian Russell?'

'It'll be a few days before they attempt to take her out of the coma. And before you ask, the burned man is still critical.'

'One of the fire victims must be Lorcan Brady.'

'If Emma is involved with him, she could be in danger.'

'Still no sign of her?' Lottie folded the letters back into the file.

Boyd shook his head. 'Disappeared into the wind.'

'I'm worried. She's had terrible shocks. First her granny, then her mother. Her father is our lead suspect and her boyfriend could be dead or dying in hospital.'

'She doesn't know about him.'

'Maybe she does. I hope she's not involved in anything drug-related. Oh, I almost forgot.'

She pulled her bag up onto the desk and took out the Culpeper book she'd taken from Marian Russell's room. Underneath, the two plastic evidence bags nestled amongst the chaos.

'I found these at the house when I went to pick up clothes for Emma.'

Boyd came and perched on the edge of her desk. He picked up the receipt. 'Danny's Bar. The evening of the attack at the Russell house. Two pints of Heineken. 19.04 p.m. Verified by PIN. Visa debit. That's where Arthur Russell works.'

'The bar manager might be able to check their records to see if it was him.'

'It's a long shot, but we can try. Arthur might've had a drink before heading home.'

'If it was him, then the coat places him at the scene of the crime. Check with the bank too to see if the transaction is his.'

Boyd glanced at the rolled-up notes. 'And this money. Tell me.'

'Bundled up in a trainer at the bottom of Emma's wardrobe.' Lottie pulled on the requisite latex gloves and took the bobbin from the notes. She flattened them on a plastic folder and counted. 'Nine hundred and fifty euros.'

'Running-away fund?'

'Well, if she has run away, she's gone without her fund. Drug money?'

'If she's mixed up with Lorcan Brady, it's a possibility.'

'He has a record?'

'Yup.' Boyd went back to his desk and brought up the PULSE database. 'Caught in possession. Not enough to say it was for supply. Suspended sentence. Last March.'

'Any known associates?'

'No. He pleaded guilty to possession. Nothing before or since. Keeping his nose clean.'

'Not clean enough. Did we find out who the registered owner of the car at Brady's house is, seeing as it was his car at the burned-out cottage?'

'Kirby got the details.'

'Where is he, by the way?' Lottie went to investigate Kirby's desk. She picked up a computer printout. 'Registered to Lorcan Brady. So, the lad has two cars in his name. Must be making more than what he gets on welfare.'

'Fingers in too many pies, I'd say,' Boyd said.

'No fingers to put anywhere now,' Lottie said. 'Jane said the body at the cottage was stabbed to death. Didn't die from the fire. Adds another dimension.'

'Has to be drugs-related.'

'Seems like it. But murdering someone for a small shed of cannabis? I don't think so.'

'The drugs unit lads will be down here so,' Boyd said.

'Corrigan will be a mile up our arses.'

'And theirs.'

'I need to think about all this. Incident team meeting first thing in the morning. We have to find out exactly what this ungodly mess is all about.' She stood up and got her jacket. 'I'm going home.'

'I'll do further searches. See what I can find out.'

'Check with the drugs unit. Lorcan Brady might be on their radar.'

'And Arthur Russell? Will I bring him in for questioning again?'

'Yes. The coat and the receipt are new evidence. See what he has to say for himself.'

'I'll get Kirby to sit in with me. Enjoy the rest of your evening,' Boyd said, without looking up.

She didn't answer, just left him there with the murmur of the radiators cooling down for the night.

CHAPTER 35

It was dark and the church bells were chiming seven when Lottie stepped outside. Almost blown away, she gripped the railing to steady herself before heading round to the yard for her car.

'There you are.'

Lottie groaned. 'You again.'

Cathal Moroney fell into step beside her, trying to keep hold of a massive golf umbrella.

'Off the record,' he yelled against the wind. 'Please.'

'You can say please, thank you, kiss my arse all you like, but I'm not making any statement on anything.' She clamped her mouth shut and searched her bag for her keys.

'It's drugs-related, isn't it?'

'No comment.'

'I heard Lorcan Brady is involved.'

'Where did you hear that?' Shit.

'I knew it!' he said triumphantly as a gust of wind took hold of his umbrella.

Lottie turned and stuck a finger in his chest. 'You know nothing until you get an official comment. Got it?'

'I want to speak to you about it. You see, I'm doing my own investigation into drugs in rural towns and I think—'

'You can stop right there, Moroney.' At last her fingers closed on the keys in the bottom of her bag. She held them aloft and pointed to the gate with them. 'This is private property, and if you don't want me to arrest you, I'd advise you to leave. Right now.'

'You're making a big mistake, Inspector.' Moroney grabbed his umbrella with both hands. 'When you realise that, come talk to me. I have a lot of information you might be interested in. Historical stuff. Think about it.'

Lottie bent down to open her car. Maybe she should talk to the journalist. See what he had. If anything. But when she turned around, he was running out the gate after his umbrella.

Not meant to be, she thought. But as she drove home, the car swaying through the deserted streets, she wondered if she'd been foolish not to listen to him. As her mother was used to saying, 'Time will tell.'

CHAPTER 36

Arthur Russell sat down heavily on the steel chair and faced the two detectives, listening as they went through the formalities and fiddled with the recording equipment.

'Any chance of a decent cup of tea?' he asked. 'I came in voluntarily without my solicitor. The least you can do is get me a cuppa.'

'Do you want us to call your solicitor?'

'Tea with two sugars would be grand.' He needed something in his bloodstream to keep him focused. Fat lot of good the solicitor had done him so far. He'd listen and keep his trap shut.

The chubby detective with the bushy hair, the one who called himself Kirby, returned with the tea. Russell savoured it, even though it was in a paper cup. At least it was hot. The sugar surged through his brain. More than two, he thought. These boys wanted him alert.

'Do you have any idea where your daughter is?'

He hadn't been expecting this. 'What are you talking about? Didn't you tell me she was at that Kelly one's house?'

'She was. But she appears to have run away from there. Have you seen her?'

Russell went to stand up. The burly detective pushed him back down. 'What's going on? Where's Emma? I'm leaving. I need to look for my girl.'

'Sit down, Mr Russell. Do you know where she might be?'

Hyperventilating now, he tried to get the words out of his mouth. 'Try my studio… shed. She sometimes comes round and listens to me play music. I was at work and came straight here when you called. She might be there.'

'We checked. She's not there. She took Natasha's bicycle earlier, and Natasha said she might have gone to her boyfriend. You know about that?'

'Emma doesn't have a boyfriend.'

'You sure?'

Running his hand furiously across his head, he tried to think. No, he'd never heard Emma mention anyone. 'What's his name?'

'Lorcan Brady. Mean anything to you?'

'Don't think so.' His brain was too tired to compute. Lorcan Brady? He thought he'd heard of him, but he wasn't about to tell these two eejits.

'Does this belong to you?' Boyd placed a folded black jacket, in a plastic bag, on the table.

'I had one like that,' Russell said. He put down his cup and pulled the bag towards him. 'Looks too new to be mine. It's not mine.'

An A4 page was put in front of him. In the centre he could see a photocopy of a receipt.

Boyd said, 'Do you want to change your story about what you did on the night Tessa Ball was murdered?'

Pushing the page back to the detective, Russell said, 'Why would I change it? It's the truth.'

'You said you went straight back to your digs after your shift ended. This tells us you didn't.'

Russell tugged at his beard. 'I had a pint, okay? No crime in that.'

'Two pints. Who was with you?'

'No one. I ordered two together. Quicker that way.' Russell looked from one detective to the other. He knew they were thinking he was talking a load of shite.

The bushy-haired one snorted.

'What's so funny?' Russell asked.

'I do that myself sometimes.'

'There. Told you so.'

Boyd said, 'You never mentioned having a drink. Why?'

'I forgot. Never thought about it until you showed me the… receipt.'

'So we find your jacket in the house and your fingerprints on the murder weapon. Can you explain that?'

'Murder weapon?'

'Baseball bat. The one belonging to your daughter.'

Thinking that offence was his best method of defence, Russell said, 'So what if my fingerprints are on the baseball bat. I bought the darn thing!'

'And the jacket?'

'It's not mine.'

'Your receipt was in the pocket.'

'I said it's not mine.'

'The receipt?'

'No, knobhead, the jacket.'

'But you said you had one just like it. The bar manager said it looked like yours when he confirmed to us that you bought the two pints.'

'It might look like mine, but it isn't. Go look around my digs and you'll find mine. It's older than that and it was wet from all the rain. I hung it up there.'

'I have an inventory of everything in your room at the B and B. No jacket.'

'That's a load of bollocks.'

'It's a fact.'

'Screw you.' Russell folded his arms and sat back in his chair. Little and Large were not going to pin Tessa's murder on him. 'No matter how many times I actually thought of killing the old crone, I didn't do it.'

'You admit you had murderous thoughts?' The bushy-haired one had woken up.

'Right now, I want to murder the two of you. Going to arrest me for that?'

'Do you admit to having a drink at Danny's the evening of the murder?'

'Yes.'

'On your own?'

'Yes.'

'And you own a black North Face jacket?'

'I won't say another word without my solicitor.'

'Thank you, Mr Russell.'

'Can I go now?'

'I'm sorry. We'll call your solicitor, and now that we have this new evidence, you will be arrested in connection with the murder of Tessa Ball. So unless you start telling us something useful, you'll be here for a while.'

Arthur eyed the two detectives as they switched off the recording device. Sealing the discs and whatever else they had to do. He drained his tea. Ran his finger around the bottom of the cup and licked off the remaining sugar.

As he was being led from the interview room to await his solicitor, he glanced at the plastic evidence bag containing the jacket. Arthur Russell knew he wouldn't sleep tonight. And it had nothing at all to do with the sugar in his tea.

CHAPTER 37

Annabelle O'Shea took a deep breath and shook off the feeling of foreboding as she opened the front door. Her hand throbbed and her legs were so sore she felt like she'd walked miles.

She poked her head around the sitting room door. Her seventeen-year-old twins, Pearse and Bronagh, were watching a US basketball game on the television. Not a sign of a school book. Two bags of popcorn lay open on the coffee table. She hoped they tidied them up before Cian came downstairs.

'Hi, Mom,' Bronagh said, waving her hand in the air without turning round.

'You're home late,' Pearse said, standing up.

Annabelle hugged her son and he began tidying up the coffee table. She mussed up her daughter's long hair. 'Why don't you both go to your rooms and make a start on homework?'

The twins gathered up their school bags, switched off the television and disappeared up the stairs. She made her way to the kitchen.

It was sparkling clean. Cian had gone into overdrive. She sighed. He did that after each outburst. All contrite. Thinking he could make things better by cleaning the house. The scent of citrus clung to everything, making her eyes water.

For a moment she wished he was dead. No, she shouldn't be thinking that. She thought of Lottie Parker, struggling through widowhood, trying to raise three teenagers and a grandchild and deal with a battleaxe mother who only helped out when the mood took her. I'm the lucky one, Annabelle told herself.

Dropping her handbag and the plastic bag of groceries she'd carried from the car onto the table, she pulled out a chair and sat down. Waiting for Cian to come down the stairs demanding his dinner. His domesticity hadn't extended to cooking. She felt like ordering a takeaway. Chinese. Maybe Indian. That would be nice. If Cian was penitent enough after yesterday, he might agree. But his outbursts were becoming more frequent and his remorse less genuine. Since he'd found out about her affair with Tom Rickard, he had morphed into something that appeared more animal than human. Had his anger and violence always been simmering beneath the surface? Had she been too caught up in her own world to notice?

He appeared in the doorway. No smile. Hands clenching and unclenching. She braced herself for the onslaught, praying it would only be verbal. He wouldn't dare touch her with the children in the house.

'You're late.' His voice a whispered snarl.

'The surgery was busy today. This rain has everyone sniffling with colds. Not that I can give them anything for a cold. Doesn't stop them appearing at my door, though.' She held his gaze. Dark unwavering eyes stared back at her. She knew she was babbling on. 'Did you have a productive day?' she added.

'What do you think?' He shut the door behind him.

Annabelle closed her eyes, tiredness seeping through her bones, pain throbbing in her burned hand.

'Look at me,' he said.

She felt his fingers jerk her chin upwards, and her eyes flew open.

'Cian. Stop. You're hurting me.' She tried to unlock his hand from her face. He squeezed harder. 'You'll leave bruises,' she muttered through pursed lips.

'I want you to relate your day to me. Minute by minute. Leave nothing out. I'll know if you're lying.'

Ever since he'd found out about her affair, he'd kept tabs on her like she was a felon and he a detective. With little choice, she related her day's activity. Leaving out Lottie's visit. No need for Cian to know about that.

The slap across the back of her head caught her unawares.

'Liar,' he said, his lips close to her ear.

'I'm telling the truth. I'll get my diary up on my laptop. You can check.'

'I know your diary. It's linked to mine.'

Annabelle tried to breathe normally. He was too close. She should have known a computer geek like her husband would have access to all her data. But Lottie hadn't been registered in her diary. She'd just shown up. There was no way Cian could have known about her.

She said, 'So then you know who was in and out all day.'

'Lottie Parker. Why didn't you mention her?'

He released her chin.

Annabelle stilled her hand from reaching to soothe her aching flesh. 'I need to put dinner on, unless you'd like a takeaway?'

'Don't attempt to change the subject. I asked you a question.'

How could he know about Lottie? Had he been following her?

'She wasn't in my diary because she just turned up. Before surgery started. What's the big deal?' Be brave, she encouraged herself.

'I'll tell you what the big deal is. You're a lying, cheating whore. And I am in control of your life now. Not you. If you do one thing, one little thing without telling me, you will never set eyes on those two again.' He nodded towards the ceiling.

'I get the message.'

His hand clutched her shoulder and his fingers pinched into the bone. Around her throat they crawled, tightening with each movement. She dared not breathe. She tried to stare him down, but had to blink. A lump choked her up and she couldn't gulp it away. His fingers pressed tighter. Her legs jellied and her knees buckled.

Then just at the moment when she felt she must surely pass out, he eased the pressure and removed his hand.

Putting his lips to her ear, he sucked hard and gnashed his teeth into the lobe. She squealed but managed to suppress a scream.

'I'm watching your every move,' he sneered. 'Every. Single. Move.'

He released her and she collapsed against the table, trying to catch her breath. When she heard the door close behind him, she ran and vomited into the sink.

*

He entered his study and locked the door behind him.

'Bitch! Stupid bitch,' he said, sitting down at his computer consoles. He had four screens. One for work, one for gaming, one to check on the webcams spread throughout the house and the other for the webcam in her office.

He checked her phone. Usual trivia. He was sure she hadn't got a new lover. But he was leaving nothing to chance this time. Not after that bastard Rickard had snared her.

No, Cian O'Shea was leaving nothing to chance.

He flicked on a screen, tapped a folder and brought up the photographs.

'You are going to pay,' he said.

But first Lottie Parker needed to be alienated.

CHAPTER 38

She was home a little earlier than usual. Didn't make any difference. The house was still the same. Her family was still the same.

Sean shouted down the stairs. 'Mam? Do you know anything about photosynthesis?'

'Ask Chloe or Katie.'

'They won't help me and this homework has to be in for tomorrow.'

Lottie rested against the door. Closed her eyes. Took a deep breath.

'Sorry, Sean. I know nothing.'

A screech from the baby alerted her to the fact that he was in the sitting room. She poked her head around the door. Katie was lying on the floor, fast asleep, little Louis swaddled in a blanket in the crook of her arm.

Lottie lifted him up without waking her daughter. Cuddling the little boy to her chest, she brought him to the kitchen. She snapped on the electric heater and glanced at the clock, wondering where Chloe might be. Finding a full bottle of formula beside the steriliser, she sat in her armchair and began to feed the baby. Maybe her own rumbling tummy might soothe him.

As Louis sucked at the bottle, Lottie thought how this serenity was a million miles from the hectic day she'd endured. Work–life balance. Wasn't that what management expounded? She doubted any of the suits resident on the top floor lived the life she did. And then there was Moroney, with his bloodhound nose, sniffing for a story, and her mother still refusing to tell her anything about her dad's death.

Her grandson's blue eyes closed and she admired the length of his lashes. She thought of Jason Rickard, the child's father. Tom and Melanie had a right to know about their grandchild. She had to talk to Katie about it. Soon. Tomorrow, maybe.

'Are you going to cook any dinner?' Sean swung through the kitchen door, his head almost touching the lintel. If he grew any taller, she'd have to raise the roof. She smiled. Was it the baby relaxing her?

'I'll finish feeding him and then put something on.'

'I can get stuff from the freezer,' he offered.

She supposed this was easier for him than trying to do his homework.

Sean disappeared to the utility room and returned with a frozen pizza and a bag of oven chips.

'Which switch is for the oven?'

*

Sean fed everyone. Chloe arrived home. In a tantrum, she pounded up the stairs and banged her bedroom door behind her.

'Boy trouble?' Sean said, and escaped to his own room.

Lottie was thinking of asking Chloe about Emma. The girls had been friends at one stage, though Emma was a year ahead of Chloe in school. But did she want to involve her daughter in a case again? No, maybe not, especially after the last time.

Katie put Louis into his buggy and pushed him up and down the hall trying to get him to sleep.

Boyd rang to say they were in the process of preparing to arrest Arthur Russell. Good. Now maybe they'd get the Tessa Ball case closed.

Deciding it was time to have a serious conversation with her mother, Lottie left her kids and headed out into the storm.

*

Rose was stirring soup in a pot on the stove.

'Will you sit down for five minutes?' Lottie asked, trying to flatten her flyaway hair. Ten seconds running from the car to the door and she'd nearly done a Mary Poppins up into the sky.

'I can talk just as well standing up, missy.'

This was not going to be easy. She'd have to grovel.

'Mother, please. This is important. I need to talk to you.'

'Go ahead. I can hear you.' Rose Fitzpatrick was trying Lottie's patience to the nth degree.

'I've spoken to everyone I could find who worked with Dad.'

'I'd say that was enlightening. Old fogeys.'

Lottie smiled to herself. Her mother would never admit she was old herself.

'I can't get my head around the fact that he… that he did it in the shed. Here at home.'

'Your father wasn't himself those last few months. Things were not going well at work. It all got too much for him.'

'But to steal a revolver from the station and bring it home? Why not do it at the barracks, or out at the lake? Anywhere but here.'

'Lottie, this is exactly why I didn't want you investigating it. You end up with more questions than answers.'

Twirling the end of the linen tablecloth around her fingers, Lottie said, 'It doesn't make sense. And no note. Why not?'

Rose turned, ladle in hand, dripping soup to the floor. 'You're making a dog's dinner of that tablecloth.'

Letting go of the cloth, Lottie was about to tell her mother about the soup, but restrained herself.

'I gave you the box file. That's all there is.' Rose shook the ladle.

'There has to be more.'

'You never know when to quit, young lady.'

'Young? I actually feel quite old. Can I have another look around in the attic?'

'No!' Rose slammed the ladle on the table. Orange liquid splashed across the white linen and up into Lottie's face.

Jumping up, she grabbed her mother's arm. 'Please, sit down.'

'What did I just do?' Rose dropped the ladle and sat on a chair. She suddenly looked very old.

'Is everything all right?' Lottie asked. 'You don't look well.'

'I'm fine.'

'Shouldn't you give up running around at all hours of the night? I heard the HSE might be clamping down anyway. Something about registering the soup kitchen as a charity.'

'It's not a soup kitchen. We just do soup runs. Different thing altogether.'

'All the same—'

'No, Lottie. I want to do it.'

'At least visit the doctor. You might need vitamins in this bad weather.'

'I don't need vitamins. I need to keep myself busy. Keep my brain active.'

Lottie sighed. There was no way she was going to win an argument with Rose tonight. She switched the subject. 'Did you have your knitting group today?'

'We said the rosary for Tessa.'

'Anyone have any idea why someone would want to murder her?'

'No. But…'

'But what?' Lottie leaned over, interested now. She made a mental note to see if Kirby had followed up with the members of the knitting group.

Rose got up and put the ladle under running water. 'I don't know. It's just a feeling. You know that house belonged to Tessa before she signed it over to Marian and went to live in her flat.'

'I'll follow that up.'

The soup was burning. Without alerting her mother, Lottie went over and switched off the stove. 'I think this is done,' she said.

'So it is.'

'Are you sure you're okay?'

'Why wouldn't I be? I'm fine.'

'And I can't have a look up in—'

'No, Lottie. Leave it be.'

She'd come back another time, when she was sure the house was empty.

As she left her mother, water still running over the ladle and splashing on the floor, Lottie knew without a doubt that there was something very wrong with Rose Fitzpatrick.

*

Turning off the tap, Rose looked around at the mess she had made. This wasn't like her. Not like her at all. She ran the mop over the floor, bundled up the tablecloth and opened the washing machine. A small pile of clothes was already in the drum. She checked the drawer. Detergent still there. She'd forgotten to switch it on.

With a sigh she shoved in the tablecloth, then turned the knob and pressed the button to start the wash.

What else had she been about to do? Lottie's words twirled around in her head like the drum of the washer. Back at the table, she tried to recall the conversation. Oh yes, the attic.

She fetched the pole from above the sitting room door and pulled down the attic stairs. At the top of the ladder, she put on the light and peered into the loft space. Boxes and papers were scattered everywhere. She paused and thought for a moment. She always kept her attic in perfect order. Everything shelved, with labels and markings, so she knew exactly where to find things.

Now it was in chaos.

Had she done this? Had Lottie come round while she'd been out? If so, she definitely wouldn't have left it in a shambles.

A chill seized her body. She couldn't move. Wind howled through the slates and down the chimney breast. It sounded like the roof was about to be lifted from the rafters.

With one last look at the vortex of memorabilia, she flicked off the light and carefully descended the ladder. Could she have left that mess without remembering? And if she had, what had she been looking for? She wasn't at all sure of the answer to either question.

CHAPTER 39

Emma shivered beneath the rough blanket and stifled her tears. No point in crying. Her grandmother was dead, her mother was in a coma and her dad was a murder suspect. And it was all her fault. She never should have listened to the big ideas and small-town talk. Some people were just bad news. She knew that now. But things had gone too far. Too much had been covered up. And now her family had paid the ultimate price.

She heard him downstairs, pottering around, making dinner. She wasn't hungry. Couldn't eat. Wouldn't eat. Wanted to die. Serve her right if she died. Why had she even come here? Because she'd been told that if anything happened to her family – if she was ever in trouble – Mick O'Dowd was the man to go to for help. He was supposed to keep her safe. Oh my God! She didn't even know him. He could rape and murder her and dump her body in his slurry pit, and no one would ever know. Why had she come here? Was it the biggest mistake of her life?

Picking up her phone, she debated putting the SIM and battery back in. If she did, it could be traced. Did she really need to make the call? She knew she had to tell someone about what she'd overheard; what she'd seen. Could she wait another day?

A burst of wind rattled the glass in the window frame. Cans and bins clattered across the yard below. The dog howled. She heard O'Dowd whistling in tune to the gale.

What should she do?

Pulling the blanket up over her head, its musty scent telling her it was years since it had been out of the linen box, she lay in the darkness and listened to the storm blowing outside.

She missed her mother.

She wanted her father.

Emma Russell was terrified. Not of the storm, but of what might happen next.

CHAPTER 40

Wind and rain crashed against the window pane and Lottie lay awake with the curtains open, staring out at the storm.

She craved the arms of a man. She craved another drink. She craved escape to oblivion.

The glass in her hand shook. She drained the clear liquid and, still in darkness, poured another drink from the bottle in the bed beside her.

There was something wrong with her mother. There always had been. Now it was worse. Had it to do with Lottie snooping into her father's suicide? But in the few days since Tessa Ball had been murdered, Rose seemed to have deteriorated. Did she know something? What had she said about Tessa's past?

As the alcohol wended its way through her veins, Lottie felt a light relief in her head. She put down the glass, then the bottle, and fell asleep to the sound of the wind.

CHAPTER 41

Alexis didn't like using Skype. She didn't like it when they could see her. And in all honesty, she didn't want to see them either. Standing to one side of her black glass-topped desk, she hit the connect button.

'Be short and quick,' she said.

'Things are going well…'

'I hear a but. Tell me.' Alexis didn't want any buts. They usually heralded new problems. She walked away from the desk and looked out at the afternoon lower Manhattan skyline.

There was silence from the computer. She was beginning to think the caller had disconnected when she heard the cough.

'You're right. There is a but. Nothing we can't handle at this end, though.'

'I'm waiting.'

'It's to do with the other problem.'

Alexis knew what was being referred to.

'Go ahead.'

'Well, I got what you wanted from the old lady's attic, but the pathologist has accessed the post-mortem file.'

'The original file?'

'Yes, ma'am.'

Alexis hated that term. She wasn't anyone's ma'am.

'Can you destroy it?' she asked.

'Not unless I get it from her.'

'Her?'

'The state pathologist.'

Alexis wondered if there was anything in the file to warrant the case being reopened. She couldn't take the chance.

'Get it. Don't contact me again unless you have it.' She walked back to her desk and disconnected the call.

She had a dinner party to attend. She knew it was one way to dispel any gnawing concern she might have about events in Ragmullin. She had handled it all before; she would do so again. Not even Detective Inspector Lottie Parker was going to stop her.

The late seventies: The Child

I don't know what age I am and they won't tell me. But I know I'm young. A child. They call me 'the child'.

Why is everyone here so old?

Shuffling in and out of their ragged slippers. Peeling the paint off the walls with their fingernails. Banging their heads against the iron radiators. Blood pouring unhindered from wounds and sores.

And the noise.

Yelling and screaming. Do they not realise there's no one to hear? No one to care about them. We're all alone, together.

Today they've put me working in the laundry room.

It's so hot, I think I might die.

The ceilings are so high, I feel so small. Maybe I am a midget.

The laundry.

Stinking shitty sheets and towels. Hundreds of them. Piled high in baskets attached to trolleys.

My shrivelled stomach turns with the stench. I retch and gag; slam my fist into my mouth to hold in the vomit. The thump to the back of my head knocks me sideways into the sheets already piled up on the floor. If I'm not careful, I could end up in the washer.

I slip my feet back into my slippers that are about ten sizes too big and begin hauling the soiled linen out of the basket onto the floor. Eventually I drag it to the washing machine.

I think I'm going to faint. It's too warm. Stifling hot. Bubbles of sweat drip down my pale nose and I wipe them away. I have to do this quickly so I can go back to my bed.

I hear the voices.

Calling.

Whispering a name I do not know.

Then shouting a name I do know.

'Carrie,' they say. 'Where is Carrie?'

And I wonder that too.

Where is *Carrie?*

It is her fault I was brought here. Her fault I've been left here. Her fault they've all forgotten about me. Carrie, the bitch.

DAY FOUR

CHAPTER 42

The smell of paint had faded but a scent of newness oozed from the furniture in Superintendent Corrigan's office. The fact that it was 7.30 in the morning and he had called her in even before she'd had time to take off her jacket didn't help Lottie's mood. Nor his either, she thought.

'Sit,' he ordered.

She sat. What was going on? She put her hand to her mouth, blew out and sniffed. No smell of alcohol. Good.

'Where were you at eight o'clock yesterday feckin' morning?'

'Here, sir.' She didn't like the look he was giving her over the rim of his spectacles.

He wagged a thick finger in her direction. 'Think very feckin' carefully before answering, Detective Inspector Parker.'

Lottie sat stock still. What was he talking about? Yesterday morning? Seemed a lifetime ago. She tried hard to think. She had worked the case with Boyd. Talked to Emma. Searched Marian Russell's house. Lost Emma. Called to Lorcan Brady's house. Before all that, early morning... Annabelle's surgery. Surely he couldn't mean that?

'I... I... don't understand, sir.'

'Let me help you understand, Detective Inspector Parker. You visited Dr O'Shea's surgery. Remember now?'

Lottie gulped. A visit to her doctor wasn't a crime, as far as she knew. 'That was a private matter, sir. Annabelle's a friend of mine.'

'Go on.'

'I had to ask her something about Louis.' Thinking fast now. Concocting the tale as quickly as the words were leaving her mouth. 'He's my grandson.'

'I know who Louis is!'

She thought Corrigan might explode. His bald pate turned red, his cheeks flushed and his eyes bulged behind his spectacles. He kept tapping a piece of paper with a silver pen, louder with each tap.

'You're lying to me. Last chance. Why did you—'

'Okay, okay, sir.' Lottie held up her hands. 'I visited my doctor because I wasn't feeling well. Thought I was getting the flu.'

'Flu, my arse.'

She could feel his stare burning through her. 'Sir, what is this about?'

'I'll tell you what it's about,' he snapped. 'I've an email here disputing everything you just said. So when are you going to tell me the truth?'

Lottie felt sweat break out on her forehead. Her T-shirt clung to her spine. If she hadn't had the flu before, she just might have it now.

'Are you going to sit there with your mouth feckin' glued shut, or are you going to tell me?' he roared.

She shook her head slowly. 'I've no idea what's in that email, sir. What's it about?'

'It's damning, that's what. You know, if you've got health problems, you're supposed to report to me. Then I can decide if you're fit to work a case as serious as the one you're working on right now.'

Shit. 'I went to see Annabelle because I… I…'

'Go on.'

Deciding on something resembling the truth, she said, 'I needed something to help me cope. At home. It's a bit mental since the baby arrived, and—'

'I don't want your family history,' Corrigan interrupted, waving the printed page. 'This email claims that you're an alcoholic and a drug addict.'

'What?' Lottie jumped up so quickly, she knocked over the chair. She went to snatch the page but Corrigan grabbed it at the same time, tearing it down the centre.

'Who sent this? Anonymous, I bet.' She looked at the scrap of paper in her hand.

'Yes, but I wanted to hear from you if there was any truth in it.' She righted the chair and slumped down on it.

'Are you drinking again, Detective Inspector Parker?' he asked, his voice way too soft to be soothing. Dangerous.

'Everyone takes a drink.' Lame, she knew, racking her brain to figure a way out of this. The only positive thing was that the email was anonymous. The force had a policy of not dealing with such correspondence. Then again, this was personal. Shit.

Corrigan pulled off his spectacles and rubbed his bad eye, which had improved slightly over the last few months, then put the glasses back on again. 'Every so often you do things that drive me to distraction,' he said. 'I'm starting to believe you'll have me in an early grave.'

'Sir, I'm sorry. But that is a malicious piece of junk. Bin it.'

'I will. But first I need to have an idea of your state of mind. Your work isn't up to scratch these last few months. You're behind on your admin.'

'I know. I'm sorry sir.'

'And you've been upsetting old folks with talk about your father's suicide. That was forty years ago. Drop it.'

'Yes, sir.'

Corrigan leaned into his chair. 'You're telling me there's no truth in this email?'

'Yes, sir.' Fingers tightly crossed on her lap.

He sighed. 'I think you have a problem, Detective Inspector Parker. A big feckin' problem. One step out of line and I'll hear about it. Understood?'

She nodded, lips in a thin, tight line. Thinking. Who the hell had sent that email?

'Can I have a copy of the correspondence, sir?'

'Why?'

'I'd like to investigate who's been making false accusations against me.'

'You won't be doing any investigating. I'll look into this. You just stay on the straight and narrow. Do what you're supposed to be doing.'

'Yes, sir.'

She got out of his office before he could say another word. Pulled the door shut behind her and leaned against it.

Surely Annabelle hadn't ratted her out? No. There was doctor–patient confidentiality to consider. And she hadn't been scheduled for a visit. She'd just turned up. Had someone been following her? But how would they know about the pills? The drinking? Boyd. No. He wouldn't go behind her back. Definitely not Boyd.

But it had to be him, she thought, twisting her hair through her hands.

'Boyd, you… you arsehole.'

*

Before the team meeting, Lottie cornered him outside the incident room.

'Thanks a bunch,' she whispered through gritted teeth, standing legs apart, hands clenched in fists in her jeans pockets. She caught sight of the flecks of hazel in his eyes sparkling under the tubed light.

'What are you on about?' Boyd said. His jawline hardened. 'You on something? You look as wild as the weather.'

'Don't, Boyd. Don't get me started. Someone sent an anonymous email to Corrigan about me and I won't stand for it. You hear?'

The light faded in his eyes. 'You think I'd do something like that?'

Shit, wrong call, Parker. She clasped his hand.

'I'm sorry. I'm just wound up. Who would do that to me?'

He pulled away from her pressing fingers. 'Well, it wasn't me.' Turned on his heel. Pushed open the door to the incident room and disappeared.

Leaning against the wall, Lottie rubbed her fingers round her eye sockets, attempting to dispel the pain that was about to explode. Taking a pill from her jeans pocket, she snapped it out of the blister and swallowed it dry. Now she had to face the troops with possibly one of them mutinous.

CHAPTER 43

Standing in front of the incident boards, Lottie said, 'Today is the day we find Emma Russell, and cement the evidence against her father, Arthur Russell, for the murder of his mother-in-law, Tessa Ball, and the GBH of his wife Marian. We put this to bed! Right?'

An unenthusiastic murmur rippled through the assembly. Maria Lynch sat with her phone in her hand, texting. Kirby lounged back on two legs of his chair, puffing on his e-cigarette. Lottie wasn't entirely sure it was allowed indoors, but now wasn't the time to raise it. The rest of the detectives and uniformed gardaí were equally unmotivated. And Boyd was glaring.

'Come on. We have a couple of murders to solve and we're not going to do it by sleeping on the job.'

'A couple?' Lynch looked up, pocketing her phone.

At last they were engaged.

She pointed to Tessa Ball's photograph. Not the death-mask one – her driver's licence photo, where she looked like a human being. The two pictures hung side by side on the board.

'Okay. So far this is what we have. Tessa Ball, aged seventy-six. Retired solicitor. Signed her house over to her daughter Marian Russell five months ago. Up until then, Tessa had lived there herself. She then moved to an apartment beside the defunct St Declan's Hospital.'

Kirby shuffled uneasily on his chair. They all had memories of what had happened last May inside the corroded walls of St Declan's.

Lottie outlined the details of the assault, concluding with, 'Death was blunt-force trauma to the back of the skull, causing a fatal brain aneurysm. A baseball bat found outside the back door is consistent with the weapon used. Traces of Tessa's DNA were found on it. Also fingerprints that we can attribute to Marian and Arthur Russell and their daughter Emma. Russell says he bought the bat as a gift for Emma about five years ago—'

'Odd gift for a young girl,' Boyd interjected.

Ignoring his comment, Lottie continued. 'No other fingerprints or DNA were found on it. Either the killer wore gloves, or he may be a lot closer to home.'

'Or she,' Boyd said.

'You know what I mean.' Lottie flicked through the pages on the desk in front of her.

'Motive?' Boyd pressed.

'I'm getting there. Arthur Russell is our number one suspect. He had the opportunity as well as motive. Marian had a barring order against him.'

'He is currently in custody,' Boyd said. 'We arrested him late last night once his solicitor eventually arrived. Superintendent Corrigan has extended it for another six hours.'

'Okay, we need to work fast because when that time expires he will have to apply to the Chief Superintendent for the additional twelve hours. After that it is charge or release time. We need more evidence. On the night of the attack, Marian went missing from her home. The following day she was dumped from a car outside the hospital. She'd been beaten and her tongue cut out. She is currently in an induced coma. CCTV from the hospital, Kirby?'

'I reviewed it with the security guys and the car was a blue Toyota. Registration clear enough to identify it as Marian Russell's car.'

'Anyone visible in it?'

'Marian was thrown out from the back seat, so there had to be two people involved. Both wore hoodies and balaclavas. So no way of identifying who they were or indeed if they were male or female.'

'See if the technical guys can enhance the images.'

'Working on it.'

'How was the tongue cut out?' Lynch asked.

A few groans permeated the room. Lottie took a breath, shifted her pages and found the doctor's report. Her stomach clenched as she read his words. 'Possibly small pruning shears.'

'How would they even get shears into her mouth?' Kirby asked, his hand up to his face as if protecting his own tongue.

'Shears used for pruning shrubs or plants are just bigger than household scissors. And Marian had been beaten, so she was possibly unconscious at the time of mutilation.'

'Were they trying to silence her?' Boyd, this time.

'Probably. Perhaps she was going to tell someone something they didn't want revealed. Maybe they were sending a warning to others.'

'Or maybe they were sadists,' Boyd said.

'And we've no notion of where she was kept for the hours that she'd been missing?' Kirby said.

'Not as yet,' Lottie conceded.

'Wherever it was, it had to be very bloody,' Lynch said.

'We find the abductors – case closed,' Kirby offered.

'Which brings me to the cottage fire at Dolanstown.' Lottie pointed to a photograph of the burned-out remains. 'Initial investigation points to petrol, possibly poured through the letter box. One male body recovered from the scene and one barely alive. And the deceased did not die in the fire. He'd been stabbed numerous times.'

'Dead before the fire,' Boyd said. 'Murdered.'

Lottie silently counted to five. Why did he keep interrupting her? Maybe she should've had the argument with him *after* the team meeting and not before.

'That is the opinion of the state pathologist. The deceased was the older of the two victims but we have no identity as yet. The other victim had the fingers of his right hand hacked off. He is suffering from severe burns and is on life support. We believe this man could be Lorcan Brady. Arrested for possession of a class C drug in March. Suspended sentence. We need to get back out to his house and do a thorough search.

'Maybe that's where Marian Russell was held.' Boyd again.

'There's no connection other than Natasha Kelly saying Brady was Emma Russell's boyfriend. Our technical team has removed cannabis plants from an insulated building to the rear of the cottage. We're still awaiting clearance to enter the burned structure. Later today we will know if it warrants the drug unit getting involved.

'Now to add to the mix, Emma Russell has absconded from the neighbour's house where she was staying. As I said, according to her friend Natasha, Emma was involved with Lorcan Brady. We need to establish where Brady was on the night of Tessa's murder, and for that matter to determine if Emma was indeed at Natasha's house where she said she was. I need to speak to the Kellys again. I have a suspicion Emma might not have been with them that night. Whether it was an innocent absence to meet a boyfriend, or to engage in criminal activity, we need to find out.' She pointed to photographs of the money found in Emma's wardrobe. 'And where did she get nine hundred and fifty euros?'

'She had a part-time job,' Boyd offered.

Lottie studiously ignored him. 'We have teams out looking for her. Time to ramp up her disappearance on social media. I'll get the press office to issue another statement. We need to find her.' She felt her face pale at the thought of feeding Moroney more ammunition with which to ambush her.

'On to Mick O'Dowd, who discovered the cottage on fire. Anyone know anything about him?'

Kirby said, 'He has great taste in cigars.'

Lottie shook her head. 'I spoke with him yesterday afternoon. I can't quite make up my mind about him.' She didn't want to say how much he had troubled her. She continued, 'He mentioned hearing a car with a loud exhaust from time to time. Other than that, he says he knew nothing of the cottage residents.'

'If they were boisterous, having drug parties and the like,' Boyd said, 'they might've given O'Dowd a reason to burn the cottage himself.'

'Why didn't he call us in that case? No need to go to those sort of lengths,' Lottie said.

'Did he give a formal statement?' Lynch asked.

'He's coming in today.'

'Back to motive,' Boyd said. 'The only person linking the murder of Tessa Ball and the murder of the man at the cottage is Lorcan Brady. A tenuous link, based on hearsay.'

'It's all we've got, except for Arthur Russell,' Lottie said. 'I think they should be treated as separate investigations. For now.'

'Right so.' Boyd shrugged, folded his arms and said no more. Everyone turned to look at him. Lottie silently fumed. He was playing silly buggers with her team.

'I think—' he began.

'*I* think,' Lottie interrupted. She waited until his voice drained to a whisper. Two can play your game. 'I think we tread carefully around both incidents until we know we can tie them together. We need to firmly plant Arthur Russell at the scene of Tessa Ball's murder. We have a jacket found at the house that has been sent for forensic analysis. Possibly Arthur's. The murder weapon has his fingerprints. Motive? Money? Drugs?

'Kirby, figure out why Tessa signed over her house to Marian and if it has any significance to this investigation. We need to establish if Tessa was the primary target or was unfortunate enough to have been in the wrong place at the wrong time. We know Marian phoned her mother that night. Was it friendly, or under coercion? Whatever it was, it resulted in Tessa calling round.' Lottie paused to catch her breath. 'Once Marian is out of her induced coma, we'll see what she can tell us.'

'She won't be able—' Boyd said.

'To talk,' Lottie said. 'I know. But I'm sure she can still write. Was anything discovered on her laptop or phone?'

Rustling through a file on his knee, Kirby extracted a printout. 'Confirms the call to her mother at 21.07. That was the only call she made that day other than to Emma. Historical calls throw up nothing significant either. No reports of a partner in her life.'

'What was she studying?' Lottie asked.

'Social studies and genealogy. Online course. The hard drive is corrupt from the smashing the laptop got, but we've sent it off to see if anything can be salvaged.'

'Contact whoever is running the course.'

'I did. The tutor is holidaying in Australia and the girl I spoke with wasn't very helpful. She thought the course had finished.'

'Dead end there, so.' Lottie thought for a moment. The case had to do with either family or drugs. 'Kirby, check with the land registry to find the owner of that cottage.'

'Will do, boss.'

'The knitting club. Any leads there?'

Shuffling uneasily on his chair, Kirby frowned, put away one file and took up another. 'Jesus, boss, a group of little old ladies clicking away with needles and wool. Not my cup of tea at all.'

Lottie smiled. 'Interesting interviews, were they?'

'I could tell you everything from how to cure a cold to where the Pope was born.'

Everyone laughed and Lottie felt some of the tension ease from the room. 'Anything about Tessa?'

'Not a bad word from anyone. You'd think she was a saint.'

'Maybe she was,' Boyd offered.

Lottie scowled.

Kirby said, 'Except maybe for one woman.' He slid his finger down a list and then took his notebook from his breast pocket. 'Here it is. Kitty Belfield. She started to say something – not about Tessa; about the fire at the cottage. Said, and I quote, "It's not the first time a fire in Ragmullin ruined a family", end quote. She clammed up once the room went silent with them all earwigging.'

'Belfield?' Lottie mused. 'Belfield and Ball were a firm of solicitors at one time. Speak with this Kitty Belfield again. Without an audience.'

'Will do.' Kirby rose, taking his e-cigarette from his trouser pocket followed by the stub of a fat cigar. He seemed to consider both before putting the electronic device back and heading out.

'Are you all clear on what you've to do?'

'As mud,' Boyd muttered.

'Do you have something to add?' Lottie didn't want to lose the support of her team. Not now, when someone was sneaking behind her back to Superintendent Corrigan.

'No. It's all good.'

'A word, Detective Boyd,' Lottie said as the group moved chairs out of the way, making for the door.

When the room was empty, she sat on an abandoned chair and looked up at Boyd lounging near the door, hands in pockets, one foot up against the wall.

'You know you don't have to be a complete arsehole,' she said. 'That was totally disruptive behaviour.'

Boyd said nothing.

She hated apologising. Particularly to Boyd. Especially since she had been in the wrong. But she was right about one thing. He was being an absolute pain.

'Right. I'm sorry for accusing you about the email. I was out of line,' she said.

He still said nothing.

She raised her hands to the ceiling. 'Do you want me to grovel? I shouldn't have suspected you'd do such a thing. I'd just come out of Corrigan's office and you were the first person I bumped into, so I took it out on you. You were in the wrong place at the wrong time.' But she *had* suspected him. A flush crept up her face. Shit. She knew Boyd could read her. 'Do you accept my apology?'

'I'll think about it.' He pushed himself away from the wall and stood up straight. 'Lottie, I didn't go behind your back. I don't know who did, but you need to watch your step, because someone is waiting for you to make a mistake.'

Lottie thought of Maria Lynch. Was it payback for making her stand in for the FLO? She looked up. Boyd was standing in front of her. He was smiling.

Thank God, she thought.

'Come on. We've work to do,' he said.

She laughed. 'Hey! That's my line.'

CHAPTER 44

The wind refused to let up or calm down, and the scabby collie dog looked cold and hungry sitting on the porch when Lottie and Boyd pulled into Lorcan Brady's driveway. Everywhere was dank and black. Branches on the trees surrounding the house dipped and swirled, cracking against the roof tiles.

'It's awful weather for October,' Lottie remarked.

'Doesn't matter what month it is, it's like bloody winter.'

'Lighten up, will you. You're making me depressed.'

'That poor dog looks like he should be in the dog pound,' Boyd said.

'They'd put him down.'

'Exactly.'

'You're a cruel—'

'Don't say it,' Boyd said.

They got out of the car. The dog raised its head but didn't move.

'Maybe you could bring him home. Little Louis would love a dog.'

'Will you stop?'

Lottie opened the front door with the key they'd recovered from the remnants of Lorcan Brady's burned jeans. A pile of mail shifted as she shoved the door inwards. With gloved hands she picked it up and scanned through it.

'Junk,' she said, and dropped the pile on the table in the hall. It was already overflowing with rubbish.

'Smells a bit rank in here,' Boyd said, sniffing the air.

'Damp,' Lottie said. She walked into the room to her left. A sitting room at one time, it now looked like it had evolved into some kind of a den.

'Easy to tell his mother isn't around any more,' Boyd said.

'Poor woman. Maybe she's better off.' They'd discovered that Lorcan's mum had died two years previously from cancer. There was no record of a father.

A small table with crooked legs stood in the centre of the room, cluttered with empty beer cans and a candle melted to its wick.

'Yuck,' Lottie said, looking through the detritus on the table. Crisp bags, chip bags, two half-eaten burgers. The carpet was littered with crumbs and dirt. The fireplace was piled high with fast-food wrappers, and a pizza box containing a few crusts lay on the floor. Shelves in the corner were stacked with beer cans rather than books. The arms of the chairs had served as ashtrays, with burns tracked along them.

'No sign of drug paraphernalia,' Boyd said.

'As if it would be left out on view,' Lottie said.

'Everything else is.'

She examined one of the shelves. 'Boyd, do you see a fish tank anywhere?'

'No. Maybe in the kitchen. Why?'

'Look at all that fish food.' She counted twenty-seven containers.

'Let's have a look in the kitchen.'

The door was open and Lottie was about to step in but stopped. She put out a hand, preventing Boyd from entering.

'I think we've found where Marian Russell was held,' she said.

Boyd peered over her shoulder. 'Jesus! It's like something out of *The Walking Dead*.'

'Contact SOCOs. I'm going to have a quick look upstairs.'

'Don't you think we should wait?'

'You can. I need to know what type of lunatics we're dealing with.'

Boyd pointed into the kitchen. 'And that doesn't tell you?'

Lottie hardly heard what he said. She was already at the top of the stairs. The landing floor was constructed of old wood, and above her head, a light bulb was screwed into a makeshift electrical fitting attached to a cross-beam. There was no ceiling. All the studding appeared to have been stripped away. Electrical cables ran along the beams. The light switch was missing screws and hung at an angle from the wall. There were two bedrooms and a bathroom.

Entering the nearest room, Lottie deduced it had been Lorcan's mother's. Untouched since the day she died, most likely. Mounds of dust had collected on the gold satin bedspread. A yellow-ochre hue sliced the room in two, escaping from the space between the closed curtains. She shut the door and entered the second room.

The smell hit her. Rancid dirty clothes. She held a gloved hand to her mouth. Used condoms were strewn across the bare wooden floor, lying among dust and discarded beer cans. A jumbled mound of filthy sheets was scrunched up on top of the mattress, and the velour headboard was covered with cigarette burns. A chest of drawers stood under the window, and Lottie braced herself for the trek across the floor, expecting at any minute for vermin to scuttle out from beneath the bed.

About six tins of Lynx deodorant stood haphazardly amongst drink cans and empty cigarette packets. Three deep drawers. She opened the first one. A whiff of puke rose to her nose.

'Jesus Christ,' she muttered.

'What?'

Lottie jumped, jostling the collection on the dresser.

'Boyd, you bastard. You frightened the shite out of me.'

'The state of this place. What kind of tramp is Brady?'

'A filthy one. Everything stinks. How could Emma Russell be involved with him?'

'Love is blind,' Boyd said.

'Love would want to have no sense of smell to come into this room. I really can't see Emma in this pigsty.'

'What's in the drawers?'

'Give me a chance.' Lottie gingerly moved the underwear around, her gloved fingers searching beneath them. Finding nothing, she closed the drawer and opened the next one. T-shirts and vests. The bottom drawer too had little to offer. 'More clothes. Hey, wait a minute.'

'Is that what I think it is?' Boyd leaned over her shoulder.

'If you thought it was a bag of heroin, then yes.' She held it aloft.

'That's worth a fair bit.'

'How much do you think?'

'There must be at least ten ounces in there.'

'Worth killing for?'

'There has to be more. I'll look in the bathroom.'

'You might want a gas mask.' Lottie opened her handbag, found a plastic evidence bag and deposited the heroin. Giving the drawer a final glance, she closed it.

As she was passing the bed, she flicked up the bundled sheeting. Snagged up in the clump of dirty linen, she caught sight of a snatch of purple material. Carefully she plucked out a girl's hoodie. She'd seen one similar to it recently, but in a different colour. Where? Who'd been wearing it? Emma Russell! Had the girl really been in here? Having sex with Brady? It didn't fit with the image she had of her. But she'd been proven wrong before.

'Found more!' Boyd shouted from the bathroom.

With a shake of her head, Lottie folded the hoodie and took it with her. Boyd was on his hands and knees, having removed the avocado-green plastic covering from the side of the bath.

'Shit,' she said. 'That's some haul.' Boyd had extracted three more bags of heroin.

'But it's not a lot in the scheme of things, is it?'

'Lorcan Brady's fingers were chopped off, Marian Russell had her tongue cut out and was left for dead, and an unidentified male was stabbed and burned. There must be more drugs.'

'Maybe they went up in smoke in the cottage fire?'

'I think we'd better find out before someone else is murdered,' she said.

'We need to identify the dead man. It might lead us to his killer.' Boyd got up from his knees. 'Want to look in the cistern?'

Lottie lifted the lid from the toilet cistern. 'Water. Nothing else. But…'

'What?'

Shifting the lid back on the cistern, Lottie glanced around the dingy bathroom with its plastic decor and drab tiles. 'If Lorcan Brady was big into the drugs game, don't you think he would be living somewhere better than this?'

'Possibly.'

'The hacking-off of his fingers – I think he was stealing from the big guys. Got caught out. Was he a middleman, or the lowest link of the chain? Is something bigger going on?'

The trundle of a heavy van and the screech of brakes from outside caused her to look up. 'That'll be McGlynn and his team.'

Boyd said, 'Wait until he sees the amount of blood in that kitchen.'

Lottie had another look into the bedroom and a familiar icy chill settled between her shoulder blades.

'Boyd?'

'What?'

'We'd better find Emma.'

CHAPTER 45

Jim McGlynn wasn't a happy camper.

'I wish you two would toddle off to some other division. Didn't I tell ye I've been looking forward to a nice easy ride into retirement? You keep screwing up my journey.'

'Not our fault,' Lottie said.

McGlynn was busy setting up his equipment to photograph the scene. 'When I've finished here, I'm going to the cottage. It's been deemed safe to enter at last.'

'Let me know if you find anything.' At the door, Lottie turned. 'Will you get your team to go through the rubbish bags out the back?'

McGlynn nodded. 'It all looks a bit too frantic in here.'

Boyd said, 'Maybe the assailants were high on drugs.'

'Possibly.'

Lottie looked at the streaks of blood lining the surface of the gnarled wooden table lying on its side. Chairs had been overturned. Doors were hanging off the cupboards and crockery had been smashed on the floor. Envelopes and paper were scattered everywhere and the sink looked like no one had washed anything in it in months. Food littered the counter tops along with two dead mice.

'No fish tank,' Lottie said. 'Why all the fish food?'

'Maybe that's what he fed the dog with.'

'Let us know your findings,' Lottie said to McGlynn, and eased past Boyd into the hall. She got an evidence bag from one of the SOCOs and placed the purple hoodie into it.

Passing the acquiescent collie on the doorstep, she bent down to rub his head, but stopped. His fur was a crawling knot of maggots.

'Jesus, Boyd! This dog needs a vet.'

Boyd shrugged his shoulders. 'I'll contact the dog warden.'

'But—'

'He needs to be put down.'

Boyd took her elbow and guided her to the car.

*

Back at the station, after Boyd had gone off to log the heroin into evidence, Lottie stood in the middle of the office wondering which direction to lead the investigation.

'Inspector Parker, my office,' said Superintendent Corrigan, bursting through the door.

'This is getting to be a habit,' Lottie muttered at his retreating back.

Kirby raised his head. 'A *bad* habit.'

Lottie strolled down the hall and into the superintendent's office. Second time in the space of a couple of hours. Not good.

'Sit.'

'What's up, sir?'

'I've a report here detailing the findings at the cottage.'

'That was quick.'

'What do you mean?'

'I was speaking to Jim McGlynn fifteen minutes ago, and he said the cottage had only just been cleared as safe to enter.'

'Not the feckin' cottage. The shed behind it, if you want to be so particular about it.'

'Oh, right. Sorry, sir.'

He pressed his spectacles tighter to his nose and read from the report in his hand. 'A hundred and sixty kilograms of cannabis with a potential street value of three million euros.'

'Holy cow. Under everyone's noses.'

'Some of it was still growing, but the bulk of it was packaged and found in crates buried under clay. Did you get any further with identifying the victims?'

'Yes, sir. I suspect the man still alive is Lorcan Brady. He's twenty-one, so he fits the description. I've just come from his house. Besides the kitchen looking like an abattoir, we found a substantial quantity of heroin. Not sure of the street value as yet.'

'I made the right move so.'

Lottie shifted in her seat. She knew where this was going.

Corrigan continued. 'I've informed the national drugs unit. They're sending someone down to take over. Should be here in the morning. So what does that mean for your investigation, Inspector?'

'I have until the morning to complete it.'

'Correct. Get your skates on and find that runaway girl. She could be the link to all this.'

Lottie nodded and left as fast as she could. She knew Emma could be a link, but whichever way she looked at it, she didn't see the girl fitting in with a drug ring. Something just wasn't right with that scenario.

*

McGlynn contacted them to say he'd left his deputy at Brady's house and was back at the cottage sifting through ashes. Lottie grabbed Boyd and they sped out to Dolanstown. Approaching the burned-out structure, she saw McGlynn's white protective suit moving like a ghost in the blackened shell.

'It's hard to believe there was that amount of cannabis plants housed in the shed. What was going on?' she said.

'Someone tried to murder two men and succeeded in killing just one. Then the suspect burned the cottage down but didn't take the cannabis. Weird,' Boyd said.

'Did the assailant even know about the drugs? What are we missing here, Boyd?'

'I don't know, but maybe SOCOs can find something to help us identify the other victim.'

They pulled on protective clothing, overshoes and gloves. The wind almost lifted Lottie from her feet as she walked up the path to the incinerated cottage. SOCOs had covered over as much of it as they could manage with tents, but the wind was playing with them as if they were kites.

Giving up on the hood of her Teflon boiler suit, Lottie let her hair fly about her face as she entered the charred remains.

'Ah, the grim reapers,' McGlynn said through his paper mask.

'What's that?' Lottie pointed to the scorched object in McGlynn's hand. She had no idea which room they were standing in. All furniture and fittings had been destroyed.

'A bone,' McGlynn said.

'A bone?' Lottie took a step closer.

'Human?' Boyd asked.

McGlynn remained silent as he placed it in an evidence bag, then bent down and picked up another one.

'Jesus,' Lottie exclaimed. 'Are they… fingers?' A gulp of saliva formed at the back of her throat and she thought she might be sick. Wind caterwauled through the gaps where windows had once protected the interior from the elements. It sounded like a banshee. A forewarning of death? She shivered.

'I'll collect everything and tag them, then inspect them back at the lab,' McGlynn said. 'I'll let you know my findings.'

'Anything else?' Lottie asked.

The forensic man's eyebrows arched. She was glad she couldn't see his face. She knew it was a mask of scorn.

'Okay, okay,' she said. 'We'll let you get on with it.'

Her phone pinged with a message as she and Boyd headed back
to the car.

'Who's that?' he asked.

'Kirby. Guess who owns the cottage?'

'I'm in no mood for guessing games, Lottie.'

'Mick O'Dowd. The liar.'

CHAPTER 46

The door to the milking shed was closed and there was no sign of the dog or O'Dowd's Land Rover.

'Maybe he's at the station giving a statement,' Boyd said.

'Lying bastard,' Lottie said. 'I asked him if he knew who owned the cottage and he said he didn't.'

Boyd marched up to the front door. No doorbell. He hammered with the knocker. 'What's up with you?' he asked.

Lottie remained standing, buffeted by the gale, in the middle of the dung-covered yard.

'I'm trying to recall exactly what I asked him.'

Boyd moved back to her. 'About what?'

'The cottage.' She slapped her forehead. 'Shit. I don't think I asked him who owned it. I only enquired if he knew who *rented* it.'

'But why didn't he volunteer the information? Did he not want to implicate himself in a murder investigation?'

'He was already implicated. He found the cottage on fire and reported it.'

'I think if he'd been involved,' Boyd said, 'he would have stayed well away from it.'

Lottie shook her head. 'He struck me as being devious. I don't know what he's up to, but I'm going to find out.'

Boyd shrugged and thumped on the door with his fist. 'No one home,' he said.

A dog barked inside.

Lottie shook off her frustration at her ineptitude with O'Dowd. She spied a shed door swinging open, crashing against the wall, and made for it.

'Hey, we need a search warrant to go in there.' Boyd appeared at her shoulder.

'Door was open. Inviting us.' She stepped into the dusky interior. Scrabbled around for a light switch. Unable to find one, she said, 'Got a torch?'

Boyd tapped the flashlight app on his phone. A cone of light shone into the murky depths. A quad bike with stinking mucky wheels was parked next to a red tractor, which appeared to rise up from the shadows.

'A Massey Ferguson,' Boyd said.

'How'd you know that?' Lottie asked.

'Says it here. On the insignia.'

He dipped the phone downwards, immersing Lottie in darkness. The wind shook the wooden structure and it appeared to shiver around her. She picked her way carefully as Boyd followed with the light.

'What's that?' She pointed to an implement among shovels and spades.

'A scythe. Used for cutting hay in the old days.'

'Dangerous-looking weapon. Could it chop off fingers?' Lottie lifted the tool. 'Bit heavy.'

Boyd inspected the blade under the glare of his phone light. 'No trace of blood. We shouldn't be in here without a warrant. We'll be in big trouble.'

'Never stopped me before.' She put the scythe back where she'd picked it up from and began inspecting the rest of the tools. 'Everything in here could be used as a weapon.'

'They're farm tools. You're reading too much into them.'

Through the flapping galvanised sheets on the roof, a squall penetrated with a sinister whistle.

Suddenly Lottie stopped and her hand flew up to her mouth.

'Oh my God,' she said.

*

Driving past the incinerated cottage, Mick O'Dowd wondered how long it would take the guards to figure out he owned the place. Not long, he supposed, now that Tessa Ball was dead. Didn't leave him much time to get his affairs sorted. He'd already started on his accounts and needed to get back to them quickly.

A hundred metres along the road, he slowed the Land Rover and idled the engine. He looked in his rear-view mirror. Men in white suits were flocking like geese around the blackened ruins. They'd have found the stash in the shed by now, not that it was anything to do with him. But what else would they find? He needed to hurry.

A gust shook the vehicle. O'Dowd glared at the sky. At least the cattle were in the outer barn. He wouldn't have to go trudging through saturated fields to bring them in.

He lit a cigar and inhaled two puffs before setting it down. He knew what he had to do. He released the handbrake and slowly made his way home.

CHAPTER 47

The light danced around them as Boyd attempted to shine the phone on what had alarmed Lottie.

'It's just a bicycle,' he said.

'It's hers,' Lottie whispered.

'Whose?'

'Emma's. I mean Natasha Kelly's.' She stepped closer to the red racing bike. Let her gloved hand stroke the handlebars.

'You've never seen her bike. How can you know it's this particular one?'

'You know bikes. Tell me, is this for ladies or gents?'

'It's a lady's. But that doesn't mean anything.'

'Why is it in Mick O'Dowd's barn?'

'Maybe it belongs to his mother or sister, or a friend. Jesus, Lottie, I don't know.' Boyd swept his hand through his hair. 'Come on. We have to get out of here.'

'I'm not going without the bike.'

Boyd scanned the interior of the barn with his phone light. 'See those cameras, up there? They're CCTV. O'Dowd is recording us.'

'What? Why have cameras in a barn?'

'To protect his tractor? I don't know, but I do know I don't like this.'

The flashlight dimmed. Lottie waited a moment for her eyes to refocus with the narrow strip of daylight coming from the doorway.

'We can't just leave the bicycle here. It's evidence,' she said.

'From an illegal search. Use your head. We have to go back to the station and process a warrant.'

'On what grounds? We can't say we know it's here.' Boyd got the light working again. He bent down and inspected the tyres. 'All pumped up. Plenty of mud and dung caked dry on them. It wasn't ridden today.'

'If Emma had it, why did she come here? And where is she?'

A terrifying thought struck Lottie as starkly as the bird that flew from the roof and clipped her hair.

She screamed. 'I hate birds. Let's get outside.'

Boyd didn't argue and she followed him out. Clouds were scudding like missiles across the sky and a drizzle of rain had resumed. She looked up at the farmhouse windows.

'She could be inside. Held against her will.'

'If – and it's a big if – she came here on that bike, it looks like she came voluntarily.'

'Yes, but she could have ridden into the arms of a madman. Or maybe he picked her up on the road.'

Boyd sighed. 'I think your mind is warped to expect the worst in every situation.'

'Grim reapers. That's what McGlynn called us. Maybe we are.'

She headed for the other shed. Inside, both sides were lined with cattle, chewing on meal and hay. She moved down the aisle and glanced at the slatted floor, where dung and urine seeped. She looked up. 'More cameras.'

'He's protecting an expensive herd. That's all. Nothing sinister.'

With a disgruntled sigh, Lottie left the shed and marched over to the back door of the house. She banged loudly.

'Emma? Emma Russell, are you in there? I just want to be sure you're okay and then I'll go away.'

Pressing her ear to the wood, she listened. 'Nothing. We'll try the front door again.'

Boyd beat her to it. Hammered as hard as he could. Banged the knocker. Shook the handle. Still no answer. The howl of the dog barking catapulted him away from the door.

'Mason,' Lottie said.

'Look, there's no one else here. And don't go telling me she's tied up or murdered. We do our job. We'll process a warrant and go find O'Dowd.'

Lottie turned at the sound of a vehicle approaching along the road. 'I think he's found us.' Leaning against the front door, she folded her arms, and waited for O'Dowd to park at the side of the house.

'What are you two doing here?' O'Dowd jumped out of the vehicle almost as soon as it stopped, leaving the door open in his haste. 'Get off my property. I've had enough of your crowd.' He raised his fist and shook it, pushing his face into Lottie's.

'Hey, just a minute…' Boyd said, straightening his shoulders.

'No, let him finish,' Lottie said. 'I want to hear what he has to say.'

'I don't have to say anything to you. Clear off, ye pair of bollockses.'

'Have a nice lunch in town?' she goaded, spying the remnants of gravy caked dry at the corners of his mouth.

O'Dowd took a step back and appeared to mentally calm himself. 'What do you want?' he asked after a moment.

A blast of wind swept around the side of the house, stealing his words.

'We need a formal statement on the events surrounding the fire at the cottage,' Lottie said.

'Where do you think I've been half the day?'

'I've no idea.'

'In town, at your station, waiting for someone to listen to me.'

'And did they?'

'What?'

'Listen to you?'

'Done and dusted. Now if you'd be so kind as to leave…'

Lottie forced a smile. 'Kind? Mmm. I'm really not that type of person.'

'I'll call the—' O'Dowd stopped mid sentence.

'Guards?' Lottie smirked. 'Oh, how fortunate. We're already here.'

'You think you're a smart bitch, don't you? Like that father of yours. Remember where it got him?'

Though she worked hard not to lose it, the smile died on Lottie's face.

'Mr O'Dowd, my colleague DS Boyd and I would like to have a civil conversation with you. Won't you ask us in?' She wished she could mention the bicycle in the shed.

O'Dowd leaned in towards her. She plastered a stoical expression on her face. Boyd hovered behind, ready to intervene.

Spittle settled around O'Dowd's teeth as he drew his lips back in a snarl. 'You have no right to be on my property.' His voice a threatening growl.

'Speaking of property,' she said, 'how come you never mentioned you owned the cottage?'

He eyed her up and down, his mouth hardening into a grimace. 'You never asked.'

'You should have said.' Lottie ran her hand through her hair. He was succeeding in giving her the feeling of lice crawling around her scalp, taking hold of the roots of her hair. 'If you own it, surely you know who rented it?'

'I told you that already. I don't know.'

'I think you're being very economical with the truth, Mr O'Dowd.'

'And I think that if you're not careful, you might end up jamming your service weapon to your own forehead.'

Gulping down a spurt of bile, Lottie lifted her hand and slapped him as hard as she could across his face. His proximity to her didn't allow her to put any strength behind the blow, but it gave her a smidgen of satisfaction.

O'Dowd laughed, a grating-on-glass sound. 'Assault along with trespassing. I think I have you sewn up nice and neatly now, Inspector.'

Boyd grabbed Lottie away from the farmer's towering body. 'We're leaving.'

'I'll be lodging a complaint against you, Inspector. And don't come back here unless you have a warrant.'

Lottie planted her feet so Boyd couldn't pull her further away.

'Tell us about the b—' she began.

'Lottie!' Boyd forcibly seized her elbow and steered her towards the car. 'Now isn't the time. Okay?'

All fight left her body and she slumped onto the seat when Boyd opened the door. She looked out through the windscreen at O'Dowd. He rubbed a hand over his mouth and down the stubble of his chin. With his other hand he pinched the bridge of his nose and sneezed out a long snot before summoning phlegm from this throat. A globule of mucus landed on the hood of the car.

As Boyd reversed out of the yard, Lottie opened the door, leaned out and shouted, 'You're an ignoramus! You old fucker!'

The brakes screeched. She felt Boyd haul her back in before he leaned over and shut the door with a bang and sped from the farm.

*

From the first-floor window, Emma watched Mick O'Dowd fuming in his own yard. Should she have come down and opened the door when the detectives had knocked? But he'd told her to stay put. Plus his rabid dog was chained up at the bottom of the stairs, inside the front door. Definitely not going down there, she thought.

When she heard him below in the kitchen, she shrank further against the wall and pulled the old blanket up to her chin. The roughness of the wool grated against her cheek and she wanted to scream. Why hadn't she done that when the guards were here? She didn't know who she could trust. But she'd been told to trust O'Dowd, hadn't she?

'Girleen, I'll put a few spuds in the pot and have a bite of dinner for you in a short while. That okay?' His shout came up the stairs.

Emma nodded.

'Are you up there?'

She heard the dog bark and a foot stamp on the bottom step.

'Yes, yes. That's grand, but I'm not hungry,' she yelled back.

'You have to eat, missy. Food for the body is food for the soul.'

She heard him laughing his sharp, clinking laugh on his way back down the stairs.

He hadn't touched her. Not a finger had he laid on her, but she was now more scared of him than the others she'd originally been frightened of.

'I've a bit of written work to do here, if you care to give me a hand while the dinner is cooking?' She heard his voice echo up through the kitchen ceiling to her room.

'In a minute, maybe,' she said, and stuck her fist in her mouth to stop herself from screaming.

Was there anyone she could trust?

CHAPTER 48

Lottie didn't utter a word on the short drive back to the station. Her temper simmered just below the surface of her indignation.

As Boyd swung the car onto Main Street, she said, 'He could've chopped her up and fed her to the cows or his dog. You saw that scythe and that… that rotor machine thing. Jesus, Boyd, we need that warrant.'

'Calm down.'

'You're telling me to calm down? After that… that excuse for a man threatened me?' She struggled to spin her words together in a coherent sentence.

'You were out of order. You shouldn't have hit him and he was within his rights to tell us to get off his property.'

Arms folded tightly, chin buried to her chest, Lottie smouldered.

'If you keep that up,' Boyd said, 'there'll be smoke coming out of your ears.'

'We need to get a full description of the bicycle from Natasha.' Lottie fumbled in her bag for her phone, then stopped. 'Better still, drive over to the Kellys' house. I'll talk to her myself.'

'We have a description back at the station,' he said. 'And you have to delegate. It's impossible to do everything yourself.'

'Go to Kelly's. I need to talk to Natasha,' she said abruptly.

He swung the car around the roundabout and headed in the direction of Carnmore.

Lottie seethed for the rest of the short journey. She thought of her own children and how she'd felt when Sean, and then Chloe, had gone missing. There really wasn't anyone left to miss Emma, except her dad, and he could be a murderer. She took out her phone and called home. Just to hear they were all okay, that was all, she told herself.

*

A dishevelled-looking Bernie Kelly opened the door. The make-up she'd worn so confidently the other day was now streaked, and her hair looked like it nested robins.

'What now?' she said.

'I have to speak to Natasha,' Lottie said.

'It's not a good time, and I'm getting mighty fed up with all this interference.'

Lottie moved past her along the hallway and into the kitchen. Natasha was leaning against the jamb of the open back door, puffing vigorously on a cigarette. The table evidenced the remains of a half-eaten dinner, and a plate lay in pieces on the floor, strings of spaghetti and sauce clinging to the legs of the table and congealing on the tiles.

'What happened here?' Lottie asked.

Natasha flicked the cigarette outside, then came in and closed the door. She faced Lottie, taunting her with a smirk.

'None of your business,' she said, folding her arms defiantly.

From behind her, Lottie heard Bernie say, 'Just a family argument. Like she says, none of your business.'

'We only want to have a chat,' Boyd said.

Lottie had forgotten he was there. She turned to see him with his arm around Bernie Kelly's trembling shoulders. The woman was clutching a black cardigan tight to her chest and her jeans were streaked with red sauce.

'I really think you should leave,' Bernie said. 'I want to have a word with my daughter.'

'Natasha,' Lottie said, 'sit down.'

'I prefer to stand.'

'I don't care what went on between you and your mother. You can sort that out yourselves. I'm here to ask about your bicycle. What colour is it?'

'My bike? I don't know. It's years since I used it.'

'Is it black or white? Red or blue?'

'Red. I think.'

Lottie looked up at Boyd, then to Bernie. 'Do you have a serial number for it? On insurance documents maybe?'

Bernie shook her head.

Turning her attention back to Natasha, Lottie said, 'The night Tessa Ball was murdered, can you tell me exactly what you and Emma did?'

'Watched telly. Told you that already.'

'I don't believe you.'

'That's not my problem.' She unfolded her arms and clenched her hands into fists by her sides.

Calling Boyd over, Lottie whispered in his ear. He headed out to the car, returning a few moments later with a large plastic evidence bag. He held it up.

'Do you know who owns this?'

Natasha's eyes widened, but she kept her lips sealed shut.

Bernie butted in, 'You have one just like it, love.'

'Maybe,' Natasha said, her lips curving upwards. Slowly she drew her eyes back to Lottie. 'Where'd you find it?'

'Lorcan Brady's house. Have you ever been there?'

'I told you, he's Emma's boyfriend. She must be with him.'

'No, she's not. Lorcan is in hospital.'

'Hospital?' Bernie said. 'I thought… Is he okay? What happened to him?'

'Had a bit of an accident with a fire.'

'Is he all right?' Natasha asked, her teenage cockiness slipping.

'Not really. No.'

'Is he going to die?' Bernie again.

'I'm no doctor,' Lottie said, 'so I can't answer that. Back to the hoodie. I need to determine ownership.'

Bernie studied it for a moment and said, 'Emma was wearing Natasha's clothes while she was here. If Lorcan's in hospital, do you know where Emma is?'

'I don't know,' Lottie admitted. 'Do you know a Mick O'Dowd?'

Bernie shook her head. 'No. I don't think I recognise that name.'

Looking at the red mess decorating the kitchen, Lottie said, 'Are you going to tell me what happened here?'

'Just family stuff,' Bernie said. 'Isn't that right, Natasha?'

Lottie watched as Natasha stood stock still, her face as unreadable as her mother's. 'Suppose so.'

'If you remember anything about the hoodie or where you think Emma might be, let us know,' Lottie said, and walked slowly behind Boyd as they left the house.

She wasn't sure what she had witnessed here. But she was sure of one thing. There was no one better experienced than her to know how tumultuous the relationship could be between mothers and teenage children.

CHAPTER 49

'I want a transcript of O'Dowd's statement.' Lottie banged a bundle of files from one side of her desk to the other.

Boyd walked over and began straightening them. She slapped her hand down on top of his.

'Stop!' she said and looked up at him.

'*You* stop,' he said. 'You're driving yourself mad. And the rest of us along with you.'

'We need to speak to Arthur Russell about Mick O'Dowd,' she said.

Kirby walked into the office brandishing his notebook. 'Spoke to Kitty Belfield again, after a feed of bacon and cabbage. Jaysus, it was mighty.'

'He's been released,' Lynch said, raising her head from her computer.

'Who?' Lottie, Boyd and Kirby said together.

'Arthur Russell,' Lynch said. 'Superintendent Corrigan said, quote, we "couldn't pin a straight line on a seam to hold it together", unquote. Said the Chief Superintendent told him we had nothing new other than circumstantial evidence, so he's been released.'

'Ah, for Christ's sake!' Lottie jumped up, knocking the files from her desk to the floor.

'And we have to hand everything over to the drugs unit. Pronto. Superintendent's word, not mine,' Lynch said.

Lottie slapped the lid of the photocopier down and switched off its hum. On her way back to her desk, she knocked over a stack of box files.

'Who do you think is going to sort that lot now?' Boyd asked.

'Sorry. I'll do it later.' She flopped back onto her chair and held her face in her hands.

Silence reigned in the office. Everyone afraid to breathe. All waiting for the next outburst.

'I'm really sorry,' Lottie said. She took a few deep breaths and looked up. 'Okay, Kirby. Tell me about Kitty Belfield.'

CHAPTER 50

After getting rid of his solicitor, Arthur headed for Danny's Bar. He needed a pint. He needed a feed. Hell, he only needed a pint.

As he walked down Main Street, his bare head getting clipped by useless umbrellas, the rain sheeted down and he realised the guards still had his coat. Or *was* it his coat? He'd have to go back to the digs and check. After he'd had his pint.

Outside the door to Danny's, he stopped. Sirens and commotion sounded towards him from Friars Street. He stared through the rain. Two fire engines were parked haphazardly across the road, figures frantically unfurling hoses. Water was everywhere. The deluge from the storm must have caused the river that wended its way through the town to burst its banks.

A thought struck him about the night old Tessa was murdered. About his jacket. Shit, he thought, I have to find Emma.

Abandoning all thoughts of his much-needed pint, he ran back up the street.

CHAPTER 51

To pacify him, once he'd put the dog outside in the yard, Emma ate the dinner of mashed potatoes, beans and a fried egg. She tasted none of it, just let it slide into her tummy.

'I've to check the heifers,' O'Dowd said. 'Will you wash up?'

She nodded.

'Keep an eye on the cameras. Can't be too careful, you know. With all that's happened.'

She glanced at the small television in the corner, beside the refrigerator, with its split screens showing the gate, yard, barns and sheds. She cleared the table as he pulled on his wellington boots and went out the back door, calling for Mason.

She filled the sink with water, then, unable to find any washing-up liquid, scrubbed as best she could to get the grease off the pots, wishing she was back home, where she'd gladly stack the dishwasher for her mum without a row. Holding back a sob, she dried the dishes and put them in the cupboard. She looked at the pile of accounting books he'd stacked up on the centre of the table.

The square panes of glass rattled and sheets of rain hammered against the window behind her. Feeling in her jeans pocket for her phone, she thought of the call she had made earlier. Maybe she should have waited. Was there still too much danger around? Taking the phone out, she sat at the table to dismantle it. She snapped out the battery and then the SIM card. Her fingers shook from fear and cold and she dropped the card. Where had it gone? She scanned the floor.

Nothing. Maybe it was still on the table. As she searched around the pile of books, she noticed one sticking out obliquely. Lifting the stack, she pulled it towards her. It looked familiar. Opening it, she glanced at the name inscribed on the inside cover. A gasp of recognition escaped her lips. What was going on? Just who the hell was O'Dowd?

She tugged off her spectacles, wiped them with the end of her shirt and replaced them on her nose. Picked up the book again. Wind crashed against the window and rain pounded like pellets on the tiled roof. Emma sat still. Waiting. Listening. Shivering.

The door opened.

'What is this?' she said, vaulting up from the chair, waving the book.

She stopped. Felt the blood drain not just from her face, but from her entire body.

The first punch knocked her back across the table. The book flew out of her hand and her phone crashed to the floor. The second smashed her spectacles into her face, glass shattering, cutting her skin and breaking her nose.

Emma Russell never felt the third blow as she slipped into unconsciousness.

CHAPTER 52

Kirby pulled a chair across and sat beside Lottie's desk. She felt like asking him for a hug, just to feel human contact, but thought better of it. A sense of loneliness descended on her shoulders and she longed for one of her pills. Impossible to sneak one with them all looking at her like she should be locked up.

'Kitty Belfield,' Kirby began as he flicked over pages of his notebook.

'Just the outline,' Lottie advised.

'Her husband Stan Belfield was a partner with Tessa Ball in the firm of solicitors, Belfield and Ball. This was from the sixties to the early eighties. Closed up shop in 1982.'

'Okay. What's your punchline?'

'Kitty told me the firm were involved with some very contentious cases in the early to mid seventies. There was one in particular that Tessa dealt with. According to Kitty, Tessa had an unhealthy interest in it and wouldn't let Stan in on any meetings or consultations.'

'What was the case?'

'She was very vague. She's ninety if she's a day. I pressed her and she said she only recalled that it resulted in a mother apparently trying to burn down her home with two children in it. The mother was sectioned and placed in St Declan's Asylum. Apparently every file in the office pertaining to that case was stolen in a burglary in 1976. Nothing else was taken. The place wasn't ransacked. It seemed the burglar knew where to look. Interesting, isn't it?'

'Enlighten me.'

'It points to Tessa, doesn't it? She handled the case. She knew where all the files were kept. She had to be in on it.'

'I can't see how one incident in 1976 has anything to do with Tessa's murder forty years later.'

Kirby grunted. 'Well, I thought it was significant.'

'Were the files ever found?'

'No.'

'Who was the woman who tried to kill her children?'

Kirby ran a finger down his notebook. 'Carrie King.'

'Okay,' Lottie said. 'This could lead us into a rabbit's warren. We haven't the manpower, so let's park it for now and we'll see what develops.'

'Right, boss.' Kirby stood up and with slumped shoulders wheeled his chair back to his own desk.

'Where's the transcript of the statement O'Dowd made today?'

Boyd tapped at his computer. 'Odd.'

'What's odd?' Lottie said. When she was sure none of her colleagues were watching, she snuck a pill from her bag and quickly swallowed it. Keep calm, she commanded herself.

'There's nothing on the system relating to it.' Boyd turned round. 'Lynch? Did you take O'Dowd's statement?'

'No.'

'Kirby?'

'Not me. I'll check with the front desk.' He lifted his phone. After a moment he said, 'Desk sergeant has no record of O'Dowd coming in.'

Lottie shoved her chair back and stood.

'That's priceless. Just priceless,' she said. 'Kirby, how did you find out O'Dowd owned the cottage?'

'Land registry.'

'No idea of who rented it then?'

'Not through any of the estate agents in town. I even broadened my query outside of town.'

'Back up a bit,' Lottie said. She moved over and sat on the edge of Kirby's desk. 'Have you a copy of the land folio or deeds?'

'I'll bring it up.'

Lottie breathed deeply, watching Kirby's chunky fingers stamp down on the keys. He clicked on a document.

'Print it.'

'Done.'

Lottie took the page. 'Boyd, have a look at this. See who owned the cottage before O'Dowd?'

'Jesus!'

She picked up her bag and rolled her jacket over her arm. 'Kirby, process a search warrant for Mick O'Dowd's farmhouse and lands. Come on, Boyd, we need to speak to O'Dowd again. And this time he will tell me the truth.'

CHAPTER 53

The car lurched from side to side as Boyd tried to avoid the water-filled potholes along the gloomy country road. Ebony clouds chased each other across the starless sky. Torrential rain crashed against the windscreen; the wipers couldn't keep up.

'Should've brought a pair of wellingtons,' Lottie muttered.

'Bit of a move up the fashion ladder for you.' Boyd wrestled with the steering wheel.

'O'Dowd's yard will be like a swimming pool.'

'More like a slurry pit.'

'Hey, there's the turn.'

'Can't see a thing. Hold on tight.'

Lottie clamped her feet to the floor as Boyd swerved, taking a sharp right. She felt herself being flung sideways. Her seat belt jerked against her shoulder. 'Take it easy. I know I said to hurry, but I want to get there alive.'

'Not a light on anywhere,' Boyd said, screeching the car to a halt in O'Dowd's yard.

'The Land Rover's here. Let's take a look.' She zipped up her jacket and exited the car. Boyd switched off the headlights, plunging them into darkness.

'Can't you leave them on?'

'I've got flashlights.'

He produced two from the boot. Lottie took one, checked it worked and followed the cone of light up to the front door.

Hammering the knocker on the door, she shone her torch through. It reflected back, blinding her.

'Thought I saw a ghost.' She turned to Boyd. He was nowhere in sight. 'Boyd? Where are you? The dog could be loose. Come back.' She flashed the light about wildly.

'He's not loose.' The wind carried his voice around the side of the house to Lottie's ears. 'He's injured.'

'What? How?' She ran, splashing through puddles, wind buffeting her against the gable end, and fell over the crouched figure of Boyd.

'Ouch,' she cried.

Lying on her back on the slimy dung-splattered ground, she tried to get traction with her elbows; slipped again.

'Lottie? Are you okay? Give me your hand.'

'Where's the damn torch?' She dragged herself to her knees.

Boyd shone his beam around the yard and she saw the dog.

'Oh my God? What happened?'

'Poor bugger's dead.'

Holding a hand to her mouth, she said, 'He was a nasty dog, but he didn't deserve this.'

'Surely O'Dowd didn't kill his own dog?' Boyd asked, picking up her torch.

Reaching for Boyd's hand, Lottie allowed him to haul her to her feet. The warmth of his fingers did little to dispel the chill cartwheeling along her skin.

'This is not good,' she said, shaking off his hold.

'We should come back in daylight.'

A strong gust flung a tin can across the yard.

'Just a minute. Let's try the back door first. Give me the torch.' She took it and led Boyd round to the rear of the house, where she knocked on the door.

'This is pointless,' Boyd said.

A pane of glass rattled in the door. 'We'll search it in the morning. Get a squad car to come and housesit.'

'What for?'

'In case O'Dowd comes back.'

'But his car is here.'

'He's not, though, and his dog is dead. I need to check if the bike is still in the shed.'

Shivering from her fall, Lottie walked in the illuminated cone cast by the torch. The rain continued unabated. At the door of the shed, water dripped down into one of the blue plastic barrels. Inside, the tractor loomed like an iridescent monster. No sign of the quad. No sign of the…

'Boyd. Quick. Come here.'

She sensed him moving to her shoulder. Felt his breath on her neck.

'The bicycle is gone,' he said.

'You wouldn't let me take it earlier. It was evidence that Emma was here.' Her voice was even. The pill was working. Keeping her from screaming at him.

Boyd spoke in an even-tempered tone. 'You know you couldn't take it then. We needed a warrant.'

She turned. He was so close, she could see the pores of his skin in the light from the torch in his hand. All around, shadows swarmed at her, the galvanised roof rising and falling with the force of the tempest raging outside. Something howled in the distance and a massive crunch, then a bang, signalled a falling tree. Lottie flinched and moved towards Boyd. He wrapped his arm around her. Too close. But she wanted to feel his closeness. To feel safe. Leaning into him, she let her cheek touch his. Briefly. Breathed in his scent.

And then he spoke. Almost breaking the spell. Almost.

'You're tired. Soaking wet. It's been a long day. You need to go home.' He trailed his fingers through her sopping hair.

She said, 'You're right. As usual. Let's go.'

But she didn't move. Couldn't move.

He lowered the torch as his mouth met hers. Their lips brushed silently, quickly, and something stirred within her. Something that had been dormant for so long, she hardly recognised it.

'Oh Boyd. Don't do this to me.'

'You want me to stop?'

'No.'

His hands slid around her back and her body was drawn tightly into his. She could sense it in him too. A longing. A craving. Call it whatever… she wanted it. Her muddy hand rose automatically, up around his neck, and she pulled him down to her lips.

Another loud crash separated them. The wind had succeeded in lifting the roof clear from the rafters, flinging it high into the black sky and out over the field. Rain gushed in.

'The gods are in some temper,' Boyd said, with a strained laugh. He shone the torch up into the heavens. 'All O'Dowd's equipment will be destroyed without the roof.'

'Serves the bastard right.' Lottie walked with measured steps around the side of the tractor, her body still tingling. 'I see the drainpipe took off with the roof.' She glanced at the plastic barrel as she passed.

A flash of lightning cracked the sky and emblazoned the yard. In a spark of clarity, she halted. The warmth that had coursed through her body a moment ago fled. Her blood froze midstream to a solid icicle.

Taking a step backwards, she whispered, 'Boyd… In… in there. Look.' She pointed to the barrel. 'I… I saw something.'

'Probably a drowned rat. Like us.'

He swung his torch around and the beam settled on the water in the barrel that once held O'Dowd's Propcorn. Lottie followed the glow with her eyes, felt her legs go weak, cried out, lost her breath, gulped down the acidic bilge.

She dared to look again.

A swathe of hair rippled around two open eyes looking up at her from the depths of the watery grave.

It wasn't a drowned rat.

Lottie screamed.

CHAPTER 54

The man circled the car, rain pounding on his head.

He had a call to make. A very difficult call. He wasn't at all sure of the reception his message would get. He tapped the number, rainwater drenching his iPhone screen. No signal. Good… or was it?

He turned round at the sound of sirens blaring, coming towards him. The shrieking noise seemed to be in competition with the storm that had yet to reach its peak.

Watching until the garda cars and the ambulance disappeared over the hill, he decided the call could wait. He got into his car and followed the lights into the night.

He knew where they were headed.

CHAPTER 55

Even with Boyd's coat over her shoulders, Lottie continued to shiver. Her jeans settled like a damp sheath on her legs, hair matted to her scalp. Balling up her fists, she thumped them against her head.

'She was here, Boyd. All the time. God almighty, this is all my fault.'

'No use going there, Lottie.'

'That's the point. We were here. Earlier. We saw the bike. We should have gone inside the house.' She stared up into his eyes. The sparkle of hazel had turned to black. 'Leave me alone.'

Without answering, Boyd shrugged and went to direct the SOCOs towards the barn.

She slumped down onto the doorstep. Looking up at the sky, she allowed the rain to run down her face, along with tears of helplessness. The white-suited SOCOs swarmed around the barrel holding the body of Emma Russell, sightless in her watery grave.

There were no stars in the sky, only bullets of rain shooting down the darkness. The storm howled like a banshee welcoming the dead, and branches crunched and cracked and fell to earth. The cattle in the second shed lowed long and hard. Another flash of lightning lit up the heavens, and a thunderclap followed.

Spotlights were erected by the team, and as she sat there on the lonely wet step, Lottie thought how surreal the night had become. A seventeen-year-old girl, submerged until she drowned. Without sympathy or pity. Without prayer or penance. Without remorse or guilt. Shoved into a barrel while rain pummelled her body and water flooded her lungs until her last breath left her being, her life extinguished in a strangled gulp.

Lottie felt her brain helter-skeltering inside her skull. A flutter of movement caused her to shift her focus down to her feet. A small bird, its wings drenched so badly it probably couldn't fly. Its tiny body shivering. It was useless. So was she. Forcing herself, she tried to comprehend what had happened. Who was this monster she was dealing with? One thing was definite: Lorcan Brady and his partner had had nothing to do with Emma's death. Brady was lying in hospital and the nameless man was already dead. So who then? Had O'Dowd killed the girl? It seemed most likely. Everything pointed to him. The bicycle in the shed. The fact that he had vanished. The lies he had told and the truth he had kept hidden.

Why had Emma's grandmother, Tessa Ball, signed over the cottage to O'Dowd? How did she even come to own it? And who was the man stabbed to death in its embers? Why had Emma come here? Why was she dead? Why?

Sensing Boyd's presence, Lottie glanced up. Silhouetted by the lights, the rain for a backdrop, he stood like a weary Grecian god, smoke from his cigarette swirling and dying in the cold night.

'Want one?' he asked.

'Please,' she whispered.

Crouching down beside her, he lit it for her.

The sound of tyres crashing through water caused them to look at each other. Lottie heaved herself up. A door slammed and heavy footsteps followed.

'What the feck is going on here?' Superintendent Corrigan bellowed against the storm.

'Emma Russell. We found her. Drowned,' Boyd said.

'Drowned? What happened?'

'Yes, sir. In a barrel used for Propcorn.' Boyd started to explain. 'It's acid, used for animal feed. You mix it—'

'All right. All right. What was she doing out here?' Corrigan stretched his hand towards the activity in the barn.

'I have to figure that out yet, sir,' Lottie said. Throwing down the cigarette, she shoved her hands into her damp pockets and awaited the tirade.

'Figure it out soon.' Corrigan marched towards the SOCOs.

Boyd exhaled. 'Narrow escape.'

'Don't speak too soon.' Lottie watched the superintendent chatting with McGlynn, before he promptly returned.

'First thing in the morning. My office.' And he rushed back to his car.

Jane Dore arrived and suited herself up under an enormous umbrella held by a garda. Lottie nodded acknowledgement of the state pathologist's presence and walked with Boyd to watch the SOCOs removing the teenager's body from the barrel.

A man with a gurney and a body bag waited inside the roofless barn as incessant rain spilled down on top of it.

Boyd clutched Lottie's elbow. She shook him off.

'I'm fine. I've seen bodies before.'

The barrel was now on its side, water emptying quickly until only Emma's fully clothed body remained inside.

Lottie caught McGlynn eyeing her above his mouth mask. Pools of emeralds, dimmed by the scenes he witnessed. Just like her own, she supposed. Along with another SOCO, he gently eased Emma free from the plastic drum and onto a Teflon sheet.

Stepping closer, Lottie looked down. The girl's open eyes appeared to glare at her, questioning her, asking why she had let her down. Why she hadn't saved her. There were scratches across her nose and forehead.

'I won't know cause of death until I do the post-mortem,' Jane said, pre-empting Lottie's question. She assessed the body. 'Fully clothed. Jeans, shirt and sweater.' Her fingers felt under the wet wool and cotton, checking carefully for wounds.

'I assume she drowned,' Lottie said.

'You know what I say about assuming anything?' Jane said.

Lottie sighed. 'Let me know your findings.'

'Of course.'

'You didn't give me a chance,' Lottie whispered and reached out a hand to wipe a strand of hair from Emma's death mask.

McGlynn dipped his eyes in warning, but Lottie had already turned away.

CHAPTER 56

After sending Boyd off to tell Arthur Russell about his daughter's death and to verify his whereabouts since his release from custody, Lottie watched two crime-scene officers meticulously identify, bag and tag potential evidence in O'Dowd's kitchen.

Emma's broken spectacles. Her phone, with a cracked screen. SIM card and battery, separate from the phone. These were the only signs she had left behind that she had been here.

And accounting ledgers. Stepping closer, Lottie flipped open one of the ledgers with a gloved finger. Columns of words and figures. They meant nothing to her. Another had a list of numbered livestock. Who would feed the heifers and milk O'Dowd's cows now, she wondered? If he didn't return. If he had murdered the girl. If…

Flicking through the pages, a light of recognition dawned. She knew that handwriting.

'Hand me an evidence bag,' she said.

With the ledger sealed, she took another quick glance around. She was sure this was where Emma had been attacked. The CCTV monitor was smashed on the floor.

'Any tapes?' she asked the SOCO who was dusting the counter top for fingerprints.

'Haven't noticed any yet. But if I come across them, I'll notify you.'

'Do that, please.'

She'd seen enough. With the evidence bag under her arm, she left the house, wondering why Emma had been here and what Mick

O'Dowd's role was in the whole sorry mess. Soon, she hoped, Marian Russell would be able to give them answers.

*

At the front of the house, Lynch jumped out of a squad car, dipped under the crime-scene tape and caught up with Lottie.

'Do you want the good news or the bad news?' she said.

'Now isn't the time for games,' Lottie said, shoving the evidence bag under her jacket to keep the rain off it. 'I need to get home to my children.'

'Just trying to soften the blow,' Lynch persisted.

'Okay,' Lottie relented. 'Good news?'

Lynch took a deep breath and exhaled. 'The man we suspect is Lorcan Brady is off life support but unable to talk for the moment.'

'That's the good news?'

'Yes, boss. The bad news now?'

'Oh, go on. It can only add to the day I've had.'

'Marian Russell died half an hour ago.'

*

'Inspector Parker?'

Cathal Moroney had appeared from behind a white van with a satellite dish on the roof. He got no further than the gate. Two gardaí succeeded in keeping him behind the crime-scene tape.

'Have you a comment on what you think happened here, please?'

'Do you honestly want to know what I think?' Lottie tightened her grip on the evidence bag under her jacket, and walked up to the tape, careful not to slip in the downpour.

Moroney slid his microphone under her nose. 'Yes, please. Is it another murder? The girl who went AWOL from under your very eyes?'

Stepping forward, jabbing towards him with her finger, Lottie said, 'You are the lowest of the low. How do you live with yourself?'

Moroney grabbed her hand before it connected with him.

'Detective Inspector Parker, I'll let that go for this one time only. I'll put it down to the shock of whatever you've witnessed in there. But let me tell you, I could do you for assault.'

Lottie kept her mouth shut. He had a point.

'So it's no comment, is it?'

She nodded and ducked under the tape, heading for the squad car Lynch had exited. Before she reached it, she felt Moroney tug her sleeve.

'Meet me in the Joyce Hotel. Tomorrow. Say twelve thirty p.m. There's something you need to know.'

She shrugged off his hand and opened the car door.

'Don't forget,' he said.

'If I do, I'm sure you'll remind me.'

She got into the car and slammed the door. She had more to be doing than meeting Cathal fecking Moroney tomorrow. She leaned her head into the seat and closed her eyes tightly. She could still see Emma Russell's staring back at her. And she immediately thought of her children. It had been one long, merciless day.

*

His coat had been there all the time. Folded in a ball under his music desk. Or had he got two? He couldn't remember. God, but he had to cut down on the weed. He had no idea what was real or imagined any more.

The guitar held no solace for him. He plucked at a string, sighed, and laid the instrument back in its stand. He scanned his small cabin of refuge and felt the walls encroach on his very soul.

Where would he begin to look for Emma?

Perhaps he should rush over to the hospital and shake the life out of Marian. See what she had to say for herself. The witch. With her plants and her spells and whatnot. Most times he was sure she was insane; other times he was convinced she was just plain sad.

A knock roused him from his reverie. Before he could move, the door swung inwards and Arthur Russell's sorrowful little world was once again rocked on its axis.

CHAPTER 57

The young garda parked the squad car in the station yard. It took Lottie a moment to realise where she was. A sharp knock on the window and she jumped in her seat.

'What the…?'

A face peered in at her, the light attached to the wall beaming down behind it.

She stepped out of the car in a daze.

A hand was thrust towards her. She looked down at it and then up at the face. No one she recognised. A head of black hair meant he was probably younger than her. Even in the obscure light she could see his skin was dark. Tanned? She couldn't make out the colour of the eyes. Not here, anyway. As he stepped back to give her room to shut the car door, she noticed he was a good head taller than her, with shoulders broad enough on which to hang a door. He smirked, and before he opened his mouth, she knew arrogance percolated in the pores of his skin.

'David,' he said. 'Detective Inspector David McMahon. National Drugs Unit. Seconded from Dublin Castle to take command. You must be Detective Inspector Parker.'

Take command? Arrogant prick, she thought. 'You can take all you like, but I'm still SIO on the murder cases. And the new one.'

'New what?'

'Murder.' Lottie brushed past him and glided up the steps and in through the door. She wanted to bang it in his face, but it was on a slow hinge. She left him standing in the rain. And she knew his mouth was open.

*

'I'll take this office, shall I?'

He was heading into what would soon be her new office, as yet unfinished, without a door.

'No you won't. That's mine.'

'Looks like no one has moved in. It'll do.' In he marched, pulling off his coat, shaking rainwater over the new beige carpet. He moved a ladder from one wall to the other and eyed the decorator's table.

She slapped the ledger she'd taken from O'Dowd's house onto her desk and flopped into her chair.

'Can I get a chair and a computer?' he asked.

'You can piss off back to Dublin,' she muttered under her breath.

'What was that?'

'You can talk to Superintendent Corrigan about that.'

'I will.'

His voice was deep: a baritone. Or was it a bass? Jesus, she was so exhausted she could cry.

'Didn't think you'd be here until tomorrow,' she said.

He came and sat at Boyd's desk. She wanted to yell at him to get his arse off her friend's chair, but she hadn't the energy.

'After the fire victim was identified, I knew you wouldn't have the expertise to handle it,' he said.

'What are you talking about? Lorcan Brady is a small-time crook. No need for you to disturb your evening.'

'Lorcan Brady? No, not that whippersnapper.'

'Who then?'

But she knew. McMahon had got word before she had. The stabbed and burned man must have been identified through his dental records. Big-time crook, if it brought a detective inspector out of his cushy Dublin office while a biblical storm raged.

'Jerome Quinn,' he said.

'One of *the* Quinns?'

'Second biggest drug family in the country. Jerome split from his half-brother a couple of years ago and disappeared from our radar. Interesting to note he'd most probably been living under your very nose here in Ragmullin.'

'He never came to our attention.'

'Correct, but it was some haul of cannabis he had growing, wasn't it?'

Lottie could hear the reprimand in his tone. Wait till he found out about the heroin they'd discovered in Brady's house.

'Not to mention the value of the heroin from Brady's house.'

So he already knew. Unable to think of a suitable reply, she remained mute.

'You look tired,' he said. 'I'll check into my hotel and we'll take this up in the morning. Should be an open-and-shut case. I'll be out of your hair in no time.'

She felt her hand reach up to her straggly locks. A natural reflex. Maybe he wouldn't be too bad after all.

'And I want a computer in here, first thing.' He fetched his coat and was out of the door before she could pull her thoughts together to frame a suitable reply.

'What the hell?' she said to the four walls.

Her phone beeped. Katie.

'I meant to ask when you rang earlier, Mam, will you pick something up from the supermarket for dinner? And a tin of formula for Louis. Oh, and while you're at it, maybe another pack of nappies. Ta. You're the best.'

'Sure,' Lottie said, and the call died. She leaned over and rested her head on the desk. She didn't realise she'd fallen asleep until she felt a tap on her shoulder.

'You'd better go home, Lottie.' Boyd.

She stretched and glanced at the ledger, still in the evidence bag. 'I need you to have a look at this.'

'Tomorrow,' he said. 'And there's no sign of Arthur Russell at the B and B or at Danny's. No one has laid eyes on him since he was released.'

'Shit. Surely he didn't kill his own daughter?'

'Anything is possible.'

'I wonder if he knows Marian is dead?'

'I've no idea.'

'Let's recap.' She sat up as straight as her tired spine allowed. 'Tessa Ball is dead. Marian Russell, her daughter, is dead. Marian's daughter Emma is dead. Three members of one family. Who benefited from their deaths? What is the motive? And who had it? Arthur? O'Dowd? I can't get my head around it.'

'Lottie?'

'Yes?'

'It can wait until tomorrow. Go home.'

'Where's everyone?'

'Still at O'Dowd's. There is a search party out for him and Arthur Russell. But the storm is playing havoc. The town is flooded. The river burst its banks. I had to drive here the long way round.'

Lottie jumped up.

'I hope my house is okay.' The river skirted around the side of the estate where she lived. She remembered Katie's call. Surely she would have mentioned if the house was in danger of flooding? Then again…

'Will you come grocery shopping with me, Boyd? I haven't the energy.'

'What?'

'Please?'

'The things I do for you.'

CHAPTER 58

Every night it was the same. Stepping carefully around him, like the floor was covered in sharp shards of glass. And no matter how hard she tried, something invariably tipped him over.

Tonight Annabelle vowed it would be different.

Every last surface in the house was shining. The counter tops were immaculate. The floor – you could eat your dinner off it, and she had, once, with his shoe resting on the back of her neck.

There had to be a way out of this hellhole. Going to a hostel might be an option. But he would find her. And she had to keep her practice going. She had to keep the twins.

Her life had always been boring with Cian, and she no longer remembered why she had married him. At one time she had plugged the gap with affairs, but her disastrous liaison with Tom Rickard had been the final straw for Cian. Something had snapped inside him when he found out. The man she thought she'd been married to for twenty years had altered within weeks into a raging control freak.

It was all her doing, he'd said. She was the one who'd slept in other men's beds, the one who'd let other men shag her. She was the one who'd deceived her husband with a myriad of lies. She was the worthless one. Wasn't she? So she deserved every slap and humiliation he threw at her. Didn't she?

No she did not, she told herself. Annabelle O'Shea was not going to be trampled into worthlessness. She had to do something.

She undressed her burned wrist, tended it with ointment and wrapped a clean bandage over the seeping wound. It should be healing by now, but it wasn't. She limped over to the stove and, like a robot, stirred the stew.

The twins were in their rooms, finishing their homework. There was no sound from Cian's study. Come to think of it, she had not heard anything from him since she arrived home from work. She glanced at the clock. He usually visited the kitchen around now, to check on her and call her names.

But this evening there was silence.

She ceased stirring and listened intently. The hum of Bronagh singing along to a tune. The stomp of Pearse's foot on the floor. Not a sound from Cian's study.

Opening the back door, she peered through the rain at the raised door of the garage. His car wasn't there. She never asked where he went or what he did, because she didn't care. It gave her a few hours of uninterrupted peace. But to go out this early? The clock indicated that it was 19.05.

Slipping off her boots, she climbed the stairs in her Calvin Klein socks. Holding her breath outside his study, she waited. Listened. Nothing. She eased out a breath as her fingers clutched the handle. And then she noticed the coded keypad attached to the door. When had he put that there?

What was Cian involved in that warranted keeping his own family out of his study? She tried the handle anyway. No give. With a sigh of resignation, she was turning to go back down the stairs when she heard, above the cacophony of the storm, the sound of a car screeching up the drive, rounding the gable of the house and entering the garage.

She ran down the stairs and flew into the kitchen, and was stirring the stew when he walked in. Not a word. Not a glance. She didn't raise her head until she sensed the icy chill as he walked up behind her, eased his arm around her waist and dragged her body to his in a rough embrace. A damp smell of staleness rose from his clothes as his fingers began to probe.

Her long neck, which she had once loved him to caress, froze with the touch of his cold lips on her most sensual spot. And then the pinch, where no one could see. Biting her lip, she willed the scream to lock itself down. To stay silent until she was free to acknowledge the pain.

His hand circled her body and delved under the waistband of her jeans, toying with the lace of her knickers, his fingers exploring. She breathed out, hoping he wouldn't mistake it for consent. He didn't. With a final pinch, and without having uttered a word, he extricated himself and hit her behind the knees. She buckled but didn't fall. He left her with her hand still holding the spoon above the saucepan. Straining her ears, she heard him enter his study and shut the door. Slowly she sank to the floor.

Wiping away her tears, a resolution formed in the depths of her soul.

This could not go on.

Twins or no twins, Cian had to go. If he didn't, she would. Eventually.

But first she would find out what was so precious to her husband that he kept it locked away in his study.

CHAPTER 59

Lottie pushed down an urge to turn at her front door and walk straight back out again. It was like living with three adults who insisted on acting like two-year-olds. They crowded out her four-bedroomed semi-detached house and overwhelmed her with tasks after work each evening. But she loved them. And she needed them more than they would ever know. They kept her grounded in brightness and helped keep the darkness of her job outside her front door.

This evening, though, she needed a drink. No, she thought. Not yet.

Hauling the bag of groceries onto the counter, she began putting the supplies in the cupboards. It looked like her mother hadn't been in today. The kitchen was a mess. Working, trying to manage the house, watching the children… it was too much. Leaning her head against the cupboard door, she banged a tin of beans down on the counter without hearing the noise she was making. And banged it again.

'Mam!' Katie ran in. 'What do you think you're doing? You woke up Louis. I'll have to rock him for another hour to get him asleep again.'

'I told you not to get into the habit of rocking him.'

'I'm so tired… Anything that gets him to sleep is fine by me.'

Lottie shoved a jar of curry sauce and two packets of soup into the cupboard. There were three soups in there already. She automatically checked the use-by dates. Two years out of date. What the hell?

'Are you listening to me, Mam?'

Lottie turned round. Her eyes glazed over, and without knowing what she was doing, she flung the packets to the floor.

'Jesus, Mam. Stop. What's wrong with you?'

Lottie squinted over at her daughter. 'Katie?'

'I'm getting Chloe.' Katie flew out of the kitchen.

A black shadow crept across Lottie's vision. She clutched for the counter top but her legs slipped out from under her and she slid to the ground. Tipping back her head, she gulped for air. Couldn't catch her breath.

'Katie…'

Breathe, she warned herself. Breathe. She was no use to her kids dead. Unable to catch hold of a breath, she saw black stars swim in front of her eyes. Then darkness.

*

When she opened her eyes, for a moment she didn't know where she was. She pulled her legs underneath her and knelt up. At last she could draw breath. Her hands. What was on her hands? She looked around. The floor was covered in powder. The soup packets had burst open. It was splattered everywhere. Had she done that? Of course she had. Mad, mad woman!

In that moment, she didn't care how many resolutions she had made; she needed a drink.

Katie rushed in, Louis in her arms.

'Mam, there's something wrong with you. Are you drunk?'

'No, I'm just exhausted.'

'I can't stand living here. Do you know that? I'm going to have to leave. I don't care what you say. I have to get out of this house.'

'Don't be stupid. Where can you go? You've no money. And it's raining.' Lottie wondered who was talking. Surely it wasn't her?

'My son has a grandad.'

'What? Tom Rickard? Don't be daft, Katie.'

'Mam, we need to talk.' Katie sat herself at the table.

Lottie dragged herself over and sat down. 'Tom Rickard doesn't know about Louis.'

'I traced him. Emailed him. And he wants to see his grandson. You can't cope with us all here, so in a few weeks I'm going to take Louis to visit him.'

'After all I've done for you and little Louis! I've been so worried about you. You can't just up and leave.'

'It will only be for a holiday. Nothing's finalised. I just sent a few emails.'

'Louis is too young.'

'No he's not. I've applied for his passport.'

'You can't do that.'

'I can. I did. Mam, we need a break from each other. I need a few weeks away. You need the space too.'

Lottie felt her mouth opening and closing. No words came out. Only a few minutes ago she'd been half wishing them out of the house, and now she didn't know what was going on. Be careful what you wish for. Sure.

CHAPTER 60

Boyd was standing on the doorstep.

'Are you going to invite me in, or what?'

'Or what,' Lottie said, opening the door wider.

'Is it raining in there?'

'I've just got out of the shower. Come in.'

He shoved a brown bag containing a plastic bottle into her hand, shuffled out of his jacket and made for the kitchen. 'Something smells good.'

'You're an awful liar. Dinner is well over. Unless you'd like some Pot Noodles.'

'I'd rather be shot than poisoned any day,' he said, sitting at the table.

'Make yourself comfortable.' Lottie inspected the bottle. 'Diet Coke? No wine in Tesco?'

'Beggars can't be choosers.'

'You're in some mood tonight.'

'Pot and kettle.'

'Why are you here?'

'I… Lottie, give me a break. I just came round to see if you're doing okay. After today, you know…'

'I'm fine.' She chewed the inside of her lip, not liking where the conversation was headed.

'That's not what Katie… Shit!'

Bottle of Coke in one hand, a glass in the other, Lottie stared open-mouthed at him. She hadn't expected that. 'What are you saying? Come on, Boyd. Out with it.'

'It's nothing. Katie rang me. Said you were having a meltdown and would I come have a chat with you.'

'Jesus Christ.' She handed him the glass. 'You should have brought wine.'

'Thanks.' He twisted it around in his hand.

She poured a glass for herself. Her phone rang. She glanced at it. Saw the caller ID.

'Are you not answering it?' he asked.

'It's only Annabelle. She can leave a message. I suppose Katie contacted her too. She's probably checking up that I didn't take an overdose.'

'Don't be so disparaging. People care about you. Sometimes you reach a stage where you have to admit you need help, and when it's offered, you should take it.'

'So it's Dr Phil sitting at my table, not my friend Boyd.'

'I *am* your friend. Don't you get it, Lottie? You had a bitch of a day today, a horrible week, and you need to talk about it. No use burying your head in the sand.'

They sipped their drinks to the sound of Louis whimpering and Katie soothing him in the other room, and the rain bashing against the windows.

'I don't know what's wrong with me. No one can understand,' Lottie said.

'Try me.'

She kept her eyes downcast, swirling the Coke in the glass.

'I'm drowning, Boyd. That's what it feels like. I have this feeling inside, just here.' She drummed her chest with her fist. 'It's consuming me. I feel so selfish. I can't love anyone. Not even my children. Do you know why?'

'Tell me.' His face was etched with concern; his eyes swimming with unspoken words.

'I'm afraid,' she said, lowering her eyes from his gaze. 'If I love, I will lose. And I can't lose them. Not my children. Oh God, if anything happened to them, to any one of them or to little Louis, I'd throw myself into Lough Cullion. Can you understand that?'

'I understand that you love your children and Louis. You love them so much you're afraid to reveal it. You think that if you show how much you care, you'll get hurt or you'll hurt them. This is life, Lottie. We all get hurt. But we are the grown-ups. We can handle it. Right? You loved Adam, then he died. And that is your only problem. You don't know how to cope with the guilt.'

'Guilt?'

'Maybe not guilt. Maybe it's fear. I'm not Dr Phil, but I believe you're so consumed with a fear of losing all you love that you push everyone away. There's this giant barrier, like a... like a force field around you, repelling each and every person you care for. You need to break it down, Lottie, or it will break you.'

She smiled weakly. 'Thanks, Boyd. You've put into words exactly how I feel.' She knew he was so right. Her fear of loss meant she kept him away too. 'Now no more talk about me. I'll be fine.'

A soft silence descended on them.

'I can't understand why Emma was killed,' he said at last. His words immediately brought a chill to the room. It settled on Lottie's shoulders.

'Maybe she saw or knew something,' she said. 'I suspect there's something about the night Tessa was murdered that we've missed. We'll go back over every bit of evidence in the morning. I won't rest until this is solved.'

'Stop. Don't beat yourself up. Whoever killed her wanted to wipe that whole family out. They're on a mission and I don't think you or anyone else would have stopped them.'

'But why? We need to dig beneath the surface of this.'

The front door opened and closed.

'Well, if it isn't himself… Boyd. Am I right?'

'Hello, Mrs Fitzpatrick.' Boyd stood and shook her hand.

Rose dropped her umbrella into the sink and shifted out of her raincoat, handing it to Boyd to hang up in the hall. 'It's an awful night to be out.'

'What has *you* out in it?' Lottie asked, taking no notice of Boyd's cautionary look from behind her mother's back.

'Dropped in to see if everything was all right.'

Had Katie called her mother? She was going to kill that girl.

'Everything is fine. Why wouldn't it be?'

'I heard about that poor child. Tessa Ball's granddaughter. Terrible business altogether.'

'Would you like a cup of tea?' Boyd offered.

Lottie glared. It was her house!

'Sure, why not?'

As Boyd filled the kettle, Lottie asked, 'Did you hear Marian Russell died today too?'

Rose paled. 'No, I never heard that.'

'Are you sure you can't tell me anything about Tessa and her family?'

'I'm sure.'

'She was a solicitor in the seventies and eighties. You or Dad have any dealings with her?'

Lottie studied her mother. Rose's hand shook slightly, but her eyes were focused straight ahead, unwavering.

'I can't recall that we had anything to do with her.'

'Dad's will, maybe?'

'No. You know he left everything to me. And once I'm gone, it'll be yours.'

'Mick O'Dowd. Do you know him?'

Rose shook her head. 'Can't say that I do. Why? What did he do?'

'I don't know yet. I think maybe he was an old boyfriend of Tessa's.'

'I doubt that very much. She had no time for anyone other than her daughter, Marian. Spoiled that girl rotten, she did. Compensating for the loss of her husband at such a young age.'

Lottie searched for the insinuation, but couldn't find it. Rose was quiet. Too quiet. Lottie studied her mother. She seemed to be lost in her own world, a film of tears shrouding her eyes.

'Mother, what's wrong? Are you okay?'

Shrugging off Lottie's hand, Rose stood. 'I'd better get home. You're in good hands here.'

'Kettle's almost boiled,' Boyd said.

Rose smiled. Trust Boyd to get her mother on his side.

'Next time.'

At the door, Rose turned. 'Mick O'Dowd? A right ladies' man in his day, if it's the same fellow I'm thinking of.'

'Lives out by Dolanstown,' Lottie said.

'That's him.'

'We think he might have killed Emma,' Boyd said.

'Emma? He wouldn't hurt a hair on her head.'

'Why not? Did he know her? She was killed at his farmhouse. He is one of our suspects.'

'He wouldn't hurt that girl. You'd better look elsewhere.' Rose stepped out into the rain, opened up her umbrella then closed it again before the wind could take hold of it.

'What do you mean?' Lottie asked her mother's departing figure.

'Do you want a lift?' Boyd offered.

'I have my car.' And Rose disappeared out onto the road.

Lottie stared at Boyd as the rain beat in on top of them.

'Close the door,' Boyd said.

In the kitchen, seated at the table, they sat in silence digesting what Rose Fitzpatrick had said.

'First she knew nothing, then she knew an awful lot. I can't figure her out at all.'

'Could Mick O'Dowd have been the writer of Tessa's love letters?' Boyd said.

'It's all a bit mad. And I really think my mother isn't well. Did you notice how pale she is?'

'A bit thinner, maybe.'

'I'm going to have a word with Annabelle about her. Book her in for a check-up.'

'Did Annabelle leave you a message?'

'I never checked my phone. She'll ring back if it's urgent, but knowing her…'

'Lottie? *You* need a check-up, never mind your mother.'

'Don't start. Finish your drink, then I'm going to bed.'

Boyd drained his Coke, and Lottie took the glass and put it in the sink. 'I'll see you in the morning.'

He got up and headed for the door. 'You know, if what your mother insinuated is correct, then Marian Russell could've been Tessa and O'Dowd's daughter.'

'There's no point in speculating. Whether she was or not, what relevance can it have to anything we're dealing with?'

'Maybe nothing, or…'

'Or maybe everything. At this stage, we don't know. Goodnight, Boyd.' She gave him a quick hug.

Chloe came down the stairs. 'I've an appointment with my therapist in the morning. But don't worry, I can go on my own.'

'See you,' Boyd said with a wink.

'Bye,' Chloe said.

Lottie locked the front door and switched off the sitting room light.

'Hey, I'm going to watch some telly,' Chloe said.

'Don't be up half the night,' Lottie warned as her daughter passed her in the hall, rolling her eyes like only a teenager could.

Lottie's heart stopped for a moment. There was one Ragmullin teenager who would never roll her eyes again.

She reached out and touched Chloe's arm. The girl stopped. 'Are you okay now, Mum?'

Lottie gripped her middle child in a hug, and received one back. Holding Chloe at arm's length, she said, 'Once I have my family, I'll always be okay.'

'Good. You scared us earlier. You are a good mum, if a little wacky at times.'

'Thanks for that, Chloe.'

'Any time. Now can I watch the telly?'

'And you're okay too, aren't you?'

Chloe turned up her sleeves. Lottie gulped at the sight of the old scars ridged along her arms. But there were no fresh cuts. 'I'm doing fine. And I know I've to talk to my therapist or to you if I ever feel that bad again.'

'And Sean and Katie? Are they okay?'

'Mum, you need to ask them, not me.'

Lottie gave Chloe one last squeeze and watched her beautiful, intelligent daughter walk tall into the sitting room.

Yes, she really must talk with Sean and Katie.

But first she needed to sleep.

CHAPTER 61

Alexis sat at the head of the long table, where she could see her seated guests. They lined the length of it, eight on each side. Sixteen of the most influential people in New York's computer gaming industry. The place that had been set at the end of the table, facing her, remained empty. As it had done for the last few weeks.

But her child would return. Once things were sorted.

It was an important time. A busy time. She needed to ensure she sorted out the mess in Ragmullin. A mess that was now threatening the world she had spent her life building up. A mess that she had fled from forty years ago, hoping she was leaving it all behind forever. She should have known that the death of an inconsequential garda sergeant in 1975 would one day resurrect itself; that skeletons would fall out of closets and come knocking on her door. Bones had been resurrected, and it was then her worries began in earnest.

Not that his death had much to do with her. No. It was what had happened the year before it that caused her intense worry. But after the discovery of the boy's bones last January, Alexis knew it was the one thing that could unhinge the old woman to reveal what she might or might not have suspected for years. And Alexis needed to be in control of all possibilities. Plans had been put in place. But as it turned out, she'd been blindsided. No matter what happened now, she had to make sure her child never found out.

As laughter mingled with the rise and fall of the chatter around the table, Alexis tuned it out and devised the next steps she must take.

This time the past would stay buried.
She could not risk losing the child.
Once was enough for that to happen.
She would make damn sure it would not happen again.

The eighties: The Child

That's what they call me. The Child.

Do they not know I have a name? I did have one once. So long ago, I don't even remember it.

Doesn't matter now. I can be who or what I want to be.

I'm working on the farm now. A farm? Ha, that's a laugh. I even laugh when I say it. It's just a patch of ground within the high walls surrounding the asylum. Yes, I can call it an asylum now. Because that is what it is. This is where I have been abandoned. I'll most likely die within these walls.

But today I am outside.

Johnny Joe shows me how to sow herbs. Herbs that heal, he says. Pity he didn't use them on himself. The mad old man with his crooked brown fingers and his smoke-ridden cough.

I don't think about my mother much any more. The voices have stopped calling her name. Maybe she is dead. Or maybe someone released her. Why didn't they release me? Has everyone forgotten that I'm here? I asked a nurse one day when I'd be going home. She laughed and mussed up my hair.

'You're never going home.'

'Why not?'

'Your home was burned to the ground, you mad child.'

'I'm not mad. Not like the others. I just want to get out.'

'The only way you can get out of here, child, is when whoever signed you in comes back for you and signs you out.'

'Why haven't they come back?'

'I think they've forgotten you exist.'

And she walked away from me.

I think of that conversation as I place another seed into the gnarled old hands of Johnny Joe. I watch his fingers curl over the little source of life before he drops it on the dry earth. I spread the clay over the seed with my fingers and dip them into the pot for another one. We repeat this process six hundred and sixty-five times before I start to cry.

He looks up at me, the whites of his eyes yellow. He grabs my hand and raises it to his lips. I think he's going to bite my fingers off. But no, he gently kisses the tips of them.

'No crying in here, child. The time for crying is done. The devil is all around us. Crying won't keep him away. He is in your very soul. Now back to work.'

I hand him the final seed.

'Six hundred and sixty-six.'

DAY FIVE

CHAPTER 62

The morning awoke with a sepia sky, the clouds low and watery. The storm died with the night but it left a trail of destruction in its wake.

Lottie was in the station before any of the others. No sign of McMahon, either. She flicked through the news on her phone app.

Farming land in the midlands had flooded; rivers had burst their banks and overflowed. There was a special report from Ragmullin. Cathal Moroney, with his flashy white teeth. The lower end of the town was now sinking in the waters of the river. The greyhound stadium was a mini lake; all racing cancelled for the foreseeable future. One picture showed mucky brown water streaming from the front of Carey's electrical shop; a plastic-covered washing machine bobbing just inside the door. The council had a *Boil Water* notice in place as Lough Cullion, the drinking water supply, had been contaminated with run-off from surrounding farms.

She wondered what state Mick O'Dowd's farm was in this morning. And where had he disappeared to? Could he have killed Emma? Was she related to him?

She lifted the phone and called Jane Dore to ask about Emma's post-mortem.

'Later today, I hope. Marian Russell's body is here also. She succumbed to septicemia as a result of her wounds. I'll send over the prelims when I have them completed.'

Lottie hung up. Marian's death would be officially classed as murder. Three victims from one family. Was it the same murderer?

Could there be more than one psycho at work around the town? She hoped not.

Kirby shuffled in, his coat hanging over his arm, and grunted, 'Good morning, boss. Some mess out there after the storm.'

'Some mess in here too,' Lottie said. 'Get everyone into the incident room as soon as they come in. We need to get a handle on this.'

'Handle on what?'

Lottie looked up. Detective Inspector David McMahon stood in the doorway, his mop of dark hair glistening with dampness.

'Sir,' she said, picking up a file and making a hasty exit. Why had she called him sir? He was the same rank as her. Get it together, Lottie, she scolded.

At the incident boards, she moved Emma Russell's photo to the victims' side, joining her mother and grandmother. She folded one hand around her waist, then rested her elbow on her wrist and contemplated the pictures. The burned man now had a name. Jerome Quinn.

'He's the odd one out,' she said aloud.

'Maybe he's the link that holds it all together.'

She hadn't heard McMahon enter the room. Now he stood beside her, tall and arrogant. The prick.

'What evidence do you have to support your theory?' she asked.

'I could ask you the same question,' he said.

Boyd, Kirby and Lynch joined them and sat down with a few other tired-looking detectives. This should be interesting, Lottie thought, as McMahon turned in unison with her to face the troops.

'Will you introduce yourself?' she asked.

Buttoning the jacket of his suit over a slim-fitting shirt, he took a step forward, leaving Lottie in his shadow.

'Detective Inspector David McMahon. And don't call me Big Mac or anything like that. I'll answer to sir or David.' He smiled, reminding Lottie of Cathal Moroney's white veneer grin. He was still speaking as she uncrossed her arms and held them straight by her sides. Trying to appear as tall as him because she knew she would fail in making herself look as important.

'I'm with the Garda National Drugs Unit. As your investigations into the murder of Tessa Ball have uncovered a substantial quantity of drugs, this investigation now falls under my remit.'

'Hey, hold on a minute!' Lottie jerked alive and grabbed his sleeve, quickly dropping her hand when he looked down his nose at her. 'Sorry. But we retain the right to investigate alongside you. I believe there's more to this than just a drug crime.'

McMahon turned slowly and pointed a finger at the picture of the burned man.

'Jerome Quinn,' he said. 'Second in command to his half-brother Henry "Hammer" Quinn. Do you all appreciate who we are dealing with now?'

A murmur greeted his question. He continued. 'We suspected he had a long-time girlfriend, but he's unmarried. Plenty of bimbos sniffing around him.'

'Bimbos! Ah, come on now, you know you can't speak like that,' Lottie said.

'You know what I mean. Hangers-on, wanting a bit of the action. Free swag and all that.'

Lottie scowled.

McMahon said, 'Jerome disappeared over fifteen months ago and went to ground.'

'Underground in Ragmullin?' Boyd said.

'There's a criminal element operating out of this town. Someone got greedy. The Russell family was slap bang in the middle of it.'

'Their murders might have absolutely nothing to do with the drugs,' Lottie said when none of her team were forthcoming.

McMahon unbuttoned his jacket, shoved his hands into his trouser pockets and strutted around the perimeter of the room. 'Marian's tongue was cut out. Her daughter was in a relationship with small-time crook Lorcan Brady. Was Marian about to squeal? Did someone try to stop her?'

'Hold on a minute there.' Boyd was up and out of his chair. 'We only have it on hearsay that Emma Russell was involved with Lorcan Brady.'

'Didn't you find cash hidden in her room, Inspector?' McMahon said, without looking at Boyd. 'Didn't you find a hoodie she may have been wearing?'

'That's true, but—' Lottie began.

'Wasn't her body found a few miles down the road from where Brady and Quinn were assaulted and burned?'

'Yes, but—'

'Didn't you find unidentified plants hidden at the Russell home?'

Lottie nodded.

'I rest my case.'

'Bollocks,' Kirby said, and jammed his e-cig into his mouth.

Lottie closed her eyes, waited for an arrogant tirade. Deathly silence reigned as she counted. She reached nineteen before McMahon spoke.

'Have you a more reasonable hypothesis to offer, Detective Kirby?'

When Lottie opened her eyes, McMahon's suit jacket was once again buttoned up and he was standing at the opposite end of the incident boards.

'If I was to go along with your scenario,' she said, 'which I'm not ready to, tell me why Tessa Ball was killed.'

'Wrong place, wrong time,' he offered.

'Bullshit.' Boyd.

'You have the floor,' McMahon said, and folded his arms. Lottie didn't dare turn her head, but she could imagine he had a sneer plastered over his closely shaven face.

'Right,' Boyd said, and mimicked McMahon's earlier tour of the room. 'Marian Russell rang her mother Tessa at 21.07 on the night of Tessa's murder. We believe Emma left to go to Natasha's at 18.30 and arrived home sometime after 22.30. We can assume that Marian let someone she knew into her house, as there was no sign of forced entry. Whoever it was wanted Tessa there. That was the reason for the phone call. We could assume the person was Arthur Russell, as he has no alibi from 19.30 on that evening – a domestic situation that got out of hand.'

'I will indulge this line of thought for the moment,' McMahon said. 'Tessa was attacked and murdered. Marian was taken away, in her own car, to Lorcan Brady's house. There she was tortured and mutilated. The next day she was pushed out of the car at the hospital. It's been confirmed that was the car found burned out at Lough Cullion the same morning that Lorcan Brady and Jerome Quinn were tortured and burned in a cottage just outside Ragmullin.'

'That cottage was once owned by Tessa Ball,' Lottie said. Time to get her investigation back in her own hands.

'And a criminal was renting it.'

'She signed it over to Mick O'Dowd.'

'The farmer on whose property her granddaughter was found murdered. He rented the cottage to Quinn, therefore he may also be involved in the drugs ring.'

Lottie couldn't dispute his argument. Didn't mean she had to buy into it. 'We're still looking for O'Dowd. When we find him, we'll get some answers.'

'Depending on whether he's still alive or not.'

'Of course he's alive.'

'Appears to me you haven't been successful in keeping many suspects, or witnesses for that matter, alive so far. Where do you think this O'Dowd character could be? His Land Rover is still at the farm, I believe.'

'A quad bike is missing,' Lottie said.

'Not an ideal getaway vehicle, is it?'

'He might've had—'

'Enough!'

Superintendent Corrigan moved to the front of the room. Lottie hadn't noticed him arriving.

He shook hands with McMahon and clapped him on the back. 'Good to have you in our neck of the woods.'

The two-faced bastard. Lottie planted a smile on her face, careful not to catch Boyd's eye.

'Great to be here, Superintendent. I'll have this solved in a matter of hours. I'm heading to speak with Lorcan Brady once I wrap up this meeting.'

'Brady can't speak…' Lottie stopped. Had she been kept out of that loop also?

'I was informed earlier that he's ready to have a wee chat with me,' McMahon said.

'I think I should be the one to—'

'Great stuff,' said Superintendent Corrigan, cutting her short. 'Off you go, David, and I'll have a wee chat with my team.'

Lottie noticed the realisation dawning on McMahon. He'd been outsmarted at his own game. She couldn't help a grin curling at the corner of her mouth as she watched the Dublin DI shake Corrigan's hand and leave the room.

'Shut the feckin' door,' Corrigan instructed once McMahon had left.

'With pleasure,' Kirby said, dragging himself out of his chair.

'Now, I want a full update from the senior investigating officer. Inspector Parker, that's you, in case you had been misled by that Dublin hotshot in a suit. You have ten minutes to consult with your team. Then I want you in my office. With answers. Understood?'

'Yes, sir.'

CHAPTER 63

The relief was palpable once the two men had left. Lottie thought the four walls also breathed a welcome sigh. The air seemed to lift. If only momentarily.

'I don't want this going on a day longer than necessary. I want Arthur Russell and Mick O'Dowd found. What are you doing about it?'

Lynch sat up straight. 'Every officer in the district is mobilised and there's a manhunt throughout the state for them. Checkpoints are operational since Emma's body was found. Airports and ports have been notified. Everyone is watching for them.'

'So what have we got in the line of answers to our overall investigation?'

'I've just received a transcript of the information that was salvaged from Marian Russell's laptop hard drive,' Lynch said. 'I'll give you a summary as soon as I get a chance to examine it.'

'Good. Kirby, you look like the dog that got the bone. What's your news?'

Kirby grinned, and Lottie had to smile back, even though she wanted to tell him to get a haircut.

'The bones found at the cottage yesterday...'

'Brady's missing fingers?'

'Yes, boss.'

'The gun we found in Tessa's apartment,' Lottie said, moving on swiftly. 'Any information from ballistics?'

Kirby shifted in his chair, from one buttock to the other.

'Out with it,' Lottie said.

'You might not like this.'

'Let me be the judge of that.' Her phone vibrated in her jeans pocket. Ignoring it, she braced herself for whatever it was Kirby thought she wasn't going to like.

'The revolver is a Webley and Scott. Used by the Garda Special Branch back in the seventies.'

'The Special Branch?' Lottie said. 'How did it end up in Tessa Ball's possession?'

'I've no idea,' Kirby said. 'But the weird thing is…'

'Go on.'

Kirby took a deep breath and blurted out, 'Ballistics show it's a match with the bullet from an old suicide.'

Lottie's next question died on her lips. She knew where this was leading. She formed a new question.

'You mean to tell me that the gun we found in a murder victim's home the other day is the same gun that my father used to kill himself forty years ago?'

Kirby was biting his lip, nodding his bushy head of hair.

Boyd said, 'That's… that's the most far-fetched thing I've heard in… in ages.'

Lottie walked around the room, mulling over the significance of this. Had Tessa known her father? How did she come to have the gun? In all the reports she'd read so far in her own private investigations, it was stated that Peter Fitzpatrick had stolen the gun from a secure cabinet in the garda station. She banged her fists against her forehead. Nowhere had she read what had happened to the gun afterwards. Nowhere had she seen any connection to Tessa Ball. But had she? Think, Lottie, she told herself. Think. Then it came to her. Her father's notebook. The one with the name of the solicitors scrawled across the centre of a page.

'Oh my God,' she said.

'What?' Boyd said.

'Remember the notebook I showed you? It had "Belfield and Ball" written in my father's handwriting. Someone please tell me what is going on.'

'Just a minute,' Boyd said. 'No point in jumping to conclusions. They were probably the only firm of solicitors in Ragmullin in the seventies. Your father was a garda sergeant. He would've been dealing with the courts on a weekly basis, so it's not unusual that he had the name written down.'

'But I don't understand why Tessa had the gun.'

'It's probably nothing to do with our current investigation,' Lynch said. 'Just an odd coincidence.'

'I don't like coincidences,' Lottie snapped. 'Odd or otherwise.'

'Then there are the files that were stolen from Belfield and Ball. Files that Tessa had been dealing with,' Kirby said, scratching his head with the end of his e-cigarette.

'I agree this may have nothing to do with the murders,' Lottie said, 'but I'll talk with Kitty Belfield myself and maybe have a chat with that old journalist, Buzz Flynn. He might remember something from his newspaper days. You know him, Kirby; will you tell him I'll be calling?'

Kirby nodded.

'Do you think I should inform Bernie and Natasha Kelly about Emma's murder?' Lynch asked.

'I forgot about them. Boyd and I will call later. I'm sure they know already, but no harm in a formal visit to wrap things up with them.' Lottie paused then added, 'I wonder what Lorcan Brady has to say for himself about it all.'

'I'm sure our Dublin friend will tell us when he returns,' Boyd said.

'One other thing,' Kirby said, flicking through McGlynn's report. 'Brady's house.'

Lottie turned to look at him. 'The blood in the kitchen is that of Marian Russell?'

'Confirmed. But this has to do with the bags of rubbish out the back. They proved to hold vital evidence.'

'Bloody clothes?'

'Yes. They've been sent for DNA analysis.'

'Let me know as soon as you know.'

'That's not all…' Kirby hesitated. 'In amongst the rubbish they also found Marian's tongue.'

CHAPTER 64

In her office, Lottie tried to keep the churning in her stomach to a minimum.

'Will I get coffees?' Boyd offered.

'No, I think I might puke. The bastards. Why torture her? Why not just kill her and be done with it? Something is not adding up here, Boyd.'

'Talking of adding up, what's with that ledger you took from O'Dowd's house?'

Lottie pulled on protective gloves, laid a sheet of plastic on her desk and retrieved the ledger from the evidence bag. From her drawer she took the copies of the letters they'd found in Tessa's apartment. Laying them beside the ledger, she pointed to the handwriting.

'Notice anything?'

Boyd sat on the edge of the desk and leaned over her shoulder, his voice close to her ear. 'The writing looks similar.'

'Not similar. It's the same.' She turned to look up into his eyes, their hazel flecks dancing. 'Is this the missing link?'

'Perhaps another link, but I don't think we have the full chain yet.'

Lottie picked up the letter from the top of the pile. No signature. No date. She read it aloud:

> *My dearest love,*
> *I know we cannot be together, but I want you to know that I*
> *think of you every day. Others have decided that we are to be*

apart. Not me. I want you to believe that. If I had my way, we
would be together. You deserve to be loved. I would give you
mountains of it. I want to. But that is not to be, unfortunately.
I will write again as soon as I can.
Please believe that I really do love you.
Love you always.

'That's it,' she said. 'The rest of the letters are in a similar vein.'

Boyd picked up another. 'So if we get the handwriting analysed, and allowing for passage of time, are we going to be able to categorically say that Mick O'Dowd wrote these letters?'

'I think so.' Lottie put them back in the folder. She closed the ledger and replaced it in the evidence bag. 'But they read kind of… weird, as Kirby would say. Don't you think?'

'We have no clue as to what this separation was. Her husband might still have been alive at the time.'

'He died early in the marriage, leaving Tessa free. Something isn't right with them. I can't fathom it.'

'We know there's a connection between Tessa and O'Dowd. She sold or gave him the cottage, for Christ's sake.'

'She was a solicitor. Maybe she was a go-between for O'Dowd and someone else.'

'But she kept the letters. Never sent them on.'

'Yeah.' Lottie wiped a hand over her throbbing head. 'And that gun… I'm going to have a chat with Buzz Flynn. See if he can enlighten me about anything my father might've been involved with.'

'You're right. Newspaper hounds know even more than us guards. And I'll check to see if there's been any sighting of our two missing men.'

'Do. One of them must be a murderer.'

'Or both?'

'We also need to find out what McMahon gets from Brady. Better still, we could go talk to Brady ourselves.'

As she grabbed her jacket, her phone vibrated. She saw a red circle indicating that she had an earlier voice message. She should ring Annabelle. She answered the call.

'Hi, Jane. Any news on Emma's PM?'

'Can you take a quick trip over here? There's something you need to know.'

'I was just on my way to interview someone, but I'll call to you first if you think it's important.'

'It is.'

'I should be there in half an hour.'

CHAPTER 65

The morning had lapsed back into its familiar greyness. Rain was spitting against the windscreen as Lottie drove along the motorway, chasing the clouds.

The Dead House seemed colder than usual, which Lottie thought heightened its odour, and she couldn't help the feeling of unease scratching behind her eyes. Two bodies were laid out on the autopsy tables. Covered. Good, she thought, glad she hadn't to look at the terrified, dead eyes of young Emma.

'Come into my office. I need to speak to you in private,' Jane said. There was no one else around and she hadn't yet robed up. Why the delay? Lottie wondered.

She ushered Lottie into the cramped office. Lottie pulled off her jacket and hung it on the back of a chair. Jane sat down facing her, clutching her hands together like they might escape their wrists if she let go. Her face, usually like a fine porcelain teacup, now looked like a cracked ceramic mug.

'Coffee?' she offered.

Lottie shook her head. 'I'm grand, thanks. You look awful. Has something happened?'

'There was a break-in here,' Jane said, her voice just above a whisper. 'Last night.'

'That's terrible,' Lottie said, thinking of all the evidence that could potentially be interfered with. 'Tell me.'

'The alarm was disabled and all the CCTV cameras were either smashed or covered. I was first in at seven thirty this morning...'

'Was anything taken? Evidence damaged or tampered with?'

'No evidence or bodies were interfered with that we could determine. But it might throw a shadow over chain of custody and verification of samples. No equipment was damaged, except for the CCTV, of course. I called Tullamore gardaí and they were excellent.'

'All logged and reported?'

'Yes.'

'So why the break-in?'

Jane hauled a large leather bag from beneath her desk. With trembling hands she extracted a bulky green folder. 'I brought this home with me last night. What if they were after it?'

Lottie frowned. 'What is it?'

'Your father's post-mortem file and relevant inquest documents.'

Lottie felt her mouth hanging open. She blinked and leaned forward, grabbed Jane's hand. 'You got it? After all this time? Why do you think someone was after it?'

Shoving the file across the desk, Jane said, 'I made a copy. I wanted to replace it without anyone knowing I had it. Of course it must have flagged on a computer system somewhere.'

'So this is a copy?'

'No, this is the original. I made the copy yesterday but I hadn't time to return the original, so I took it home with me to have a read-through. And maybe somewhere in the back of my mind I thought it was safer with me.' She buckled up her bag and laid her hands on top of it. 'The copy was here, on my desk. It's the only thing missing.'

'Oh God. I'm so sorry about all this.'

'It's not your fault. I went through the correct channels to get the file. I had no reason to suspect it might send a red flag to someone.

But Lottie, this may mean you were right to suspect that your father's death wasn't all it seemed.'

'I know. And I apologise for putting you in an awkward position. Did you tell the investigating guards?'

'I don't know why, but I said nothing. Anyway, I still had the original.'

Lottie put a protective hand on top of the file. At last she might get some answers. Or had she opened a Pandora's box? 'You said you read it last night.'

'I did.'

'Anything strike you as odd about his death?'

'I think your father *did* kill himself.'

Lottie slumped back in the chair. Unwanted tears stabbed the corners of her eyes. She brushed them away angrily.

Jane continued. 'But I think he may have done it under duress. I studied the PM photographs and found evidence of excess pressure on his thorax. There were strange indents across his chest too. I think he may have been tied to a chair. I believe someone forced him to pull that trigger. Then they untied the ropes.'

Lottie sucked in her bottom lip, desperately trying not to cry. She had been right all along. All these years, struggling with the idea that her father hadn't loved her enough to want to live.

'Thanks, Jane,' she whispered. 'Thank you so much.'

She felt the pressure of Jane's hand on hers.

'Lottie, you need to drop it now. Don't keep after it. You won't find answers. It will destroy you.'

'But don't you see? My father was murdered. I have to find out why, and then I have to bring the perpetrator to justice.' She wondered once again why Tessa Ball had had in her possession the gun that had killed her father.

'Whoever it was, they're probably dead by now,' the pathologist said.

'Someone knows, Jane. Someone, somewhere knows. Why else were they prepared to steal that file?'

CHAPTER 66

Arriving back in Ragmullin, Lottie drove through the flooded streets and parked outside Willie 'The Buzz' Flynn's apartment.

Buzz brought her into a cluttered living room. A two-bar electric heater blazed in the fireplace and a gas heater flamed out a noxious heat in the centre of the room. She searched for somewhere to leave her jacket, but there didn't seem to be anywhere free to put it. The room was packed to the ceiling with memorabilia relating to the late singer Joe Dolan. The old man, one hand gripping a Zimmer frame, pointed out each prized possession, documenting its significance.

'I've a few videos here too, of Joe singing. I'll put one on for you.' Buzz pulled a cassette from a bookcase.

Lottie placed her hand on his arm. 'Not now, if you don't mind. I'm in a bit of a hurry. I'd like to ask you a few questions. About your time working with the *Midland Tribune*.'

He croaked a laugh. 'I'm retired out of there donkey's years. What could a pretty young lady like yourself want to know about the old days?'

'I'm not altogether sure, to be honest.'

'Start at the beginning.' He lowered his thin body into an armchair and sat on top of a bundle of newspapers.

Looking around, Lottie spied a stool with a frayed leather seat. She pulled it over and sat down gingerly, hoping the bandy legs wouldn't give way under her weight.

'Have you heard about Tessa Ball's murder?' she asked.

'Nothing goes on in this town without Buzz knowing.' He tapped his nose with a thin finger, the skin almost transparent.

'Tell me about her.'

'Didn't know her at all, at all. Not recently anyway. She used to be a solicitor. At a time when there weren't many women in the profession. Not like nowadays. Tough-nosed biddy she was.'

'Why do you say that?'

'She had a reputation.'

'Reputation? Not a good one?'

'Depends on what you mean by good.' He leaned into the chair, newspapers rustling as he made room for himself. 'From what I can remember, Tessa Ball was good at winning cases in the district court. She mainly dealt with what you'd now call family law. Though there was no such title then.'

'What sort of cases?'

'Father against son, brother against brother – land stuff. Husbands beating their wives – abuse stuff. That kind of thing. It was a long time ago. My memory is not what it used to be.'

'You're doing fine,' Lottie encouraged him. 'Is there any case in particular that you can recall?'

He closed his eyes. She thought he had nodded off when he started to speak. 'Not a case. No. A bit of a scandal, you could say. She sorted it out, though. Oh yes, Tessa was the go-to woman to get things sorted.'

'What scandal? Would I find it listed in the newspaper's archives?'

'No, you won't, because it was never reported. All hush-hush, covered up. Ha! But every dog in the street knew about it.'

'Can you remember it?' Lottie wondered what she was doing here. Surely this old man's unreliable recollections had nothing to do with her investigation. She wanted answers to things she didn't even know the questions to.

'Let me think,' he said, knotting his fingers together. 'It was the time of the IRA bombings in Dublin. You can look it up on the goggle thing you use nowadays. Seventy-two or three, I think. It was all over the press. God, that was a time when the Special Branch were sprouting up everywhere like wild ivy. Shocking times. Shocking.'

'I was only a child then,' Lottie said. 'What was this thing that Tessa was involved in?'

'There was a local woman… Carrie… I can't remember the surname. I remember the name Carrie, because wasn't there a horror film of the same name?'

'Yes.'

'Well, this Carrie was a bit of a horror show herself. A right madam. Into drugs and drink in a fierce way. Must've been from Woodstock or somewhere that she got her barmy ideas. A hippy. That's what she was. Wild clothes, every colour under the sun; hair all matted… What do you call it? Dreadlocks? Aye, that's it.'

'What happened to her?'

'Don't know.'

'So, Mr Flynn, what's your point?'

'Buzz. Call me Buzz. It's the only name I answer to nowadays.'

'You were telling me about this Carrie woman,' Lottie prompted.

'I know what I was telling you. Not senile yet.'

'I'm sorry. Go ahead.'

'She slept around. Anyone that'd give her a few bob or a drop of whiskey was welcomed. You know what I mean?'

'I think I do.'

'Got herself caught with buns in the oven a fair few times.' He tapped his nose again.

'She had more than one pregnancy?' Where was this going?

'There was a rumour doing the rounds that young Mick O'Dowd and even a couple of the guards up in the station were regular visitors to her.'

Lottie felt her stomach lurch, then somersault. Shit, this wasn't what she'd been expecting. 'Really? Did you hear any names?'

'No. All part of the hush-hush,' he said. 'Here's the thing. The rumour mill sizzled with the news that Carrie had a child, but there was no sign of it. One day she was pregnant, and the next she wasn't. Don't know what went on there, now do I? A few months later, wasn't your woman going around with another bun in the oven. No contraceptive pill available in them days, was there? Until the women took the train to Belfast protesting about its availability in the North…'

'Go on,' Lottie said.

'The story went that Tessa Ball took the child and reared it as her own. I don't know if that was fact or fiction. And this is the best bit so far. It must only have been two years later and your woman was pregnant again. Like a rabbit, she was. Sorry. I didn't mean to be so vulgar.'

'Back up a minute. You think Tessa took a child away from this woman?'

'Rumour, that's all. Will I go on?'

'Yes, do.' Some memory, for an old man, Lottie thought. Or perhaps he was making it up, now that he had an audience.

'Twins she had that time. And this is the really interesting thing. The two mites were taken from her and placed with a foster mother, and Carrie was shunted into St Declan's. About a year, maybe two years later, she was back out. Tessa Ball was involved. Got her released, so the story goes. And Carrie had her twins back.'

'So what happened then?'

'Tried to burn the bloody house down, she did. The mad witch.'

'Jesus. Did the children die?' Lottie was now convinced this was the same Carrie that Kirby had mentioned.

'I don't rightly know what happened to them, though I heard one of them was fostered.'

'And Carrie, did *she* die?'

'No, she didn't. Sure you can't kill a bad thing. Great saying that. Back into the asylum she went. Come to think of it now, one of the children was placed there with her until they could find a home for it.'

'Is there any way I can get verification for any of this? St Declan's records?'

'That monstrosity closed down years ago. Run by the Health Board then. What's that called now?'

'The Health Services Executive.'

'Fancy name for the same bloody thing. You should try them.'

'So you think Tessa Ball was complicit in everything to do with Carrie and her children?'

'That was the talk at the time. And sure, then all the files were stolen out of the solicitor's office. Any evidence of her supposed involvement gone.'

'I must say, Buzz, you have a great memory, to recall all this after so long.'

'Told you I'm not senile yet. But it's just with Tessa's murder the other day, and talking to you now, it all came back to me. Different times now. That carry-on wouldn't happen today, sure it wouldn't.'

Lottie thought for a moment. Maybe the murders, though linked to criminal and drug activity, were in fact intrinsically rooted in the past. Had Rose been right with her offhand remark about Tessa's past come back to haunt her? Tessa was dead; her daughter and grand-daughter were dead. Who else was left to be haunted by that past?

She stood up, her legs like jelly. 'Thank you, Buzz. You've been very helpful. I'll see myself out.'

'Just me and Joe here now.' He dragged his old body out of the armchair and put a cassette into the VHS recorder. 'I go to the day-care centre on Thursdays; other than that, I'm here all the time. Call and visit. I'll boil the kettle for you next time.'

As Lottie stepped outside and the clouds gave way to another downpour, her phone vibrated in her pocket.

Shit. Moroney.

CHAPTER 67

The Joyce Hotel had commanded the centre of Ragmullin for over one hundred and fifty years. Having undergone many facelifts and name changes, it was currently named after the Irish novelist who it was said had once stayed a night in the establishment. As Lottie entered the lounge bar, it took a few seconds for her eyes to adjust to the dark interior.

'Over here, Inspector.'

She squinted and turned on her heel. Cathal Moroney sat nestled in a red velour armchair nursing a pint of Guinness. A fake coal fire burned gas up a blocked-off chimney.

'Thanks for agreeing to meet me. Will you have a drink?' He wiped froth from his upper lip.

'A cup of tea would be nice.'

As he beckoned to the barman, Lottie sat opposite the reporter, wishing she had asked for a double vodka. But she needed her wits about her where Moroney was concerned. She pulled off her jacket, folded it into a ball and squashed it between the iron legs of the small round table.

'You intrigue me, Inspector.'

'I can't say the feeling is mutual.' She shifted on the chair, dipping her head slightly to avoid his scrutiny.

'Can we be friends?' He held out a hand.

'Not on your life.' She folded her arms. This was going to be painful. The barman arrived with a pot of tea, and without waiting for it to brew, Lottie poured the weak liquid into a cup. At least it might warm up her hands. 'What do you want to speak to me about?'

'No time for chit-chat, then?'

'Come on, Moroney, you know how busy I am. Out with it.'

He sipped his pint. Slowly. Lottie felt her patience tip over. She stood up.

'I'm leaving.'

'I think you'll want to sit down,' he said, slapping his glass onto the table. 'It's about the drug link to these murders you're investigating. And possibly your private investigation into your father's death.'

Lottie stopped, bent halfway under the table retrieving her jacket. Raising her head, she glared at the reporter. If he didn't try so hard, she might even go so far as admitting he could be handsome. She supposed he flossed his teeth and dyed his hair. Even a little Botox on the forehead to help his television appearance. For all that, his green eyes were bloodshot, probably from drinking whiskey alone in a one-bedroom flat at night, and his belly strained against his shirt buttons.

She sat back down. 'Go on.'

'Nothing for nothing,' he said, curling his lip in a knowing smirk. 'Thought as much.'

'I want the inside track on these drug-related deaths.'

'What are you on about?' She wasn't giving him anything.

'I believe there's an organised-crime element involved in the Ball and Russell murders. I've been working on a story for years and I think this is the apex of it. I want in.'

'You're delusional.' Lottie poured more tea, well brewed now.

A waiter arrived with a plate of food on a tray. 'Mr Moroney, you ordered chicken, mash, veg and gravy. That right?'

'Good lad. Put it right there.' Moroney made room on the table for the plate of food. 'Hungry, Inspector? Can I order anything for you?'

'No thank you,' Lottie said. Her stomach growled in protest.

She watched Moroney dig a fork into the chicken, stuff it into his mouth and chomp with his white veneers. She realised she had never met him outside of his confrontational reporting work. But he might have information to help her, so she'd have to put up with his disgusting eating, for a few minutes at least.

'My father,' she said. 'What makes you think I've been looking into his death?'

He tapped the side of his nose with his fork, leaving a streak of gravy behind.

'It's my business to know these things. So what's in it for me?'

Sipping the cup of tea, Lottie gripped the handle tightly. She had to find out what he had, if anything. She made her decision.

'If you tell me what you know, I'll *try* to give you first call on whatever we discover with regard to the murder investigations. Before any other media outlet is informed. I can't promise anything, but I'll do my best.'

'Not good enough.'

'Goodbye, Mr Moroney.' She clattered her cup to the saucer and made to get up again.

'No… sit down.' Moroney flapped the hand holding the knife. Reluctantly Lottie resumed her seat. Chewing, he said, 'My father started out as a reporter on the local *Tribune*. Worked his fingers to the bone with black ink from the presses. Ended up owning the damn thing. Luckily, he didn't live to see his life's work taken over by a digital corporation.'

'And what has that got to do with—'

'My father was a meticulous reporter. Never lost the skill, even when he was managing a shitload of trouble at the paper. Kept files on everything and anything.'

'And it's all digitised now?'

'Mostly, but not what I'm referring to.'

'I don't follow you, Mr Moroney.'

'Cathal, please. Can I call you Lottie?'

'No way, *Mister* Moroney.'

'Jaysus, but you're very contrary.' He pulled his drink towards him and drained it to the dregs. Signalled the barman for another, sat back and folded his arms. He'd left the knife and fork resting on either side of the plate. Boyd would lose it if he saw that, Lottie thought, and smiled.

'Nice smile,' he said.

She dropped it and frowned.

'Now where was I?' he said.

'Your father and his files.'

'When I was growing up, he was always talking about this one story he had uncovered but couldn't print. As a young boy I remember him being very angry about it. My mother used to shush him to stop him talking about it in front of me. He smoked a pipe and he would be sucking and pulling frantically on it, slamming papers around the desk he had built in the corner of the living room. Once I overhead him talking about two children. His words chilled me.'

'What did he say?' Lottie wasn't sure there was any merit in listening to Moroney and his childhood recollections, but something was telling her to give him another few minutes. Especially as what he'd said so far resonated with what Buzz had told her.

'He said, "Those little children didn't deserve what happened to them, and neither did Sergeant Fitzpatrick." I heard him say those words many times.'

Lottie moved to the edge of her chair, hands gripping the armrests. 'What children? Who were they?'

'I didn't know then, but I do now.'

'And they had something to do with my father?'

'He mentioned them in the same sentence.'

'How can you recall that? Surely you were just a child yourself?'

'I knew you'd ask. That's why you need to see the file I found among my father's things. He ended up with dementia; died five years ago. A heart attack took him in the end. But even in his ramblings, these children were always mentioned in some context. And he was never allowed to print the story.'

'How do you know?'

'Because I have his original report in my possession. Attached to it is a formal letter from the garda commissioner threatening to close down the newspaper if the story saw the light of day.'

'Jesus!' Lottie sat back in her chair and ran a hand through her hair. 'Was the story to do with these children or my father's suicide?'

'Both.'

'Do you realise what you have in your possession, Mr Moroney?'

'I do. And I think you suspect your father didn't kill himself. At least not voluntarily.'

The barman arrived with Moroney's drink and cleared away the plate and cutlery.

'What do you mean?' Lottie said, when he'd gone.

'Do we have a deal?' Moroney said.

She sat still, eyeing the reporter as he paused with his pint halfway to his lips. Could she really risk her job by going behind Superintendent Corrigan's back? Perhaps she could feed Moroney inconsequential information. Something that was ready to be released anyway.

'And I don't want any shite from you,' he said, as if he had read her mind.

'Deal.' She could get fired for this, but she had spent all her life trying to figure out why her father had killed himself, and the last four months actively pursuing it, getting nowhere. And today everything seemed to be flowing towards her like molten lava. 'When can I see the file? Do you have it with you?'

'You may think I'm stupid, but don't underestimate me. I've spent years on this drug story; what can you give me on the murders?'

Thinking frantically, Lottie wondered how much information she could realistically release to a television reporter without the leak being attributed to her. Not much. She'd have to bluff Moroney.

'I'll pull together what I have and prepare a document for you,' she said.

He took a notebook and pen from his breast pocket. Scribbled, then tore out a page. 'This is my home address. Call to me tomorrow night. Say around eight. That will give me enough time to make a copy of my father's file. If you don't arrive with solid information, something concrete I can use, our deal is off. Is that clear?'

'Clear,' Lottie said, wishing she had Boyd with her to bestow reassurance that she was doing the right thing.

Somehow she knew what he would say: 'Career suicide.'

CHAPTER 68

Lottie caught up with Boyd at the station and they drove to inform Bernie and Natasha Kelly what had befallen Emma Russell; even though they were not family, she felt a duty to them. She had decided it was best Boyd knew nothing of her conversation with Moroney. What he didn't know wouldn't worry him, as her mother was apt to quote.

The front door was open, rain sweeping in on the hall carpet. The car in the drive had the boot and four doors open.

'What the…?' Boyd said.

Lottie shoved by him and entered the house.

'What's going on, Bernie?' She put out a hand to stall the woman's progress towards the door with an armful of clothes.

'I'm getting out of this hole of a town, that's what I'm doing.'

'Why?'

Bernie laughed. 'Why! Did you come down in that last shower out there or what? My daughter's best friend and family were murdered and you ask me why. We're getting out before we're next.'

'Let's put these down for a moment.' Lottie took the clothes from Bernie and dropped them on the couch. It was already covered with boxes and crates. She noticed that all the ornaments had been removed from the room. She heard crockery and cutlery rattling in the kitchen. Glanced in. Natasha was methodically packing kitchen utensils into a plastic crate. One by one, trance-like. Turning back, she saw that Bernie was seated on an armchair with Boyd perched on the arm beside her.

'I'm sorry about Emma,' Lottie began, standing with her back to the empty grate. 'Every officer in the division is working flat out to find who murdered her.'

'So I've been told.'

'What do you mean?'

'You're not the first to call today. Had a visit from a prick of a detective inspector.'

If she wasn't so angry, Lottie would have laughed. Bernie had McMahon well summed up.

'I'm sorry, but DI McMahon neglected to inform us that he was calling to you.'

'He seemed to be on something of a one-man mission.' Bernie appeared to have calmed a little.

Lottie ploughed on. 'How long have you lived here?'

'Why do you want to know that?'

'We went through this before, but I really need to find out how well you knew the Russell family. The comings and goings of people to their house. Any unusual cars or individuals you can recall. There are only these two houses on this part of the road. It's very isolated, so I'm sure you would've been aware of any odd characters hanging around.'

'You don't suspect Arthur any more, then?'

'Everyone is a suspect until we can arrest the culprit.'

'Even me and Natasha?'

'I'm only asking if you've seen—'

'I know what you're asking. And no. I didn't notice anything. Don't you think I would have told you if I had?'

'Have you seen Arthur recently?'

'No.'

'Can I have a word with Natasha? Alone?'

'No. She's not yet eighteen and I'm entitled to be with her. What do you want to ask her?'

Ignoring the question, Lottie said, 'Where are you going to move to, Bernie? Do you have family anywhere?'

'Family? Huh. Natasha is the only family I need. I have to protect her. After all that's happened this last week, the girl is inconsolable. We have to get out of here. Don't you understand that? Are you a mother?'

'I am,' Lottie said. Not a very good one, she thought, recalling her meltdown last night.

'Surely then you can understand how I have to shield my daughter from all this mayhem?'

'I understand. But I don't think running away from it is going to erase the memories. Natasha will carry the scars no matter where she is. Stay; get her help. See a doctor yourself, even. You're too distraught to drive anywhere.'

Bernie sighed and seemed to relax, then jumped out of the chair, unbalancing Boyd, who almost hit the floor. She lunged for the bundle of clothes Lottie had deposited on the couch before dropping them again.

'I honestly don't know what the right thing to do is,' she cried, crumpling to her knees.

Natasha rushed from the kitchen and stared, jaw clenched, a vein throbbing in her neck. 'What have you done to upset her now?'

Lottie winced at the tone of the teenager's words. Not for the first time, she wondered how Emma had really got on with Natasha. Too late to ask her now. She could ask Natasha, but maybe now was not the right time.

'I think you should stay here until all this is resolved,' Boyd said in his soft, calm voice. He put a hand on Bernie's shoulder. Lottie was surprised to see the woman reach up and caress Boyd's long fingers. Before she could put what she was seeing into words, Natasha leapt forward and pushed him away.

'Don't you dare touch my mother! Leave us alone.' She wrapped her arms around Bernie.

'I think you should go,' Bernie said. 'Maybe we will stay for a few more days.' She allowed Natasha to lead her into the kitchen.

As the door closed, Lottie exchanged a look with Boyd.

'Before I get waylaid again,' she said, 'let's go to the hospital to check if Mr Brady has anything to say for himself.'

They left the Kelly women to each other.

CHAPTER 69

They showed their IDs to the guard outside the hospital ward and signed in.

Lottie had been up close with a victim of burns before, but was not prepared for the scene before her.

'Oh shit, Boyd, he looks bad.'

'Understatement of the century.'

'This amount of tubing and machinery could operate a small factory for a year, let alone keep one man alive.'

A groan from the bed and she jumped. Moving closer, she dragged a chair behind her, but decided she was better off standing. Boyd sat down and took out his notebook.

'Lorcan, I'm Detective Inspector Lottie Parker. This is my colleague Detective Sergeant Boyd. We want to ask you a few questions.'

'His vocal cords are damaged,' said a nurse, entering the room with a bag of fluid. 'You'll have to lean in close if you want to hear him. Though I doubt you'll make out anything he says. Your last man left in a fluster. He couldn't understand a word. Though I didn't tell him what I'm telling you.'

'Thank you,' Lottie said.

The nurse said, 'Ring the bell when you're done and I'll come back.'

When they were alone, Lottie did as the nurse had said and crouched down beside the bandaged Brady.

'Lorcan, I'd like to know who was behind the killing of Tessa Ball and the torture of Marian Russell.'

Brady groaned; a gurgle emanated from his throat and a wheeze escaped his melted lips.

'Did you catch that, Boyd?' Lottie glanced round. She certainly had no idea what the injured man had said.

'No.'

'I know you were only involved in minor drug dealing, Lorcan.' She automatically crossed her fingers at the lie. 'That doesn't concern me. I think you're too nice a lad to be up for murder, so can you tell me anything at all that will help me find who is behind all this?'

The swollen eyelids flickered without opening. His blistered lips stretched slightly. God, she thought, he'd be better off dead. Then she noticed his hand, cannula protruding from bandages, twitching. The hand with just a thumb and index finger remaining.

'This is useless,' she said, turning back to Boyd.

In an instant, she froze as her own hand was gripped by the two-fingered man.

'You scared me half to death there, Lorcan,' she said. Realising he wanted her to come closer, she crouched down at the side of the bed, her ear to what was left of his mouth. 'Who was behind the murders, Lorcan?'

His voice was cracked from fire damage, but she could make out a word.

'Wuinnie.'

'Quinnie?' She looked back at Boyd. 'I think he means Jerome Quinn.' She leaned closer to the injured man. 'Who did this to you?'

'Wuinnie.'

Her hand was released from the thumb and finger and the machines began to emit high-pitched beeps. Lottie indicated to Boyd that it was time to leave.

'We won't get anything out of him. Not today, at any rate.'

The nurse breezed into the room. 'Time you two left.' She busied herself, flicking switches on the machine until the room was restored to the relative calm of a monotonous hum.

Lottie waited until Boyd had pocketed his notebook, then followed him out.

'He can't mean Jerome Quinn,' Boyd said when they were at the elevator. 'He was stabbed; burned to death. It has to be the half-brother, Hammer Quinn.'

Deep in thought, Lottie stepped inside when the door slid open.

'Brady is so badly injured, he could've been saying something completely different.'

The door shut and the elevator descended.

'We'll see what McMahon has to say.'

*

Lottie figured McMahon was a man used to getting what he wanted, when he wanted it. He was seated in his office, *her* office, on a new leather chair, behind a desk with a laptop.

'I went to see Lorcan Brady,' she said.

He eyed her from under his black fringe.

'I thought I told you *I'd* be speaking to Lorcan Brady,' he said.

'How did you get on?' She stood in the doorway.

He shuffled in his seat, the leather squeaking under him. 'Couldn't get a word out of him.'

'Do you think Jerome Quinn's half-brother Hammer has anything to do with it?' she ventured.

'He has everything to do with it.'

'But why now? Why wait until this very week to go for him? He must've known where he was all along.'

'Did you stop to think that Marian might have talked before they ripped her tongue out?'

Lottie felt her stomach shrivel at the thought of what the woman had suffered. And they had found her tongue in black refuse sacks, thrown out like a piece of rotting detritus.

'Where is all the money? We only found nine hundred and fifty euros,' she said. 'And I have doubts that it is drug money.'

'Offshore accounts, probably. I'll get to the bottom of it.'

'I'm sure you will,' Lottie said. 'And I'd like to know what business you had calling to the Kellys this morning?'

'I would've thought that was obvious.'

Lottie balled her hands into fists. Why did bastards in authority succeed in making her feel inadequate? She straightened her spine, tried to look important. 'I know they were neighbours, but—'

'They were the only neighbours on that road,' he interrupted. 'So they were the obvious people from whom to get information.'

'And did you?' From whom! Where the hell did he go to school?

'What?'

'Get information?' Jesus, he was a first-class bollocks.

'I need to confirm a few details.'

'Look here, DI McMahon. I'm SIO and I'm entitled to know what you know.'

'On the contrary, I think it works the other way round. So unless you have anything useful to tell me, let me get on with my work and I suggest you do likewise.'

'I'll see what Lynch found out about the data on Marian's hard drive.'

'No need,' he said. 'I've looked through it myself. Nothing of interest. Don't waste your time.'

'It's my job, whether you like it or not.'

'I don't mean to sound arrogant, but you're out of line, Inspector. Be careful whose toes you step on.'

She would have slammed the door on him if there had actually been one there to slam.

CHAPTER 70

Lynch was tying and untying her ponytail, wrapping her hair around her fingers.

'You look stressed,' Lottie said.

'A bit. I've spent all morning trying to piece together what Marian was working on. But it's like trying to do a jigsaw puzzle with nothing only blue sky.'

'At least it's not a black cloudy one,' Boyd said.

Two pairs of eyes scowled at him.

'Right, I'll check with Kirby to see where he's at,' he said.

'He should be following up with the land registry to see if Tessa had any more property. Will you get on to the HSE and find out if they have any records relating to St Declan's in the seventies?'

'What has that got to do with anything?'

'Boyd, can you do what you're asked without questioning it?'

'I can and I will, but I'd like to know why. Okay, okay. I'm going.' He left the office muttering to himself.

'You were saying.' Lottie pulled her chair over beside Lynch, conscious of McMahon sitting in what should be her office. He had a good view of them but hopefully he couldn't hear them.

Lynch pointed to the printout. 'It's all to do with the course she was studying. I didn't discover anything relating to drugs. Unless you count pages and pages about herbs and plants.'

'I found a herbal book on her bedside cabinet. Wait a minute.' Lottie rushed over to her desk and picked up the book. The outer jacket was torn and discoloured, the pages inside faded.

'Awfully small print,' Lynch said.

Lottie sat down again. '*Culpeper's Complete Herbal*. She might have had an interest in this field. Any word on the haul from the coal bunker?'

'*Hypericum perforatum*.'

'What?

'St John's Wort. It's a medicinal plant. Used to be sold for treating depression. Off the market now.'

Lottie ran her finger along the index and found St John's Wort. Highlighted in pencil. Interesting.

'By growing the plants in the bunker, Marian might've been trying to recreate its natural habitat – shady woods. Says here it is used for the treatment of melancholy and madness. I could do with some of that treatment.' She closed the book. 'What else on the transcript?'

'It looks like she was attempting a family tree. We only have her Word documents. It'd be great if we could retrieve her internet history.'

'Can we get access to her emails?'

'I can check it out, if you think it's of any use.'

'Be good to know who, if anyone, she was in contact with. How far had she got with the family tree?'

'Not far at all. She had Arthur's family mapped out, linking into her marriage with him, and then down to Emma.'

'And we still have no idea where he is,' Lottie said. 'On her own side, what did she have?'

'Not a lot,' Lynch said. 'Parents – Tessa and Timothy Ball. But wait for this.'

Lottie glanced at the page Lynch was holding. 'I haven't got all day.'

'She wrote a name, in brackets, beside Tessa's. It is O'Dowd.'

'What?' Lottie took the page and read, scrunching her brow in a frown. Was it there because Marian had found out that Tessa had

had an affair with Mick O'Dowd? Or were Tessa and Mick related somehow. Cousins? Brother and sister? Wouldn't locals have known? Maybe it explained why Emma had fled to O'Dowd's farmhouse. Or did it? 'This is very confusing. Any other theories?'

'Nope.'

'You're a font of information today, Lynch.'

'That's why I've been tearing my hair out.'

'Keep going through it. Something might turn up.'

'Right, but I don't think it's going to help us solve who killed Tessa and her family. If you ask me…'

'Go on.'

'I tend to agree with Inspector McMahon's viewpoint: this is a drugs feud.'

Sure you do, Lottie thought. 'We have to explore all avenues. Leave him and his cronies to follow up with his drug buddies, and we'll do our side of things. Understood?'

Wheeling her chair back to her desk, Lottie realised she was beginning to sound a lot like Superintendent Corrigan.

*

The email icon flashed on her computer. She clicked open Emma Russell's post-mortem preliminary report. Scanning through the document, her eyes zeroed in on the cause of death.

'Boyd!'

'You don't have to shout, I'm just across from you.'

'Cause of death… asphyxia due to aspiration of fluid in the lungs. Emma was drowned. And Jane found lacerations consistent with her spectacles being smashed into her face. Also a contusion on the back of her skull. Unable to determine if this was from a fall or from being hit with an as-yet-unknown implement.'

'Poor girl. Someone beat her up and shoved her into a barrel of water while she was still alive.'

'And there's still no sight or sound of O'Dowd?'

'Nope.'

Lottie told Boyd about the data from Marian's laptop. 'So were Tessa and O'Dowd related?' she wondered.

'I'll check their birth certificates,' he said.

'We need to start looking at the why of all this, rather than the how. We know everything that has happened and most of how it happened. But we have no idea why.'

'The drugs angle?'

'McMahon can work on that. More than likely it has a role somewhere. I just don't think it's a major one.'

'So where do we start?'

She wanted to tell Boyd about her conversation with Buzz Flynn, but she wasn't sure how he would react.

'Why was the gun in Tessa's possession?'

'What?' Boyd said.

'Nothing.'

'You mentioned the gun.'

'Thinking out loud again. Why did Tessa have it? The old woman Kirby interviewed seemed to know her. Kitty Belfield. Let's see if she's at home. She might have some answers.' Picking up her jacket from the floor, Lottie headed for the door.

'Kirby already spoke with her,' Boyd countered.

She turned, one arm in the sleeve of her jacket.

'Are you coming or what?'

'I suppose I am.'

CHAPTER 71

The drive up to Farranstown House provided a view of the churning black waters of Lough Cullion in the distance.

When she stepped out of the car, Lottie held onto the roof to steady herself against the rising swirl of wind. With waterlogged pebbles crunching beneath her boots, she reached the door of the eighteenth-century country manor ahead of Boyd. She dragged down on the worn piece of twine, ringing the ancient brass bell.

'This is how the other half lives,' Boyd whispered as they stood on the cracked concrete step, shielding themselves from the tempest.

'Looks a bit sad,' Lottie said, and pulled the string again.

'I'm coming! I'm coming.' The door swung inwards and a woman, bent double, her head almost touching her knees, appeared. 'You youngsters have no patience. None whatsoever.'

Restraining herself from stooping down to the woman's level, Lottie introduced herself and Boyd.

'Can we have a few words please, Mrs Belfield?'

'The name is Kitty. And where is that lovely young man who was here the other day? Did you not bring him with you?'

'He's busy,' Lottie said, realising that Kitty was talking about Kirby.

'Come in so. He loved my bacon and cabbage. A great chat he was. Don't get many round here to talk to nowadays. Sorry about the cold. I usually don't put down a fire until seven.' She led the way inside.

It was colder inside than out. The wide stone-floored hall, naked of any adornments, gave way to a large high-ceilinged living room.

The walls were dressed in hanging tapestries depicting long-ago battles, and the ceiling, decorated with alabaster coving, seemed to creak with the weight of the upper level. Two couches that had once been upholstered in black leather, now stripped to their lining, were the only furniture in front of the vast cast-iron fireplace. A couple of logs sat in the grate with rolled-up sheets of newspaper protruding.

'Sit down,' Kitty said. 'I can't see you when you're standing up. Scoliosis of the spine has me crippled. I won't offer tea, because it isn't teatime, so let's be hearing what you have to say for yourselves.'

'It's about Tessa Ball,' Lottie began.

'Well, it's hardly about the weather, young lady. What do you want to know about Tessa that you haven't heard from your friend Larry?'

'Larry?' Boyd frowned.

'Kirby,' Lottie whispered.

'Lovely young man – I'd say he's a right hit with the ladies.'

'You'd be correct there,' Boyd said.

'About Tessa,' Lottie insisted. 'We know she worked in partnership with your husband. Was there anything she might have been involved in that could have resulted in her murder?'

'As a solicitor, Tessa would have dealt with a lot of ordinary folk, but she'd also have dealt with unsavoury characters. I'm sure there's a list of people out there who were only too glad to hear she'd kicked the bucket.'

'The files that were stolen from the office. You told Detective… Larry that they related to a case involving a woman called Carrie King who tried to burn down her home. Can you tell me anything else about that?'

Kitty turned up her nose and folded her arms as best she could around her shrunken frame. 'I shouldn't have said anything. The words were out of my mouth before I knew what I was saying. He is very disarming, that young man.'

'We are interested in hearing the story.'

'There is no story.'

'Tell me about your husband's business.' Lottie tried to sidetrack Kitty before the woman clammed up totally.

'I wasn't allowed near the business. My role was to look after this monstrosity of a house. Left to my husband by a grateful client, if you can believe that. Back then, property was currency. I don't know what type of characters he and Tessa dealt with, but I'm sure criminal elements were involved.'

'And Carrie King. What was all that about?'

Kitty appeared to hesitate, though it was hard to see the old woman's face.

'I know nothing about her. Tessa dealt with that. Stan gave me the impression he was put out by it. But he let Tessa run the show.'

'The files that were stolen. I suppose there were no copies kept.'

'You suppose correctly, Inspector.'

'And no one was ever apprehended.'

'No one.'

'Do you know why Tessa would have had a gun in her home?'

'A gun?' The old lady clutched a hand to her chest, catching her nylon blouse in a fist.

Lottie ploughed on. 'It was an old Webley and Scott revolver. Used mainly by the Special Branch in the seventies. And by the IRA when they could get their hands on them.'

'That's another story,' Boyd said.

'Tessa,' Kitty said, 'wasn't all sugar and spice. She was tough. A woman before her time, if I was to quote a cliché. Today, I think she would have made president. A crooked one, but she'd have made it.'

'Crooked? How?'

'She was in cahoots with a guard. And her brother thought he was Casanova. Ended up mucking out cow dung on a bankrupt farm.'

'Brother?' Lottie felt the cold wind whining down the chimney and rustling the newspaper in the grate. A shock of soot fell out onto the threadbare mat at her feet.

'Well, it was said they were brother and sister but I suspect there may have been something more between those two. Too close for comfort they were.'

'Is it Mick O'Dowd you're referring to?' Boyd asked.

'It is. Put his hand up my dress once. First and last time he did it.' Kitty patted her pleated tweed skirt down over her knee.

'Tessa owned a lot of property and signed a cottage over to O'Dowd. Would you know about that?'

'No. But like I said, property was currency.'

'We can't find Mick O'Dowd. Is there anywhere he would go to hide?' Lottie said.

'How would I know?' Kitty sniffed indignantly, turning up her already wrinkled nose. At last Lottie could see her face, and noticed the old woman's eyes blazing a cold shade of blue.

'Just thought I'd ask.'

Kitty said, 'But it was odd when Tessa had Marian.'

'Odd how?' Lottie leaned closer as the old woman's voice lowered to a conspiratorial whisper.

'The child was the spitting image of O'Dowd. Something was going on between those two, mark my words.'

'But…' Pausing, Lottie tried to line up her thoughts. 'I thought O'Dowd might have been in a relationship with Carrie King.'

'O'Dowd got himself into a relationship with any woman willing to spread her legs for him. Pardon my vulgarity, but it's the truth.'

'What can you remember about Carrie King?' Lottie wondered if Kitty had the same recollections as Buzz Flynn.

'Carrie was a lost soul, God love her.' Kitty shook her head and stared at the lifeless fire. 'She abused herself and she allowed others to abuse her. Locked up in the asylum eventually. But she wasn't mad. No, Carrie was plain sad. She'd stand outside the post office on a Friday, when the old lads would be picking up their pensions, looking for pennies to buy drink. Turned to prostitution in the end, poor girl.'

'Where did she come from? Was she from Ragmullin?'

'How would I know? God himself only knows where Carrie hailed from. She arrived one day, probably off the Dublin train. Wherever she came from, Ragmullin didn't welcome her.' Kitty seemed to swallow a sob.

'You seem to have a lot of sympathy for her. Did you do anything to help?' Boyd said. Lottie threw him a look telling him to shut up. He shrugged his shoulders.

'Carrie was beyond help.'

'You knew her personally?'

'I didn't *know* her. Made her acquaintance… once. She crawled on her hands and knees up that avenue out there… on a day not unlike today.' Kitty was staring at the window. 'Wind and rain. It was Halloween. I don't remember the year, but it was awful miserable. We didn't have all the razzmatazz you get nowadays. The only pumpkin we knew about was a turnip. Well, she looked like a turnip that day. Ready to pop out a baby.'

'Why did she come here?'

Kitty turned and lifted her head as far as it would go. Lottie recoiled. A shot of venom would have been less poisonous.

'How would I know?' the old woman said. 'She fell through the front door when I opened it. Walked the whole way from town, she had. Nearly two miles in the rain. How she didn't die of pneumonia, I'll never know. I hauled her in – I was forty years younger than I am today, and a lot straighter too – got her onto that very couch you're sitting on now, and boiled the kettle for a cup of tea. I thought she was drunk or high, or maybe both. She was spouting gibberish. I can't recall it now, but every sentence contained the words "Tessa" and "bitch". I telephoned Stan and told him to get himself home.'

Kitty stopped speaking and Lottie tried to envisage what had happened. She knew she was dealing with something very dark.

'Stan sent Tessa here instead,' Kitty continued. 'The screams. The screeches that young woman howled when she saw Tessa walk into this room. I can tell you, I still hear them when I go to bed at night. The lights flickered and the fire almost died in the grate. It was like the devil himself had entered my house and all the inhabitants of hell were on his heels.'

'Jesus,' Boyd said.

'No, there was no Jesus nor God here that evening. Only evil. I can tell you this… Carrie was terrified of Tessa Ball. So terrified, she flung herself off that couch, crawled to the fire and tried to throw herself into it.'

Lottie watched Kitty intently, hanging on her every word.

'What did Tessa do?'

'Tessa was so cold hearted it's a wonder she didn't douse the fire with her words alone. She walked over there,' Kitty pointed to the fireplace, 'lifted the poker and threatened to beat the baby out of Carrie if she didn't get up on her feet.'

Lottie tried to imagine the then thirty-five-year-old Tessa Ball turning into this demonic individual as painted by Kitty. A woman who in later years kept a prayer to St Anthony pinned to her bedside locker with a Bible resting atop. 'Did you try to help?'

'I was as terrified as poor Carrie. I helped her up, her babies straining to escape her womb. She screamed and Tessa dragged her out to her car. That was the last I ever saw of her.'

'Surely, as a concerned citizen, you should have reported the incident to the authorities?'

'Authorities? Young lady, this was the early seventies. Everyone was in everyone else's pocket. The priests and nuns ruled the roost. The guards were as twisted as the priests and the health boards had crooked people in every organisation you could think of. That girl was destined for a mother-and-baby home, or the asylum. I don't know which was the lesser of the two evils, but she ended up in the asylum.'

'I heard she was released at one stage, and committed again after trying to burn down a house.'

'Mmm... I heard that too. But I don't know the story behind it.' She folded her arms, twitched her nose and set her mouth in a straight line. 'I only know that when Stan came home that day and I told him what had happened, he told me to forget all about it. Never repeat it to a sinner, he said. And I never did. I'm only telling you because Stan is no longer around to know and now Tessa is dead too. And you're not a sinner, are you, Inspector? So no harm done.'

Kitty leaned over and, with the aid of a walking stick, stood up, still doubled over. Lottie wondered if perhaps the old lady had paid with her health for not helping the young woman who had come to her door seeking refuge.

'I still don't understand why Carrie came all the way out here in the bad weather you've described. Why would she do that?'

'I ask myself that question quite often. And I don't like the answer I come up with.'

'And what answer is that?'

'That perhaps my Stan was one of those men who took advantage of her.'

'Surely not,' Lottie said.

'This was a town of secrets. Open secrets. People knew everything and said nothing.'

Lottie knew only too well how the town worked. And she didn't like it one bit.

'I felt sorry for Carrie that day,' Kitty said, her voice cracking. 'Mainly because of her helplessness, but also because of her fear. But she made her own bed, as they say, and she had to lie in it, even if it did turn out to be in a padded cell in the asylum.'

'I heard that one of her children was placed in the asylum too. I didn't think that could happen.'

'I know nothing about that.' Kitty shuddered and gripped the mantelpiece for support. 'But those were different times. Back then, children who were not wanted were put in any damn place an adult pleased.'

Lottie put out her hand to steady the old woman, who brushed away the help and flicked a long plastic flint. As the newspaper in the grate ignited, sparks shot out and a flame took hold. Another snarl of wind sent more soot trickling down the chimney. A gust appeared to shake the house to its roots. Should she ask the question or let it die? It would fester if she didn't ask.

'One last question,' she said. 'You mentioned Tessa was in cahoots with a guard. What were they involved in?'

'Let me think.' Picking up the poker, Kitty thrust it into the grate, moving the logs about. 'The two of them eventually signed Carrie's life away.'

Holding her breath for a moment, Lottie exhaled as she said, 'What was his name?'

'Detective Inspector Parker, are you sure you want me to answer that question?' Two crystal eyes shot a look at her.

'Yes,' Lottie said.

'I think you already know the answer,' Kitty said and replaced the poker in the companion set. 'Sometimes knowing is worse than not knowing. Can you understand that?'

'I'm not sure, Kitty. I'm honestly not sure of anything.'

'Well then, my dear, I think I've said all that I'm going to say. I'll show you out.'

CHAPTER 72

Detective Larry Kirby sucked hard on his e-cigarette, wishing he had never started the thing. A cigar, a nice fat Cuban. Yeah, that would be nice. He thought of Mick O'Dowd and how he had given him one the morning of the fire.

'You know, Lynch,' he said, 'I've been thinking.'

'You know, Kirby,' she said, 'that's a dangerous thing.'

'This Mick O'Dowd character. I can't figure him out at all. If he had something to do with the fire or the drugs found there, wouldn't he have been five hundred miles away at the time rather than reporting it and sitting waiting for us with no alibi other than his blasted cattle?'

'Maybe it's because he had nothing to do with it.'

'But then Emma is killed on his farm and he disappears.' He took a deep pull on his e-cig and let the vapour exit through his nostrils. Catching Lynch raising an eye, arching her eyebrow, he said, 'And don't even think about telling me to stop smoking this.'

'I wasn't going to. But I hope Superintendent Corrigan doesn't arrive,' Lynch said. 'Back to Emma. If she went to O'Dowd's voluntarily, then she thought she was safe there. So there has to be some connection between Emma's family and O'Dowd, and the only thing I've found so far is his name in brackets next to Tessa's on Marian's family tree.'

'That and the fact that the cottage he owned once belonged to Tessa Ball. Wait a minute.' Kirby stood up and rooted through files on his desk. Not finding what he was looking for, he started thumping his keyboard. 'Here it is.'

'Here what is?'

'There's a map accompanying the folio number for the cottage.' He stood beside the photocopier that doubled as a printer.

'Come on. Come on.' He tapped his foot on the floor, as if that would speed up the process. 'Here.'

At his desk he lined up the pages of an outline property map. Lynch joined him to examine it.

'That's the folio number for the cottage.' He pointed to the plot of land where the cottage was situated. 'And that there is O'Dowd's farm. We can assume he owns that. So why did Tessa transfer to him the piece of land with the cottage?'

'Maybe because it was next door to him and she wanted a few quid, and he wanted to expand?'

'But he didn't expand. A drug king from Dublin moved in. Started a cannabis grow house.'

'Perhaps he was fed up with farming. Wanted to branch out.'

'That means he knew about the illegal activities. So why not let someone else report it when it went up in flames? That's what's stumping me.'

'He reported it because he didn't know what was going on. Maybe Tessa maintained overall control.'

'Used him as a patsy?'

'Yeah. Look and see who owned the farm before O'Dowd.'

'I can't see it from this. I'll get back to land registry... Wait a minute, Lynch.'

'What now?'

Kirby pointed to the map on his screen. Dragging the mouse, he zoomed in. 'Okay,' he said. 'That there is Lough Cullion. Agreed?'

'Agreed,' Lynch said, sitting forward.

'And there is Dolanstown, O'Dowd's farm, the cottage.'

'Agreed.'

'And that, on the other side, is Carnmore.'

'I think I see where this is leading.'

'Marian and Arthur Russell lived in Carnmore. And the land backs on to Dolanstown. Not accessed by road because of the new road. But the two are back to back.'

'What's that?' With a pen in her hand, Lynch pointed to a square on the edge of Carnmore.

'A big house?' He zoomed in. 'Feck this.' He closed off the screen, brought up Google Maps. 'That's better.' He keyed in Carnmore. 'Okay. This is what you were looking at. It *is* a house.'

Lynch read from the screen. 'Farranstown House.'

'I recognise it.' Kirby said. 'I'd better ring the boss.'

'I'm the boss.' McMahon strode into the office, wet coat dripping water from his arm. 'What is it I need to know?'

'With all due respect, sir,' Kirby said, 'it's nothing to do with the drugs angle. Just a little digging we were doing into land ownership. Nothing for you to concern yourself with.'

'That is tantamount to insubordination. You had better tell me.'

CHAPTER 73

The windows were as old as the house.

Kitty leaned on the window seat, pressing her face against the glass and looking out at the red hue tinting the darkness until the tail lights of the car disappeared at the end of the drive. As the black veil of night descended again, she withdrew back into the living room. The fire was struggling to ignite, but she wasn't concerned enough with the cold to bother with it any further.

With the aid of her stick, she left the room and hobbled down the stone-floored hallway to the kitchen. In the darkness, from memory and by touch, she made her way to the phone hanging on the wall beside the bolted door that led to the old cellar.

Lifting the receiver, she hit the speed-dial button and waited for the pick-up.

'I can't lie for you any more. I think the prophet of doom is landing on your shoulders as we speak. I'm sorry.'

She hung up before there was time for a reply.

Still in darkness, she pulled back the bolt on the cellar door, flicked on the light switch and stared into the space below. Could she make it without falling head first? But she needed to destroy what was down there. The only evidence the guards could use to make sense of everything.

Her spine pained her more than her knees. She could make it down, but would she make it back up again? And if she didn't, there was no one to come looking for her.

Switching off the light, she locked the door.

'Another time,' she said, and listened to her voice echoing back at her from the icy walls.

CHAPTER 74

Lottie entered the office with Boyd behind her.

Sensing a stand-off, she said, 'DI McMahon, just the man I need to have a word with.'

He indicated the office with no door, and she followed.

'What is it you want?' McMahon said, all pretence at congeniality lost in his tone.

'I wanted to get an update from you on how your side of the investigation is progressing,' Lottie said.

'I didn't come down in the last shower of rain.'

'Looks like it from here.' Why did she have to say what she was thinking?

'Detective Inspector Parker, first your detective out there, the one who badly needs a haircut…'

'Kirby?'

'Yes. First he insults my intelligence, and now you're doing the same.'

'You have a nicer team up in Dublin, do you?'

'As a matter of fact, I'm treated with the utmost respect.'

'Well then, why don't you piss off back up there?' No going back now.

'What… what did you just say?'

'I said, why don't you—'

'Stop right there.' He was out of his chair and standing in her space. 'I want an apology this instant or I'm on my way to your superintendent.'

'Good. And you might ask Superintendent Corrigan when this refurbishment is going to be completed. I'm itching to get back into *my* office.'

Lottie felt the backdraught of hot air as McMahon rushed past her out of the doorless space and through the main office, heading for Corrigan's.

'You handled that well,' Boyd said sarcastically.

'Don't you start,' Lottie said.

'Can I have your attention for a minute.' Kirby clicked his keyboard.

'Fire away.'

Pulling her chair across, Lottie inched in beside him and forced herself to concentrate on what he had to show her. But her mind was in turmoil. She'd been out of line, allowing McMahon to rile her. But she couldn't dislodge the image planted in her brain by Kitty Belfield. A pregnant Carrie King's terror of Tessa Ball. Had the past caught up with Tessa? Where was Carrie King now, if she was still alive? Where were her children? And did Lottie even believe the half of what Kitty had said?

'Tell me what I'm looking at.'

Pointing with the tip of his biro, he said, 'That's O'Dowd's farm. The small square is the cottage.'

'How many acres is the farm?'

'According to the land registry, it's two hundred and fifty. But that's not what I want to show you.'

'I'm waiting.' Lottie leaned in as Boyd peered over her shoulder.

'That's Farranstown House,' Kirby said.

'What is?' Lottie asked, knitting her brow in a frown.

He clicked the mouse to zoom in. 'Farranstown House is situated on another five hundred acres, leading down to the shores of Lough Cullion. Following me so far?'

'I think so,' Lottie said.

'The land on the other side of Farranstown House is where Tessa Ball lived before she signed her home over to her daughter, Marian Russell.'

'So let me get this straight,' Lottie said, holding up her hand to halt Kirby. 'It's possible that at one time all that land had been part of the Farranstown estate.'

'Correct.'

'And we didn't twig how close the Russell and O'Dowd places were, because the land is accessed by two different roads,' Lottie said, realisation dawning on her.

'Never entered into the equation,' Boyd said.

'If all this land was at one time owned by the Farranstown estate, when was it broken up and sold?'

'Does it even matter to our investigation?' Boyd asked.

'Besides the drugs angle being pursued by McMahon,' Lottie said, 'we haven't come up with anything else. But this might be another way to approach it.'

'You've lost me,' Boyd said, stretching and walking back to his own desk.

Lottie put out a hand to call him back. 'Whoever owned Farranstown also held all that land. Now, Mick O'Dowd owns two hundred and fifty acres and the burned cottage. The portion of land on the other side of the manor house contains two houses. One was originally Tessa Ball's, where Marian lived, and the other is where Bernie Kelly lives. Kirby, does Bernie own her house?'

'I'll find out,' he said. 'What difference does it make?'

'We know Tessa signed over the cottage to Mick O'Dowd. What if she owned the land on the other side also?' Lottie pointed to the screen. 'How would a town solicitor acquire all that wealth?'

'Kitty Belfield told us her husband inherited Farranstown House,' Boyd said.

'Right. If the Belfields owned the whole lot, what are we talking about in terms of size? Almost a thousand acres? That's a lot of land for—'

'A small-town solicitor,' Boyd said.

'O'Dowd told Kirby that the family who originally owned the farm left for America forty years ago…' Lottie stopped mid sentence. 'That's around the time all the trouble was going on with Carrie King.'

'Who's Carrie King?' Lynch asked.

'I don't rightly know, but I intend to find out,' Lottie said, shoving back her chair and standing up. 'Unearth everything you can about that land. Go back as far as possible. I want to know who owned, sold, leased or bequeathed every blade of grass on it.'

'I think you're a bit spooked after Kitty Belfield's tale,' Boyd said.

'I am. Will you get me a list of all St Declan's patients for the last forty-odd years? I want to see what happened to Carrie King.'

'You're chasing a shadow,' he said.

'That may be so, but I need to catch up with it before someone else ends up dead.'

'It's the proverbial wild goose chase,' Boyd said, lining up his pens on his desk. 'We have a direct link to a Dublin drug gang and you have me checking out asylum patients who are probably dead by now.'

Lottie whirled round. 'There is not one shred of evidence pointing to Marian Russell or her daughter having anything to do with drugs.'

'A hoodie that Emma might have been wearing was found in Lorcan Brady's house,' Boyd said. 'He was shacked up with Jerome Quinn before they were burned. And Marian Russell had her tongue cut out. It all points to criminal involvement in… in something or other.'

'Boyd, you talk pure shite sometimes. Get me an update on those searches for O'Dowd and Arthur Russell.' As she grabbed her bag and jacket, she heard Superintendent Corrigan's footsteps hammering down the corridor. 'And cover for me. I'm out of here.'

'Where?'

'To look at land.'

Running out of the door, she ignored Corrigan's roar behind her and fled down the stairs and out of the station.

CHAPTER 75

On impulse, Lottie found herself driving towards O'Dowd's farm. She wasn't about to hang around to get a bollocking from Corrigan. McMahon would've painted a dim enough picture without her adding to its bleakness. She needed air and time to clear her head. She grabbed at her bag to search for a pill and immediately thought of Annabelle. After she was finished here, she'd call her to see what she'd been ringing about. She threw the bag back on the seat.

The wind had stolen the crime-scene tape from the gates at the entrance to the farm – it now swung from the bare branches of a tree. She parked up and stepped out carefully, avoiding the mucky puddles. Listening, she found the only sound was the downpour and the wind roaring across the barren fields. The house stood like a lost icon from a museum. Curtains drawn over the grey windows; stonework black from the rain; door tightly closed against the elements and intruders. Too late now.

Walking around the side of the house, she wondered how Emma was related to O'Dowd. It had to be the reason she'd come here. And where the hell was he?

At the rear of the building she looked over at the barns and sheds. The SOCOs had completed their work and departed, leaving a trail of evidence easy for the trained eye to see.

Glancing into the milking shed, she noted the empty stalls, machinery hanging limply. She remembered standing here with

O'Dowd as he busied himself with his animals, a raw anger burning beneath the surface of his skin. Why hadn't she probed deeper? Somehow the O'Dowd she'd met was hard to marry with the younger version she'd learned about earlier. Had his dalliance with Carrie King and her subsequent fate forced him to exile himself to a solitary life with animals?

'They were taken to the mart.'

Lottie turned round, her heart stopping its beating for a second.

'What the…?' She took a step back as the tall figure of McMahon loomed out of the shadows and stood at the open barn doorway. She hadn't heard his car. 'What are you doing here?'

'Same thing as you, I imagine,' he said. 'Trying to figure out what brought young Emma here.'

'I thought you were convinced everything was drugs-related?' She stood her ground.

He stepped closer and leaned one arm on the railing. 'That's my theory, but the only thing not fitting in nice and neat is Emma.'

'Thing? You're a cold-hearted bastard.'

'You know what I mean.'

She moved closer to him, deciding to fight this out. 'If Emma was in a relationship with Lorcan Brady, which I must say I doubt, then there's your link.'

'That may be so, but I just don't buy it.'

'Me neither,' Lottie conceded.

'Will we have a look through the house?' he said. 'This place gives me the heebie-jeebies.'

Lottie caught him eyeing the slatted floor. 'Not a farm boy, then?'

'City slicker, that's me.' He smiled.

Lottie was no fool. She could see his smile was forced. Despite her misgivings, she led the way to the rear door, digging around in her handbag for the evidence bag containing the key. Putting it in the lock, she glanced over her shoulder. McMahon had moved towards the other shed.

'Are you coming in?' she asked.

'What the hell is that?' He indicated the large machine with rotors.

'An agitator,' she said, recalling O'Dowd's words.

'Used for what?'

'Stirring shit.'

He followed her into the kitchen.

The CCTV monitor had been taken away, as had the accounting books. Specks of dark brown on the table and floor were circled and numbered. They were the only remaining evidence of the trauma suffered by Emma before she was forcibly submerged in a barrel until she drowned.

'Did the killer have help?' Lottie wondered aloud. 'If Emma was attacked in here, she'd be a dead weight. She had to be carried outside and then put in the barrel.'

'How big is O'Dowd?'

Lottie thought for a moment, recalling his broad shoulders – a man used to hauling animals and feedstuff.

'He's a farmer. Worked alone. He looked strong and relatively fit, despite his age. But I can't see him killing Emma.'

'Why not?'

'She came here after her grandmother was murdered and her mother left lying in a coma in hospital. She didn't seek out her father. She came to O'Dowd. Why?'

'Some prearranged code?'

'Perhaps. But what danger did she pose that warranted her being killed?'

'Maybe, like her mother, she knew something and was going to blab.'

'Then we have to find out what that something was.'

Lottie turned to find that McMahon had divested himself of his coat and was sitting at the table, fingers tapping the grained wood. Even though the house had been thoroughly searched, she felt the need to do something. She began opening and shutting cupboard doors.

'You won't find anything,' he said. Tap, tap, tap, his fingers continued.

'You never know.' He was grating on every nerve in her body. She stood back and visualised the scene as it might've been just before Emma was attacked.

Dinner dishes washed up. Draining board wiped clean. Accounting ledgers on the table. Her spectacles and phone on the floor. The floor. Dropping to her knees, Lottie lay flat on her stomach and looked around.

'What in the name of…?' McMahon began.

'Shush.'

A horde of people had trooped through the house. Everywhere had been searched, fingerprinted; DNA collected. Had something been missed? Like a predator, Lottie crawled on her belly, arms outstretched as she moved towards the sink area. A gap, about three inches, between the cupboard and the floor. Reaching out her hands in front of her, she eased them into the space. They touched something solid. She flicked her fingers, trying to draw the object out.

'It's a book.'

'More of O'Dowd's accounts, no doubt. Did that man never hear of a computer?'

She heard McMahon shove back his chair. His footsteps echoed on the stone floor. An icy shiver escaped from the bottom of her skull and travelled down the nape of her neck. If McMahon wanted to pay her back for her enmity, now was the time. Get a grip, Parker. Her fingers edged round the corner of the book and she slid it towards the aperture. Blowing dust out of her nostrils, she grabbed it in her hand and sat back on her haunches.

'Well, fuck me pink,' she said.

'Are you offering?'

Lottie swung round. Boyd was framed in the doorway, dousing a cigarette between his fingertips.

He nodded to McMahon.

Standing up and brushing herself down, Lottie didn't bother to ask Boyd why he'd followed her. She was just glad he had.

'What did you find?' McMahon peered over her shoulder.

'An old book.'

'Probably down there since the kitchen was installed a hundred years ago. I'll see you two back at the station. I hope you can come up with some answers for Emma's involvement. I want to wrap this up as soon as I can.'

'Wrap it up and get back to your castle,' Lottie said, between gritted teeth. She knew he'd heard her by the force of the door banging after his exit.

Boyd said, 'You know that blacklist management keep? I reckon your name is in the brightest of red letters, commanding top spot.'

'It's the same book,' Lottie said.

'What book?'

'Have you an evidence bag?'

'Out in the boot of the car. Why?'

'Doesn't matter. It's well contaminated by now.' She laid the hardback on the table, stood it on its side and read the gold lettering on the brown linen spine. '*Culpeper's Complete Herbal*. Similar to the one Marian had.'

'Looks different.'

'This hasn't got the dust jacket.' She flicked open the old pages, some with colour illustrations of plants; most lined in a tiny font. 'Look, Boyd.'

Small cursive strokes in blue ink, now faded, at the top right-hand corner of the index page: *Carrie King*.

CHAPTER 76

Sitting on a boulder on the shore of Lough Cullion, Arthur Russell scanned the dark horizon, then glanced behind him up the hill at the big old house.

Only one window had a light shining. He couldn't see any shadows but he knew she was up there – looking out on the expanse of her once immense fortune. Marian had told him the story but he hadn't believed her. When had that been? Back when she'd started her cursed study course. He'd thought she'd been making it all up. But now, after all that had happened, he suspected she might have been telling the truth. He should go to the guards and tell them. Shouldn't he?

They already suspected him of murdering Tessa and possibly mutilating and killing Marian. If that was all, he might have told them. But then Cathal Moroney had arrived at his door looking for a comment on the murder of Emma. His daughter. His beautiful princess, who'd been taken from him by Marian and Tessa. His little treasure – his reason for living. And now she was gone. He drained the can of cider and pulled up the tab on another.

The black waves on the usually calm lake, now dappled with heavy raindrops, churned up an angry white froth and sloshed against his feet on the stony shore. The boat shed, to his left, appeared like a shroud in the darkness, beckoning him with a watery finger.

His tears mingled with corpulent raindrops as he heaved his guitar in its leather case higher onto his shoulder and took his first step into the water. The second step was harder. The third almost impossible. By the time he stopped counting, the water was swirling about his waist, pulling against him. He kept on going.

CHAPTER 77

Annabelle slid her phone from one hand to the other. Why hadn't Lottie returned her call last night? If she wanted happy pills, she'd be here in an instant.

Cian was out. Again. His usual night-time forays. Hopefully he had another woman and he might disappear for good with her. God help her when she got to know the real Cian. Annabelle's one regret was that she hadn't held onto Tom Rickard when she'd had the chance.

Pacing the hallway, her eyes darting up the stairs, she knew she had to see what was hidden behind that locked door. Making up her mind without any thought for the consequences, she ran up the stairs. She'd try every conceivable combination and hopefully something would work.

At the top landing, she stared. The door to Cian's study was slightly ajar. Could she be this lucky? No. Cian was too careful. But he'd left in an awful hurry. Had he really gone out? She felt her heartbeat reverberating in her ears. Quickly she flew back down the stairs. Checked the kitchen, the living and utility rooms. Opening the back door, she could see that the garage was open and empty. He was definitely out. And the twins were at after-school study.

Back up the stairs. Back to stand outside her husband's study with its open door.

Forcing her feet to move, she sidled up to the door. Pushed it with her index finger. Waited as it slid inwards.

The sight before her stopped her breath and silenced her heart. Taking another step inside, careful to make sure that the door didn't close and lock her in, she bit her lip and gripped her arms around her sides. She hadn't been in here in recent months. She'd expected the computer, monitor and lights. But not to the extent that she now witnessed.

'What is this?' she whispered.

'Mine,' Cian said from behind her, and the door clicked shut.

Annabelle whirled around on the balls of her feet, eyes widening in terror.

'I'm s-sorry… the… the d-door was open.'

'It was a test, you dumb bitch. A test to see if you would respect my privacy. And do you know what? Come on, answer me. No? I'll tell you. You failed!'

His balled-up fist didn't connect with her face. Cian O'Shea wasn't that stupid. Instead it thumped into her solar plexus. Doubling over, she fell to her knees.

'Cian, no… no. I saw nothing. Honestly.' Coughing, she curled into a ball as he kicked out with his booted foot, catching her on the kneecap.

She felt his breath at her ear as he crouched down beside her.

'There's nothing to see. Just my work. It's all that's important to me in this world. My children and this. Not you. Do you get that?'

As he bit down on the lobe of her ear, pulling out the stud earring, she cried out again. 'Please stop.'

'You go around town, the important doctor following in daddy's footsteps. But inside the walls of this house, you are mine. And you know I monitor your phone calls, so tell me why you were ringing that stupid bitch Parker last night? Don't deny it, because I know.'

'I didn't get to talk to her. She didn't pick up.'

'That's not the point, is it? The point is you fucking phoned her!'

'I… I'm sorry.'

'You will be.'

She felt his fingers tighten around her burned wrist; she sensed the blister bursting and pain shot up her arm and across her chest. 'I wish I was dead,' she cried.

'Be careful what you wish for.'

A high-pitched beep sounded above her head and a screen burst into light.

'Out you go,' he said, pulling her by her damaged wrist and dragging her to her feet.

She looked into his mad eyes before he opened the door and pushed her outside. As the door closed, she heard him say, 'One minute, please, I'm just getting rid of the dog.'

*

Walking around her office, Alexis tapped a manicured fingernail against her hip.

'Who was that?' she asked, working hard at keeping her temper even. She was fed up with phone calls. Nuisance individuals interfering in all she was trying to do. But this one was important.

'Nothing for you to worry about.'

'I know you don't have a dog. I asked you a question!'

'Just my wife. She's gone now. No worries.'

'I pay you well so that I shouldn't have to worry. I insisted that no one else should know.'

'No one knows. I guarantee it. She heard nothing. Do you want this update?'

Listening to his breath panting down the line, she picked up a cigarette and lit it, careful not to stand too close to the smoke alarm. Exhaling fumes through her nostrils, she eased relaxation into her body.

'Please tell me the old woman is no longer a threat.'

'I'm afraid you've more to be concerned about than her. I've discovered that someone else has a potentially damning file.'

'Why are you telling me this? Go and get it.'

'It's not that easy.'

'You are the computer geek; find it.'

'It's a hard copy. Compiled by hand, years ago. I got you the post-mortem file, didn't I?'

'I wasn't aware there was another file in existence. What's in it?'

'I don't know and I can't go breaking and entering again. I prefer the technical stuff.'

'You have to get it.'

'No. I can't do it. And that's final.'

She walked more and more slowly, her finger-tapping becoming increasingly insistent against her Michael Kors black jersey dress. In front of the life-size portrait on the end wall, she stopped and allowed her hand to slowly glide over the ridges of oil left by the brush. An artist's interpretation of the only person she loved. Letting her hand linger on the painted chin, then the eyes, she smiled. 'I won't let anything come back to haunt you.'

'What?'

'I wasn't talking to you.' She marched to her desk. Sitting down, she said, 'But now I am.'

She could see the man pulling away from the camera. Shock? She would give him a shock.

'You're to get that file. Do whatever it takes. And make sure there are no more nasty surprises waiting to crawl out and slither into my world. You got that?'

'But—'

'No buts! Do you want me to divert my million dollars away from your piss-poor company? Because I will. And those lovely twins of yours – you really don't want anything to happen to them. Do you? So lift your lazy ass out of that chair and get the file.'

She waited as he struggled to find a suitable retort. But she knew there was none. Money talked, and her money was now shouting the loudest of all.

'Don't you dare threaten my children.'

'Oh, it wasn't a threat. It was a promise.' She reached out a finger to stab the monitor, and his image filled the screen. 'Little man, you have no idea who you are dealing with.'

'What did you just call me?'

'Go and do as I ordered. I'm paying you well. And I want that file. That's final.'

She jabbed the keyboard and the screen went black, plunging her desk space into darkness. Sitting back in her chair, she puffed on her cigarette and closed her eyes.

CHAPTER 78

When dinner was finished, Sean remained seated at the table.

'Mam, are you okay?'

'I'm fine, Sean. How are you, though?'

'I feel great, honestly. But you…'

'It's just this case I'm working on. It's draining me.'

'Chloe said a girl from her school was murdered. Is that what's upsetting you?'

Lottie smiled wanly and reached out a hand, laying it on top of her son's. 'Yes, it is upsetting, because I have no idea why she was killed. It's so sad.'

'It's not your fault, Mam.'

'I should have looked out for her more.' It occurred to her that she should be looking out for her own family more too.

'Did you know she was in danger?' Sean asked.

'The fact that her grandmother had been murdered… well, I should've been more diligent with her care.'

'Ah, Mam. Don't beat yourself up over it. You can only do so much. You're only one person. You can't do everything for everyone.'

'Sean, you are so wise at times…' Just like his father.

'But?'

'But you need to do your homework. Please don't spend so much time on those computer games. They're not good for your brain.'

'I got this really good one, Mam. You'd love it. A bit like GTA, but it's set in Ireland. Guards and all.'

'I hope I'm not featured in it.'

Sean smiled. 'Actually, Mam, I think you are.'

'What do you mean?'

'There's this woman guard and she is a real pain in the arse. Just like you.'

Lottie laughed. 'Sean Parker, you take that back.'

'She even looks like you. It's so weird. There I am, playing this game, and the cop is just like my mam. Do you want a go?'

'Maybe first I should solve a real crime. Go on. Do some homework and try to get to sleep early.'

'Don't I always?'

Without any warning, Sean stood up and wrapped his arms around Lottie, kissing her cheek. 'You be careful, Mam. I don't want to lose you too.'

She couldn't answer. Just sat there staring at the door easing closed as her son left the kitchen. When had he grown up so much? As tall now as his father had been, and he was only fourteen. Her brave, strong son. Growing up to be just like his dad.

Linking her fingers, Lottie looked down at them. Long and freckled. Were they like her father's? Was *she* like her father? What had he really been like? What drove a family man to pull the trigger of a gun and obliterate his own life and that of his family? She knew that his actions had indirectly caused the death of her brother Eddie. What had Peter Fitzpatrick been involved in for his life to end in such a bloody finale?

Her throat felt dry and she craved a drink. No. She had to think of her children and grandson. She couldn't self-destruct like her father had. History couldn't repeat itself.

Making up her mind, she shoved back her chair and ran up to her bedroom. Opening her bedside cabinet, she took out the bottle of vodka. Back down in the kitchen, she unscrewed the cap and watched the clear liquid swim through the plughole. When she turned round, Katie was standing in the doorway, rocking little Louis in her arms. Chloe lounged behind her. They were both smiling.

It was those smiles, more than anything, that gave Lottie hope for the future of her family. She took little Louis in her arms and inhaled his baby smell. She felt the soft pads of the palms of his hands beneath her fingers, and on either side of her, Katie and Chloe linking her arms.

CHAPTER 79

The reality of staking out a house was nothing like he had imagined. He'd been following the key players for ten months or more, and he still couldn't get used to it. Couldn't get used to being used. He parked his car half a mile away and walked through the terrain he had scoured on Google Maps. The flashlight from his phone lit up his steps and he was careful to hold it downwards so as not to alert any night owls of his progress. Not that many were out in the incessant rain.

Vaulting the back wall, he lowered himself easily into the garden. No lights on in the house. All in bed. Slowly he walked around the side, the drumming of the torrent masking his footsteps. No alarm system. But he already knew that. Better to be sure, though. Returning to the back door, he checked how the lock worked, then extracted a small toolkit from his wallet and got to work.

He knew the layout of the house. The drawings were online, attached to the developer's planning application from seven years ago. Easy. Acclimatising himself to the lack of light, he waited for his eyes to focus via the illumination from the red digits on the cooker clock. Listened. The tinkle of water trickling through radiators on a night timer. The creak of furniture settling. The whoosh of the wind against the back door. Checking once more that the blinds were down and no one was moving upstairs, he switched on the torch again.

The settings for breakfast chilled him.

There were children in this house.

He thought of leaving.

Could he walk away?

No. Not now.

Too much at stake.

With no time left to waste, he pushed open the kitchen door and entered the rest of the house.

The late eighties: The Child

I have no concept of the passage of time.

I have no idea how old I am.

I know Johnny-Joe died.

They say he overdosed after digesting the seeds he was supposed to be planting. Ha.

Six hundred and sixty-six. Johnny-Joe's favourite number. Never less; never more. Wail at the sky, he would, if I miscounted. Sickened me. Every time I had to go into that garden with him. Well, I put an end to that little job. Stuffed all six hundred and sixty-six seeds down his old yellow throat. One by fucking one. I did it, and I never want to hear that number again. He didn't protest much. I told him the devil said he needed him to eat them. Johnny-Joe. Ha!

Today, I have a visitor. Not once, in all the time I've been here, however long that may have been, has anyone called to see me. I've no idea what this is about. Could someone have finally remembered about me? I often wonder about the other one. The other part of me they didn't lock away. Or maybe they did. Somewhere else.

My head hurts as the nurse pulls the shirt tight to my chest and closes up the buttons. An awful yellow yoke, with white daisies. Daisies! I hate daisies almost as much as I hated Johnny-Joe and his fairy seeds. I don't mind the trousers, with their wide flare, though they are a little too tight.

I'm brought to the other side of this mad place. None of that peeling paint and shitty smells. It's painted and shiny. Keep the sunny side out, at all times. I leave my ward, with its screaming and shrieking, and after a walk down a never-ending wide corridor and out through a dozen tall doors, unlocked and locked again behind me, I am deposited in a room with three chairs and a small square table. The windows are high and arched. The paint on the walls is yellow. Like my shirt. Yuck.

I pull up my socks from where they have slipped down in my shoes and pick at the elastic until it snaps and the sock folds once again around my ankle. I do the same to the other one. They have cut my hair tight to my head and combed it straight. I quickly run my fingers through it and shake my head vigorously until I'm sure it is all standing on end. Now I feel contented. I'm not going to play their game. I'm planning my own.

When the woman walks in, I feel my breath stick in my throat and the words I wanted to yell smother down into my chest. Somewhere in the dark recesses of my brain I remember her. My mother? No, she is not my mother. She's the one who brought us here that day. Signed the papers and walked away. Along with a man in uniform.

It's all coming back in such a rush, my head hurts. He's not here today but he was with her that day. Wasn't he upset? I close my eyes and drag the memory to my conscious state. I was so young. He was yelling something about how the foster mother should have taken both. Now I remember. The presence of the woman before me has sparked those memories of when she was here with that man, and I feel another sensation taking root in my soul. The same one that caused me to count to six hundred and sixty-six as I stuffed the miserable little seeds down Johnny-Joe's throat.

'You're sixteen.' Her voice is high and cold. 'You probably thought I'd forgotten about you. Well, I've come to let you know that you're staying here until you're twenty-one. I think that is the right age to let you out into the world again. If I don't die in the meantime.'

She laughs in a shrill, high-pitched way that drills a hole into my head. And I want to drill a hole in hers.

'Behave yourself in here and I'll be back to sign you out. A few more years. That's all.'

She hasn't sat down. Standing. Holding a black leather handbag tight under her arm. The sun outside comes from behind a cloud and shines in through the stained glass at the top of the window, painting her in a myriad of colours.

She opens her bag, takes out a book. Holds it out to me. Should I take it or let her hold it until her arm weakens and she has to put it back in her bag?

I step towards her. She steps backwards.

I smile. I know I have a smile that can strike fear into others. Her mouth droops and I think she's going to scream. She doesn't. Her eyes seem blinded by the light coming from the window. I could jump on her and bite out her tongue and spit it against the sickly yellow walls. And no one would hear until it was too late.

I want to do that. I really do.

But I also want to get out of here.

And if that means waiting another five years for her to come back, then I will keep on smiling at her until she leaves.

I take the book from her hand, my fingers lightly brushing against her skin.

She shivers, as if I've stuck an icicle through her heart.

She turns to open the door, her mission complete.

'Where is my twin?' The only words I have spoken aloud to anyone in years. The sound of my voice frightens even me.

'You don't need to know.'

She opens the door and escapes to her world, condemning me to another five years in mine.

I am patient.

I can wait.

DAY SIX

'No let-up in the weather, then,' Boyd said as Lottie bumped into him on the station steps.

She keyed in the code on the interior door and together they made their way up the stairs to the office.

'The sandbags holding back the river are at breaking point,' she said, hanging up her jacket. No sign of McMahon in her office.

'I thought it burst its banks already?'

'That was in the centre of town; up near my house, the water is above the banks and the council put down sandbags. No idea how long they'll last.'

'The weather!' McMahon strode into the office shaking his coat, splashing drips over desks and paperwork. 'I'm sick of listening to people moaning.'

'Don't listen then. Why don't you—'

'Lottie!' Boyd said, his hazel eyes firing a warning at her across the office.

'I was just going to say why don't you get a warm mug of coffee.' She attempted an eye roll, but when Boyd laughed, she was sure her efforts had resulted in something completely different.

'Good idea,' McMahon said. 'Two sugars. I like it sweet.'

'I wasn't suggesting—'

'I'll get it,' Boyd interjected.

Lottie followed him to the makeshift canteen.

'I can't believe we still have no sightings of either O'Dowd or Arthur Russell,' Boyd said.

'And I can't believe Corrigan hasn't called me in after McMahon complained yesterday,' Lottie said.

'I think our super is in your corner.'

'I am. For now.' Corrigan stuck his head into the confined space. 'But if you don't solve this and get rid of that shithead back to Dublin soon, I think I'll throw in the feckin' towel myself.'

Lottie looked at Boyd and they burst out laughing. She felt tension easing out of her shoulders as Corrigan stomped off down the corridor muttering to himself about getting a press release ready.

With mugs of coffee in hand, they went back to the office. Lottie had taken one sip when Kirby rushed in.

'We've an emergency call out at Gaddstown,' he panted. 'I've sent a squad to follow the ambulance. A neighbour reported blood oozing out beneath the back door of a house.'

'Whereabouts in Gaddstown?' Lottie asked, half rising from her chair.

'Number 2 Treetops. Why?'

The saliva in her throat dried up and she thought her legs would give way. She gripped the edge of her desk with one hand while scrabbling around the mound of paperwork with the other. Files tumbled to the floor.

'What the hell!' Boyd jumped up and began gathering the fallen reports. 'What are you looking for?'

Lottie held up a page torn from a small notebook.

'Number 2 Treetops,' she whispered.

'So?' Boyd placed the files on her desk. 'What about it?'

'It's where Cathal Moroney lives.'

First responders had strewn crime-scene tape across the gateway pillars at the front of the house. An ambulance was parked up behind a Ford Focus. In front of that, a people carrier.

Lottie glanced into the seven-seater. Two child seats were strapped in the back.

'Is Moroney married?' she asked Boyd, realising how little she knew about the reporter.

'I'm sure we're about to find out.'

The uniformed officer standing outside the front door held up his hand. 'We're waiting for SOCOs, Inspector.'

'I have to see for myself,' Lottie said. Boyd went back to the car for protective clothing. 'What's it like in there?'

'Bad. Very bad.'

'Who broke down the door?'

'My colleague.' He pointed to a man leaning against a tree, his face greener than any leaf that might have once adorned the branches. 'He was in and out before I got further than the kitchen. We called for reinforcements and forensics, secured the site and waited.'

Lottie hurriedly pulled on overalls, overshoes, gloves and mouth mask. The garda stood to one side and she entered through the damaged front door.

The familiar metallic scent of blood wafted towards her. To her right, a staircase leading to the first floor; to her left, an open door. She peered inside. A family room. Fireplace with ashes, a floral suite, cushions scattered higgledy-piggledy. In the corner, a plastic box overflowing with toys.

'I've a bad feeling about this, Lottie,' Boyd said.

She was shaking. 'Me too.'

They backed out of the room and made their way down the hall to the kitchen. Modern, open-plan, with an island in the centre. It was laid for breakfast. Orange juice carton. Smooth, no bits. Cereal boxes. Coco Pops, muesli. Two ceramic mugs. Two plastic beakers. One blue. One pink. Two plastic bowls. One blue. One pink.

Lying against the cupboard beneath the sink was a woman with long black hair matted to her scalp. Blood had ceased pouring. It streaked the side of her face and neck and saturated her white cotton nightie. Her eyes were closed. She looked like a doll that had been dropped by a careless child. Her legs were spread out; hands by her sides, palms upwards. Her blood had flowed towards the back door. This must be what the neighbour had witnessed seeping out onto the step.

'Where are the kids, Boyd? Where's Moroney?' Lottie asked, knowing that the answer to one or both of those questions lay beyond the breakfast bar.

She took a step on to the satin-finish cream floor tiles.

'McGlynn will have your guts for garters,' Boyd said.

She continued around the side of the island, holding her breath, almost closing her eyes.

She exhaled loudly. 'It's Moroney.'

The man she had seen as her nemesis lay supine on the floor, a black-handled knife protruding from his stomach, still clutched in his hand. Had he been trying to extract it, or had he stabbed himself? His face was bruised and bloody. His mouth hung open, his once sparkling megawatt smile no more.

Boyd said, 'Domestic drama?'

Lottie looked around wildly, clutched Boyd's outstretched hand. 'Where are the children?'

She rushed back to the garda at the front door. 'Did you check upstairs?'

'No, Inspector. Waiting for you lot and SOCOs.'

'You didn't check to see if the children were here? Good God!' She turned and took two steps at a time up the stairs.

'Lottie, wait!' Boyd called.

'They might be alive,' she shouted over her shoulder.

A landing spread out in front of her. With gloved fingers she tapped the first door open. Bathroom.

'There's no blood trail,' Boyd said.

'What do you mean?'

'If Moroney went apeshit and killed his family before himself, there'd be blood everywhere.'

'Shut up.'

The next door was wide open. Master bedroom. Duvet thrown back and sheets crumpled, as if the occupants had just jumped out of bed. They would never be getting back in, she thought.

The next door had the name JAKE in blue plastic lettering pinned to the door. Glancing across the landing, she saw a door with pink lettering. ANNIE.

'Oh my God, Boyd. I can't do it.'

She leaned back, took a deep breath and pushed the door open. Jake's room was empty. She followed Boyd into the little girl's room. Also empty.

'Where are the children?' she cried.

A whimper from the corner of the room alerted her.

'The wardrobe!'

Running across the shaggy pink carpet, she pulled back the sliding door, tugged the hanging clothes apart and dropped to her knees.

'Annie? Sweetheart, I'm a friend. You're okay now. No one is going to hurt you.' Stroking the arm of the curled-up trembling child, she pulled down her mask and hood, not wanting to terrorise the little girl further.

'Mommy? Where's m-m-my m-mommy?'

Lottie gently lifted Annie out of her refuge. Boyd leaned in to search further. He shook his head.

'Annie darling, where's your brother? Where's Jake?'

The child in her arms screamed.

Boyd rushed across to the boy's room. Lottie heard him pulling at doors and drawers. He returned. 'He's not in his room.'

The sound of commotion downstairs reached Lottie's ears.

'Let's get this little one to an ambulance,' she said.

At the bottom of the stairs she directed Jim McGlynn towards the kitchen. Boyd passed by and out of the front door, calling for a paramedic.

'I want my mommy,' Annie cried, clinging to Lottie's neck.

'Find the neighbour who reported this,' Lottie instructed Boyd.

Sitting on the bottom stair, she pulled a fleece jacket from the banister to wrap around the child, then realised that she could compromise any evidence that might be on the girl. She waited. Had Moroney killed his wife and then himself, as Boyd had surmised? Hadn't Moroney told her only yesterday that he'd been working for years on an organised crime story? Maybe he'd got too close to the truth and had to be taken out. But why kill his wife? Jesus, she didn't even know the woman's name, hadn't even known Moroney was married with kids. She had him all wrong.

Boyd returned with a woman, tear-streaked cheeks, hair hanging untidily around her shoulders.

'This is Dee White. Jake was having a sleepover with her son last night. She brought him home this morning and got no response at the front door. When she went round the back… she saw the blood.'

'I had Jake with me. I just bundled him up in my arms and ran home to call the emergency services. I knew something was wrong.'

'What age is Jake?'

'He's five. Annie is three. Will you come with me, sweetie?'

Lottie said, 'Annie, I want you to go with Dee. You'll see Jake soon. Would you like that?'

The little girl murmured and wriggled from Lottie's grip. Dee took her in her arms and Boyd guided them to the ambulance. Lottie assigned a detective to remain with them at all times. Maybe the little girl had seen something. Heard something. They'd have to interview her at some stage. But she's only three, Lottie thought, and turned back to the kitchen of death.

CHAPTER 82

McGlynn and his team worked in silence. There had to be a study or an office. Lottie tried the door to her left. Utility room – the washing machine with a late-night wash. An empty basket sat on the floor ready for the clothes. Clothes that would never again be worn.

Coats hung on hooks, wellingtons lined up neatly beneath them. A shelf with a pair of small football boots, mud and grass clogged in the studs.

'Out,' McGlynn said. 'You've trampled all over my crime scene. Enough is enough.'

'Later, then. After the state pathologist arrives.'

Without glancing at the bodies, she moved back to the hallway and into the living room. Beyond the fireplace a door lay open. Before McGlynn or any of his team could stop her, she entered.

Moroney's home office. The only thing not upturned was an old desk with its drawers hanging open. It looked hand-made. Roughly hewn timber planks nailed together. A filing cabinet, on its side, had the drawers ripped from its rollers. They were piled on top of each other, contents spilled and ripped apart. The blinds were pulled down behind the desk but a little light crept in at the sides. Lottie noticed the framed photograph hanging on the wall. A seated Moroney, with his usual megawatt smile, his shoulders draped with the arms of the beautiful black-haired woman standing behind him, so different from how she now looked on the kitchen floor. Two children, smiling out at the camera, on his knees, their arms wrapped around his neck.

Choking back a sob, Lottie silently mourned the man she had never liked and the family she'd never known he had.

'Inspector?' Jane Dore stood, suited up in the hallway.

Totally convinced now that Moroney had not murdered his wife before taking his own life, Lottie walked out of the office with determination in every step. Someone had been looking for something. And she'd no idea if it had been found or not. But once the SOCOs had finished their work, she would be back.

'It's an ugly one,' she said.

'Aren't they all?' Jane said, and set off for the kitchen.

Outside the tent that had been erected at the front door, the cold air had turned to rain once more, and with her mouth set in a grim line, Lottie hurried round the back of the house to look for Boyd.

*

'Cathal and Lauren Moroney were murdered sometime between five and seven this morning,' Boyd said, lighting two cigarettes.

'Very careful murderer to get in and out unseen by neighbours.' Lottie took one of the cigarettes.

Boyd consulted his notebook. 'We have a report from a man who lives down the road. Says he heard a car around six. Looked out of his bedroom window. It was still quite dark so he can't be sure of the colour, but it was definitely a saloon type.'

'That's a lot of good.'

'Better than nothing.'

'I can't stop thinking of that poor little girl. What did she hear to make her terrified enough to hide?'

'Maybe the killer shoved her into the wardrobe?'

'I don't think there was time for that.' Lottie pulled hard on the cigarette, trying to shield it from the rain with her other hand. 'I'd say Moroney was in the bedroom getting dressed. Heard his wife scream or something. Instinct kicked in. He hid his daughter and ran down the stairs to see what was happening.'

'That sounds daft. His wife could've screamed if she'd burned herself on the cooker or such. Why would he immediately think something was seriously wrong?'

Lottie watched Boyd pacing in small circles, avoiding the puddles on the ground. Cigarette smoke hung low, suspended around him in the mist.

'Moroney was investigating a drugs ring,' she said, taking a final drag before stamping out the butt beneath her boot.

Boyd ceased his pacing. 'And how do you know that?'

'He told me.'

Boyd stood still.

'What?' she said. 'Don't be looking at me like that.'

'Like what? Lottie, what were you up to with Moroney?'

'I wasn't up to anything.'

He grabbed her arm. She smelled the freshness of the rain rising from his clothes. Drops dripped from his hair to his cheeks and nose. Too close. She took a step back, shook her head and walked away.

'You'd better tell me,' he shouted after her.

CHAPTER 83

McMahon was pacing the office, as pent up as Boyd had been earlier. Lottie slammed her bag on the floor beneath her desk.

'I think your friend Henry "Hammer" Quinn might be behind the Moroneys' murders,' she said.

'That's not possible.' He came to a stop beside her desk.

'Why not? Moroney told me he was investigating a drugs ring. He must've had something worth killing him for.'

'Well, it wasn't Hammer, because I had him arrested late last night. Picked up from his home. He spent the night in Store Street garda station.'

'Shite. It had to be one of his associates then,' she said, biting her lip, wondering if she had it all wrong. Again.

'Hammer was interviewed extensively. He admitted a few things but he swears he hasn't seen or heard from Jerome in two years. Says he had nothing to do with the murders here in Ragmullin. Much as I hate to admit it, I tend to believe him.'

'Jesus, that's some turnaround. You're the one pontificating that all this has to do with drugs.' Lottie slapped her hand on the desk and a stack of files shuddered without falling. The whole investigation had started off with the murder of Tessa Ball. Was she the crucial link in everything?

'I'm not saying it's not to do with the drugs. Just that Hammer and his gang aren't involved. I believe we need to find out who was supplying Lorcan Brady and Jerome Quinn with the heroin, and who they were supplying the cannabis to,' he said.

'And the fish food we found in Brady's house,' Lottie fumed. 'Add that to your list while you're at it.'

'What about it?'

'There was no fish tank.'

'Ha! It's used to cut the heroin. Makes it go further. Makes more money.'

'I've heard it all now.'

'Oh I doubt that.'

Lottie shuffled her chair into her desk, then took the first file from the bundle and opened it. The typed words swam before her eyes as she tried to divert her attention from McMahon going into her office.

Her phone rang.

'Yes, Don,' she said to the desk sergeant.

'There's an Annabelle O'Shea down here asking for you. I told her you were busy but she's insistent.'

She'd never phoned Annabelle back. What could be so urgent? But her friend might be the welcome relief she needed. 'Show her into the interview room if there's nowhere else available and I'll be down in two minutes.'

McMahon said, 'I'm calling a team meeting. Five minutes in the incident room.'

'I'm busy,' Lottie said, and made her escape.

*

Might as well be on Mars, Lottie thought as she entered the airless interview room. The outside world ceased to exist once you seated yourself at the steel table, its legs screwed to the floor.

Her breath caught in her throat. 'Annabelle! What happened to you?'

'I need to speak with you, Lottie.'

Dragging a chair across, she sat beside her friend, who didn't look at all like the confident doctor she'd known for most of her life.

Annabelle raised a bandaged hand and pushed back a loose strand of hair behind her ear, the lobe of which was covered in dried blood. With her other hand she traced a line around her neck and her trembling fingers drew down the roll of her black polo-neck sweater.

'Jesus Christ.' Lottie stared at the marks circling her throat. 'What happened?'

'Have you to switch on that recorder before I say anything?'

'If you're making a formal complaint, I'll get someone to sit in with us and I can record the conversation.' Lottie sat rigid, unsure whether to wrap her arms around her friend or to call an ambulance.

'No, I don't want anyone else. I'll tell you first. Then you can decide what you want to do.'

'Maybe I'll record it to be on the safe side. It might not stand up in court, but if you don't want another witness, that is your choice.'

Flicking the switches, Lottie formally identified herself and got Annabelle to say her name for the tape. She really should be upstairs dealing with the Moroney killings. But her friend looked too distraught for this to be anything other than serious.

'Now, Annabelle, tell me what happened to you. How you come to have those injuries.'

'I'm not sure, Lottie. It's kind of personal, but at the same time, I'm so afraid.'

'You've presented with visible injuries to your hand, neck and ear. They will have to be photographed. Who assaulted you?'

Annabelle whispered something.

Lottie said, 'I'm sorry, but you need to speak up for the tape.' Had she just accused her husband of assault? Oh God, she needed Boyd to sit in.

'My husband, Cian O'Shea.' Annabelle's voice was stronger now. 'But that's not the reason I'm here.'

'If that bastard did that, he must be charged.'

'Hear me out. Then I'll decide what I want to do.'

Gripping her friend's hand, Lottie looked into her eyes and felt the reflection of intense sadness. She knew Annabelle was a master of her own circumstances, but not even one of her affairs warranted the abuse she must be suffering. And what could be more important than reporting her husband for assault? 'Go ahead.'

She waited as Annabelle swallowed, blinked back tears and pulled her hand away.

'I know you thought Cian was a good man. A quiet guy. Waiting patiently by while I partied and shagged my way though life. Maybe that was true, but once he found out about my affair with Tom Rickard, something shifted dramatically inside him. It was like that affair snapped his heart in two.' She paused, swallowed, took a deep breath, exhaled and continued. 'I could handle the taunts. The dagger stares. The name-calling. I could handle all that… I thought. I wanted to leave many times, but the twins… You see, he would never let them go with me. He repeated that so often, Lottie, I feared he meant more than just not letting them leave. Do you follow me?'

Lottie thought for a moment. This didn't sound like the Cian she thought she knew. But she had felt something was wrong when she visited the other day.

'I do follow you. But even if Cian did those horrible things to you, I don't think he would harm his own children.'

Annabelle laughed, and Lottie flinched at the manic sound. It was like the wail of an injured animal.

'He would, you know. If he can rape me in our own kitchen, with the twins not far away, he can do anything he damn well pleases. But Lottie—'

'Rape? Jesus, Annabelle! I'm getting Boyd. This has to be formal.'

'Hear me out first. I think Cian is involved in something very dark. Dangerous. He spends hours locked away in his study, and I mean locked. He put a code device on the door to stop me entering and snooping. But I did go in. He left it open on purpose, to test me. I was suspicious before… but now… now I'm sure.'

'Sure of what?'

'He's doing something dreadful. He disappears from the house every night and doesn't come back until morning. I don't know where he goes, but last night I heard him leave around four a.m. He came home as I was leaving for work. He was… Oh Lottie. He was covered in blood.'

'What!'

'Blood.' Annabelle paused. 'Can I have a drink of water?'

'Sure, and I'm getting Boyd. Wait here a minute.'

She went to the door and shouted for someone to fetch Boyd and bring water. She sat back down, checked the recorder and waited while Annabelle stared at an invisible spot on the wall.

'You wanted me?' Boyd entered the room carrying a pitcher of water and a couple of paper cups. 'Annabelle! What happened to you?'

Lottie brought him up to date. 'Are you okay to continue, Annabelle?'

Annabelle drained her cup of water and Boyd refilled it. She sipped, then bit her lip before continuing.

'Cian came into the kitchen literally drenched from the rain and I could see blood on his hands. I think he'd tried to wash it off, but I'm a doctor, I know blood streaks when I see them. I must've been standing with my mouth open, because before I knew it, he'd thumped me in the stomach. When I fell to the ground, he held me down with his foot. I thought he was going to kick my head in, but he changed his mind, hauled me up and grabbed me by the throat. I could smell it on him then. The blood. I could smell it on his skin.'

'What happened then?' Lottie asked, keeping her voice low and calm though she wanted to shake the story out of Annabelle.

'He snarled, like a dog. Told me to keep my mouth shut and then he wouldn't have to kill me too.'

'Kill you too? Who did he kill?'

'I don't know, but then I heard on the car radio about a suspected murder out in Gaddstown and I had to come here. Am I married to a murderer?'

Lottie eyed Boyd. He looked as incredulous as she felt. 'Tell me what happened after he told you to say nothing.'

'He stripped off his clothes and put on a wash, then walked naked up to his study. Not caring if the twins saw him. No matter how he is with me, he usually remains visibly calm to others. Now he's gone mad. Insane? I don't know, but he seriously frightened me. What has he done, Lottie?'

'I intend to find out,' Lottie said. 'Where is he now?'

'At home.'

'Where are the twins?'

'At a friend's house. I waited until they were up and had had their breakfast. Stuck a smile on my face and dropped them off. I couldn't face going into the surgery, so I drove out to the lake and sat in my car for a few hours deciding what to do. And now I'm here.'

'Annabelle, we are going to pick Cian up and bring him in for questioning. You have to sign your statement. Then I think you should collect the kids and book into a hotel for tonight.'

'Why can't I go home once you get Cian?'

'We need to interview him and see if we can get evidence to link him to a crime. You will be safer away from home until we have a clearer picture of what we're dealing with. Do I have permission to enter your house?'

Unhooking a key from her key ring, Annabelle handed it over. 'You'll need the alarm code too.' She called it out and Boyd wrote it down.

'It's all my fault,' she cried. 'If I had remained faithful, this would never have happened.'

'Don't blame yourself. None of us knows what drives someone to alter their behaviour. And Cian is responsible for his.'

CHAPTER 84

Once Annabelle had left, Lottie and Boyd returned to the incident room. No sign of McMahon.

Kirby said, 'We got updated data from Emma's phone. She made one call after she went missing.'

'Just the one? To who?'

'Whom,' Boyd said.

'Not now, Boyd. Who did she call?'

'Natasha Kelly.'

'Oh. I thought maybe it was someone we could pin her murder on. Looking for moral support, I suppose. Girl talk. When did she make the call?'

'12.05 p.m. Lasted four minutes and three seconds.'

'And no other calls? None to her father?'

'Nope. That's it. As we couldn't track the phone before, I reckon she had taken the battery out.'

'Figures, seeing as we found the SIM card and battery separate from the phone, in the kitchen.' She thought for a moment. 'What was so important that Natasha was the only person Emma felt safe enough to contact? We need to interview Natasha Kelly. Have you Emma's phone data for the night of Tessa Ball's murder?'

Kirby flicked through the pages. 'Nothing until the 999 call. Jaysus, I thought youngsters were always on their phones.'

'They very seldom ring or text any more,' Lottie said, thinking of her own children. 'Facebook, Snapchat and WhatsApp. Check out her social media accounts. See if that turns up anything.'

'Right, boss,' Kirby said, scratching his head.

Maria Lynch piped up. 'I checked her Facebook already. Nothing unusual. She had no Twitter account.'

'Did you check out Natasha's accounts?'

'No, but I will.'

Lottie said, 'We have a development that might answer a few questions about Cathal and Lauren Moroney's deaths.'

'At last. Answers.' Superintendent Corrigan marched in. 'I'm sick of the media calling us headless chickens. These murders are like an aggressive cancer, spreading too fast. We need to halt it. And I mean today.'

He was gone almost as soon as he had arrived.

'You heard the man,' Lottie said. 'And if Tessa's murder had to do with land, figure out how much she was worth and who would benefit by wiping out her entire family.'

'Besides, O'Dowd, Arthur Russell is the last man standing,' Lynch said.

'Well find them. Boyd, you come with me.'

'Do we need backup?'

'Let's see who or what we're dealing with first. Okay?'

Boyd shook his head. 'Cian O'Shea. Who would believe it?'

Lottie said, 'Not many, I'm sure. Let's get to his house before he gets to a solicitor.'

*

The house looked grimmer today than Lottie remembered. She got out the key ready to put it in the door.

'The alarm code. Do you have it ready?' she asked.

'In my head,' Boyd said.

'Annabelle wasn't sure it would be activated, but if the keypad is beeping, it's on.'

Lottie stuck the key in the door and turned it. They stepped onto the black and white diamond-shaped tiles and listened. No beep from the alarm. Not a sound. She crept into the kitchen, looked around quickly. No one. At the door to the utility room, she paused. No sound from the washing machine. She peered in. The door of the machine hung open. Empty.

'Where did he put the clothes?' she whispered.

Boyd was looking out at the back garden. 'There's a car in the garage. He must be here.'

As she turned to leave, Lottie spied a laundry basket on top of a counter. With protective gloves on her hands, she picked through the clothes. A man's outer jacket, sweater, shirt, trousers and underwear. 'Where did he leave his shoes? We'll need to bag this lot once we've found him.'

Back in the hall, she wondered if maybe they should get a warrant. No. It'd be fine. At the top of the stairs, she saw the door with the keypad. Open. She raised an eyebrow at Boyd, questioning. But then she realised that Cian would have no need to lock his study during the day while his family was out.

With a nod of her head, she indicated for Boyd to follow her.

At the door, she kept her hand on her gun, unsure of how this was going to develop. With the tip of her boot, she edged the door inwards.

'He's not here,' Boyd said, stating, as he usually did, the obvious.

'All this equipment. It's like something out of a Hollywood studio.'

'You're trespassing on my property.'

Lottie swung round, crashing into Boyd.

Standing on the landing, naked, was Cian O'Shea. And he looked feral.

'Ah, the very man we're looking for,' Lottie said, winging it.

'Get out of my house. Now.'

Visually assessing him, Lottie couldn't see any obvious wounds on his body. She concentrated on the knife in his hand.

'I think you should put down that weapon and get dressed, then we can have a chat.'

'I said, get out!'

He moved into the study. Lottie stood unmoving. His eyes were predatory. Was this the same man who had been married to her friend for twenty years? She didn't recognise him. His mouth drooped and his hair was wild.

As Cian advanced further, Boyd pounced. The knife fell to the floor, and before Lottie could react, Boyd had snapped handcuffs on the naked man. Cian crumbled and began to cry. 'I didn't mean to kill them. That wasn't supposed to happen.'

'Call SOCOs and get him out of here,' Lottie said.

Boyd led the man to his bedroom, where he found a robe to hide his nakedness, before bringing him down the stairs, reading him his rights as he went. O'Shea had presented as a dangerous threat to two detectives, armed with a lethal weapon. They could probably hold him for twenty-four hours on that charge alone. He would likely retract the words he had just uttered. Lottie needed evidence to support Annabelle's statement.

The study had multiple screens hanging on the wall. Wide screens. Flat screens. Two computer desktops and laptops. Wires were neatly pinned and secured along the walls. A set of headphones hung on a hook and the leather chair was situated in front of a desk full of technology.

With her finger still gloved, she hit the return button on one of the laptops. A screen burst into life.

'Jesus Christ,' she said, exhaling a long breath. What the hell was Cian O'Shea involved in?

CHAPTER 85

Kirby and Lynch were going over the information they'd received from the land registry when Boyd's computer pinged with an email.

'Have a look at that, Lynch. Might be important.'

Lynch went over and tapped Boyd's keyboard. Kirby joined her.

'Health service records?' he said.

'The list of St Declan's patients. This is a wild goose chase.'

'Open it up,' Kirby said.

'You do it. I'm not a snoop.'

'Ah, for Christ's sake.' Kirby jabbed a thick finger on the email, opening it up. 'Screenshots of handwritten originals. I'll print them off and let Boyd chase his own goose when he returns.'

He ambled back to his desk.

'So,' he said, 'all this land was owned by Stan and Kitty Belfield in 1970.'

'Who owned it before them?'

'What matters is who owned it afterwards. I don't know why or how, but by 1976, this portion here, consisting of two hundred and sixty acres, was in Tessa Ball's name. This piece here, where Marian lived, twenty acres, was also in Ball's name. The Belfields retained ownership of the manor house and the land banking down towards the lake. With me so far?'

Lynch nodded. 'Yes.'

'Over the last couple of years, the two hundred and sixty acres of farmland, including the cottage, was transferred over to Mick

O'Dowd. He was just a farm tenant before that. Why the transfer? And the land at Carnmore containing two houses was transferred to Marian Russell. Nothing remained in Tessa's name except her apartment. She wasn't dying or anything, was she?'

'Nothing showed up at the post-mortem.'

'So the question is, what prompted a wealthy former solicitor to divest herself of her wealth?' Kirby said.

'Does it even matter?'

'This might all have to do with land ownership, not drugs.'

'Money,' Lynch said, 'the root of all evil.'

'We need to run this by the boss,' Kirby said. 'They're taking their time getting back.'

'Who's taking their time?' McMahon asked, entering the office with a swish of his shoulders.

'Shit,' Lynch said.

CHAPTER 86

Dressed in a white forensic suit, Cian O'Shea cut a morose figure in his sterile cell. Lottie left him to ponder the walls and walked up towards the office with Boyd.

'Bastard, saying nothing until he gets his solicitor.' Boyd thumped his hand against the wall with every step he took ascending the stairs.

'We can nail him for the Moroney murders once SOCOs lift something from the washed clothes.'

'If what Annabelle said about the blood is correct, then they will.'

'And his DNA should be in Moroney's house. But why did he do it?' Lottie headed for the car pool yard. 'I'd kill for a cigarette. We deserve a break.'

Huddled in the rear doorway, Boyd lit the cigarettes.

Lottie dragged heartily and stared up at the misty sky. 'Will it ever end?'

'The rain?'

'Boyd, will you give me a hug. Just a quick one. In the face of all this insanity, I want to feel a little bit human.' She turned to him, and he dipped his head and kissed her cheek before wrapping his arms about her.

'You are the most human person I know,' he said into her hair.

'The world is so full of monsters, I fear for my family. I panic when I think of what we'll find next.' She drew away from his embrace, took another drag of her cigarette and stubbed it out. 'And then I wonder if my father had any involvement with Carrie King's incarceration in St Declan's.'

'What difference does it make?'

'Maybe he was a monster too.' She glanced up at the clouds as they burst with a thunderous downpour. 'If he was into something illegal, maybe he didn't like what he had become.'

'You think that's why he killed himself?'

'If he did in fact kill himself.'

Boyd threw down his cigarette. 'You may never know, and you have enough to concern yourself with right now.' He gave her one final squeeze. 'Let's go back inside before we drown.'

'We'll get nowhere until O'Shea's solicitor arrives. But first I want to speak with Natasha Kelly. Will you be a star and pull the car up to the door?'

*

They passed Marian Russell's house on the way. It stood ghostlike; a spectre in the rain.

'Where can Arthur Russell be hiding out?' Lottie asked.

'We've interviewed all his known friends. Searched everywhere. He hasn't left the country. We'll find him.'

'I don't think he killed his own daughter. When we spoke with him, he seemed to genuinely love her.'

'You never know what can drive people to murder. Look at Cian O'Shea,' Boyd said.

'What was his motive for killing the Moroneys? That's what I'd like to know.'

'We don't know that he killed anyone.'

'Not yet.'

'Do you think he murdered the others too?'

'I don't know, Boyd. I honestly don't know what to think. But we really need to find Mick O'Dowd as well as Arthur.'

He parked outside the Kellys'. 'No car.'

'They might be at the shops,' Lottie said. The house looked as empty as Marian Russell's. She rang the bell, hammered on the door until her knuckles turned red.

'No one home,' Boyd said.

'Check the rear.' Lottie took off at a run and Boyd followed.

'Definitely no one here,' she said after a minute. 'I thought they'd decided to stay. So where are they? I need to find out why Emma phoned Natasha.'

'Calm down. They'll be back.'

'I've a bad feeling about this.'

'You've a bad feeling about everything.'

'Check their car registration number and radio traffic to watch for them. Shit, there isn't even a neighbour to ask when they were last seen.'

'Will you quit panicking? They're not gone far.'

'And how do you deduce that?'

'Oh for Christ's sake.'

Lottie watched as Boyd stomped back to the car. He leaned in and grabbed the radio. Looking around the house once again, she noted the lie of the land and wondered if Kirby had received any additional information about the land. Next on her list.

From the car, Boyd shouted, 'McGlynn wants us at O'Shea's house.'

CHAPTER 87

'We've sent the clothes for analysis,' McGlynn said, leading the way up the stairs.

'They were washed. Will you get anything from them?' Lottie asked.

'Fingers crossed we will.'

'I didn't know you were the superstitious type.'

'Detective Inspector Parker, you don't know anything about me.'

'True,' Lottie said as they reached Cian's study. 'So, what did you want to show us?'

'This here is Gary. He's a technical genius.'

Lottie nodded at the young man. He was suited up, as she was, but she assumed he was young. Not too many technical geniuses in her age group. 'What did you find, Gary?'

'This is some set-up,' he said, and she could hear the admiration in his voice. 'There's a whole games development suite here. I could sift through it all day long.'

'Gary,' McGlynn said. 'Tell the detectives what you discovered.'

The technician reluctantly walked away from his prize. 'This is an impressive CCTV system. Remotely linked. And from what I can see, it's mainly via mobile phone network.'

'So he was spying on people via their phones?'

'And computer webcams.' He tapped a keyboard with his gloved fingers.

The screen Lottie had accidentally accessed earlier popped open. Annabelle's surgery. She looked back at Boyd.

'This is what I told you about.'

'So the bastard was spying on her,' Boyd said.

Gary clicked a mouse and another screen sprang life.

'Looks very modern,' Lottie said.

'It's an office. But have a look at the reflection on the glass wall behind the desk.'

Leaning over, Lottie squinted at the image. 'A skyscraper?'

'I think this office is in Manhattan.'

'Jesus,' Boyd said. 'Was he spying on someone in New York?'

'Can you access the address of the building?' Lottie asked.

'The image is a still, not live. I tried accessing the code, but no luck.'

Tiredness and frustration seeped into her bones; she just wanted Gary to get to the point.

'And brace yourself for this one.' The technician clicked a third screen open.

'What the…?' Lottie gaped open-mouthed. 'That's my son's room.' She stared incredulously. 'How…?'

'He hacked into his computer with a game download.'

'But why was he spying on Sean?'

'I don't know. Maybe it was the only way he could access your home.'

'Why would Cian O'Shea be spying on me and my family?'

'And for how long?' Boyd said.

'I'll let you know more once I get stuck in.'

She could only see his eyes, but Lottie knew the young man was itching to get started on Cian O'Shea's project. Whatever the hell that was.

'And all that is live feed?' she asked.

'Yes, it's in real time.'

'Copies? Recordings? Tapes or anything?'

'I don't know yet.'

'O'Shea has some serious questions to answer.'

McGlynn handed Lottie a file. 'This was in the cabinet. Know anything about it?'

Lottie stared at the copy Jane Dore had made of her father's post-mortem file. With all Cian's expertise, she supposed it was a simple task for him to hack into the state computer systems and put a flag on the file. But why did he need to do that, and then steal the hard copy?

Feeling the confinement of the room and the heat from the equipment, Lottie turned and rushed out. It suddenly felt way too small. And she felt even smaller.

CHAPTER 88

Lottie wanted to go home. Instead she sent a technician to her house to check out Sean's computer equipment and to search for further intrusions. Exhaustion caused her knees to creak, but Kirby wanted everyone in the incident room. He'd pinned maps up on one of the incident boards.

She tried to hide a yawn with the back of her hand. 'Explain.'

'For some reason, in 1976 all this land was transferred from Kitty and Stan Belfield to Tessa Ball. Then two years ago, Tessa transferred the farmland, including the cottage, to O'Dowd, and six months ago, the land containing the Russell and Kelly houses to Marian.' Kirby smiled triumphantly.

'So?' Lottie said.

'Why?'

'I wanted answers, not more questions.'

'This might explain part of it.' Lynch pinned two sheets of paper on the board alongside the maps. 'Birth certificates.'

Lottie rose from her chair and stood beside Lynch.

'Tessa was born Teresa O'Dowd.' She glanced at the other certificate, noted the parents' names. 'She was Mick O'Dowd's sister.'

'Maybe that explains why she signed the land over to him,' Lynch said.

'Answers one question,' Kirby said.

'But why did she only do it two years ago? What happened in her life then to force her hand?'

'The only thing I can come up with is that the cottage was rented out around then. So it might have been the start of their involvement with the drug lord.'

'Jerome Quinn?'

'Yup.'

'Was she trying to distance herself by formally signing the land to O'Dowd?'

'How does Cian O'Shea fit in?' Boyd said.

'This gets more complicated by the minute.' Lottie paced in small circles. 'We need to find O'Dowd. He's the only one who can tell us about Tessa.'

She thought of her search of O'Dowd's house and the book she'd found under the sink cupboard, with its inscription inside.

'Carrie King,' she said. 'Did you come across any connection to her?'

'No, don't think so,' Kirby said.

'No,' Lynch said.

'Let me get this straight.' Lottie sat down and drummed her knuckles against her forehead. 'The Belfields owned all that land. Stan was in partnership with Tessa Ball. Something occurred in the early to mid seventies to warrant him signing a large part of his fortune over to Tessa. What?'

Boyd said. 'What do you know about this Carrie King?'

'She was supposedly into drugs and alcohol. Had a number of children taken from her and was eventually locked up in St Declan's. Kitty Belfield said Tessa was heavily involved in the circumstances surrounding Carrie King's incarcerations. She even suggested to me that Mick O'Dowd could have fathered at least one of Carrie's children, and she remarked how alike Marian was to O'Dowd. But if Tessa and Mick were brother and sister, perhaps that's the reason for the resemblance.'

'Or, as you first thought, O'Dowd fathered Marian with Carrie King and Tessa cobbled together a birth certificate and raised her as her own.'

'Let's go with that for a minute,' Lottie said. 'It still doesn't explain all that land transfer. What hold could Tessa have had over the Belfields?'

'Maybe they had no children of their own and saw Tessa as an heir,' Lynch said.

'Kirby, check it out,' Lottie said. 'Boyd, we're going to have a go at Cian O'Shea.'

She wasted a full hour with Cian O'Shea and his solicitor. She'd be hearing 'no comment' in her sleep for a year.

'The bastard,' she said, entering Cathal Moroney's house.

'He's afraid, though,' Boyd said.

'He should be very afraid. By the time I finish with him he—'

'Lottie, there's nothing you can do. Let's find the evidence.'

'Right.'

'What do you hope to discover?'

'I have no idea, but if it was Cian O'Shea who broke in and murdered the Moroneys, you can be sure it wasn't something on a computer he was looking for. It had to be the file Moroney told me about.' She headed straight for the study.

'So it *is* drug-related.'

'If I knew that, O'Shea would be in front of a judge this minute. As it is, we still have to look. This place is a mess.'

On her knees, Lottie carefully stacked pages. Once she had a good sheaf, she handed them to Boyd. 'Make yourself useful.'

'Doing what?'

'These were all in the drawers and filing cabinet. So at one time they were in some sort of order. You're good at that.'

'But I don't even know what they relate to.' Boyd took the papers and sat on a chair by the desk.

'Use your head.'

'Is there anything in particular you want me to highlight for you?'

'Something that caused a murderer to break in and kill Cathal and Lauren Moroney, while one of their terrified children hid upstairs.'

'Murder might not have been the intention.'

'Probably not. If he'd found what he was after, I think he'd have been in and out without being discovered. Just sort the papers and I'll go through them.'

Should she tell Boyd about her conversation with Moroney? But surely his murder had nothing to do with what his father had wanted to print back in the seventies. Had it? No. It was something Moroney himself had uncovered about the drugs ring. Had to be. And if the killer hadn't had enough time or couldn't wrangle it out of him, then that information was still here. Somewhere.

*

'It's all stuff he's already reported on,' Boyd said three hours later as he surveyed his handiwork. Lottie was still on her knees, wading through the morass of paper.

'It's here somewhere and I'm going to find it.'

'You don't even know what you're looking for. Let's call it a night and we can get back to it tomorrow.'

'Tomorrow?' Lottie threw her hands in the air. 'We have case files as high as the body count. Something links them all together. Moroney was on to it.' Sitting back on the floor, she caught sight of the clock on the wall. 'God! Is that the time?' She jumped up, scattering paper and files in her haste.

'Hey! I just sorted those. And yes, it's 12.03, madam inspector. Just after the witching hour.'

'I should've been home hours ago.' She edged out past Boyd to the living room. Catching sight of the box of toys, she faltered. Thank God the children had not been harmed physically, though they would suffer psychological damage. And she knew how bad that could be. Picking up her jacket, she felt her phone vibrate in the pocket. She checked it. Chloe.

'Hi, hon. I'm sorry, I got held up at work. All okay?'

'Mom, you'd better come home. Now.'

'What's the matter?'

'It's Katie. You need to speak to her. Little Louis is driving me and Sean mad. Sean even threatened to stuff him up the chimney. He's only joking, but please hurry.'

'I'm on my way.'

Lottie stood with the phone in her hand, staring at the fireplace. Then back to the toy box. Where would a man hide something he didn't want found? Rushing over, she pulled toys from the plastic container. Lego, Peppa Pig, a fire truck, a garda car with a siren that blared loudly as her hand touched it.

'Slow down. You're like a lunatic,' Boyd said, shrugging on his coat.

Her fingers touched it before her eyes registered it. She yanked it out. A faded manila folder. Similar to the one she had kept all those years in her desk drawer until she had solved the mystery last January. A green treasury tag was looped through a double-punched hole at the edge. She stared. Her hand feathered the old paperwork. Sensing Boyd standing over her, she didn't know whether to hide the file under the toys or show it to him. Gulping down a sob, she felt his hand on her shoulder.

'What is it?'

'The answer, Boyd. I think it might be the answer I've been looking for.'

CHAPTER 90

Boyd retrieved a plastic evidence bag from the car and Lottie carefully slid the folder inside. Time. She would need time and peace to go through it. But the title scripted on the front told her enough. This was Moroney's bargaining chip. But was it what the killer had been after, or was that something else entirely?

Tiredness creased her legs as she hobbled towards the car, nodding goodnight to the officer manning the crime-scene tape at the gate.

'Will I drop you at yours or do you want to pick up your car at the station?' Boyd asked.

'I'd best get home and sort out the war.' Lottie clicked on her seat belt.

'Care to tell me why that file has your father's name on it?'

'Not now. I can't think straight.'

But she *was* thinking. Thinking how her father's post-mortem file had gone missing from the Dead House. How Cathal Moroney and his wife had been murdered in their own home. How this file had lain hidden among his children's toys. She wouldn't sleep tonight. Her mind was in overdrive.

As Boyd idled the engine outside her house, she saw that all the lights were blazing.

'Your kids still up?' he asked.

'Probably killing each other. Thanks for the lift.' She put her hand out to open the car door, but felt Boyd tug at her sleeve.

'You need to be careful,' he said, his voice as soft as the rain pitter-pattering against the windscreen.

Twisting to face him, Lottie smiled. 'You know me, I'm always careful.'

She leaned over to peck his cheek, but he turned his head and their lips met, fleetingly. A warm sensation travelled the length of her body and settled nicely in the pit of her stomach. She wanted more. Now. To help warm the chill that had slipped over her body like a coat.

The moment was broken when he drew back and faced towards the rain falling outside. With a sigh, she stepped out onto the pavement and watched him drive off. Clutching the file tight to her chest, she walked towards her front door.

*

She sensed nothing until the shock of the whack to the back of her neck caused her to lunge towards the door, cracking her head against the weather-beaten timber. The file in its plastic covering slipped from her fingers to the ground. She fell to her knees, blood pouring from a gash in her forehead. The second punch landed in her ribs. As a gloved hand whipped up the file, Lottie grabbed for the ankle beside her. What if he got into her house? To her children. Her grandson. No!

She turned over and glanced around wildly. Alone. Staggered to her feet. Where had he gone? No car speeding away. Had he escaped on foot? She dragged herself down the path, veering onto the grass patch, blinded by her own blood. Glimpsing a shadow vaulting her neighbour's wall, she felt adrenaline kick in and took off after him, shedding her bag and jacket as she ran. Would Boyd have heard anything as he left? Her feet were moving quicker than her brain. She swiped away the blood now streaming down her face. As long as the assailant was ahead of her, her children were safe.

Over the wall. Around the side of the house. Where had he gone? A bat-like figure was scrambling up the embankment at the end of the garden. The train tracks. He was heading for the railway. She had no idea which way he would go. She followed.

Grasping at bushes and shrubs, she made her way upwards, slipping and sliding, until eventually she was standing on the tracks. The bells in one of the cathedral spires rang out the half-hour. Rain pelted down on top of her and the wind roared around her. She couldn't see him anywhere.

'Scumbag! Come back. Come back here!' she yelled at the top of her voice, but her words were carried away on the wind.

Swinging round, trying to see where he could have gone, she lost her footing on the wet steel girders and tumbled head over heels down the opposite embankment. Crashing into long grass, she yelped in pain. Blackness all around. The amber glow from street lights, distorted by the wind and rain, flitted in and out of focus. Grabbing the branch of a bramble bush, oblivious to the thorns piercing her skin, she pulled herself upright. Pain shot from her ankle and she stumbled. Attempting a step forward, she tried to think what Boyd would do in this situation. Head back and check on her family? Call for reinforcements? Or continue her quest? Damn it, there wasn't much she could do with tears of blood blinding her more than the driving rain. She couldn't go back up the slope, so the only way was forward to the road, then she could limp back to the house and call for backup.

As she began to walk, dragging her leg, a figure stepped up out of the long grass, silhouetted by the warped lights in the distance. Lean, not too tall, clothed from head to toe in black. Waving the plastic evidence bag containing Moroney's file.

'Who are you?' Lottie shouted. 'I want that file.'

Silence. The figure advanced. One step at a time.

Hightail it the hell out of here? Or stand her ground? The reverberation of little Louis crying and the memory of Chloe's anxious phone call reminded her that she needed to get home. But she also wanted to know the truth. The truth Cathal Moroney's father had been prevented from publishing in his newspaper all those years ago. The truth Cathal Moroney had been murdered for. And was it this truth that had wiped out Tessa Ball and her family?

Tugged by indecision, she heard the wind kick up as the rain washed blood from her forehead into her eyes. Refocusing her vision, she saw that the figure was not alone. Another person was skidding down the embankment, coming to a standing stop in front of her. Images of her children, alone without a mother or father, flashed and died in her mind. She would never see little Louis grow up. Her mother was right. Irresponsible was her middle name.

This time the blow to the side of her head smashed the light out of her eyes like an exploding bulb. As she fell into the darkness of the night, she glimpsed the glint of a knife before her knees hit the swampy grass. She had one last thought before she fell unconscious – she knew exactly who they were.

CHAPTER 91

The fire in the stove had long died when Rose Fitzpatrick awoke, cramped, at her kitchen table. She sat up and let her eyes wander through the darkness. Too many nights she had sat like this. Alone. Too much time to think. And now she thought of Tessa Ball and how the woman had interfered in her life.

She stood up and checked all the electrical appliances were switched off. They were. At least I'm not totally losing my mind, she thought. Out in the dark hallway, she looked up at the fuse box. She knew that someone had purposely knocked off her electricity the other day, just as she knew someone other than Lottie had ransacked her attic. All led to the past.

If they came for her too, she knew she would be sorry to die. She'd miss seeing her grandchildren and great-grandson grow into adulthood. She smiled sadly. She'd also miss seeing Lottie rush head first through her life. Maybe one day her daughter would settle down again. Boyd. He was a nice man. Rose thought of her own husband, Peter. The bastard.

She flicked on the bedroom light and drew the curtains. Without undressing, she lay on her lonely double bed and closed her eyes. For more than forty years she had kept her secrets. But perhaps now was the time to reveal them.

*

Alexis was sure something had gone wrong. She knew O'Shea had hacked her webcam, so she was careful to remain on the other side of her office. Beside the painting.

She had done everything in her power to protect the child. Everything. But she hadn't counted on murder. Her finger slid along the news app on her phone. Two more dead. Two children orphaned. What would happen to them now?

Her mind was unceremoniously dragged back to a time long ago. Ragmullin. Where it had all begun. Where she had acted beyond her years and put a plan in motion to ensure she could raise at least one of Carrie's children. Trying to make up for her sister's madness. It had taken a lot of money. But her parents had had plenty. Now she herself had more than she would ever need. And it still brought her nothing but trouble.

Her phone vibrated with an incoming call. She glanced casually at the caller ID and cancelled it.

She had called up her own computer expert and ordered a virus to be placed on everything O'Shea had been connected with. Nothing could be traced back to her. She had had enough of Ragmullin, with its warped citizens.

And now there was somewhere more important she needed to be.

The late eighties: The Child

They put me back in the laundry room after the woman's visit. I liked the book she left with me. It had my mother's name inscribed on the inside. Did she think I would take after my mother and sow herbal plants? Huh, I did enough of that with Johnny-Joe. Perhaps one day I will meet that woman and return the book.

I hate this laundry so much.

The smell. That's what I hate. Dirty stinking vermin living in this place. All of them. The nurses and the shit-faced lunatics I have to share with.

Another basket is wheeled towards me. A woman with a slack, crooked face pushes it.

'What you looking at?' she says.

'Just trying to figure it out.'

'You're so mean.'

'An alien? No, maybe you're a big fat rat.'

'No! Don't say that. I'm going to tell them and you'll have to work here until you die.'

I turn round so rapidly I catch her off guard. My fist clips the side of her head and she falls face down on top of the dirty linen. Right place for her, with her shitty arse sticking up in the air.

Sweat drips down my forehead and along my nose. The air is boiling. I feel like stripping off. Maybe I will.

She moans.

'*Oh shut up, will you? You're giving me a headache.*'

I open the machine to throw in the sheets, and then I get a mad thought. I am in the madhouse after all. Wheeling the basket over in front of the machine, I grab her ankles and pull. She is heavy, the old cow. More sweat. Pouring now like rain down my face. Swelling under my armpits. Pull and tug. Pull once more and haul her up and out, and in.

'*There now, ugly face. You'll be nice and clean after a few cycles.*'

I close the door. Press the button. Turn the dial. And she's off.

Sitting down amongst the soiled sheets, I cross my legs yoga style and watch.

Big Chief Sitting Bull.

Yeah!

I hear someone laughing.

Oh, it's only me.

I keep on laughing until the machine stops.

There's something quite soothing about watching someone die.

DAY SEVEN

CHAPTER 92

Boyd's mobile chirped as he got out of the shower.

'Hi, Chloe. What's up?'

'Is Mam with you?'

'With me? What gave you that idea?' He reached for a towel.

'She never came home last night.'

'She did. I dropped her off. It was late. After twelve thirty. She should be there. Have another look.' He dried himself vigorously, the phone clamped between chin and shoulder.

'What sort of a dope do you take me for? I've checked. Not a sign of her anywhere.'

'Calm down, Chloe. Don't be worrying. I'll call round to yours on my way into work. Give me ten, fifteen minutes. Okay?'

'Hurry up.'

Boyd quit the call and dressed in his grey suit, white shirt and blue tie. He ran a hand through his hair, grabbed a jacket and ran to his car.

'Where are you, Lottie?' he said through clenched teeth.

*

Chloe opened the door, with Katie and Sean standing behind her.

'You're sure she didn't come inside last night?' Boyd walked into the kitchen behind Chloe. When the girl glared, he held up his hands. 'Okay. Okay.'

'I thought I heard her at the door about twenty minutes after I rang her. But it must've been the wind, because no one came in. After a few minutes, I even went outside to look. No one around the place. Just rain and wind.'

Boyd walked back to the door. Checked the lock. No key. Searched around the step. Nothing. Where did she go after he dropped her? The memory of her lips on his suddenly erupted and he knew immediately that something had happened to her. She'd been anxious to get home and read the file they'd taken from Moroney's. But she'd wanted to see her children even more. He phoned Kirby.

'Any sign of the boss this morning?' he asked.

'Nope.' Dropping his voice to a whisper, Kirby said, 'McMahon and Corrigan are having a big conflab about something or other. We haven't been invited to the party because—'

'Wait. Listen. The boss never arrived home last night.' He explained where they'd been. 'Will you send a couple of uniforms over to watch her family. Just in case.'

'Sure thing. On it straight—'

Boyd hung up and called Superintendent Corrigan to inform him of Lottie's disappearance before returning to the kitchen. Sean, Chloe and Katie, holding baby Louis, were sitting in silence at the table. They had heard every word he'd said on the phone.

'Is Mam going to be okay?' Sean asked.

Boyd stared at the tall young teenager, the spitting image of his dead dad, and felt his heart lurch in his chest.

'I hope so.'

But he wasn't sure. He tried to line up his thoughts. O'Shea was in a cell at the station, ruling him out of the equation. They still had no information on the whereabouts of O'Dowd or Russell. Could one of them have approached Lottie last night? Would she have left voluntarily with one or the other? Probably. If she thought it would lead to solving the murders. Why hadn't she called him? He flexed his fingers, beginning to fear for Lottie's safety. Shit, he feared for her, full stop.

'Once gardaí arrive to watch you, I'm off out to look for your mother. Don't be worrying. Okay?'

'It's not okay,' Chloe said. 'Go and look for her now. We don't need you babysitting us. I'll phone Granny again. She'll be over in two minutes. Go and do your bloody job.'

Boyd couldn't help the half-smile that broke out on his face. Chloe was so like her mother it was uncanny. He couldn't help but notice her scratching at the skin of her arm with her fingernail. Fresh pink lines of trouble.

Hearing a car pull up outside, he rushed out. Garda Gilly O'Donoghue jumped out of the squad car.

'Go on,' she said, taking over.

Boyd leapt into his own car. Before turning the key in the ignition, he thought for a moment. He had dropped Lottie at her door. She never made it inside. What had occurred? Had she been abducted? Or had she noticed someone acting suspiciously and taken off after them?

He got out of the car and searched again around the front step and the pathway. If anything had happened here, the rain had washed everything away. Walking across the small overgrown lawn, he noticed indents filled with water. His feet squelched in the grass. He hunkered down. Checked with his finger. Footprints.

Following their trail, he found they stopped at the wall. Out on the pavement he glanced up and down, and over the neighbour's wall. A dark bundle caught his eye. Rushing over, he picked up what he knew to be Lottie's black puffa jacket and her handbag. With them in either hand, he ran around the side of the house and into a garden. Here he could see distinct footprints leading up to the embankment to the railway tracks. At least two sets.

'Boyd?'

He turned to face Kirby huffing towards him, a fat cigar clenched between his teeth. 'What's going on?'

'I think she saw someone suspicious and followed them. Up there.' Boyd pointed upwards.

'Jaysus, she could've gone in any direction after that,' Kirby said, stuffing the cigar into his jacket pocket.

'Take these' Boyd handed over Lottie's belongings. 'I'm going to have a look.'

'After that, I think you need to come to the station. I have new info you need to look at.'

Catching onto a bush, Boyd vaulted a small fence and began climbing up the embankment. Once on the railway tracks, he looked all around. The rooftops of Ragmullin lay like some Old Master's monochrome sketch, faded with time, contorted with their secretive history and drowning in a deluge of murders. He crossed the tracks and checked the other side. A steep hill of grass and shrubs. At the bottom, a short pathway led to the main road. The reeds and grass were dampened down. From the weather? Or had someone slid down there in the night? Wishing he had on a pair of hiking boots rather than his leather loafers, he made a slippery descent. At the bottom, he determined that the reeds were damaged from more than the rain. To his left, the path led to the main road.

He gazed up the way he had come and concluded he'd have to take the long way round. As he walked, he kept his eyes to the ground. But anything that might have indicated that Lottie had taken this route had been obliterated.

He had no idea where she was.

CHAPTER 93

The sound of water trickling down the inside of a copper drainpipe woke Lottie up.

'Ohhh,' she groaned. 'My head.'

Dragging her body to a sitting position, she found her limbs were free from restraints. A thin sliver of light gleamed through a crack between a door and its jamb in front of her, up high. Where the hell was she?

Her hand, pricked with thorns, flew to her forehead, her fingers touching dried blood. The back of her skull felt like it had been hit with a steel bat. Running her hands down her body, checking, she was sure she had no major injuries. The knife had not been used on her. And she was still clothed in her filthy shirt and jeans. Her feet were bare and her ankle swollen. Unbound. Why? Must be somewhere her captor believed she could not escape from. We'll see about that, she thought, parking her pain, steeling her body with resolve. No way was she going to die in this musty black hole.

In the sliver of light, she determined that the walls and floor were naked stone. She turned round on to her hands and knees, and crawled. There was a wooden table with sturdy legs. Could they be used as a weapon? She tried. They wouldn't budge. No chairs. At the far wall – cupboards. No doors. Shelves. Cans and containers. Dipping her finger into one, she touched hard clay.

She took out the can and peered inside. A small green shoot struggled for life in the dry piece of earth. Ten cans, in five cupboards. Then an old washing machine. A twin tub, with its rubber hose sticking out. Not perfect, but it would do. Past the washer, a wooden staircase with open slats. She gazed upwards at the door at the top. High and foreboding. Was she alone in the cellar of some old house? She tried to recall if O'Dowd's farmhouse had a cellar, but her mind was blank.

Up the stairs, as quietly as she could manage, each step causing her to wince with her throbbing ankle. Tried the round brass handle. Of course it was locked. Sitting on the top step, she peered down into the cavern to which she'd been brought in the dead of night.

There had been two of them. It had taken two people to possibly haul her into a car and drive her here. They must have knocked her out with the blow to her head. She remembered no more. Who had stolen the file, then assaulted and abducted her? At the back of her mind, she thought she had known at the time. That didn't matter now. All that mattered was getting home to…

Dear God. Her children. Clamping a hand to her mouth, preventing a cry escaping, Lottie felt tears brim, then flow. They'd better not touch my kids, she thought, or so help me, I'll kill them myself. She needed a plan. This was not the time to dissolve into a bubbling wreck.

Dismissing the pain in her body, she made her way on her buttocks back down the steps, crawled to the cupboard and set to work.

CHAPTER 94

Back at the station, Boyd checked in with Superintendent Corrigan, who had activated a district-wide search for Lottie. He left Corrigan on the phone to McMahon, who was at the hospital trying to extract further information from the recovering Lorcan Brady.

Pulling off his suit jacket, Boyd said, 'So, Kirby, what's this information you have?'

'Number one, you need to check those printouts on your desk. They came in via your email yesterday. I got Lynch to print them off but forgot to tell you.'

'I'll have a look in a minute. What's number two?'

'After we got Tessa and Mick's birth certificates, the boss told me to find out if the Belfields had any kids.'

'Go on.'

Kirby chewed on the end of his e-cig, twirling it from one side of his mouth to the other as he searched his desk. 'I got the Belfields' marriage cert. Guess what Kitty's name was before she married Stan Belfield?'

'O'Dowd?'

'Nope. King.'

'King?' Boyd rushed over to Kirby's desk and took the page from him. 'Any relation to Carrie King?'

Kirby held up another page. 'Kitty King had a child before she was married, called Carrie. Born out of wedlock, as they used to say.'

Boyd said, 'What happened to Carrie?'

'Have a look at the printouts on your desk. Records from St Declan's Asylum.'

Boyd sat down and scanned through the documents, his mind swirling with thoughts of Lottie. God, he hoped she was okay.

'Carrie King was in and out of St Declan's for most of her life,' Kirby said.

Looking up, Boyd said, 'These are just for the seventies. How do you know she was in and out all her life?'

'I rang the HSE records office, pulled in a few favours. They've emailed me the relevant pages. From what I can see, Carrie King was incarcerated in that hellhole in the sixties until she was nineteen and on two other occasions in the seventies. I've also traced that she lived in the cottage that was burned down the other day.'

'Let me get this straight,' Boyd said. 'Kitty Belfield was Carrie's mother. So did Tessa help cover up Carrie's indiscretions? If so, she was paid in land by the Belfields. Kitty did say land was currency.'

'And Marian Russell's mother was Carrie and Mick O'Dowd was her father.'

'Therefore O'Dowd was Emma's grandfather,' Boyd said.

'That's the way it looks,' Kirby said.

'But signing over all their land in payment?' Boyd scratched his head. 'What exactly did Tessa have to do?'

'Look at the two entries I've highlighted in the St Declan's records.'

Boyd flipped over the page. 'Carrie was signed into St Declan's in 1973 by Tessa Ball and... Jesus, Kirby!'

'I know. The town sergeant. Lottie's dad, Peter Fitzpatrick. Read on.'

'Signed out by Peter Fitzpatrick and Kitty Belfield. Okay, so she spent a couple of months inside that time.'

'Yes. Having already spent most of her childhood there. Now read on.'

'Another order was signed by Tessa Ball in November 1974 and Carrie was sectioned again. No record of a release date. Why?'

'She tried to burn down the cottage with her twins inside,' Kirby said.

'Jesus, Kirby, this isn't straightforward at all.' Boyd marched around the office, pulling at his chin. 'Last night we found an old file in Moroney's house. The name on the cover was Peter Fitzpatrick. Maybe it relates to the incarceration of Carrie King. Carrie gave birth to Marian. And now you say she also had twins. What happened to them?'

Kirby checked his notes. 'I don't know. I've just had a chat with my old friend Buzz Flynn and he told me they were born about a year after she was released from St Declan's the first time.'

Boyd shook his head. 'This is a bit of a minefield, isn't it?'

'Yup.'

'I think the Belfields, because they were well off, thought they were above placing Carrie in a mother-and-baby home.'

'And the asylum was the lesser of two evils?'

'Seems that way. They were prepared to shed their wealth to keep their family lunacy hidden.'

'But why?' Kirby said.

'This was the early seventies. Things were different then. Rich families didn't like to have their dirty linen washed in public.'

'So they locked away their shame in the asylum.'

'Did Kitty have just the one child? Carrie.'

'Nope,' Kirby said, and waved another page. 'After she married Stan, she had another daughter—'

The door pushed open and McMahon rushed in. 'Brady's been talking.'

'We're in the middle of sorting this mystery out,' Boyd said, without raising his head.

'Yes, but you're going to want to hear this. I know who killed Tessa Ball and abducted Marian Russell.' McMahon shoved his hands into his pockets and stuck out his chest.

'Lorcan Brady and Jerome Quinn?'

'They killed no one. They were paid to abduct the two women. But the person who was bankrolling them, that's who did the killing.'

'Go on then, tell us,' Boyd said.

'You're not going to believe it…'

CHAPTER 95

With cans stacked behind her and the hose strategically near her hand, Lottie resumed the position she had been left in by her abductor. She didn't have long to wait.

The screech of a bolt being shot back and the door at the top of the staircase opening caused the hairs on her arms to stand to attention. She was in pain, but ready. Shielding her eyes from the light, she made out the silhouette of a slight figure coming down the stairs.

'Natasha.'

'Don't say anything. Just be quiet and you won't get hurt.'

Lottie laughed. She couldn't help it.

'Natasha, how are you involved in this?'

'I'm bringing you some food, so shut up and eat. You don't want *her* coming down. She's in a bad mood and that's not good.' She placed a tray on the ground, four feet from where Lottie sat.

Without a glance at the food, Lottie stood up and gingerly took a step towards the girl. She was dressed in black Converses, jeans and long-sleeved T-shirt. Her hair was tied back and she looked younger than her seventeen years.

'What do you want with me? Why have you brought me here?' Another step forward. The girl retreated up the stairs.

'You couldn't leave us alone! If you'd stayed away, we could've left without any fuss. But you had to come around upsetting my mum. Now she says she's staying until the end. I hate you.'

Before Lottie could utter another word, Natasha had slipped through the door and snapped the bolt shut.

Kneeling down to the tray of toast and tea, Lottie tried to assimilate everything that had happened in the last week. How did Bernie Kelly fit into the equation? At the back of her mind she'd always felt that something was off with Bernie and her daughter. But events had occurred so quickly, she hadn't explored the possibility of Bernie's involvement. Now she had to figure it out. Her life depended on it.

If Bernie Kelly was behind the murders of Tessa, Marian and Emma, then Lottie knew exactly what the woman was capable of.

*

She must have fallen asleep after the tea and toast, because she awoke with a jolt. Bernie Kelly was sitting on the bottom step, tapping a long knife against her thigh. The door above her was open, light streaming in.

'Sleeping Beauty awakes,' she snarled. 'Though I don't see much beauty.'

'What do you want? Why did you abduct me?' Lottie scrambled her thoughts and tried to sit up straight.

'I followed you to Moroney's house. Saw you leave with that file.'

'I don't know what you're talking about,' Lottie said. 'Where am I?'

'In the cellar of what should be my rightful inheritance.'

'What?'

'You didn't read the story in the file, did you?'

'I had no time to read it. You attacked me.'

'Yes, me and my sweet girl. Strong, aren't we?'

'You're insane.'

Bernie Kelly laughed. 'I wasn't always insane, you know. But when that greedy bitch Tessa Ball had me locked away with my mother in the asylum, I was condemned to a life of madness. If you can't beat them, join them. You ever hear that saying?'

'I did, but I think you know exactly what you are doing, Bernie. And this is wrong. I'm a detective inspector. You need to let me go. We can work this out.'

Another laugh, louder, more demonic. The woman stood up, the light behind shrouding her. She looked like the devil rising up from the flames of hell.

Lottie eased back against the arsenal she'd built up. She couldn't let Bernie see it. It might be her only hope of getting out alive.

'This is Kitty's house, isn't it?' she said.

'Ah, so you *are* a detective. How did you figure that out?'

'It's either O'Dowd's or Belfield's, and I can't smell cow shite, so…'

'Your deduction skills are a little primitive. You didn't figure *me* out, did you? You or your team. Incompetence.'

'What did you do with Kitty Belfield?'

'My grandmother?'

'What?'

'You heard me.'

'Kitty Belfield is your grandmother?'

'*Was* is the correct grammar. The old witch.'

'I don't understand.'

'I'll enlighten you, shall I?'

As long as she kept Bernie talking, Lottie thought she might get a chance to use her makeshift ammunition. Boyd and the team had better have got their act together. But how would they figure it out in time? She would just have to trust them, she told herself.

'I hope you didn't harm the old lady,' she said.

'Lady? Don't make me laugh.' Bernie sniggered. 'Now see what you made me do!'

'Tell me your story. I want to know what happened to you.'

'I'm not sure I want to tell you anything,' Bernie said, wrinkling her nose. She wandered towards the old washing machine. 'I'm fascinated by this. It's so small. Not like the ones I had to work with in the madhouse.'

'What do you mean?'

'Don't keep interrupting me!' The eyes glaring in the half-light were ferocious. Pinpricks in a white face. Daggers of evil. 'Are you going to be quiet?' Her whisper was laced with menace.

Lottie nodded, one hand behind her back encircling a can, the other around the hose beneath her legs. She might only have one chance, and she'd have to take it wisely. She watched intently as Bernie heaved herself up on top of one of the cupboards and folded her arms, the knife still in her hand. She didn't appear to see Lottie as a threat. That would work in her favour.

'My mother spent most of her young life inside St Declan's. Money greased hands for that to happen. That's fine. I can understand that. But I can't understand why I was also consigned to the asylum. And I'd never have found out the truth about the history of my sordid family if Marian Russell hadn't decided to burrow a little deeper during her course. Marian. My older sister, or half-sister, depending on who her father was. But I'd never have known she was related to me if she hadn't started digging with an industrial-sized spade. I know it now. I knew it before I ripped her tongue out of her head. The bitch and her adoptive mother. Tessa, the cow, got rid of all her property so that I could get nothing from her. She thought I'd be happy renting that poxy house. And me in league with one of the biggest drug families in the country.' She swung her legs like a little girl.

Lottie felt pieces of the puzzle begin to click into place. She struggled against slipping into detective mode, asking questions. Remain silent. Safest option, she concluded.

'You didn't figure that out either, did you? Me and Jerome Quinn. We were an item. I coaxed him away from the city, brought him down here. Got him into the cottage. The same one my twin and I were almost burned to death in by our mother. Seemed only right that I succeeded in burning it to the ground.'

'With two men, including your lover, inside?' Lottie couldn't help herself. She tried to bite her tongue, but failed. 'How did you manage it?'

'Easy. Once I doctored their weed, they turned into two laughing imbeciles. I stabbed Jerome and knocked out Lorcan as he stood there with his mouth open. I knew he was stealing from us, so I exacted retribution by hacking off his grubby fingers. Don't know how he didn't die, but I reckon he's not far off it.'

'You are a heartless bitch.'

'I am what others made me.'

'What had Emma to do with Lorcan?'

'Nothing. Great idea to lead you to believe he was Emma's boyfriend. You fell for that. Like you assumed I was with the two girls the night I killed the old bag, Tessa.' She paused before continuing. 'Jerome and Lorcan helped me bring Marian to Lorcan's. I left her for dead. Then those two fools had a change of heart and dumped her at the hospital. Almost ruined everything. I think they met a suitable fate for their sins.'

'And Emma. Why did you have to kill her?' Lottie couldn't understand anything Bernie had done, especially the murder of Emma. 'She was no threat to you.'

'I gave her food and shelter and she repaid me by running off to that old man. Her grandfather! I don't think she knew who he was. Only that Tessa had once said that if anything bad happened, he was the only person who could help her. So she stole Natasha's bike and fled.'

'But Emma was no danger to you.'

'Are you stupid or what? She knew I wasn't with her and Natasha at the crucial time that night. I returned as she was leaving to go home. She said nothing because she didn't think it was important. Not then. But she had time to think about it out on that stinking old farm, because she rang Natasha and said she was going to tell the guards. She believed I might have seen something to help *solve* the murders. The innocent cow.'

Lottie tried to understand what she was hearing. One thing she knew for certain – Bernie Kelly had no intention of releasing her alive. Otherwise she wouldn't be relating her murderous story. The woman's cold-blooded monotone poked at every nerve in her body. She wanted to lash out with the can, smash it into Bernie's face. But she was too far away. Bide your time, she warned herself.

She said, 'Mick O'Dowd. Where is he?'

'Mincemeat, I should think. Before we dragged Emma outside, I went looking for him. Found him working in the cow shed. He tried to come at me with a slash hook, but I *accidentally* kicked aside one of those slats on the floor. Down he sank into the shithole. Very effective tool, that agitator. I don't believe you'll find even a fingernail intact. Slurry whence he came, slurry to where he rests. Is that a line from a poem? If not, it should be.' More laughter.

Biting down nausea, blocking the image of O'Dowd's last horrendous moments, Lottie said, 'He could've been your biological father.'

'What of it? I don't care. He certainly didn't care enough to stand up and claim me. No one did. They paid off the asylum manager so that they would take me in with my mother. Me. A child.' A derisory snort.

'What became of your twin?'

'I don't know. I remember having a foster mother at one stage. But I honestly don't know and I really don't care any more, because now I've got rid of the witches.'

'Why did you torture Marian?'

'She knew too much, with all her genealogy stuff. I tried to be her friend. But she wasn't anything like I believed a sister should be. Too interested in her herbal remedies. Thought she could grow something to help my depression, as she called it. Then she wanted to go public with what had happened to me as a child – being thrown into the asylum. Said I could make money out of it. The stupid woman.'

Lottie turned this around in her head. Marian had had her tongue cut out because if she went public, Bernie's association with criminals would be discovered. 'Your mother, Carrie, was she into herbal remedies also?'

'How would I know?'

'There was a book on herbs at O'Dowd's, and another one at Marian's house. The name Carrie King was written inside the book I found at the farmhouse.'

She watched Bernie jump off the countertop and walk up and down. 'Seeds. Herbal stuff. Now I see.'

'What do you see?'

'I think it was my mother who started Johnny-Joe growing seeds in the asylum. Tessa brought me the book. I gave it to Marian. A peace offering.'

'But I found two copies.'

'Maybe she gave one to O'Dowd too. How the hell would I know? Does it even matter?'

'In the larger scheme of things, Bernie, no it doesn't.'

'They said Carrie was mad, but the real mad one was that Kitty Belfield bitch. She abandoned her daughter so that she could marry a wealthy man. And disowned Carrie over and over again by not acknowledging her children. That is the worst sin of all. Abandonment.' She paused. Lottie felt the heat of her fiery stare. 'You said you have children. Are they safe? Do you watch out for them? Care for them? Nurture them? Kitty Belfield didn't. She felt only shame. She did nothing for her daughter or her grandchildren. She disowned them all.'

'How do you know so much about the family?'

'I knew a little through Marian, but I got to read some files here. The first day I called. I must look like Carrie, because it was as if Kitty recognised a ghost from the past. I frightened her so much, she showed them to me. She said they'd supposedly been taken in a burglary. She eventually told me that Stan and Tessa orchestrated it so that no one would ever lay eyes on the files. I can't understand why they didn't burn them. Oh shit, I should have asked the old bag that before I suffocated her. I suppose I'll never know now. But who cares? I don't.'

Lottie tightened her grip on the can behind her back, gritted her teeth. She couldn't afford to say the wrong thing, but she probably would. Bide your time, Parker. Once her children had reported her missing, Boyd would find her. He was diligent, and if he studied the land maps, wouldn't something resonate with him? Maybe. Maybe not.

She kept watch as Bernie continued her silent march up and down the confined cellar. And silently prayed for the knowledge to know when to strike.

CHAPTER 96

'We thought he was saying Quinnie,' Boyd said, grabbing his jacket.

McMahon said, 'No, he definitely said Bernie. She was behind it. He can't talk much, but I'm sure that's what he said. Where are you going?'

Boyd stopped at the door, turned back. 'I don't know.' Flopping down in the nearest chair, he said, 'We need to think. Where could Lottie be?'

Kirby said, 'If this has to do with revenge over land or inheritance, it might link back to the Belfields. I think Lottie could be at Farranstown House.'

'I think you're right,' Boyd said. 'Come on, let's get moving.'

'Hold on a minute,' McMahon said. 'Why would Bernie go there, and why would she take DI Parker?'

'We have no other bright ideas, have we?' Boyd looked around at the faces of Kirby, Lynch and McMahon. Corrigan was standing at the door.

'Well what are you waiting for, DS Boyd,' the superintendent said. 'Get out there and bring back your boss. In one piece. Right?'

'Feckin' right, sir.'

*

Keep her talking. I must keep her talking, Lottie thought. And even though the woman was brandishing a knife, its blade sharp and glittering, she felt no fear. A gentle calmness settled in her heart.

She felt as if her soul was suspended above her, guiding her body. She could do this.

'Do you blame O'Dowd for what happened to Carrie?' she said.

'Don't make me puke. That pig only wanted what he could get for nothing. Abused my mother over and over again. He, and too many others, destroyed her.'

'I heard she did that all by herself.'

'What do you mean?'

'Drugs and drink. You must know she was self-destructive. O'Dowd and the other men facilitated her to do whatever she wanted to do.'

Was she justifying what she suspected were her own father's actions? No. She had no proof he had had anything to do with Carrie King. Except, perhaps, being complicit with Tessa in having Carrie admitted to the asylum. The Moroney file might hold the answers.

Bernie said, 'O'Dowd took advantage of an already damaged mentally ill woman. Tessa and Kitty, they committed the mortal sin. Punishable by death.'

'So why kill O'Dowd if Tessa and Kitty were to blame?'

'He got in the way.'

'We thought he'd escaped on his quad. Where is that?'

'Natasha drove it across the fields. It's in the bottom of Lough Cullion.'

'She was with you when you killed Emma?' Dear God, what kind of monster was this woman?

'You hardly think I hauled an unconscious teenager into that barrel all by myself? My daughter is my right hand. Isn't that right, sweetheart?'

Lottie looked up as Natasha appeared on the top step.

'Yes, Mum.'

Shaking her head, Lottie couldn't fathom how Bernie's insanity had wormed its way into her daughter.

'And you contracted Cian O'Shea into your plans. How'd you manage that?'

'Who? I don't know anyone by that name.'

'He… I thought he… Did you kill the Moroneys?'

'No. And I didn't contract anyone to do it either. But I'm glad to have the file.'

'I don't understand…'

Bernie stopped pacing and tapped the knife on the edge of the washer. 'Have I missed something? You think I killed Moroney? Perhaps if I had known about the file I would have, but someone got to him first.'

The tapping ceased. Lottie held her breath. Was it time? She couldn't make a sound. The can might scrape on the stone floor. How could she work this?

'How come you were following me?' she asked.

'You called the other day when we were planning on leaving. Got me wondering if you were on my trail, though now I see I was wrong there. You really had no idea, did you?'

'I had my suspicions.'

'No you did not. You came snooping again yesterday and I decided to follow you, just out of curiosity. Little did I think I would come up with a surprise prize.' She laughed loudly. 'Oh, I think I just made a joke there.'

'Mum?' Natasha's voice echoed from the top of the stairs. She flicked a switch to her left and the cellar filled with light.

The girl took one careful step forward. Another step.

'I think we're done here,' she said.

A third step.

Four more to go, Lottie thought. Enough time to grab the can from behind her back and aim?

'What are you talking about?' Bernie said.

A fourth step.

'I'm tired, Mum. Enough.'

A fifth step.

'Go back, Natasha. You don't need to see this.' Bernie turned towards her daughter.

A sixth step.

'You're right. I don't want to see anything you do any more.'

Bottom step. Lottie's hand tightened on the can. Rising to her knees, she flung it with full force at Bernie. Too low. Caught her on the leg.

'You bitch,' Bernie yelled, springing forward, the knife tight in her hand.

Lottie held on to the hose, and as Bernie reached her, she whipped it across the woman's ankles, trying to topple her. No effect. With a shriek, Bernie lunged, thrusting the knife downwards. Lottie ducked, threw her body sideways. Too late.

A scream pierced the damp air. Had it come from her own throat? She wasn't sure, but the pain searing through her upper back caused her heart to palpitate in rapid uncontrollable beats. Blood rushed from her brain; gushed from her body. She heard her heartbeat slowing. Stars twinkled in the dark. Red, white… No, not yet, she thought. I have to see my children. I have to tell them I love them. I love them… love…

Falling prostrate on the stone floor, she glimpsed Natasha jumping on Bernie's shoulders. She had picked up the can that Lottie had thrown, and now she brought it down on the back of her mother's head.

The cellar was filled with screams.

Sirens in the distance.

Car doors slamming. Footsteps running. Shouts.

Boyd?

I'm dying, she thought. You're all too late. Too late, Boyd…

The world dimmed and went dark.

CHAPTER 97

Boyd crashed through the door and flew down the stairs with Kirby and Lynch behind him. He made straight for Lottie, with just a sideways glance at Natasha Kelly sitting on the floor, hugging her knees to her chest, her mother lying at her feet.

'Lottie?' he whispered, turning her over on her side. He lowered his ear to her mouth. A faint breath. 'Thank God.'

Tearing off his shirt, he used it to stem the flow of blood. Then he held her in his arms and waited for the paramedics to arrive. He watched Lynch handcuff Natasha and Kirby check Bernie for a pulse. The woman's eyes snapped open. Kirby jumped back for an instant before he dragged her hands behind her back and handcuffed her.

'She's under the stairs,' Natasha cried. 'I think she's still alive.'

'Shut your mouth,' Bernie groaned.

'Who?' Kirby asked.

'Kitty,' Natasha said. 'Mum told me to shove her in there and lock the door. She stuffed seeds into her mouth. She wanted her to suffocate.'

Kirby started up the narrow staircase, but stood aside to allow two paramedics to descend.

'They're here now,' Boyd whispered in Lottie's ear. 'You're going to be fine.' He thought he heard her murmur as he reluctantly allowed the paramedics to take over. He looked on helplessly as one of them applied an oxygen mask and another checked Lottie's vital signs.

'Is she going to be okay?' he asked, rubbing his hands vigorously together, oblivious to Lottie's blood staining them.

'Appears to be substantial blood loss,' one said. 'Heart rate is slow. BP too low. We need to get her out of here now.'

'What are you waiting for?' Boyd shouted. Lottie couldn't die. He needed her. Her kids needed her. He ran to help with a gurney.

Within a few minutes they had Lottie strapped on, a drip inserted and a monitor attached. Then they were gone.

Boyd looked around, biting his lip, trying to still his racing heart. Let her survive.

He helped Lynch bring the two women up the steps.

'I need a doctor,' Bernie said.

'You need a fucking shrink,' Boyd said.

Kirby met them at the top of the stairs. 'I've called another ambulance. Kitty Belfield is barely alive. I don't think she's going to make it.'

'May she rot in hell,' Bernie spat.

'I think she will have plenty of company,' Boyd said, and shoved her through the door.

CHAPTER 98

Superintendent Corrigan was pacing the incident room when Boyd returned.

'Any news?' he asked.

'She's in surgery. Doctors will know more in a few hours. I dropped her mother and her kids at the hospital. They're very upset.'

'Understandable. This is a right feckin' mess,' Corrigan said. 'Glad you got there in time.'

'Just about,' Boyd said.

'Why don't you go home and pick up a shirt?'

Boyd looked down at himself. 'I think I've one in my locker.'

'Did you find anything at Farranstown house?'

'Kirby is there with a few uniforms. They should find the file that was stolen from Lottie.'

'Moroney's father's file?'

'Yes, sir.'

'And still no sign of O'Dowd or Arthur Russell?'

'No, sir.'

'If this Kelly woman is responsible for all the murders, why have we got Cian O'Shea in the cells?'

'I think he killed the Moroneys but I'm still trying to figure it all out, sir.'

'Figure it out pronto. Once you've found a shirt, go and interview him again.'

'Yes, sir.'

Boyd stood in front of the incident boards as Corrigan left the room. Nowhere could he see how Cian O'Shea fitted into the equation. If he continued to refuse to speak, forensics would have to do the job for them.

As he was heading back up from the locker room, Kirby came down the stairs.

'Found it!' He held up Moroney's manila folder.

'Okay,' Boyd said. 'Time to find out why two innocent people lost their lives.'

'There's more than two innocent people dead in all this mess.'

'Don't start, Kirby. Because I might just throw you down those stairs.'

He took the file and stormed past Kirby, who looked at him, slack-jawed.

*

The light was fading as Boyd finished reading the file. He rubbed his chin and leaned back in the chair. The historical events that had happened in Ragmullin were tantamount to depravity. No words could describe it, but Paddy Moroney, in his unpublished report, had done his best. Boyd could see why it had never been printed.

McMahon strolled into the office, hung up his coat and started to unplug his laptop.

'You done here, sir?' Boyd asked.

'I'll be back for Lorcan Brady's court appearance, though the doctors say it will be months before he can attempt rehabilitation.'

'Did Brady have anything further to add?'

'Solved the mystery of Arthur Russell's jacket and the receipt.'

'Go on.'

'It took a while to understand him but I got the gist of it. Bernie Kelly sent Brady to keep track of Arthur's movements the evening of Tessa's murder. She needed him to be the prime suspect. Brady watched Russell have his two pints after his shift ended. When he left, Brady lifted the receipt and put it in the new jacket Bernie had purchased. She left it hanging on the rack in the house later that evening.'

'Conniving bitch,' Boyd said. 'By the way, Detective Inspector Parker is out of surgery. In case you were wondering.'

'I was, actually. But she should have joined the dots before she nearly got herself killed.'

'Hey, wait a minute there.' Boyd stood up and faced McMahon. 'If you'd been doing your job, you'd have known Bernie Kelly was in a relationship with Jerome Quinn.'

'No need for insubordination, Boyd. For your information, her name never came up in relation to Quinn. So back yourself down off that high horse.'

Sighing, Boyd shook his head. He was too tired to go into battle. He wanted to visit Lottie. To see with his own eyes that she was going to recover.

'I've heard from Mr O'Shea's solicitor,' McMahon said, zipping the laptop into a black nylon bag. 'He continues to claim he never laid a hand on the Moroneys.'

'Maybe not, but once I have the forensic report back, it will tell us he laid a hand on the knife that was sticking out of Cathal Moroney's chest.'

'Ever think of doing a bit of drama?' McMahon said.

'What type of bullshit is that?'

'You seem to love performing, once you have an audience.'

Boyd did a Lottie on it and counted to ten.

'And just so you know,' McMahon continued, 'I've sent a SOCO team out to O'Dowd's farm. Natasha Kelly insists her mother knocked him into the slurry pit and activated the agitator machine.'

'Right, so,' Boyd said, preventing himself from saying he wished he could knock McMahon into a slurry pit. He caught sight of Superintendent Corrigan entering the cramped office with his hand outstretched.

'Great job, David. Thanks for coming to Ragmullin. Now drive safely on your way back to the city.'

'Glad to be able to help,' McMahon said, ending the handshake and picking up his laptop. 'Whenever you're thinking of retiring, give me the heads-up. I might be interested in coming down the country. I think I might be able to straighten out a few of your troops.'

'Don't you worry about us. We cracked this case and will stand with our heads held high. My troops are a credit to this force. And now you'd better be off, before another storm hits. What're they calling this one, Boyd?'

'Would you believe it,' Boyd said, 'it's Carrie.'

'On that note, I'll leave you to it,' McMahon said, pausing to put on his coat. 'Give Detective Inspector Parker my good wishes.'

Corrigan waited until McMahon was down the corridor and out of earshot. 'He's a feckin' arsehole.'

'Agreed,' Boyd said.

'When you visit Parker, give her my good wishes and tell her that our Dublin friend has returned home.'

'She'll be happy to hear that, sir,' Boyd said, but his mind was curdling with the thought of how Lottie would react to the contents of the folder on his desk.

CHAPTER 99

It was evening before Boyd was allowed into the ICU to visit Lottie. Rose had taken the children home. He stood in the doorway, clutching the folder, studying the various machines with their staggered lines and blipping numbers. Not that long ago, he himself had lain in such a state after he too had been stabbed. Pulling up a chair, he sat by her bedside and watched her slowly breathe.

'You were lucky,' he said. 'Though you won't be able to throw a shot putt for a while.'

Her eyelids flickered and opened slightly.

'Welcome back,' he said.

He thought he caught her smile from behind the multitude of tubes.

He kept talking. 'I've read Paddy Moroney's file.' Was that a twitch of an eyebrow? Here he was, imagining things. 'It's comprehensive. You need to read it when you get better. I'm telling you this now because you're going to have to be brave. And those kids of yours are pretty shocked, so you need to hurry up and get your strength back.'

A high-pitched beep screeched from one of the monitors, emptying the room of its easy silence.

'What the hell?'

A nurse ran in. 'It's okay. Nothing to worry about. Mrs Parker needs rest. She's endured a terrible ordeal. Why don't you come back tomorrow?'

'I will,' Boyd said. 'Are you certain that's nothing to be concerned about?' He pointed to the machine as the nurse successfully muted it.

'She'll be fine. She's in very good hands here.'

He felt like he was back in school, being scolded by a teacher for doing something naughty, something someone else had done.

'I'll see you tomorrow, Lottie.' He squeezed her hand, and for a fraction of a second he felt her squeeze back.

CHAPTER 100

Alexis smiled up at the NYPD's newly appointed captain. At last he was getting the recognition he deserved. The chief of police and the New York City mayor stood by his side. This was the most rewarding moment of her life. She was so proud of him. As proud as a mother should be.

He came towards her, the mayor by his side.

'Mr Mayor, I'm pleased to meet you,' Alexis said, shaking his outstretched hand.

'Likewise, Ms Belfield. You are a very influential woman, doing great things for the city, I hear. I know your son will do the same.'

'I'm sure he will, Mr Mayor.'

As the crowds began to leave the ceremony, Alexis linked her arm through Captain Leo Belfield's. Her son. Carrie's son.

She had chosen him over the girl, Bernie. When he was only a toddler, she knew she could make him great. Not once had she felt remorse for taking her half-sister's son. Not once had she felt remorse for leaving his twin sister behind. Not once had she felt remorse for making sure Carrie would die behind cold, mad walls. Not once had she felt remorse for forcing her mother and father to forfeit their land so that she could escape with Leo. Not once had she felt remorse for compelling Tessa to ensure Sergeant Fitzpatrick kept his mouth shut. And not once had she felt remorse for contracting that computer guy from Ragmullin to recover any files that might lead to the investigation being reopened.

Not once.

She had done her family a service. And now Bernie, the twin she had abandoned to the asylum with her mother, had unwittingly removed the players who could potentially make trouble for her and her son. The fact that Bernie had been involved with a drugs gang had complicated matters beautifully for the Irish police.

Not quite all the players were gone, though. She winced at the thought. There was still one of Carrie's offspring out there, besides Leo, of course, and Alexis knew she might still have more work to do to ensure that that one remained in ignorance. For now she was content that nothing could be traced back to her, no matter what stories O'Shea might tell. She was head of a computer company, after all. She knew how to eliminate all traces.

She heaved a sigh of relief. Dug her fingers into the thread of her son's uniform sleeve. Gazing up at his new captain's shield, she made a silent vow.

No one would ever take that away from him.

No one would ever take him away from her.

Absolutely no one.

The nineties : The Child

Today I'm getting out of here. You'd think I'd feel elated, wouldn't you? But if I was to tell you the truth, I feel kind of sad. That's mad. Ha! Funny ha ha.

She died in here. My mother. Carrie. I don't know when. But I've seen her grave, marked with a simple rusting iron cross, among the multitude of similar crosses in the asylum cemetery. It's the fifth one in, near the wall. Johnny-Joe's is fifteen plots ahead of her. She died some years before him, then. There are no dates on the crosses, just numbers. King, 1551. It would have been a nice symmetry if the number had been 666. But I don't care about that any more.

I fold my meagre clothes into a cotton holdall and walk out of the ward with its shitty piss smell and its screaming occupants. In an absurd kind of way, I'm going to miss them all.

Tessa is standing there. Oh yes, I know who she is. I see her in the reception when the nurse shoves me through the final door. I hear her lock it behind me.

'Come with me now and be a good girl,' Tessa says. 'I've signed all the paperwork. I've everything sorted. A nice flat for you in Dublin and a little part-time job.' She leans towards me and says in a quiet but stern voice, 'And you are never to talk about this part of your life. Forget all about it. Forget about me. Start anew and things will work out for you.'

I smirk. This causes the half-smile to slither down her face and a frown to furrow her brow. Silly cow. Did she think I was going to thank her? This building didn't make me a saint. Nothing so miraculous could happen in here. No, I was tainted with madness, and evil streaked a stake through my soul.

I know that she is going to abandon me and hope that I will never find her. But I will. One day. I can wait. I am used to waiting.

Before she pulls away after her whispered threat, I say into her waxy ear, 'I will never forget you. So don't imagine that you can ever forget me.'

TWO WEEKS LATER

CHAPTER 101

25th October 2015

Lottie sat up in bed and thanked Chloe for the tea and toast. She hadn't the heart to tell the girl she never wanted to touch either again.

'Louis is being really good,' Chloe said. 'You'd think he knows to be quiet when you're trying to sleep.'

'He's a great baby. You are all brilliant children. I'm a lucky mother to have you here with me. Did I tell you I love you?'

Chloe groaned. 'Only about a million times since you've come home. We know you love us. Always knew it. So please, please don't keep saying it. It gets kind of gross after a while.'

Lottie smiled, reached out and held Chloe's hand. 'I'm sorry for—'

'Enough!' Chloe said. 'I want my old Mum back. The cranky, contrary, fussing and rushing one. You know who I'm talking about?'

'Yes, I do. Okay. Less of the mushy stuff. I promise.'

'Whatever, but I know the next time any of us comes in here, you're going to start again.'

Lottie watched her tall, beautiful daughter pick a tendril of blonde hair from her face and head for the door.

Without turning round, Chloe said, 'Granny is on her way up to see you.' Then she escaped.

Putting the tray on the locker, Lottie flinched with the pain in her upper back. Almost two weeks she'd been made to stay in the hospital. And now, after three days in bed at home, she was itching to get out and back to work. Another month, the surgeon had said. Well, he doesn't know me, Lottie mused. But now she had to face Rose Fitzpatrick. That thought was more painful than the wound in her back.

'How are we today?' Rose said, dropping about a dozen magazines on the bed. 'Thought you could do with something to read.'

'I've plenty of reading material,' Lottie said, tapping the folder on the bed beside her.

'What's that then?' Rose enquired, leaning over to have a look.

'A story compiled by a journalist.'

'About your heroics in catching a serial killer?'

'No.' Lottie thought the best course of action was to get straight to the point. Though she wished she was standing up so she could look Rose in the eye.

'Paddy Moroney was the owner of the *Midland Tribune*,' Lottie began.

'The father of that poor murdered journalist and his wife. He's been dead years. Why would you have his story?'

Pulling herself up in the bed, Lottie went for it.

'My dad was a fraud. A sergeant on the take. Bad enough I spent my life thinking he'd killed himself, but do you know what's worse? Knowing he duped the system and conspired to put a young woman called Carrie King into the asylum. Jesus, the girl was just an alcoholic; I don't think she was ever insane.'

'That was a long time ago.' Rose stood awkwardly, pushing her hands into her pockets. She stared at a point above Lottie's head.

'Everything was a long time ago with you. I searched for the truth but you thwarted me every step of the way. You thought that if you gave me that box of Dad's things, I'd stop. But you sent me digging deeper until Cian O'Shea and Bernie Kelly's horrific actions unexpectedly led me to the truth.'

Lottie watched her mother move from foot to foot. If this were a normal conversation, Rose would sit on the edge of the bed. But she suspected Rose knew exactly where it was leading.

'There is a lot of unsubstantiated information in Paddy Moroney's file. Most of it doesn't matter to me. But some of it does. Some of it I can accept, but the one thing I don't believe is that my dad fathered Carrie King's first child. Paddy documents that that child was taken into our home. That can't be possible. There was only Eddie and me. Isn't that right?'

Rose bent her head. An imperceptible shake of her short hair. Surely not. Lottie gulped. Her heart pounded. Her wound constricted and suddenly she felt very ill.

'Mother? What are you not telling me?'

Rose bit her lip and stared at the ceiling before dropping her gaze to Lottie. 'I told you to leave it be,' she whispered, and then her voice rose. 'How many times did I tell you to stop asking questions? But no, you had to prove you could solve the problems of the world while unravelling our family history. This is not a fairy tale, Lottie. There's no happy ending. Our world has real live people in it, not cartoon characters. The dead are gone. They're not here to explain their actions. But you cannot leave it alone!'

Lottie recoiled at the vehemence in her mother's voice. 'What are you talking about?'

'The truth. Do you want to hear it? Because this is your only chance.'

Closing her eyes, Lottie blinked away tears. Did she want to know the truth? Yes. Could she handle it? Strong Lottie could, but a wounded animal, like she was now, probably couldn't. But she had to know.

'I want to hear it.'

'You won't like it. Final warning.'

Lottie flung back the covers and sat on the side of the bed, ignoring the shaft of pain.

'For Christ's sake, Mother, this isn't some game-show quiz. Spit out the truth. I'm ready. No matter what you have to say, I think I have it figured out already.'

Leaning against the wall, Rose said, 'I don't think you have. That's the problem. But you need to remember one thing. This is all your father's fault. Not yours, not mine.' She paused.

Lottie waited.

'He was a bastard. Your father. On the take. You were correct there. And do you know why? Because, and you know I don't use bad language, but I will now, because he fucked a desperately demented girl. Got her pregnant and came crying on my shoulder, apologising, asking what he could do and how it would affect his career. The selfish man. Never once did he think of that young damaged woman and how he had abused her.'

'I… I don't think I need to know any more.' Lottie looked around her room wildly. Where were her pills? She needed something. A drink. Anything.

'Yes you do. You wanted answers, and by God, I will have my say.'

Silence. She hadn't even the coordination left in her body to count the seconds that were passing.

'Your father knew Tessa Ball through court cases. Approached her to see what could be done. No abortions allowed. No access to even a back-street abortion. So they came up with a plan. When I think of it now, I want to be sick.'

'What plan?' Lottie whispered.

'Once the baby was born, Peter would take the child as his own. He only had to convince me to go along with this madness. He painted it up; dressed it in fine clothing, his story. How we would be doing young Carrie a service. She wouldn't be able to raise the child. She was a drug addict and an alcoholic. She'd spent half her life in a mental asylum, for God's sake. He pleaded. The baby was his flesh and blood, after all. The clown.'

Lottie noticed tears spilling down Rose's cheeks. Had her mother totally gone over the edge? But no, she looked saner than she had in months.

'How could you take this child in? You had Eddie, you had me...'

'That's the whole point, Lottie. Don't you get it? Come on, Detective Inspector Parker. We didn't have you. I couldn't have children after Eddie was born. Complications at birth. I was left sterile. That's why there was a seven-year gap after Eddie.'

'I don't understand...'

'You were Peter's child, but you weren't mine.' Rose convulsed in sobs. 'But I loved you. Love you.'

'No!' Lottie shot up from the bed, the ache in her back screeching objections along with her voice. 'You're not serious. You can't be. No! That cannot be true.' She rounded on her mother, gripping her shoulders. Looked into her flooded eyes.

'You called me Charlotte after Charlotte Brontë. You told me that. Didn't you? I'm yours and Dad's. Please don't tell me otherwise.'

'I'm sorry, but it's true. You are the daughter of my Peter and the Carrie King woman. Tessa Ball forged the birth certificate through her contacts at the registry office.'

Lottie dropped to her knees at the feet of the woman she had called mother for over forty years. But Rose wasn't her real mother.

Her biological mother was a woman who'd been locked up in an insane asylum and left there to die.

She shook her head repeatedly. This couldn't be true. No. Dementia, that was what it was. She would get Annabelle to run checks on Rose's brain. There were tests... special tests they could do...

Rose continued. 'Tessa had this hanging over your father's head like a giant sledgehammer, threatening to let it drop if he didn't get involved later on when she tried to cover up her own brother's involvement with Carrie. She took Marian as her child. Keeping a wealthy family happy, she was. No shame displayed for all the neighbours to see.'

'They were babies,' Lottie cried. A cold chill traversed her shoulders, slipped down her spine and back up again, coming to an icy resting place in the nape of her neck.

'You know what I mean. These people were gentry, or at least they thought they were. Covered up all they could, but then there were the twins. How were they going to hide twins?'

'How? Sign them into the asylum with their mother?' Lottie scoffed.

'No. The Belfields had a daughter, Alexis. She was a few years younger than Carrie and she agreed to take the twins. She fostered them, probably illegally, as she was young and unmarried, and poor Carrie was hauled off to the asylum once more. But this time she didn't stay quiet. Threatened to go public, so I heard.'

'But how would a supposedly insane woman be believed?'

'I don't think Kitty could take the risk. She enlisted Tessa, who forced Peter to help. Carrie was signed out and given the cottage by the Belfields, with the proviso that she get herself clean and then she could have the twins back. All was grand until she started taking drugs and drinking again. Then came the night she almost burned them all to death.'

'So Alexis took the twins again?'

'No. Apparently Alexis was heading to America to start up a business venture. She agreed to take one child. The other, Bernie, was incarcerated with Carrie in St Declan's. I think initially she was put in while the family decided what to do about her. But they just left her there. With her mother.' Rose sighed, long and deep. 'I thought they'd both died in there. But I was wrong about that, wasn't I?'

Lottie was speechless. She didn't want to believe her mother, but then hadn't most of it been in Moroney's report anyway?

'How could you do it? Agree to take me in? How could you live with Dad after what he did?'

'It was hard. I did the right thing in the long run. Look how you turned out. Good upbringing wins out in the end.'

'I can see that we are both victims in this pathetic play, and you know what? I pity you, Mother. Or whoever you are. I pity you for the choices you made.' Lottie leaned against the bed, wishing she was strong enough to run out of the door, down the stairs and out to the street, where she could howl like a wild animal at the night sky. 'Dad's suicide… had you anything to do with it?'

'How could you think that? I had nothing to do with it. Anyway, he was the one who had the affair, not me. He had to live with that sin. Remember, Lottie, no one knows what goes on behind closed doors. We all thought Annabelle had a perfect marriage, and see what her husband was doing to her.'

Annabelle, Lottie thought. She wondered how she was, now that Cian had been charged with double homicide. She'd have to make contact soon. Thinking of what her mother had just said, she'd always known Annabelle hadn't had the perfect marriage but she'd thought Cian, for all his faults, had been a good husband. Dead wrong there, Parker, she told herself. Circumstances had changed Cian, released in him something evil. And circumstances had most surely turned

Bernie into what she had become. But Rose was deflecting the conversation, in typical Rose fashion.

'This isn't about Annabelle or Cian or anyone else,' Lottie said, drawing her back to the topic in hand. 'This is about my dad.'

'He was the one who fathered a child outside of his marriage, so don't go blaming me.'

'But things must have been strained at home. Jesus, you took in another woman's daughter. Shit.'

'She was an addict. She couldn't care for you. There was no help for her back then, just the asylum.'

Lottie stared up at the ceiling. Blinded by tears. Frustration? Anger? Sorrow? She had no idea.

'No wonder I'm so fucked up.'

'I thought if I let you have your father's things, it would be the end of it. Instead you started on your mad witch-hunt. All those poor innocent people. Killed because of your meddling.'

Lottie dragged herself upright again. 'You're wrong there. Marian Russell started it with her genealogy investigations.'

'But don't you see, your snooping got Cian O'Shea involved to spy on you, and on me. And whether you care to admit it or not, Lottie, that led directly to the murder of the Moroneys. So don't play the angel here. Shoulder some of the blame.'

Bristling from the harsh words, Lottie decided that once she was well enough, she'd visit Cian O'Shea in prison to see if she could succeed where others had failed. She needed to know who had got him involved.

'I've heard enough now, Mo… Rose. I think you need to leave.'

Rose pushed away from the wall. At the door, she turned. Lottie stared at the once sprightly woman she had called her mother. Now that woman looked half her size and broken.

'I'm going,' Rose said. 'I just ask one thing. Leave it alone now. Don't go looking for more answers. It'll only cause people pain. People who have spent their lives running away from it. Remember, you have your own children and your grandson to think of. You don't want to bring more heartache into their lives.'

Lottie got up, cringing with pain. She stood as erect as she could.

'For your information, I'm not finished with this. I intend to find my last remaining half-sibling.'

Rose laughed drily. 'Don't forget, you have two.'

'Two?' Lottie felt confused. Then it struck her. 'Bernie Kelly can rot in jail for the rest of her life. I'm talking about her twin. I will find where this Alexis is and—'

'You won't. You can never fight her. Your father couldn't.'

'What do you mean?' How did Rose always get the last word?

'Your father couldn't stand up to her. He was a tired and broken man, the poor eejit. It was Tessa that made him do it, but I firmly believe that Alexis was behind her, pulling the strings. Didn't you wonder why Tessa had the gun? The gun that killed your father?'

Yes, she did.

'Alexis put it all in motion and Tessa wore your father down. Tried to convince him it would be wrong to speak the truth. He was a wreck by the time… by the time… I could never prove it, but I always thought someone tied him up, put the gun in his hand and forced him. Why else was there a rope on the floor by his feet? The rope was taken away, and after the inquest, the gun disappeared too. Tessa had it all these years.' Sighing softly, Rose added, 'In the end, I don't know if he even wanted to pull the trigger or not. But he did it.'

Feeling a weakness in her knees, Lottie sat back on the bed and studied her hands. She had no words left to utter. When she looked up, she was alone.

'I don't know who I am,' she whispered to the rectangle of light shining through the gap left by the open door. 'Who am I?'

30th October 2015: The Child

The day that woman, Tessa Ball, arrived to sign me out should have been a happy day. But it wasn't. I was leaving the only place I knew as home.

So when she stood there signing the final form, my soul was as black as the leather bag she held scrunched under her elbow.

She should have left me to my own world.

That day she unleashed a force of vengeance on herself and her family that would take another twenty-odd years to come to fruition.

I'm happy now. I've completed my life goal.

I lived with people I knew could one day help me to do what I wanted to do. My mission: to wipe out the insanity that had condemned me and my mother to live without the life to which I was rightly entitled. Even when Natasha was born some years after my release from the asylum, I never wavered. I knew she would understand and help me. She was my flesh and blood after all, and it didn't matter that I didn't know who her father was. I would prove the strength of that bond to those who had never allowed themselves to believe in it.

I wonder what they've done with Natasha. I suppose they'll try to make her stand witness against me. But my daughter will not betray me. That defiance, back in the cellar, was just fear. She thought the detective was going to kill us both. Poor girl. I had it all under control. I still do.

I'm back in here now. Well, it's not St Declan's, obviously; that's closed down. Another St Declan's, though I didn't even ask the name.

All the same to me. I'm to be left here until they decide whether I'm fit to stand trial.

I know I'm not that child who was thrust into a world of madness. I've been fully aware that every action I've taken in my life was well thought out and implemented with meticulous planning. I know I am not insane. But they don't know that. I've learned to play many roles. And this is one I was destined to play.

The child born to a mentally ill mother; locked up for nearly twenty years for no reason other than to protect family honour. How could I be anything other than insane?

Flicking through the pages of the only book I was allowed to bring with me, I study the herbal illustrations and wonder if they will let me sow some seeds. I would like that. My mother, Carrie, would be proud of me.

EPILOGUE

31st October 2015

Knocking on Boyd's door seemed more civilised than jamming her finger on the bell. Soft, tender knocks. Tap, tap, tap.

She waited. No shadow formed behind the glass of the door. No sound, no movement. Silence within while everyday sounds continued outside.

Leaning her head against the cool glass, she realised this had been a mistake. It felt right when she'd made her decision. The decision had come from thinking about the loneliness in her life; the lies her life had been founded upon; the quicksand of lies she was quickly succumbing to.

Surrounded by a beautiful family and still she was lonely. Some might laugh. Others might think she was crazy. Maybe she was. After all, wasn't there a little bit of insanity running through her veins? Or maybe she should take that DNA test, just to be sure. No, not right now. One day. Perhaps when Rose died and there was no else to get hurt, she'd get Jane to do the test.

Not now. No. Not now.

The need to feel herself wrapped in the arms of someone she'd come to rely on as more than just a friend had become so strong. So she had acted on it. No alcohol in her system this time. No happy pills. Just herself. And he wasn't even home.

Story of my life, she mumbled sadly to herself, making her way down the path. Pulling her hood up against the biting wind, hefting her bag higher on her good shoulder, she walked out on to the street.

'Hey, Lottie, where are you off to so fast?'

She stopped. Turned round.

He was standing at the door. Hair dripping, skin damp. Just out of the shower, most likely.

Why was she really here? Unable to form a coherent word, she said nothing. Just stood like an eejit, staring.

'Don't walk away now,' he said, coming down the path in his bare feet. 'Come in.' He held out his hand.

No hesitation. She moved towards him and took it.

And for now, it felt so right.

She felt like she belonged.

*

Later that evening, they sat on a boulder on the stony lake shore, looking out to where Arthur Russell's body had eventually risen with the stormy waters. An innocent man whose wife and daughter had died because of the insanity of the past. The ease with which people could cover up their secrets had confounded Lottie.

'How many other poor souls were abandoned behind high walls because of land, money, and children born out of wedlock?' she said.

'Too many,' Boyd said.

'Who am I, Boyd?

'You are Lottie Parker, that's who.'

'I'm not the Lottie I thought I was. I'm another person entirely.'

The final leaf fell from a tree, fluttered down and lay at her feet. A gust of wind lifted it and carried it to the water's edge. They sat there and watched it float out on the wild lake.

'A fragile leaf at the mercy of nature's will,' Lottie said.

'And human life, just as fragile, is at the mercy of human greed and shame,' Boyd said.

'Will it ever end?'

'The bad weather?'

'The lies, Boyd, the secrets and the lies.'

A LETTER FROM PATRICIA

Hello dear reader,

I wish to sincerely thank you for reading my third novel, *The Lost Child*.

I'm really grateful to you for sharing your precious time with Lottie Parker and company. If you enjoyed it you might like to follow Lottie throughout the series of novels. To those of you who have already read the first two Lottie Parker books, *The Missing Ones* and *The Stolen Girls*, I thank you for your support and reviews.

All characters in this story are fictional, as is the town of Ragmullin, though life events have deeply influenced my writing.

If you liked *The Lost Child*, I hate asking, but I would love if you could post a review on Amazon or Goodreads. It would mean so much to me.

The amazing reviews my books have received to date really inspire me to believe in myself.

You can connect with me on my Facebook Author page and Twitter. I also have a blog (which I try to keep up to date).

Thanks again, and I hope you will join me for book four in the series.

Love
Patricia

www.patriciagibney.com

trisha460

@trisha460

ACKNOWLEDGEMENTS

To date I have written and published three titles in the Lottie Parker series, *The Missing Ones, The Stolen Girls* and most recently this book, *The Lost Child*. Writing each one has been a different experience for me, as I am learning all the time. And the main thing I have learned is that my books would not be out there and doing so well without a magnificent team behind me.

The most important part of that team is you, the reader. You have bought my books and read them, and *The Lost Child* is no exception. Your reviews instil in me a confidence to keep on writing. Thank you.

Thank you John Quinn and Martin McCabe for advising me on policing matters. They know I take liberties with this information in order to narrow timelines and help the story progress. I take full responsibility for the fiction!

For *The Lost Child* I had to discover a little about farming matters (even though my paternal grandparents were farmers). Thanks to Michael and Veronica Daly for the grand tour of their farm and for showing me the agitator. I had nightmares for a week.

All my books are published in audio format, so I want to thank Michele Moran for her magnificent narration, giving a voice to Lottie and my cast of characters. And thank you to Adam Helal, Audio Producer.

Bookouture is more than a just a publishing house. It's like a family home, where everyone supports and advises. The hands-on approach makes my writing and editing a lot easier.

To Helen Jenner, my editor on *The Lost Child*, thank you for your insight into my writing and for guiding me in making the novel into an incredible writing experience. To everyone else from Bookouture who worked on *The Lost Child*, thank you. I must give a special shout-out to Kim Nash and Noelle Holten for their incredible media work and for organising blog tours. Your tremendous diligence (at all hours of the day and night) helps get my books noticed.

Thank you also to those who work directly on my books: Lauren Finger, Jen Hunt, Alex Crow, Jules McAdam, Kate Barker, Jane Selley and Tom Feltham.

One thing I've experienced since joining Bookouture is the tremendous support among fellow Bookouture authors. Thank you, guys!

Thank you to each and every blogger and reviewer who has read and reviewed *The Missing Ones*, *The Stolen Girls* and of course *The Lost Child*. I will continue to keep you busy!

My agent, Ger Nichol of The Book Bureau, is a font of knowledge on the book business and I value her advice. Ger's engagement on my behalf with Bookouture, especially with Oliver Rhodes, Lydia Vassar-Smith, Peta Nightingale and Jenny Geras in negotiating new contracts, is something I couldn't do without.

Early readers of first drafts are essential to me, and I wish to thank my sister Marie Brennan for taking the time to read my work. She is always on hand to sort out the nitty-gritty when I find myself in a black hole, and to fill me with confidence.

Escaping to write in remote places has become the norm for me. Jackie Walsh, you are amazing at firstly booking our trips and secondly saying, 'Pack the laptop.'

Others in the writing circle who inspired and motivated me while writing *The Lost Child* are Niamh Brennan, Grainne Daly, Louise Phillips, Vanessa O'Loughlin, Ann O'Loughlin, Liz Nugent, Arlene Hunt and Carolann Copeland.

I rode a media roller coaster for a while; thanks to all the newspapers and radio and TV shows that featured me, with special thanks to the researchers and producers who ensured I remained calm. Massive thanks to everyone in local media.

A special thanks to Eoin McHugh, Redmond O'Regan, Eamonn Brennan, Teresa Doran and Margaret Coyle.

And a huge thank you Marty Mulligan for having me on The Word stage at Electric Picnic 2017. You are one awesome Mullingar man.

There is always a core of strong stalwarts at my back keeping me focused. My friends Antoinette and Jo, my brother Gerard and sisters Marie and Catherine, and Lily Gibney and family.

I have the most pride a mother could have in my three strong children, Aisling, Orla and Cathal, who suffered much in their young lives following the death of their dad, Aidan. They have proved time and again that he lives on in each of them. Aidan would be so proud of how his family is coping after a harrowing few years. And I'm sure he would spoil Daisy and Shay. He still guides and protects us. Always in my heart, dear Aidan.

Finally, I dedicate *The Lost Child* to my parents, Kathleen and William Ward. This book deals, at one level, with some dysfunctional families. But my own family life has two of the strongest, most hard-working and caring parents I could ask for. They are always by my side and have helped me through the dark days of my life, so I dedicate this book to them, true parents.